Praise for *The Red Tent*

'Diamant has taken a little-known character from the Book of Genesis and created a fascinating story of love, betrayal and infamy' *Elle*

'Lust, sibling rivalry, infertility, jealousy, murder, ambition . . . It weaves fascinating traditions of womanhood with mesmerising storytelling. Sexy, moving and unputdownable' *She* Book of the Month

'I genuinely fell into this rich and colourful world and Dinah and Leah have stayed with me as ancestors and sisters brought to life by Anita Diamant's imaginative novel' Maureen Lipman

'A passionate saga of betrayal, grief and love, vividly bringing to life the culture of the times . . . a superb woman's read' *Bookseller* Star Choice

'An affecting tale of betrayal, grief and love' *Scotland on Sunday*

'Life lessons are implicitly woven throughout this enchanting story . . . If you don't read it you'll be missing out' *Eve*

'Diamant is a wonderful storyteller, not only bringing to life these women about whom the Bible tells us so little but also stirringly evoking a place and time. As with the best writers of historical fiction, Diamant makes readers see there's not much difference between people across the eons, at least when it comes to trial and tragedy, happiness and love' *Booklist*

The
Red Tent

The Red Tent

ANITA DIAMANT

PAN BOOKS

First published 1997 as a Wyatt Book for
St Martin's Press, New York

First published in Great Britain 2001 by Macmillan

This edition published 2002 by Pan Books
an imprint of Pan Macmillan Ltd
Pan Macmillan, 20 New Wharf Road, London N1 9RR
Basingstoke and Oxford
Associated companies throughout the world
www.panmacmillan.com

ISBN 978-0-330-48796-2

21 23 25 27 29 28 26 24 22

A CIP catalogue record for this book is available from
the British Library.

Typeset by SetSystems Ltd, Saffron Walden, Essex
Printed and bound in Great Britain by
CPI Mackays, Chatham ME5 8TD

Visit www.panmacmillan.com to read more about all our books and to buy
them. You will also find features, author interviews and news of any author
events, and you can sign up for e-newsletters so that you're always first to hear
about our new releases.

For Emilia, my daughter

GENERATIONS

FIRST GENERATIONS

Terah m. Imma

Nahor m. Milcah   Abram m. Sarai

Betheul m. Saruga

Laban m. Adah   Mer-Nefat   Huna   Tefnut   (Ruti)   Rebecca m. Isaac

Leah   Zilpah   Rachel   Bilhah   (Kemuel   Jacob
                           Beor)   Esau

THE CHILDREN OF JACOB

Jacob m.	Leah m.	Zilpah m.	Rachel m.	Bilhah
	Reuben	Gad	Joseph	Dan
	Simon	Asher	Benjamin	
	Levi			
	Judah			
	Zebulun			
	Naphtali			
	Issachar			
	Dinah			

THE CHILDREN OF ESAU

Esau m.	Adath m.	Basemath m.	Oholibama
	Eliphaz	Reuel	Jeush
	Edva	Tabea	Jalam
	Libbe		Korah
	Amat		Iti

DINAH IN EGYPT

Paser m. Nehhetany

Re-nefer m. Hamor   Nakht-re m. Herya

Shalem m. Dinah m. Benia

Re-mose

The
Red Tent

Prologue

WE HAVE BEEN lost to each other for so long.

My name means nothing to you. My memory is dust.

This is not your fault, or mine. The chain connecting mother to daughter was broken and the word passed to the keeping of men, who had no way of knowing. That is why I became a footnote, my story a brief detour between the well-known history of my father, Jacob, and the celebrated chronicle of Joseph, my brother. On those rare occasions when I was remembered, it was as a victim. Near the beginning of your holy book, there is a passage that seems to say I was raped and continues with the bloody tale of how my honor was avenged.

It's a wonder that any mother ever called a daughter Dinah again. But some did. Maybe you guessed that there was more to me than the voiceless cipher in the text. Maybe you heard it in the music of my name: the first vowel high and clear, as when a mother calls to her child at dusk; the second sound soft, for whispering secrets on pillows. Deenah.

No one recalled my skill as a midwife, or the songs I sang, or the bread I baked for my insatiable brothers. Nothing remained except a few mangled details about those weeks in Shechem.

There was far more to tell. Had I been asked to speak of it, I would have begun with the story of the generation that raised me, which is the only place to begin. If you want to understand any woman you must first ask about her mother and then listen carefully. Stories about food show a strong connection. Wistful silences demonstrate unfinished business. The more a daughter knows the details of her mother's life—without flinching or whining—the stronger the daughter.

Of course, this is more complicated for me because I had four mothers, each of them scolding, teaching, and cherishing something different about me, giving me different gifts, cursing me with different fears. Leah gave me birth and her splendid arrogance. Rachel showed me where to place the midwife's bricks and how to fix my hair. Zilpah made me think. Bilhah listened. No two of my mothers seasoned her stew the same way. No two of them spoke to my father in the same tone of voice—nor he to them. And you should know that my mothers were sisters as well, Laban's daughters by different wives, though my grandfather never acknowledged Zilpah and Bilhah; that would have cost him two more dowries, and he was a stingy pig.

Like any sisters who live together and share a husband, my mother and aunties spun a sticky web of loyalties and grudges. They traded secrets like bracelets, and these were handed down to me, the only surviving girl. They told me things I was too young to hear. They held my face between their hands and made me swear to remember.

My mothers were proud to give my father so many sons. Sons were a woman's pride and her measure. But the birth of one boy after another was not an unalloyed source of joy in the women's tents. My father boasted about his noisy tribe, and the women loved my brothers, but they longed for daughters, too, and complained among themselves about the maleness of Jacob's seed.

Daughters eased their mothers' burdens—helping with the spinning, the grinding of grain, and the endless task of looking after baby boys, who were forever peeing into the corners of the tents, no matter what you told them.

But the other reason women wanted daughters was to keep their memories alive. Sons did not hear their mothers' stories after weaning. So I was the one. My mother and my mother-aunties told me endless stories about themselves. No matter what their hands were doing—holding babies, cooking, spinning, weaving—they filled my ears.

In the ruddy shade of the red tent, the menstrual tent, they ran their fingers through my curls, repeating the escapades of their youths, the sagas of their childbirths. Their stories were like offerings of hope and strength poured out before the Queen of Heaven, only these gifts were not for any god or goddess—but for me.

I can still feel how my mothers loved me. I have cherished their love always. It sustained me. It kept me alive. Even after I left them, and even now, so long after their deaths, I am comforted by their memory.

I carried my mothers' tales into the next generation, but the stories of my life were forbidden to me, and that silence nearly killed the heart in me. I did not die but lived long enough for other stories to fill up my days and nights. I watched babies open their eyes upon a new world. I found cause for laughter and gratitude. I was loved.

And now you come to me—women with hands and feet as soft as a queen's, with more cooking pots than you need, so safe in childbed and so free with your tongues. You come hungry for the story that was lost. You crave words to fill the great silence that swallowed me, and my mothers, and my grandmothers before them.

I wish I had more to tell of my grandmothers. It is terrible how much has been forgotten, which is why, I suppose, remembering seems a holy thing.

I am so grateful that you have come. I will pour out everything inside me so you may leave this table satisfied and fortified. Blessings on your eyes. Blessings on your children. Blessings on the ground beneath you. My heart is a ladle of sweet water, brimming over.

Selah.

PART ONE

My Mothers' Stories

——

Chapter One

THEIR STORIES BEGAN with the day that my father appeared. Rachel came running into camp, knees flying, bellowing like a calf separated from its mother. But before anyone could scold her for acting like a wild boy, she launched into a breathless yarn about a stranger at the well, her words spilling out like water into sand.

A wild man without sandals. Matted hair. Dirty face. He kissed her on the mouth, a cousin, son of their aunt, who had watered sheep and goats for her and told off the ruffians at the well.

"What are you babbling?" demanded her father, Laban. "Who is come to the well? Who attends him? How many bags does he carry?"

"He is going to marry me," said Rachel matter-of-factly, once she had caught her breath. "He says I am for him and that he would marry me tomorrow, if he could. He's coming to ask you."

Leah scowled at this announcement. "Marry you?" she said, crossing her arms and throwing back her shoulders. "You won't be marriageable for another year," said the older girl, who, though only a few years older than Rachel, already acted as head woman of her father's small holdings. The fourteen-year-old mistress of Laban's house liked to take a haughty, maternal tone with her sister. "What's all this? And how did he come to kiss you?" This was a terrible breach of custom—even if he was a cousin and even though Rachel was young enough to be treated as a child.

Rachel stuck out her lower lip in a pout that would have been childlike only a few hours earlier. Something had happened since she opened her eyes that morning, when the most pressing matter on her mind had been to find the place where Leah hid her honey. Leah, that donkey, would never share it with her, but hoarded it for guests, giving tastes to pathetic little Bilhah and no one else.

All Rachel could think of now was the shaggy stranger whose eyes had met hers with a shock of recognition that had rattled her to the bone.

Rachel knew what Leah meant, but the fact that she had not yet begun to bleed meant nothing to her now. And her cheeks burned.

"What's this?" said Leah, suddenly amused. "She is smitten. Look at her," she said. "Have you ever seen the girl blush before?"

"What did he do to you?" asked Laban, growling like a dog who senses an intruder near his herd. He clenched his fists and beetled his brow and turned his full attention to Rachel, the daughter he had never once hit, the daughter whom he rarely looked at full in the face. She had frightened him from her birth—a tearing, violent entry that had killed her mother. When the baby finally emerged, the women were shocked to see that it was such a small one—a girl at that—who had caused so many days of trouble, costing her mother so much blood and finally her life.

Rachel's presence was powerful as the moon, and just as beautiful. Nobody could deny her beauty. Even as a child who worshiped my own mother's face, I knew that Leah's beauty paled before her younger sister's, a knowledge that always made me feel like a traitor. Still, denying it would have been like denying the sun's warmth.

Rachel's beauty was rare and arresting. Her brown hair shaded to bronze, and her skin was golden, honeyed, perfect. In that amber setting, her eyes were surprisingly dark, not merely dark brown but black as polished obsidian or the depth of a well. Although she was small-boned and, even when she was with child, small-breasted, she had muscular hands and a husky voice that seemed to belong to a much larger woman.

I once heard two shepherds arguing over which was Rachel's best feature, a game I, too, had played. For me, the most wonderful detail of Rachel's perfection was her cheeks, which were high and tight on her face, like figs. When I was a baby, I used to reach for them, trying to pluck the fruit that appeared when she smiled. When I realized there was no having them, I licked her instead, hoping for a taste. This made my beautiful aunt laugh, from deep in her belly. She loved me better than all her nephews put together—or so she said as she wove my hair into the elaborate braids for which my own mother's hands lacked patience or time.

It is almost impossible to exaggerate the dimensions of Rachel's beauty. Even as a baby, she was a jewel upon whatever hip bore her from place to place, an ornament, a rare pleasure—the black-eyed child with golden hair. Her nickname was Tuki, which means "sweetness."

All the women shared in Rachel's care after her mother, Huna, died. Huna was a skilled midwife known for her throaty laugh and much mourned by the women. No one grumbled about tending to Huna's motherless daughter, and even the men, for whom babies held as little fascination as cooking stones, would stoop to run a callused hand across her remarkable cheek. They would rise, smelling their fingers and shaking their heads.

Rachel smelled like water. Really! Wherever my aunt walked, there was the scent of fresh water. It was an impossible smell, green and delightful and in those dusty hills the smell of life and wealth. Indeed, for many years Laban's well was the only reason his family hadn't starved.

There were hopes, early on, that Rachel would be a water witch, one who could find hidden wells and underground streams. She did not fulfill that hope, but somehow the aroma of sweet water clung to her skin and lodged in her robes. Whenever one of the babies went missing, more often than not the little stinker would be found fast asleep on her blankets, sucking his thumb.

No wonder Jacob was enchanted at the well. The other men had grown accustomed to Rachel's looks and even to her startling perfume, but to Jacob she must have seemed an apparition. He looked directly into her eyes and was overcome. When he kissed her, Jacob cried out with a voice of a man who lies with his wife. The sound woke Rachel out of her childhood.

There was barely time to hear Rachel describe their

meeting before Jacob himself appeared. He walked up to Laban, and Rachel watched her father take his measure.

Laban noticed his empty hands first, but he also saw that the stranger's tunic and cloak were made of fine stuff, his water skin was well crafted, his knife hilt was carved of polished bone. Jacob stood directly before Laban and, dropping his head, proclaimed himself. "Uncle, I am the son of Rebecca, your sister, the daughter of Nahor and Milcah, as you are their son. My mother has sent me to you, my brother has chased me to you, my father has banished me to you. I will tell you the whole story when I am not so dirty and weary. I seek your hospitality, which is famous in the land."

Rachel opened her mouth to speak, but Leah yanked her sister's arm and shot her a warning glance; not even Rachel's youth would excuse a girl speaking out when men were addressing one another. Rachel kicked at the ground and thought poisonous thoughts about her sister, the bossy old crow, the cross-eyed goat.

Jacob's words about Laban's famous hospitality were a courteous lie, for Laban was anything but pleased by the appearance of this nephew. Not much caused the old man pleasure, and hungry strangers were unwanted surprises. Still, there was nothing to be done; he had to honor the claim of a kinsman, and there was no denying the connection between them. Jacob knew the names and Laban recognized his sister's face on the man standing before him.

"You are welcome," Laban said, without smiling or returning his nephew's salute. As he turned to walk away, Laban pointed his thumb at Leah, assigning her the task of seeing to this nuisance. My mother nodded and turned to face the first grown man who did not look away when confronted by the sight of her eyes.

Leah's vision was perfect. According to one of the more ridiculous fables embroidered around my family's history, she ruined her eyes by crying a river of tears over the prospect of marrying my uncle Esau. If you believe that, you might also be interested in purchasing a magical toad that will make all who look upon you swoon with love.

But my mother's eyes were not weak, or sick, or rheumy. The truth is, her eyes made others weak and most people looked away rather than face them—one blue as lapis, the other green as Egyptian grass.

When she was born, the midwife cried out that a witch had been brought forth and should be drowned before she could bring a curse on the family. But my grandmother Adah slapped the stupid woman and cursed her tongue. "Show me my daughter," said Adah, in a voice so loud and proud even the men outside could hear her. Adah named her beloved last-born Leah, which means "mistress," and she wept a prayer that this child would live, for she had buried seven sons and daughters.

There were plenty who remained convinced that the baby was a devil. For some reason, Laban, who was the most superstitious soul you can imagine (spitting and bowing whenever he turned to the left, howling at every lunar eclipse), refused to hear suggestions that Leah be left outside to die in the night air. He swore some mild oath about the femaleness of this child, but apart from that, Laban ignored his daughter and never mentioned her distinction. Then again, the women suspected the old man could not see color at all.

Leah's eyes never faded in color—as some of the women predicted and hoped—but became brighter in their difference and even more pronounced in their strangeness when her lashes failed to grow. Although she blinked like everyone else, the reflex was nearly invisible, so it seemed that Leah never closed her eyes. Even her most loving glance felt a bit like the stare of a snake, and few could stand to look her straight in the eye. Those who could were rewarded with kisses and laughter and bread wet with honey.

Jacob met Leah's eyes straight on, and for this she warmed to him instantly. In fact, Leah had already taken note of Jacob on account of his height. She was half a head taller than most of the men she had ever seen, and she dismissed them all because of it. She knew this was not fair. Surely there were good men among those whose heads reached only to her nose. But the thought of lying with anyone whose legs were shorter and weaker than her own disgusted her. Not that anyone had asked for her. She knew they all called her Lizard and Evil-Eye, and worse.

Her distaste for short men had been confirmed by a dream in which a tall man had whispered to her. She couldn't recall his words, but they had warmed her thighs and woken her. When she saw Jacob, she remembered the dream and her strange eyes widened.

Jacob noticed Leah with favor, too. Although he was still ringing from his encounter with Rachel, he could not ignore the sight of Leah.

She was not only tall but shapely and strong. She was

blessed with full, high breasts and muscular calves that showed to good advantage in robes that somehow never stayed closed at the hem. She had forearms like a young man's, but her walk was that of a woman with promising hips.

Leah had dreamed once of a pomegranate split open to reveal eight red seeds. Zilpah said the dream meant she would have eight healthy children, and my mother knew those words to be true the way she knew how to make bread and beer.

Leah's scent was no mystery. She smelled of the yeast she handled daily, brewing and baking. She reeked of bread and comfort, and—it seemed to Jacob—of sex. He stared at this giantess, and his mouth watered. As far as I know, he never said a word about her eyes.

My aunt Zilpah, Laban's second-born, said that she remembered everything that ever happened to her. She laid claim to memories of her own birth, and even of days in her mother's womb. She swore she could remember her mother's death in the red tent, where she sickened within days after Zilpah arrived in the world, feet first. Leah scoffed at these claims, though not to her sister's face, for Zilpah was the only one who could cause my mother to hold her tongue about anything.

Zilpah's memory of Jacob's arrival is nothing like Rachel's or Leah's, but then Zilpah had little use for men, whom she described as hairy, crude, and half human. Women needed men to make babies and to move heavy objects, but otherwise she didn't understand their purpose, much less appreciate their charms. She loved her sons passionately until they grew beards, but after that could barely bring herself to look at them.

When I was old enough to ask what it was like on the day that my father arrived, she said that the presence of El hovered over him, which is why he was worthy of notice. Zilpah told me that El was the god of thunder, high places, and awful sacrifice. El could demand that a father cut off his son—cast him out into the desert, or slaughter him outright. This was a hard, strange god, alien and cold, but, she conceded, a consort powerful enough for the Queen of Heaven, whom she loved in every shape and name.

Zilpah talked about gods and goddesses almost more than she spoke about people. I found this tiresome at times, but she used words in the most wonderful ways, and I loved her stories about Ninhursag, the great mother, and Enlil, the first father. She made up grandiose hymns in which real people met with the deities and together they danced to the sound of flutes and cymbals, singing them in a high, thin voice to the accompaniment of a small clay drum.

From the age of her first blood, Zilpah thought of herself as a kind of priestess, the keeper of the mysteries of the red tent, the daughter of Asherah the sister-Siduri who counsels women. It was a foolish idea, as only priests served the goddesses of the great city temples, while the priestesses served gods. Besides, Zilpah had none of the oracle's gifts. She lacked the talent for herbs, and could not prophesy or conjure or read goat entrails. Leah's eight-seeded pomegranate was the only dream she ever interpreted correctly.

Zilpah was Laban's daughter by a slave named Mer-Nefat, who had been purchased from an Egyptian trader in the days when Laban still had means. According to Adah, Zilpah's mother was slender, raven-haired, and so quiet it was easy to forget she had the power of speech, a trait her daughter did not inherit.

Zilpah was only a few months younger than Leah, and after Zilpah's mother died, Adah gave them suck together. They were playmates as babies, close and loving friends as children, tending the flocks together, gathering berries, making up songs, laughing. Apart from Adah, they needed no one else in the world.

Zilpah was almost as tall as Leah, but thinner and less robust in the chest and legs. Dark-haired and olive-skinned, Leah and Zilpah resembled their father and shared the family nose, not unlike Jacob's—a regal hawk's beak that seemed to grow longer when they smiled. Leah and Zilpah both talked with their hands, thumb and forefinger pressed together in emphatic ovals. When the sun made them squint, identical lines appeared around the corners of their eyes.

But where Leah's hair was curly, Zilpah's black mane was straight, and she wore it to her waist. It was her best feature, and my aunt hated to cover it. Headdresses caused her head to pound, she said, putting a hand to her cheek with silly drama. Even as a child I was permitted to laugh at her. These headaches were the reason she gave for keeping so much inside the women's tents. She did not join the rest of us to bask in the springtime sun or find the breeze on a hot night. But when the moon was young—slender and shy, barely making herself known in the sky—Zilpah walked around the camp, swinging her long hair, clapping her hands, offering songs to encourage the moon's return.

When Jacob arrived, Bilhah was a child of eight, and she remembered nothing of the day. "She was probably up in a tree somewhere, sucking on her fingers and counting the clouds," said Leah, repeating the only thing that was remembered of Bilhah's early years.

Bilhah was the family orphan. The last daughter born of Laban's seed, she was the child of a slave named Tefnut—a tiny black woman who ran off one night when Bilhah was old enough to know she had been abandoned. "She never got over that hurt," said Zilpah with great gentleness, for Zilpah respected pain.

Bilhah was alone among them. It's not just that she was the youngest and that there were three other sisters to share the work. Bilhah was a sad child and it was easier to leave her alone. She rarely smiled and hardly spoke. Not even my grandmother Adah, who adored little girls and gathered motherless Zilpah to her inner circle and doted upon Rachel, could warm to this strange, lonely bird, who never grew taller than a boy of ten years, and whose skin was the color of dark amber.

Bilhah was not beautiful like Rachel, or capable like Leah, or quick like Zilpah. She was tiny, dark, and silent. Adah was exasperated by her hair, which was springy as moss and refused to obey her hands. Compared to the two other motherless girls, Bilhah was neglected dreadfully.

Left to herself, she climbed trees and seemed to dream.

From her perch, she studied the world, the patterns in the sky, the habits of animals and birds. She came to know the flocks as individuals, giving each animal a secret name to match its personality. One evening, she came in from the fields and whispered to Adah that a black dwarf she-goat was ready to give birth to twins. It was nowhere near the season for goats to bear, and that particular animal had been barren for four seasons. Adah shook her head at Bilhah's nonsense and shooed her away.

The next day, Laban brought news of a strange event in the flocks, with a precise retelling of the little girl's prediction. Adah turned to the girl and apologized. "Bilhah sees clearly," said Adah to the other daughters, who turned to stare at this unseen sister and noticed, for the first time, the kindness in her black eyes.

If you took the time to look, you could see right away that Bilhah was good. She was good the way milk is good, the way rain is good. Bilhah watched the skies and the animals, and she watched her family, too. From the dark corners of the tents, she saw Leah hide her mortification when people stared. Bilhah noticed Rachel's fear of the dark and Zilpah's insomnia. Bilhah knew that Laban was every bit as mean-spirited as he was stupid.

Bilhah says her first clear memory of Jacob is from the day his first child was born. It was a boy—Reuben—and of course Jacob was delighted. He took his new son in his arms and danced the baby around and around outside the red tent.

"He was so gentle with the boy," Bilhah said. "He would not let Adah take Reuben away from him, even when the little one began to wail.

18

"He called his son perfect and a miracle in the world. I stood beside him and together Jacob and I worshiped the baby. We counted his fingers and stroked the soft crown of his head. We delighted in him and in each other's joy," Bilhah said. "That is when I met Jacob, your father."

Jacob arrived late in the afternoon in the week of a full moon, ate a simple meal of barley bread and olives, and fell into an exhausted sleep that lasted through most of the next day. Leah was mortified by the simplicity of the food they had offered him at first, so the next day she set out to produce a feast seen only at the great festivals.

"I suffered over that meal like nothing else I had ever cooked," said Leah, telling me the story during dull, hot afternoons while we rocked the narrow-necked jars, straining the water from goat curd.

"The father of my children was in the house, I was sure of it. I could see he was smitten by Rachel, whose beauty I saw as if for the first time. Still, he looked at me without flinching, and so I hoped.

"I slaughtered a kid, an unblemished male, as though it were a sacrifice to the gods. I beat the millet until it was as soft as a cloud. I reached deep into the pouches where I kept my most precious spices and used the last of my dried pomegranate. I pounded, chopped, and scraped in a frenzy, believing that he would understand what I was offering him.

"Nobody helped me with the cooking, not that I would have permitted anyone else to touch the lamb or the bread, or even the barley water. I wouldn't let my own mother pour water into a pot," she said and giggled.

I loved this story and asked to hear it again and again. Leah was always reliable and deliberate, and far too steady to be giddy. And yet as she recounted her first meal for Jacob, she was a foolish, weepy girl.

"I was an idiot," she said. "I burned the first bread and burst into tears. I even sacrificed a bit of the next loaf so that Jacob might fancy me. Just as we do when we bake the cakes for the Queen of Heaven on the seventh day, I broke off a piece of dough, kissed it, and offered it to the fire as an offering of hope that the man would claim me.

"Don't ever tell Zilpah about this or I'll never hear the end of it," said Leah, in a mock-conspiratorial whisper. "And of course, if Laban, your grandfather, had any idea of how much food I put together for a beggar who showed up without so much as a jug of oil as a gift, he would have flogged me. But I gave the old man enough strong beer that he made no comment.

"Or maybe he made no mention of my extravagance because he knew he'd be lucky with this kinsman. Maybe he guessed he had discovered a son-in-law who would require little by way of a dowry. It was hard to know what the old man knew or didn't know. He was like an ox, your grandfather."

"Like a post," I said.

"Like a cooking stone," said my mother.

"Like a goat turd," I said.

My mother shook her finger at me as though I were a naughty child, but then she laughed out loud, for raking Laban over the coals was great sport among his daughters.

I can still recite her menu. Lamb flavored with coriander, marinated in sour goat milk and a pomegranate sauce for dipping. Two kinds of bread: flat barley and raised wheat. Quince compote, and figs stewed with mulberries, fresh dates. Olives, of course. And to drink, a choice of sweet wine, three different beers, and barley water.

Jacob was so exhausted he nearly missed the meal that Leah brought forth with so much passion. Zilpah had a terrible time waking him and finally had to pour water on his neck, which startled him so badly that he swung out with his arms and knocked her to the ground, where she hissed like a cat.

Zilpah was not at all happy about this Jacob. She could see that his presence had changed things between the sisters and would weaken her bond to Leah. He offended her because he was so much more attractive than the other men they saw, foul-mouthed shepherds and the occasional trader who looked at the sisters as though they were a pack of ewes.

Jacob was well spoken and fair of face. And when he met Leah's gaze, Zilpah understood that their lives would never be the same. She was heartsick and angry and helpless to stop the change, though she tried.

When Jacob finally awoke and came to sit at Laban's right outside his tent, he ate well. Leah remembered his every bite. "He dipped into the lamb stew over and over again, and had three helpings of bread. I saw that he liked sweets, and that he preferred the honeyed brew to the bitter-flavored drink that Laban gulped down. I knew how to please his mouth, I thought. I will know how to please the rest of him."

This line would always get my other mothers shrieking and slapping their thighs, for although she was a practical woman, Leah was also the lewdest of her sisters.

"And then, after all that work, after all that eating, what do you think happened?" Leah asked, as though I didn't know the answer as well as I knew the little crescent-shaped scar above the joint on her right thumb.

"Jacob grew ill, that's what happened. He vomited every morsel. He threw up until he was weak and whimpering. He cried out to El, and Ishtar, and Marduk, and his blessed mother, to save him from his agonies or let him die.

"Zilpah, the brat, she sneaked into his tent to see how he fared and reported back to me, making it sound even worse than it was. She told me that he was whiter than the full moon, that he barked like a dog and spewed up frogs and snakes.

"I was mortified—and terrified, too. What if he died from my cooking? Or, just as bad, what if he recovered and blamed me for his misery?

"When no one else showed any ill effect from the meal, I knew it wasn't the food. But then, fool that I was, I started worrying that my touch was hateful to him. Or maybe I had done wrong with the bread offering, given not in homage to a god or goddess, but as an attempt at magic.

"I got religious again and poured the last of the good wine out in the name of Anath the healer. That was on the third night of his suffering, and he was healed by the next morning." At this she always shook her head and sighed. "Not a very auspicious beginning for such fruitful lovers, was it?"

Jacob made a quick recovery and stayed on, week after week, until it seemed he had always been there. He took charge of the scrawny herds so Rachel no longer had to follow the animals, a job that had fallen to her in the absence of brothers.

My grandfather laid the blame for the state of his herds and his dwindling wealth upon the fact that all his sons had died at birth or in infancy, leaving him nothing but daughters. He gave no thought to his own sloth, believing that only a son would turn his luck around. He consulted the local priests, who told him to sacrifice his best rams and a bull so that the gods might give him a boy-child. He had lain with his wives and concubines in the fields, as an old midwife suggested, and all he had gotten for that effort was an itchy backside and bruises on his knees. By the time Jacob arrived, Laban had given up his hope of a son—or of any improvement in his life.

He expected nothing from Adah, who was past childbearing and sick. His other three women had died or run off, and he couldn't afford the few coins for a homely slave girl, much less the price of a new bride. So he slept alone, except for the nights he found his way up the hills to bother the flocks, like some horny little boy. Rachel said that among the shepherds, my grandfather's lust was legendary. "The ewes run like gazelles when Laban walks up the hill," they hooted.

His daughters despised him for a hundred reasons, and I knew them all. Zilpah told me that when she was a few months away from her first blood and the task fell to her of taking my grandfather his midday meal, he reached up and put his thumb and forefinger around her nipple, squeezing it as though she were a she-goat.

Leah, too, said Laban had put his hand under her robes,

but when she told Adah, my grandmother had beaten Laban with a pestle until he bled. She broke the horns off his favorite household god, and when she threatened to curse him with boils and impotence, he swore never to touch his daughters again and made restitution. He bought gold bangles for Adah and all of his daughters—even Zilpah and Bilhah, which was the only time he acknowledged them as kin. And he brought home a beautiful asherah—a tall pillar, nearly as big as Bilhah—made by the finest potter he could find. The women placed her up on the bamah, the high place, where sacrifices were offered. The goddess's face was especially lovely, with almond eyes and an open smile. When we poured wine over her in the dark of each new moon, it seemed to us her mouth broadened even farther in pleasure.

But that was some years before Jacob came, when Laban still had a few bondsmen working for him, and their wives and children filled the camp with cooking smells and laughter. By the time my father arrived, there was only one sick wife and four daughters.

While Laban was glad enough of Jacob's presence, the two men disliked each other heartily. Although different as a raven and a donkey, they were bound by blood and soon by business.

Jacob, it turned out, was a willing worker with a talent for animals—especially dogs. He turned Laban's three useless mongrels into fine shepherds. He whistled and the dogs raced to his side. He clapped and they would run in circles and get the sheep to move after him. He yodeled and they stood guard with such ferocity that Laban's flocks never again saw harm from a fox or jackal. And if there were poachers, they ran off rather than face the bared teeth of that fierce little pack.

Jacob's dogs were soon the envy of other men, who offered to buy them. Instead, he traded a day's work for the stud of the male cur with cunning wolfish eyes. When the smallest of our bitches bore the wolf-dog's litter, Jacob trained her puppies and traded four of the five for what seemed a mountain of treasure, which he quickly converted to gifts that proved how well he had come to understand Laban's daughters.

He took Rachel to the well where they had met and gave her the blue lapis ring she wore until her death. He sought out Leah where she was combing wool and, without a word, handed her three finely hammered gold bangles. To Zilpah he gave a small votive vessel in the shape of Anath, which poured libations through the nipples. He laid a bag of salt at Adah's swollen feet. He even remembered Bilhah with a tiny amphora of honey.

Laban complained that his nephew should have turned over the profit from the puppies directly to him, since the mother was his goods. But the old man was mollified by a bag of coins, with which he ran to the village and brought back Ruti. Poor thing.

Within a year, Jacob became the overseer of Laban's domain. With his dogs, Jacob led the flocks so the lambs fed on the gentle grass, the sheep grazed on patches of juicy herbs, and the full-grown rams rummaged through the tough weeds. The flocks did so well that at the next shearing Jacob had to hire two boys to finish the work before the rains came. Rachel joined Leah, Zilpah, and Bilhah in the garden, where they enlarged the wheat patch.

Jacob made Laban agree to sacrifice two fat lambs and a kid to the god of his father, as thanks for the bounty. Leah baked raised cakes from the precious stock of wheat for the sacrifice, too, which was carried out as Jacob directed. In the manner of his fathers, he burned entire loaves and all the choice parts of the animals rather than a few portions. The women muttered among themselves at the waste.

It was a year of change for my family. The flocks multiplied, and the grain flourished, and there was a marriage in the offing. For within a month of his arrival, Jacob asked Laban about Rachel's bride price, as she had said he would that very first day. Since it was clear that his nephew had no means or property, Laban thought he could get the man cheap, and made a magnanimous show of offering his daughter for a mere seven years' service.

Jacob laughed at the idea. "Seven years? We are talking about a girl here, not a throne. In seven years' time, she might be dead. I might be dead. And most likely of all, you could be dead, old man.

"I will give you seven months," Jacob said. "And for the dowry, I'll take half your miserable herd."

Laban jumped to his feet and called Jacob a thief. "You are your mother's son, all right," he raged. "You think the world owes you anything? Don't get too proud with me, you afterbirth, or I'll send you back to your brother's long knife."

Zilpah, the best spy among them, reported on the argument, telling how they haggled back and forth over my aunt's value, about how Laban stormed out and Jacob spat. Finally, they agreed on a year's service for a bride price. As to dowry, Laban pleaded poverty. "I have so little, my son," he said, suddenly the loving patriarch. "And she is such a treasure.'

Jacob could not accept a bride without a dowry. That would have made Rachel a concubine and him a fool for paying with a year of his life for a girl who had only a grindstone, a spindle, and the clothes on her back to her name. So Laban threw Bilhah into the bargain, giving Rachel status as a dowered wife, and Jacob the possibility of a concubine in time.

"Also you must give me a tenth of the lambs and kids born to the flocks while I stand guard over them for you during my year of service," Jacob said.

At that, Laban cursed Jacob's seed and stormed away. It was a week before the men finished their negotiations, a week in which Rachel wept and carried on like a baby, while Leah said little and served nothing but cold millet porridge, food for mourners.

When they worked out the final terms, Laban went to Adah, so she could start planning the wedding. But Adah said no — "We are not barbarians who give children to wed."

Rachel could not even be promised, she told her husband. The girl might look ready to marry, but she was still unripe, having not yet bled. My grandmother claimed that Anath would curse the garden if Laban dared break this law and that she herself would find the strength to take a pestle to her husband's head again.

But threats were unnecessary. Laban saw the advantage

in this delay and went immediately to Jacob with the news he would have to wait until the girl was ready before they could plan a date for the marriage.

Jacob accepted the situation. What else could he do? Furious, Rachel yelled at Adah, who cuffed her and told her to take her temper elsewhere. Rachel, in turn, slapped Bilhah, cursed at Zilpah, and snarled at Leah. She even kicked dust at Jacob's feet, calling him a liar and a coward before bursting into pretty tears on his neck.

She began to nurse dark fears about the future. She would never bleed, never marry Jacob, never bear sons. Suddenly, the small, high breasts of which she had been so proud seemed puny to her. Perhaps she was a freak, a hermaphrodite like the gross idol in her father's tent, the one with a tree stalk between its legs and teats like a cow.

So Rachel tried to rush her season. Before the next new moon, she baked cakes of offering to the Queen of Heaven, something she had never done before, and slept a whole night with her belly pressed up against the base of the asherah. But the moon waned and grew round again, while Rachel's thighs remained dry. She walked into the village by herself to ask the midwife, Inna, for help and was given an infusion of ugly nettles that grew in a nearby wadi. But again the new moon came and again Rachel remained a child.

As the following moon waned, Rachel crushed bitter berries and called her older sisters to see the stain on her blanket. But the juice was purple, and Leah and Zilpah laughed at the seeds on her thighs.

The next month, Rachel hid in her tent, and did not even slip away once to find Jacob.

Finally, in the ninth month after Jacob's arrival, Rachel bled her first blood, and cried with relief. Adah, Leah, and Zilpah sang the piercing, throaty song that announces births, deaths, and women's ripening. As the sun set on the new moon when all the women commenced bleeding, they rubbed henna on Rachel's fingernails and on the soles of her feet. Her eyelids were painted yellow, and they slid every bangle, gem, and jewel that could be found onto her fingers, toes, ankles, and wrists. They covered her head with the finest embroidery and led her into the red tent. They sang songs for the goddesses; for Innana and the Lady Asherah of the Sea. They spoke of Elath, the mother of the seventy gods, including Anath in that number, Anath the nursemaid, defender of mothers.

They sang:

> *"Whose fairness is like Anath's fairness*
> *Whose beauty like Astarte's beauty?*
>
> *"Astarte is now in your womb,*
> *You bear the power of Elath."*

The women sang all the welcoming songs to her while Rachel ate date honey and fine wheat-flour cake, made in the three-cornered shape of woman's sex. She drank as much sweet wine as she could hold. Adah rubbed Rachel's arms and legs, back and abdomen with aromatic oils until she was nearly asleep. By the time they carried her out into the field where she married the earth, Rachel was stupid with pleasure and wine. She did not remember how her legs came to be caked with earth and crusted with blood and smiled in her sleep.

She was full of joy and anticipation, lazing in the tent for the three days, collecting the precious fluid in a bronze bowl—for the first-moon blood of a virgin was a powerful libation for the garden. During those hours, she was more relaxed and generous than anyone could remember her.

As soon as the women rose from their monthly rites, Rachel demanded that the wedding date be set. None of her foot-stamping could move Adah to change the custom of waiting seven months from first blood. So it was arranged, and although Jacob had already worked a year for Laban, the contract was sealed and the next seven months were Laban's too.

Chapter Two

THOSE WERE NOT easy months. Rachel was imperious, Leah sighed like a cow in labor, Zilpah sulked. Only Bilhah seemed untouched by the turmoil, spinning and weaving, pulling weeds from the garden, and tending Adah's fire, which was always lit now, to comfort her chilled bones.

Rachel spent as much time with Jacob as she dared, slipping away from the garden and the loom to find her beloved alone in the hills. Adah was too ill to keep her from such wild behavior, and Rachel refused to obey Leah, who had lost some of her status now that the younger sister was to become bride and mother first.

Those days in the fields with Jacob were Rachel's delight. "He would look at me with wonder," said my beautiful aunt, "his fingers in my hair. He made me stand in shade and then in the sun to see the different light play across my cheek. He wept at my beauty. He sang the songs of his family, and told me about the beauty of his mother."

Rachel said, "Jacob made up stories about how beautiful our sons would be, too. Golden boys, like me, he said. Perfect boys, who would be princes and kings."

"I know what they all thought—my sisters and the shepherds—but we never touched. Well, only once. He held me to his chest, but then he began trembling and pushed me away. After that, he kept his distance.

"Which was fine with me. He smelled, you know. Much better than most of the men. But still, the smell of goat and of man was overpowering. I would run home and bury my nose in coriander."

Rachel boasted that she was the first to hear the story of Jacob's family. He was the younger of the twin boys, making him his mother's heir. He was the prettier one, the clever one. Rebecca told her husband, Isaac, that Jacob was sickly in order to keep him at the breast for a year after she weaned the brother.

Giving birth to the twins nearly killed Rebecca, who bled so much there was nothing left to sustain another life inside her. When she realized she would have no daughters, she began whispering her stories to Jacob.

Rebecca told Jacob that Esau's blessing was rightly his, for why else had Innana made him the finer of the two? And besides, in her family, it was the mother's right to decide the heir. Isaac himself was the second-born son. Left to Abram, Ishmael would have been patriarch, but Sarai had claimed her rights and named Isaac instead. It was she who sent Isaac to seek a bride from among her family, as was the custom from the oldest days.

Even so, Jacob loved Esau and hated to do him any kind of harm. He feared that the god of Isaac his father and Abram his grandfather would punish him for following his mother's words. He was haunted by a dream that woke him in terror, a dream in which he was utterly destroyed.

Rachel stroked his cheek and told him that his fears were groundless. "I told him that had he not followed his mother's bidding, he would never have found me, and surely the god of Isaac who loved Rebecca smiled upon the love of Jacob for Rachel.

"This cheered him," she said. "He told me that I gladdened his heart like a sunrise. He said such pretty things."

While Jacob spoke sweetly to Rachel, Leah suffered. She lost weight and neglected her hair, though never her duties. The camp was always well run, clean, provisioned, and busy. The spinning never ceased, the garden flourished, and the herbs were plentiful enough to be traded in the village for new lamps.

Jacob noticed these things. He saw what Leah did and learned that it was she who had maintained order during the lean years while Laban moped. The old man was completely worthless when Jacob had a question about whether the black-bearded trader from Aleppo was trustworthy, or which of the boys to hire at shearing time. Leah was the one to ask about the flock; which ewes had borne in the previous year, which goats were the offspring of the black sire and which of the dappled. Rachel, who had worked among the animals, could not tell one beast from another, but Leah remembered what she saw, and everything that Bilhah said.

Jacob approached Leah with the same deference he showed to Adah, for after all, they were kinswomen. But he approached her far more often than necessary, or so it seemed to Zilpah.

Jacob found a new question for the eldest daughter every day. Where should he pasture the kids in the spring? Had she any extra honey to barter for a likely-looking ewe? Was she ready for the sacrifice of the barley harvest? He was always thirsty for the beer she brewed from wonderful recipes her mother had learned from an Egyptian trader.

Leah answered Jacob's questions and poured his drink with her eyes averted, her head nearly tucked into her chest, like a nesting bird. It was painful for her to look at him. And yet, every morning when she opened her eyes her first thought was of him. Would he come to speak to her again that day? Did he notice how her hand trembled when she filled his cup?

Zilpah could not bear to be anywhere near them together. "It was like being near rutting he-goats," she said. "And they were so polite. They almost bent over not to see each other, lest they fall on top of each other like dogs in heat."

Leah tried to ignore the desire of her own body and Rachel was unaware of anything but the preparations for her wedding, but Zilpah saw lust everywhere she looked. To her, the whole world suddenly seemed damp with longing.

Leah tossed and turned at night, and Zilpah had seen Jacob in the fields, leaning against a tree, his hands working his sex until he slumped over in relief. For a month before the wedding, Jacob stopped dreaming of battle or of his parents and brother. Instead, he spent his nights sleepwalking with each of the four sisters. He drank at the waters of a stream and found himself in Rachel's lap. He lifted a huge boulder to find Leah naked under it. He ran from the awful thing that chased him, and fell exhausted into the arms of Bilhah, who had begun to grow the shape of a woman. He rescued Zilpah from the acacia tree, untangling her long hair from the branches where she was caught. He woke up every morning, sweating, his sex aroused. He would roll off his blanket and squirm on the ground until he could stand without embarrassment.

Zilpah watched as the triangle of Jacob, Rachel, and Leah grew into a wedge she could use. For as much as she loved Leah, Zilpah had never cared for the lovely Rachel. (That's what Zilpah always called her—"Ah, and here comes the lovely Rachel," she would say, vinegar in her voice.) She knew there wasn't much she could do to stop Jacob from becoming the family patriarch, and indeed she was as impatient for children as everyone else. Still, she wanted to make this river flow in a direction of her choosing. Zilpah also wished to make the lovely Rachel suffer just a little.

Zilpah suspected that Rachel feared her wedding night, and encouraged her to confess every worry. The older girl sighed and shook her head in sympathy as Rachel revealed how little she knew about the mechanics of sex. She had no expectation of pleasure—only of pain. So Zilpah told her nervous sister that the shepherds spoke of Jacob's sex as a freak of nature. "Twice the size of that of any normal man," she whispered, demonstrating an impossible length between her hands. Zilpah took Rachel up to the highest pasture and showed her the boys having their way with the ewes, who bleated pitifully and bled. The older sister commiserated with the trembling girl, whispering, "Poor thing," as she stroked Rachel's hair. "Poor female thing."

And that was why, on the day of the wedding, Rachel panicked. Jacob's chaste adoration had been pleasant, but now he would demand everything of her and there would be no way to refuse. Her stomach rebelled and she retched. She pulled out handfuls of hair. She ran her fingernails down her cheeks until she drew blood. She begged her sisters to save her.

"Rachel wept as we tried to dress her for the banquet," Leah said. "She cried, claiming she was unready and unwell and too small for her husband. She even tried that trick with the crushed berries, lifting her skirt and whining that Jacob would kill her if he found moon blood in the nuptial bed. I told her to stop behaving like a child, for she wore a woman's belt."

But Rachel wailed and fell on her knees and begged her sister to take her place under the bridal veil. "Zilpah says you will do it," she cried.

"I was struck dumb," Leah remembered. "For of course, Zilpah was right. I had not permitted myself to imagine such a thing—that it might be me with him that night. I could barely admit it to myself, much less to my sister, who was not so lovely at that moment, her eyes red from crying, her cheeks streaked with blood and berry juice.

"First I said no. He would know at once, for no veil could hide the difference in our height. He would refuse to have me, and then I would be damaged goods, unmarriageable, and nothing to be done but sell me for a slave.

"But all the while I protested, my heart pounded its own yes. Rachel asked me to do what I wanted more than anything in life. So even as I argued, I agreed."

Adah was too ill to help dress the bride that morning, so Zilpah took charge of the plot, rubbing Leah's hands and feet with henna, drawing the kohl around her eyes, covering her with baubles. Rachel sat in a corner, hugged her knees to her chest, and shivered as Leah prepared for what was meant to be her wedding night.

"I was happier than I had ever been," said Leah. "But I was also filled with dread. What if he turned away from me in disgust? What if he ran out of the tent and shamed me forever? But something in me believed that he would embrace me."

It was a simple banquet with few guests. Two flute-players from the village came and went quickly; one of the shepherds brought a gift offering of oil, which he left as soon as he had filled his belly. Laban was drunk from the start, his hand under poor Ruti's dress. He stumbled over his own feet when he led Leah to Jacob's side. The bride, crouched low under her veil, circled the groom three times in one direction, three times in the other. Zilpah served the meal.

"I thought the day would never end," Leah said. "I could not be seen through my veil, nor could I see out clearly, but how could Jacob not know it was me? I waited in misery for him to expose me, to jump up and claim he had been swindled. But he did not. He sat beside me, close enough for me to feel the warmth of his thigh against mine. He ate lamb and bread, and drank both wine and beer, though not enough to make him sleepy or stupid.

"Finally, Jacob stood and helped me to my feet. He led me to the tent where we would spend our seven days, with Laban following, hooting and wishing us sons," Leah remembered.

"Jacob did not move toward me until it had fallen silent outside. Then he removed my veil. It was a beautiful garment, embroidered with many colors and worn by generations of brides who had lived through a hundred wedding nights filled with pleasure, violence, fear, delight, disappointment. I shuddered, wondering which destiny would be mine.

"It was not fully dark inside the tent. He saw my face and showed no surprise. He was breathing heavily. He took off the rest of my clothes, removing first the mantle from my shoulders, untying my girdle, and then helping me as I stepped out of my robes. I was naked before him. My mother told me my husband would only lift up my robes and enter me still wearing his. But I was uncovered, and then, in a moment, so was he, his sex pointing at me. It looked like a faceless asherah! This was such a hilarious idea, I might have laughed out loud had I been able to breathe.

"But I was afraid. I sank to the blanket, and he moved quickly to my side. He stroked my hands and he touched my cheek, and then he was on top of me. I was afraid. But I remembered my mother's counsel, and opened my hands and my feet, and listened to the sound of my breath instead of his.

"Jacob was good to me. He was slow to enter me the first time, but he finished so quickly I barely had time to calm down before he fell still and heavy upon me, like a dead man, for what seemed like hours. Then his hands came to life. They wandered over my face, through my hair, and then, oh, on my breasts and belly, to my legs and my sex, which he explored with the lightest touch. It was the touch of a mother tracing the inner ear of her newborn child, a feeling so sweet I smiled. He looked at my pleasure, and nodded. We both laughed." And then Jacob spoke tenderly to his first wife.

"My own father rarely addressed me and seemed to prefer

my brother's company," he whispered. "But once, while we were traveling, we passed a tent where a man was beating a woman—wife, concubine, or slave we had no way of knowing.

"Isaac, my father, sighed and told me that he had never taken any woman to his bed but my mother, even though she had only given him two sons early in their marriage. Rebecca had welcomed him with tenderness and passion when they first were married because as her groom he treated her as though she were the Queen of Heaven and he her consort. Their coupling was the coupling of the sea and the sky, of the rain and the parched earth. Of night and day, wind and water.

"Their nights were filled with stars and sighs as they played the part of goddess and god. Their touches engendered a thousand dreams. They slept in each other's arms every night, except when it was her time for the red tent, or when she gave suck to her sons.

"That was my father's teaching about husbands and wives," said Jacob my father to Leah my mother on their first night together. And then he wept over the loss of his father's love.

Leah wept out of sympathy for her husband, and also out of relief and joy at her good fortune. She knew that her own mother had cried on her wedding night, too, but those had been tears of despair, for Laban had been a boor from the beginning.

Leah kissed her husband. He kissed her. They embraced again and again. And even on that first night, when she was tender from being opened by a man, Leah responded to his touch. She liked the smell of him and the feel of his beard on her skin. When he entered her, she flexed her legs and her sex with a kind of strength that surprised her and delighted him. When Jacob cried out in his final pleasure, she was flooded by a sense of her own power. And when she followed her breathing, she discovered her pleasure, an opening and a fullness that made her sigh, and purr, and then sleep as she hadn't slept since she was a child. He called her Innana. She called him Baal, brother-lover of Ishtar.

They were left alone the full seven days and seven nights. Food was set out for them at dawn and at dusk, and they ate with the ravenous hunger of lovers. By the end of the week, they had made love in every hour of the day and night. They were certain they had invented a thousand new methods for giving and taking pleasure. They had slept in each other's arms. They laughed like children at Laban's stupidity, and at Zilpah's strange ways. But they did not speak of Rachel.

It was a golden week, every day sweeter but every day sadder, too. There would never be another time when Leah and Jacob could wander in each other's memories or lounge during daylight in each other's arms. These were the only meals they would ever share, talking and finding in each other kindred spirits for business and family politics.

They decided that Jacob would emerge from the week feigning anger. He would go to Laban and say, "I have been duped. I was given strong wine and you gave me the harridan Leah rather than my beloved Rachel. My labor for Rachel was repaid with a swindle, for which I demand restitution. And although I spent these seven days and seven nights with your eldest girl as my duty required, I do not consider her my wife until you make me a dowry in her name, and until Rachel is also mine."

And that is precisely what Jacob said when he left the tent. "I will take the maiden Zilpah as dowry for Leah, just as Bilhah will be dowry for Rachel. I will take another tenth of your herd for relieving you of your ill-favored daughter. And to be fair, I will work for you another seven months, as the bride-price for Leah.

"These are my terms."

Jacob made this speech before everyone in camp on the day he and Leah emerged from their seclusion. Leah kept her eyes on the ground as her husband recited the words they had rehearsed the night before, naked, sweating each other's sweat. She pretended to cry while twisting her mouth to keep from laughing.

As Jacob proclaimed himself, Adah nodded assent. Zilpah turned white at the mention of her name. Laban, who had spent the week drunk in honor of his daughter's marriage, was so stupefied he could barely sputter a protest before throwing up his hands, cursing the lot of them, and returning to the dark of his tent.

Rachel spat at Jacob's feet and stormed off. By the end of the nuptial week, she had come to regret her panic. She had lost forever her position as first wife, and then she had heard the sounds from the bridal tent—laughter and muffled cries of pleasure. Rachel had poured out her sorrow to Bilhah, who took her to see two dogs mating, and two sheep, none of whom seemed to suffer in the act. Rachel went to the village and told Inna what had happened. Inna told her tales of passion and pleasure, and took Rachel inside her hut and showed her how to unlock the secrets of her own body.

When Jacob found Rachel at their accustomed tree, she cursed him soundly, calling him a thief and a bastard, a devil and a pig who inserted himself into sheep and goats and dogs. She accused him of not loving her. She shrieked that he must have known it was Leah, even when she was veiled, sitting beside him at the wedding feast. He could have stopped it. Why hadn't he? She cried bitterly.

When her tears were spent, Jacob held her to his chest until it seemed she was asleep, and told her that she was the moon's own daughter, luminous, radiant, and perfect. That his love for her was worshipful. That he felt only duty toward Leah, who was a mere shadow of Rachel's light. That she, only Rachel, would be the bride of his heart, his first wife, first love. Such pretty treason.

So it happened that the day before the next full moon there was a second wedding feast, even simpler than the first. And Rachel took her turn in the tent with Jacob.

I do not know much about that week, for Rachel never spoke of it. No tears were heard coming from the nuptial tent of Jacob and Rachel, which was a good sign. No one overheard laughter either. When the week was over, Rachel crept to the red tent before dawn, where she slept until the following morning.

At the first new moon after Leah's bridal week, there was no blood between her legs. But she kept this news to herself. Amid the hurried preparations for Rachel's wedding, it was easy enough to conceal the fact that she did not really need to change her place on the straw or use a rag between her legs when she moved around.

Two days after Rachel entered the nuptial tent with Jacob, Leah went to her mother and put Adah's dry hand on her young belly. The older woman hugged her daughter. "I did not think I would live to see a grandchild," she said to Leah, smiling and crying at once. "Beloved girl, daughter mine."

Leah said she kept quiet about her pregnancy to protect Rachel's happiness. Her status as head wife would be assured with the birth of a son, and she knew from the first that she was carrying a boy. But Rachel was furious when she learned that Leah was with child. She thought her sister had kept the news from her as part of a complicated plot to shame her, to assure her own role as first wife, as a way to cause Jacob to abandon her.

Rachel's accusations could be heard from as far away as the well, which was a good distance from the tent where she bellowed. She accused Leah of asking Zilpah to help cheat her of her rightful place. She insinuated that Leah was pregnant not by Jacob, but by a harelipped, half-witted shepherd who loitered at the well. "You jealous bitch," Rachel screamed. "You evil-eyed lummox, you only wish Jacob loved you as he loves me, but he never will. I am the one. I am his heart. You are a brood mare. You pathetic cow."

Leah held her tongue until Rachel was finished. Then she calmly called her sister an ass and slapped her face hard, first on one cheek and then on the other. They did not speak a word to each other for months.

I suppose it only natural to assume that Leah was always jealous of Rachel. And it was true that Leah did not sing or smile much during Jacob's week with Rachel. Indeed, over the years, whenever my father took my beautiful aunt to his bed, my mother kept her head bent over her work, which grew as her sons increased and as Jacob's labors yielded more wool to be woven.

But Leah was not jealous in the way of silly girls in love songs, who die of longing. There was no bile in Leah's sadness when Jacob lay with his other wives. Indeed, she delighted in all his sons and had most of them at her own breast at one time or another. She could depend upon Jacob to call for her once or twice in a month, for talk about the herds and for an extra cup of sweet beer. On those nights she knew they would sleep together, her arms locked around his waist, and the next morning her family would bask in her smile and enjoy something good to eat.

But I am rushing my story. For it took years before Leah and Rachel finally learned how to share a husband, and at first they were like dogs, circling and growling and giving each other wide berth as they explored the boundary between them.

Even so, at first it seemed a kind of parity would prevail, because at the next new moon, Rachel, too, found she had no use for the rags or the hay. Both sisters were pregnant. The barley crop was enormous. The shepherds slapped Jacob on the back and joked about his potency. The gods were smiling.

But just as Leah's belly began to swell against her tunic, Rachel started to bleed. Early one morning, nearly three months after her wedding, she woke the whole camp with her cries. Leah and Zilpah rushed to her side, and found her sobbing, wrapped in a bloody blanket. No one could comfort her. She would not let Adah sit with her. She would not permit Jacob to see her. For a week, she huddled in a corner of the red tent, where she ate little and slept a dreamless, feverish sleep.

Leah forgave Rachel her nasty words and grieved for her. She tried to tempt her with her favorite sweets, but Rachel spat at the food and at Leah, who seemed to grow bigger and rounder every day, and as beautiful as she had ever been.

"It was so unfair. So sad," said Bilhah, who finally got Rachel to eat a few olives and coaxed her out of the stained, stiff blanket. Bilhah was the one who walked to the village where Inna lived, to see if the midwife had some potion that might rouse her sister from her half-death. Inna herself came back and spent hours with Rachel, washing her, feeding her tiny bits of bread dipped in honey, coaxing her to take sips of an aromatic red mead. Inna whispered secret words of comfort and hope into Rachel's ear. She told her that bearing children would not be easy for her, but foretold that someday Rachel would bear beautiful sons who would shine like stars and assure her memory. Inna promised to put all her skills to work to help Rachel conceive again, but only if she would do exactly what the midwife told her to do.

That is why, when Leah in her sixth month sought her sister's blessing, Rachel put her hands on Leah's belly and caressed the life there. Rachel cried in her sister's arms, kissed Adah's hands, and asked Zilpah to comb her hair. She took Bilhah aside, embraced her, and thanked her for bringing Inna. It was the first time Rachel had thanked anyone for anything.

The next morning, Leah and Rachel, side by side, walked out of the darkness of the red tent and back into the light of the world, where Jacob stood. Rachel said he wept when he saw them together, but Leah said that he smiled.

"Leah's first birth was not especially difficult," said Rachel. By the time she told me the story of Reuben's arrival, my aunt had seen hundreds of babies born. And though Rachel would forget where she put her spindle the moment she put it down, she remembered the details of every birth she ever witnessed.

She told me that even though Leah's travail began before sunset and did not end until daylight, it was a straight path. His head was down and her hips were wide enough. Still, the heat of that summer night in the red tent was stifling, and none of the sisters had ever seen a birth. Truly Leah suffered most because of her sisters' fear.

It began slowly in the afternoon, with small, grabbing pains in her back. Leah smiled after each little seizure, glad to be started, eager to be admitted to the sisterhood of mothers. Confident that her body, so broad and big, would fulfill its purpose, she sang in the early stages. Children's songs, ballads, lullabies.

But as the night wore on, and the moon rose in the sky and then started to sink, there were no more smiles or songs. Each contraction took Leah up and wrung her out, like a bit of cloth, and left her panting and fearful of the next pain. Adah held her hand. Zilpah muttered prayers to Anath. "I was of no use at all," Rachel remembered. "I wandered in and out of the tent, eaten up by jealousy. But as the hours came and went, each one harder than the last, my envy waned and I was horrified by the pain I saw on Leah, the strong one, the invincible ox who was on the ground trembling and wide-eyed. I was terrified by the thought that I might have been in her place, that I might yet be. And I'm sure that the very same thoughts made Zilpah and Bilhah shudder and keep silence while our sister labored."

Bilhah finally realized that they needed more help than Adah could provide, and she went to fetch Inna, who arrived at daybreak. By that time, Leah was whimpering like a dog. When Inna arrived, she put her hands on Leah's belly and then reached up inside her. She made her lie on her side, and rubbed her back and thighs with a mint-scented oil. Inna smiled into Leah's face and said, "The baby is nearly at the door." And while she emptied her kit, she bade the women gather around to help their sister bring the baby.

"It was the first time I'd seen a midwife's kit," Rachel said. "The knife, the string, reeds for suction, amphorae of cumin, hyssop, and mint oil. Inna put her two bricks on the ground and told Leah she would stand on them soon. She moved me and Zilpah on either side to lend support when Leah squatted over a bed of clean straw. Zilpah and I became Leah's chair, with our arms around her shoulders and beneath her thighs. 'You lucky girl,' Inna said to Leah, who by then did not feel the least bit lucky. 'Look at the royal throne of sisters you have.'"

Inna talked and talked, banishing the frightened silence that had made a wall around Leah. Inna asked Adah about her aches and pains, and teased Zilpah about the tangled mat of her hair. But whenever a contraction came, Inna had words for Leah only. She praised her, reassured her, told her, "Good, good, good, my girl. Good, good, good." Soon, all of the women in the tent joined her in repeating "Good, good, good," clucking like a clutch of doves.

Inna began to massage the skin around Leah's bottom, which was swollen out of shape. She rubbed with stronger and stronger motions as the pains came closer and closer. And then she put Rachel's hand on Leah's belly and showed her how to press downward, gently but firmly, when the time came. She told Leah not to push, not to push, until Leah bellowed curses.

Rachel said, "I saw that baby come into the world as I had seen nothing before in my life. Clearly. Without a thought to myself. I thought of my own mother who had seen this so many times, whose hands had guided so many souls into the world, but who died giving me life.

"But I had no time to be sorry for myself, because suddenly a strange red bubble emerged from between Leah's legs and then, almost immediately, a flood of bloody water washed down her thighs."

Leah tried to stand, terrified, but Inna told her not to take her feet off the bricks. This was good, she said. He was coming.

Leah pushed, her face red, her eyes bulging, blue and green, glittering. Her legs were trembling as though they would buckle at any moment, and it took all of Zilpah's and Rachel's strength to hold her. Then Inna told Bilhah to take Rachel's place so she could catch the baby; perhaps the birth blood would rouse Rachel's womb to fill again, too. And so Rachel washed in the river of life.

Leah roared and delivered her son. He was so big it took both Inna and Rachel to catch him, and he started to cry even before they raised up his head. No need for the reeds to clear out this baby's nose and mouth. They all laughed, tears streaming down their faces, panting from the effort of Leah's birth.

They passed the baby around the tent, wiping him and kissing him, praising his limbs, his torso, his head, his little sex. They all talked at the same time, making more noise than any six women can make. Jacob cried out to the women to tell him the news. "You are a father," said Inna. "Go away. We will send for you soon and then you will see your son, your firstborn, when we have finished." They heard Jacob shout with joy, and call out the news to Laban and Ruti, and his barking dogs, and the clouds in the sky.

The afterbirth fell out of Leah, who was nearly asleep with exhaustion. Inna made her drink and eat before she rested, and put the baby to Leah's breast, where he nursed. Mother and son slept, and the sisters covered them. Adah watched, a grandmother's smile lingering even after she dozed off. Inna wrapped the placenta in an old rag and they buried it that night, in the eastern corner of the bamah, as befits a firstborn son.

A few hours later when Leah awoke she named the baby Reuben. It was a joyful shout of a name, a name that fairly dared evil spirits to do him any harm. But Leah had no fears for her strapping boy. Jacob was sent for and greeted his son with great tenderness.

As Jacob walked away from his first meeting with his son, his happiness seemed to evaporate. His head sank to his chest as he contemplated what had to be done next. According to the custom of his family, the boy had to be circumcised, and there was no one to do it but him. Jacob would not let Laban touch the baby, much less take a knife to him. He knew of no other man in the village or nearby hills who knew how, much less why he would do this to his firstborn son. It would have to be him.

Jacob had seen his father cut the foreskins from his bondsmen's baby boys, and he had not looked away or even winced when it was done. But he had never done this himself, nor, he now realized, had he watched carefully enough how his father had dressed the wound. And, of course, he had never cared so much for any baby in his life.

It had to be done, though, and he began the preparations, which Zilpah watched and reported to Leah, who was sick at the prospect of having her baby, her prize, put on the altar of the bamah and mutilated. For that's what she considered it. The flap of skin on the penis meant nothing to her. Indeed, now that she had seen the look of an uncircumcised man, she preferred the look of Jacob's sex— exposed, clean, audacious even—to the tiny shroud her son wore on his member, which was the source of many silly and crude jokes in the red tent. Once, Leah threatened to take a bit of charred wood and draw a face upon Reuben's sex, so that when Jacob retracted the foreskin, he would drop his knife in wonder. The women rolled around on the mats, holding their sides, laughing about the tender equipment that men carried between their legs.

But after a few days, the joking stopped, and Leah cried so long and so hard over the boy at her breast that the dark curls on his head were salted with tears. Still, she did not object to the custom of her husband's father. Jacob had survived this, she told her sisters again and again, mostly to reassure herself. Isaac had been circumcised, and Abram before him. Nevertheless, the thought of her baby in pain and in danger made the new mother tremble, and the realization that Jacob had no experience at the task put her in a frenzy of worry. Zilpah watched and saw that Jacob was not at ease about the ritual either. Every night, he sat on the bamah with his knife and sharpened it on the altar. From sunset till moonrise three nights running, until the edge was perfect, he honed and polished the blade until it could cut a hair from his head with the slightest motion of his wrist. He asked Adah to make small bandages, woven of new wool taken from the first shearing of the firstborn lamb of the season. He sent word to Leah, inquiring whether she had any of the midwife's unguents to aid in healing.

On the seventh night after Reuben's birth, Jacob sat up, silently watching the sky, until sunrise. He poured libations and sang to the god of his fathers. He poured libations over the Asherah, too, and opened his hands before her. Zilpah watched all of this and afterward stopped referring to Jacob as "that new man" and began to call him by his name.

At dawn of the eighth day after his son's birth, Jacob killed a kid and burned it on the altar. He washed his hands, rubbing them red with straw, as though he had handled a corpse. And then he walked to the red tent and asked that the women give him Reuben, the son of Leah.

He called for Laban to follow him, and the two men walked alone to the bamah, where Jacob undressed the baby, whose eyes were open, and placed him on the altar. Jacob sighed a loud, long sigh as he stripped the boy, and then he signaled Laban to grab the baby's legs. At this, Reuben began to wail. Jacob took the knife in his hands and knotted his brow.

"There were tears in his eyes," said Zilpah. "He took the baby's sex in his hands and pulled the skin up tightly, holding it between the two long fingers of his left hand. With his right hand, he cut, with a quick, sure stroke, as though it was an old custom of his, as though he knew what he was doing," she said.

Reuben howled, and Jacob dropped the knife. Quickly, he bound the wound with Adah's bandage, and swaddled the baby, badly, the way men do. He carried his son back to the women, whispering into Reuben's perfect ear words that no one else could hear.

The red tent, which had been quiet during the baby's absence, now burst into activity. Leah dressed the wound with the cumin oil that Inna had left for her own birth wounds. Adah swaddled Reuben properly and gave him back to his mother, where he took her breast with relief and then slept.

The baby healed quickly, as did Leah during her first month as a new mother inside the shelter of the red tent. She was pampered by her sisters, who barely let her feet touch the earth. Jacob came by every day, carrying freshly dressed birds for her meals. Through the hairy wall of the tent they relayed the news of their days with a tenderness that warmed those who overheard them.

Adah beamed that whole month and saw her daughter step out of the red tent restored and rested. She delighted in her grandson's first yawns and sneezes and was the first to notice Reuben lift his head. Adah held the baby whenever Leah would put him down, and the joy of him lifted years from her face and the pain from her bones. But the illness that had wasted her strength could not be cured by even the greatest joy. And one morning she did not rise from her blanket.

Adah was the only mother any of the sisters had known, and they put ashes in their hair and honored her. Leah washed Adah's face and hands. Zilpah combed her hair smooth. Rachel dressed her in the finest tunic they owned, and Bilhah placed Adah's few rings and bangles on the withered wrists, neck, and fingers. Together, they crossed her arms and bent her knees so that she looked like a sleeping child. They whispered wishes into her ears so she could carry them to the other side of the light, where the spirits of her ancestors would greet her soul, which could now rest in the dust of the earth and suffer no more.

They wrapped her in a shroud of unbleached wool lined with sweet-smelling herbs and buried her amid the roots of the big tree where the women often gathered to watch the moon rise.

Jacob dug the grave while Laban stood and watched, ashes on his head to honor his first wife. With Adah, Laban buried his youth, his strength, and perhaps some forgotten better self. He threw the first handful of dirt, then turned and walked away before the four sisters finished tucking her in with earth, flowers, and loud lamentation.

Two months after Adah died, Bilhah entered the red tent. With Adah gone and no other elder to take the part, Leah, nursing her son, became the welcoming mother. She greeted the acolyte and taught her how to manage the flow of blood, how to rejoice in the dark of the moon, how to join her body's cycle with the repetition of life.

The wheel had turned. And even though Laban retained title as head of the clan, Jacob's time as patriarch had begun.

My mothers, too, began numbering their days with the wisdom of women.

There followed many good years. The rains came in season, and the well water was sweet and abundant. The land was spared pestilence, and there was peace among the surrounding tribes. The herds prospered so that Jacob could no longer manage the work alone and he contracted with Shibtu, the third son of a local shepherd, as a seven-year bondsman. And then he hired Nomir, who brought a wife, Zibatu, and there was a new face in the red tent.

The family's good fortune and increasing wealth were not entirely the result of Jacob's skill, nor could it all be attributed to the will of the gods. My mothers' labors accounted for much of it. While sheep and goats are a sign of wealth, their full value is realized only in the husbandry of women. Leah's cheeses never soured, and when the rust attacked wheat or millet, she saw to it that the afflicted stems were picked clean to protect the rest of the crop. Zilpah and Bilhah wove the wool from Jacob's growing flocks into patterns of black, white, and saffron that lured traders and brought new wealth.

This was also the time of great fertility among the women. Many babies were born, and most survived. Leah wore the mantle of the great mother, seemingly always pregnant or nursing. Two years after Reuben's birth, she bore a second son, Simon. Levi was born only eighteen months later. Leah miscarried after that, but within another year her sorrow was forgotten in the joy of her fourth son, Judah.

Those brothers, so close in age, were a tribe unto themselves. Reuben, always the heaviest and tallest, was gentle with the younger ones. Simon was a demon—handsome and smug, demanding and rude—but forgiven everything for his dimples. Levi was a meek mouse and Simon's slave. Judah was a quiet boy, affectionate toward everyone. He was much fairer than his brothers, and Jacob told Leah that he resembled his own brother, Esau.

While Leah was carrying Simon, Laban's Ruti showed a big belly, too, and bore a boy, Kemuel, who was followed a year later by Beor. The old man doted on his slope-browed sons, who played rough-and-tumble with Leah's boys at first, but then invented a secret language, which locked them into a narrow world of their own making. Laban thought this demonstrated his sons' superiority, but the rest of the family saw it as proof of their stunted nature and limited prospects.

The happy noise of children surrounded them, but the blessing of generation was not equally distributed. Rachel miscarried again and again. After the bloody flood washed away her hopes a fourth time, she sickened with a fever that drove her out of her mind for three days and nights. This frightened her sisters so badly they insisted she stop trying to conceive and persuaded her to drink the infusion of fennel seed that seals the womb, at least until she had regained weight and strength. Rachel, exhausted, agreed.

But she could not rest long amid the clamor of her sister's sons. Although she no longer hated Leah with the full force of the past, Rachel could not smile at her sister while her own body remained fruitless. She was often away from the family's tents, seeking the counsel of Inna, who had a seemingly endless list of concoctions and strategies to open her womb.

Rachel tried every remedy, every potion, every rumored cure. She wore only red and yellow—the colors of life's blood and the talisman for healthy menstruation. She slept with her belly against trees said to be sacred to local goddesses. Whenever she saw running water, she lay down in it, hoping for the life of the river to inspire life within her. She swallowed a tincture made with bee pollen until her tongue was coated yellow and she peed a saffron river. She dined upon snake—the animal that gives birth to itself, year after year.

Of course, when anyone, adult or child, found a mandrake—the root that looks so much like an aroused husband—it would be brought to Rachel and handed over with a wink and a prayer. Reuben once found an especially large one, and brought it to his auntie with the pride of a lion hunter. But mandrakes did nothing for Rachel's womb.

During her quest for a child of her own, Rachel assisted Inna and became her apprentice. She learned what to do when the baby presented itself feet first, and what to do when the baby came too fast and the mother's flesh tore and festered. She learned how to keep a stillborn's mother from giving up her spirit in despair. And how, when a mother died, to cut open the womb and save the child within.

Rachel brought her sisters stories that made them weep, and sigh, and wonder. Of a mother who died and a father who sold the infant before her body was cold. Of a man who swooned at the death of a beloved wife. Of a woman who cried blood for her dead child. She told of potions that worked a miracle upon one woman and seemed to kill another, of an armless monster left out to die in the night air, of blood that carried off and blood that healed.

There were triumphant stories, too, of healthy twins, of a baby born blue, the cord wrapped tight around its neck, brought to life by Inna, who sucked the death from the little one's nostrils with a river reed. Sometimes Rachel made her sisters laugh with imitations of women who roared like lions and others who held their breath and fainted rather than make a peep.

Rachel became their link to the larger world. Along with tales of life and death, Rachel brought back new herbs for seasoning vegetables, recipes for unguents that healed wounds, and ever stranger remedies for her barrenness, all of which failed.

Often, Rachel returned bearing a bracelet, a bowl, or a skein of wool—tokens of gratitude for her generosity at childbed. The imperious beauty became a tenderhearted healer in the service of mothers. She wept at every birth, the easy, happy ones as well as the ones that ended with keening and whimpering. She wept with Ruti and even with Leah.

When it came time for Zibatu to stand on the midwife's bricks, Rachel alone—without Inna—led her through the ordeal, tied off the cord, and flushed with pleasure when she held "her" first, the baby that conferred upon her the title of midwife. Leah cooked her a feast that night, and Zilpah poured out salt and wine before her, in recognition of her new status as a servant of women in the name of Anath, the healer.

As time passed, more bondsmen came to live and work

for Jacob, and with them came women who bore children and lost children. Zibatu gave birth to Nasi, but then lost her second child, a girl who came two months before her time. Iltani bore twin girls who thrived, though she died of fever before her daughters knew their mother's face. Lamassi gave birth to a son, Zinri, but her daughter was left out to die because she had the harelip.

In the red tent we knew that death was the shadow of birth, the price women pay for the honor of giving life. Thus, our sorrow was measured.

After Judah's birth, Leah grew tired. She, who had always risen the earliest and retired last, who seemed most content when doing two things at once (stirring a pot while nursing, or grinding grain as she oversaw the spinning), began to stagger in the afternoons and see shadows where there were none. Inna advised her to leave off bearing for a while, and brought her fennel seeds and also showed her how to fashion a pessary out of beeswax.

So Leah rested. She rejoiced in the sturdiness of her sons, and stopped every day to caress them and play their game of smooth stones. She baked honeyed cake as she used to, and planned a new garden where herbs would attract more bees to nearby hives. She slept soundly at night and rose in peace every morning.

Leah remembered her fallow years as a time of great contentment. She held the fullness of every day in her hands, numbering the sweetness of children, the pleasure of work. She gave thanks for the fennel seeds and the wisdom to use them. Her cake never tasted sweeter than it did that year, and she responded to Jacob's body with more ardor than she had felt for years.

When she spoke of that time, Leah said, "The flavor of gratitude is like the nectar of the hive."

After two years, she put away the fennel seeds and pessary and conceived another son, whom she bore easily and named Zebulun, by which Leah meant "exalt," because with his birth, Leah exalted in her body's ability to heal and to give life once more. She adored the new baby nearly as much as her firstborn. And when she handed her son over to Jacob for the circumcision, she smiled into her husband's face, and he kissed her hands.

Chapter Three

RACHEL GREW QUIET. She stopped attending Inna and did not rise from her blanket until Leah shook her and insisted she help the rest of the women in their work. Only then would Rachel spin or weave or work the garden, but wordlessly and without a smile. Jacob could not rouse her from her sadness. Rebuffed by her unbending silence, he stopped calling her to him at night. Her sorrow became a presence so bleak, even the babies began to avoid their pretty auntie. Rachel was alone in her own black night.

Bilhah saw Rachel's despair and went to her where she huddled on her blanket. The little sister lay down beside Rachel and held her as gently as a mother. "Let me go to Jacob on your behalf," said Bilhah, in a whisper. "Let me bear a son on your knees. Let me be your womb and your breasts. Let me bleed your blood and shed your tears. Let me become your vessel until your time comes, for your time will yet arrive. Let me be your hope, Rachel. I will not disappoint you."

Rachel made no reply. She said nothing for a long time. Bilhah wondered if her sister had slept through her words, or whether her offer had offended. Bilhah said she waited so long for a reply that she began to wonder whether the words that had been gathering in her heart had not even passed her lips.

Bilhah was accustomed to silence and waited. Finally, Rachel turned and kissed her, gathering the small woman close to her body, taking comfort from her warmth. "And the tears she shed were not bitter or even salty," said Bilhah, "but sweet as rainwater."

Bilhah knew that even though her offer to Rachel was made out of love, it also served her own heart's desire. She understood Rachel's longing because it was her own. She was well into her childbearing years. The sounds of lovemaking in the close world of our tents had roused her at night, leaving her shaken and sleepless. Attending her sister's births made her wish to become part of the great mothermystery, which is bought with pain and repaid with an infant's sparkling smile and silken skin. Her breasts ached to give suck.

Honest Bilhah revealed every corner of her heart to Rachel, who knew the emptiness her sister described. They wept together and slept in each other's arms. The next morning, Rachel sought out Jacob and asked that he sire a child upon Bilhah, in her name. This was not a request, for it was Rachel's right to have a child of Jacob.

There was no other permission to seek or get. Jacob agreed. (Why would he not? Leah nursed her latest son and Rachel's back had been turned to him for long months.) So that night, on the full moon of a chill month, Bilhah went to Jacob, and left him the next morning, no longer a maiden, though not a bride.

There was no henna for Bilhah's hands, no feast, no gifts. There were no seven days to learn the secrets of Jacob's body or the meaning of his words. When the sun rose the next day, Jacob returned to oversee the flocks, and Bilhah went to Rachel, and recounted every detail of her night to her sister. Years later, she told it to me.

She wept when she entered Jacob's tent, and she was surprised by her own tears. She had wanted to be initiated into the mystery of sex, to open her legs and learn the ancient ways of men and women. But she was lonely walking into her husband's tent alone, without sisters or ceremony or celebration. She had no right to the rituals of a dowered bride, and yet she missed them.

"Jacob was kind," Bilhah remembered. "He thought my tears were a sign of fear, so he held me like a child and gave me a woolen bracelet." It was nothing. No precious metal, or ivory, or anything of value. Just a woven braid made from leavings, the kind of thing shepherd boys make absent-mindedly, sitting under a tree in the heat of the day, out of tufts of wool caught on brambles or blown to the ground. Jacob had twirled the brown, black, and cream-colored strands against his thigh until he had enough to plait into a braid.

He took the simple thing from his arm and cut it to fit hers. Such a sad little nothing of a bride price, but she wore it throughout her first year as Jacob's third wife, until it fell apart one day and she lost it without even knowing where. Thinking of her bracelet, Bilhah smiled and with her forefinger traced the place where a bit of string had tied her to Jacob.

"He comforted me with that poor gift without a word,

and I stopped crying. I smiled into his face. And then, oh, I was so bold, I could hardly believe it was me. I put my hand upon his sex and laid his hand upon mine. He lifted my skirt and massaged my belly and my breasts. He buried his face between my thighs, and I almost laughed out loud at the shock of pleasure. When he entered me, it was as though I had fallen into a pool of water, it was as though the moon were singing my name. It was all I had hoped for.

"I slept in Jacob's long arms, cradled like a child for the first time since my mother held me, may her name be set in the stars. For that night alone, I loved Jacob."

Bilhah told all of this to Rachel. It was not easy for my beautiful aunt to hear it, but she insisted that Bilhah leave nothing out. And the younger sister repeated her story as often as Rachel asked to hear it, until the memory of Bilhah's consummation became Rachel's own memory and her sister's pleasure and gratitude became part of her own feelings for Jacob.

The day after Jacob knew Bilhah for the first time, he was called away to do business with a trader in Carchemish, a journey of two days. Bilhah suffered in his absence, for she was eager to lie with him again. Rachel suffered in the knowledge that Jacob had found happiness with Bilhah. Leah suffered because she felt so distant from her sisters' lives. Zilpah watched it all, said little, and sighed much.

Upon Jacob's return, he brought Rachel a beaded necklace and spent his first night with her. Leah was still nursing, so he called Bilhah to him again often during the next months, especially when Rachel was away attending a birth.

Jacob and his third wife spoke very little when they were together, but their bodies joined in straightforward postures, which yielded them both pleasure and release. "Jacob said I gave him peace," said Bilhah, with great satisfaction.

Bilhah conceived. Rachel greeted the news with kisses and rejoiced with her sister. As the months passed and her belly grew, Rachel coddled her and asked her to name every sensation, every twinge, every mood. Did Bilhah know at what moment life had taken root? Was the tiredness of pregnancy felt in her knees or in her eyes? Did she crave salt or sweet?

The two of them shared a blanket during Bilhah's pregnancy. The barren woman felt the slow swell of her sister's belly and the gathering heaviness of her breasts. She watched the flesh stretch in tan bands across the brown belly and thighs, and noticed the changing color of her nipples. As the child grew in Bilhah, draining her of color and energy, Rachel bloomed. She grew soft and round along with Bilhah, and the hollows that sadness had carved in her cheeks disappeared. She laughed and played with her nephews and the other children of the camp. She baked bread and made cheese without being asked. She lived so deeply inside Bilhah's pregnancy that during the ninth month, Rachel's ankles grew swollen, and when the time came for the baby to enter the world, Rachel called Inna to be midwife so that she alone could stand behind Bilhah during her travail and hold her and suffer with her.

Happily for Bilhah, the birth was as simple and quick as the pregnancy had been difficult. After a morning's worth of panting and groaning, she stood on the bricks while Rachel crouched around her. Bilhah's elbows rested on Rachel's splayed knees, and it was as if the two women shared a womb for the awful hour when the baby pushed his way out. Their faces strained and reddened together, and they cried out with a single voice when his head appeared. Inna said it was as though a two-headed woman had given birth and declared it one of the strangest things she had seen.

When the boy was delivered and the cord severed, Rachel held him first, her eyes streaming, for a very long time. Or so it seemed to Bilhah, who bit her tongue and waited for the moment she would embrace the first issue of her womb. Bilhah's eyes followed Rachel's every move as she wiped the blood from the baby's body and checked to see that he was whole and unblemished. Bilhah barely breathed as the moments passed and her arms remained empty, but she said nothing. By law, this son belonged to Rachel.

Years attending so many births had made Rachel's heart tender, and with a great sigh she placed the boy in Bilhah's arms, where he lifted his eyes to his mother's face and smiled into her eyes before he took her breast.

At that instant, Rachel woke from her dream, and saw that the baby was not her child. Her smile faded and her shoulders sagged and her hands clawed at her girlish breasts. Inna had told Rachel that if she let the baby suck there long enough, he would find milk within her and she could become his milk-mother. But Rachel had no faith in her body's ability to sustain life. Putting a child to nurse on an empty breast would cause suffering to her son, who was not hers at all but Bilhah's. Besides, Bilhah might sicken and even die if she did not empty her breasts, for she had seen that happen. And Rachel loved her sister. She hoped the baby at Bilhah's breast would be as good a man as his mother was a woman.

Rachel left Bilhah with her son and went to find Jacob. She told her husband that the baby's name was Dan, which means "judgment." To the woman who bore him, Dan sounded sweet, but to her in whose name he was borne, it had a bitter ring.

The sight of the baby in Bilhah's arms, day after day, shattered Rachel's confidence again. She was only the aunt, the bystander, the barren one. But now she did not rail against heaven or plague her sisters with temper. She sat, too unhappy to weep, under the acacia tree, sacred to Innana, where the birds gathered at dawn. She went to the asherah and prostrated herself before the wide-mouthed grinning goddess, and whispered, "Give me children or I will die."

Jacob saw her suffering and gathered her to him with the greatest tenderness. And after all the years, all the nights, all the miscarriages and broken hopes, Rachel found delight in his arms. "I really had no idea why Leah and Bilhah sought out Jacob's bed before those days," Rachel said. "I had always gone to his bed willingly enough, but mostly out of duty.

"But after Dan opened Bilhah's womb, somehow my own passion finally matched Jacob's and I understood my sisters' willingness to lie with him. And then I was newly jealous for all the years that I had missed of the wild sweetness between lovers."

Rachel and Jacob spent many nights together exploring the new heat between them, and Rachel hoped again. Some midwives said that pleasure overheated the seed and killed it. But others claimed that babies only come when women smile. This was the tale she told Jacob to inspire his caresses.

During the last months of Bilhah's pregnancy, Zilpah went to Jacob's bed for the first time. She did not offer herself as Bilhah had, though she was at least five years older, as old as Leah, who had borne five live sons by that time.

Zilpah knew it would happen someday, and she was resigned to it. But unlike Bilhah, Zilpah would never ask. Leah would have to command it. Finally, she did.

"One night, when I was walking in the light of a full moon, she appeared before me," Zilpah said. "At first, I thought I was dreaming. My sister slept as heavily as Laban and never rose at night. Even her own babies had trouble rousing her. But there she was, in the stillness. We walked in the bright white light of the lady moon, hand in hand, for a long time. And again I wondered if this was really my sister or a ghost, because the woman beside me was silent, whereas Leah always had something to say.

"Finally, she spoke with careful words about the moon. She told me how much she loved the white light, and how she spoke to the moon and called to her by name every month. Leah said the moon was the only face of the goddess that seemed open to her because of the way the moon called forth the filling and emptying of her body.

"My sister was wise," said Zilpah. "She stopped and faced me and took both my hands in hers and asked, 'Are you ready to swallow the moon at last?'

"What could I say? It was my time."

Indeed, it was possible that she had waited too long, and Zilpah half hoped she was too old, at five and twenty, to bear. Age alone was no good augury. Rachel had been barren from her youth, despite all her efforts. And Leah, fertile as a watered plain, showed no sign of giving off. The only way to discover what the mother of life had in store for Zilpah was for her to go in to Jacob and become the least of his wives.

The next morning, Leah spoke to Jacob. Bilhah offered to put henna on Zilpah's hands, but she set her mouth and refused. That night she walked slowly to Jacob's tent, where he lay with her and knew her. Zilpah took no pleasure from Jacob's touch. "I did what was required of me," she said, with such a tone that no one dared ask her to say more.

She never complained of Jacob's attentions. He did his best to calm her fears, just as he had with his other wives. He called for her many times, trying to win her. He asked her to sing songs of the goddesses and brushed her hair. But nothing he did moved Zilpah. "I never understood my sisters' eagerness to lie with Jacob," she said, with a weary wave of her long hand. "It was a duty, like grinding grain— something that wears away at the body but is necessary so that life can go on.

"Mind you, I was not disappointed," she said. "It was nothing I expected to enjoy."

Zilpah conceived during Bilhah's pregnancy. And soon after Bilhah's Dan was born, it truly did appear as though Zilpah had swallowed the moon. On her slender frame, the belly looked huge and perfectly round. Her sisters teased her, but Zilpah only smiled. She was glad to be free from Jacob's attentions, for men did not lie with pregnant women.

She gloried in her new body, and dreamed wonderful dreams of power and flight.

She dreamed of giving birth to a daughter, not a human child but a changeling of some kind, a spirit woman. Full-grown, full-breasted. She wore nothing but a girdle of string, in front and in back. She strode the earth in great steps, and her moon blood made trees grow everywhere she walked.

"I loved to go to sleep when I was with child," said Zilpah. "I traveled so far in my blankets those months."

But when her time came, the baby was slow to appear and Zilpah suffered. Her hips were too narrow, and labor lasted from sunset to sunset, for three days. Zilpah cried and wailed, sure that her daughter would die, or that she would be dead before she saw her girl, her Ashrat, for she had chosen her name already and told it to her sisters in case she did not survive.

It went hard with Zilpah. On the evening of the third day of her labor, she was all but dead from the pains, which, strong as they were, did not seem to bring the baby any closer to this world. Finally, Inna resorted to an untried potion she had bought from a Canaanite trader. She reached her hand all the way up to the stubborn door of Zilpah's womb and rubbed a strong, aromatic gum that did its work quickly, wrenching a shriek from Zilpah's throat, which by then was so hoarse from her travail that she sounded less like a woman than an animal caught in the fire. Inna whispered a fragment of an incantation in the name of the ancient goddess of healing.

> *"Gula, quicken the delivery*
> *Gula, I appeal to you, miserable and distraught*

Tortured by pain, your servant
Be merciful and hear this prayer."

Soon, Zilpah was up on the bricks, with Leah standing behind her, supporting the birth of the child conceived in her name. Zilpah had no more tears by the time Inna directed her to push. She was ashen and cold. She was half dead, and there was no strength even to scream when the baby finally came, tearing her flesh front and back.

It was not the hoped-for daughter, but a boy, long, thin, and black-haired. Leah hugged her sister and declared her lucky to have such a son, and lucky to be alive. Leah named him Gad for luck, and said, "May he bring you the moon and the stars and keep you safe in your old age."

But the rejoicing in the red tent was cut short because Zilpah cried out again. The pain had returned. "I am dying. I am dying," she sobbed, weeping for the son who would never know his mother. "He will live as I did," she wailed, "the orphan of a concubine, haunted by dreams of a cold, dead mother.

"Unlucky one," she whimpered. "Unlucky son of an unlucky mother."

Inna and Rachel crouched on either side of the despairing mother seeking the source of this new pain. Inna took Rachel's hand and placed it on Zilpah's belly, showing her a second child in the womb. "Don't give up yet, little mother," Inna said to Zilpah. "You will bear twins tonight. Didn't you dream of that? Not much of a priestess, is she?" She grinned.

The second baby came quickly, since Gad had opened

the way. He fell out of his mother's womb like ripe fruit, another boy, also dark but much smaller than the first.

But his mother did not see him. A river of blood followed in his wake, and the light in Zilpah's eyes went out. Time and again Inna and Rachel packed her womb with wool and herbs to staunch the bleeding. They wet her lips with water and strong, honeyed brews. They sang healing hymns and burned incense to keep her spirit from flying out of the tent. But Zilpah lay on the blanket, not dead but not alive either, for eight days and more. She was not aware of the circumcision of Gad or her second son, whom Leah named Asher, for the goddess Zilpah loved. Leah nursed the boys, and so did Bilhah and one of the bondswomen.

After ten days Zilpah moaned and lifted her hands. "I dreamed two sons," she croaked. "Is it so?" They brought the babies to her, dark and thriving. And Zilpah laughed. Zilpah's laughter was a rare sound, but the names made her chuckle. "Gad and Asher. Luck and the goddess. It sounded like the name of a myth from the old days," she said. "And I was Ninmah, the exalted lady, who birthed it all."

Zilpah ate and drank and healed, though she could not nurse her sons. Her breasts had gone dry in her illness. But this was a sorrow she could bear. She had two sons, both fine and strong, and she did not regret her dream daughter. When they grew to boyhood and left her side, Zilpah sorrowed over the fact that she had no girl to teach. But when she held them in her arms, she tasted only the joy of mothers, the sweetest tears.

Inna told her that she should take care not to bear for at least two years, but Zilpah had no intention of going through such pain again. She had given her family two sons. She sought out Jacob one morning before he left for the pasture, and told him that another pregnancy would surely kill her. She asked that he remember this when he called a wife to his bed, and she never slept with Jacob again.

Indeed, Jacob had trembled when he learned that he had gotten twins upon her. He was one of two himself, and it had caused him nothing but grief. "Forget that they shared their mother's womb," he ordered. It was so, not because Jacob commanded it but because the two were so different. Gad, long and lean, with his flutes and drum; Asher, the short, wiry husbandsman with his father's talent with animals.

Leah's next pregnancy also brought twin boys—Naphtali and Issachar. Unlike Zilpah's, though, these twins looked so much alike that, as children, not even their mother could always tell them apart. Only Bilhah, who could see every leaf on a tree in its own light, was never fooled by those two, who loved each other with a kind of quiet harmony that none of my other brothers knew.

Poor Bilhah. After Dan, all her babies—a boy and two girls—died before weaning. But she never let her sorrow poison her heart, and she loved the rest of us instead.

Jacob was now a man with four wives and ten sons, and his name was known among the men of the countryside. He was a good father and took his boys with him into the hills as soon as they were able to carry their own water, and he taught them the ways of sheep and goats, the secrets of good pasturage, the habits of long walking, the skills of sling and spear. There, too, far from the tents of their mothers, he told them the terrible story of his father, Isaac.

When Jacob and his sons stayed in the far pastures keeping watch where a jackal had been seen or simply to enjoy the cool night air of a summer month, he would tell his sons the story of how his grandfather, Abram, bound Isaac hand and foot, and then raised a knife above the boy's throat, to give El the sacrifice of his favorite son. El was the only god to whom Jacob bowed down—a jealous, mysterious god, too fearsome (he said) to be fashioned as an idol by human hands, too big to be contained by any place—even a place as big as the sky. El was the god of Abram, Isaac, and Jacob, and it was Jacob's wish that his sons accept this El as their god, too.

Jacob was a weaver of words, and he would catch his eager audience in the threads of his tale, telling of the glinting knife, Isaac's eyes wide with fright. The rescue came at the last possible moment, when the knife was at Isaac's throat, and a drop of blood trickled down his neck, just like the tears falling from Abram's brimming eyes. But then a fiery spirit stayed the old man's hand and brought a pure white ram to be sacrificed in Isaac's stead. Reuben and Simon, Levi and Judah would stare at their father's arm, stretched out against the starry night, and shudder to think of themselves on the altar.

"The god of my fathers is a merciful god," Jacob said. But when Zilpah heard the story from her sons, she said, "What kind of mercy is that, to scare the spit dry in poor Isaac's mouth? Your father's god may be great, but he is cruel."

Years later, when his grandsons finally met the boy of the

story, by then an old man, they were appalled to hear how Isaac stuttered, still frightened by his father's knife.

Jacob's sons adored their father, and his neighbors respected his success. But he was uneasy. Laban owned everything he had attained—the flocks, the bondsmen and their families, the fruit of the garden, the wool for trade. Nor was Jacob alone in his resentment of Laban. Leah and Rachel, Bilhah and Zilpah chafed under the rule of their father, who seemed to grow more crude and arrogant as the years passed. He treated his own daughters like slaves, and cuffed their sons. He profited from the labor of their looms without a word of thanks. He leered at the bondswomen and took their beer as a bribe against his lust. He mistreated Ruti every day.

The four sisters spoke of these things in the red tent, which they always entered a day before the rest of the women in the camp. Perhaps their early years together when they were the only women in camp created a habit in their bodies that brought on the flow of blood some hours before the bondswomen. Or perhaps it was simply the need of their hearts to spend a day among themselves. In any event, the bondswomen did not complain, nor was it their place to say anything. Besides, Jacob's wives would always greet them with sweets as they entered to celebrate the new moon and rest on the straw.

Ruti said nothing, but her blackened eyes and her bruises reproached them. No older than Leah, Ruti had grown haggard in their midst. After the birth of her sons, Laban had treated her well—the tight-fisted goat had even brought her bangles to brighten her wrists and ankles. But then she gave off bearing and he began to hit her and call her names so ugly my mothers would not repeat them to me. Ruti's shoulders stooped with despair, and several of her teeth were broken from the force of Laban's fists. Even so, he continued to use her body for his own pleasure, a thought that made my mothers shudder.

For all their pity, Jacob's wives did not embrace Ruti. She was the mother of their sons' rivals, their material enemy. The bondswomen saw how the sisters kept themselves apart from her, and they followed suit. Even her own sons laughed at her and treated her like a dog. Ruti, already alone, kept to herself. She became such a ragged, battered misery to look at that no one saw her. When she came to Rachel, desperate for help, she seemed more a ghost than a woman.

"Lady, I beg you. Give me the herbs to cast out the baby I carry," she whispered in a cold, flat hiss. "I would rather die than give him another son, and if it is a girl, I will drown her before she is old enough to suffer at his hands.

"Help me for the sake of your husband's sons," said Ruti, in a voice from the other side of the grave. "I know you will not do it for me. You hate me, all of you."

Rachel brought Ruti's words to her sisters, who listened in silence and were ashamed.

"Do you know how to do that?" asked Leah.

Rachel waved a hand, dismissing the question as beneath consideration. It was not a difficult matter, especially since Ruti was in the first month.

Bilhah's eyes blazed. "We are no better than he is to have let her suffer alone, to have given her no comfort, no help."

Zilpah turned to Rachel and asked, "When will you do it?"

"We must wait for the next new moon, when all the women come to us," Rachel answered. "Laban is too stupid to suspect anything. I don't think even the subtlest among them realizes what we know and do among ourselves, but it is better to be careful."

The sisters did not change in their apparent treatment of Ruti. They did not speak to her or show her any special kindness. But at night, when Laban snored, one of the four would find her, huddled on her filthy blanket in a far corner of the tent, and feed her broth or honeyed bread. Zilpah took on Ruti's suffering as her own. She could not bear the emptiness in her eyes, or the despair that hung about her like a fog from the world of the dead. She took to visiting her every night to whisper words of encouragement into Ruti's ears, but she only lay there, deaf to any hope.

Finally, the moon waned and all the women entered the red tent. Leah stood before the bondswomen and lied with a pure heart, "Ruti is unwell. Her courses are overdue, but her belly is hot and we fear a miscarriage tonight. Rachel will do everything she can, with herbs and incantations, to save the child. Let us care for our sister, Ruti."

But within a few minutes, it was clear to most of them that Rachel's ministrations were intended not to save the baby but to cast it out. They watched, from the far side of the red tent, where cakes and wine sat untouched, as Rachel mixed a black herbal brew, which Ruti drank in silence.

She lay still, her eyes closed. Zilpah muttered the names of Anath the healer and the ancient Gula, who attends women at childbirth, while Rachel whispered words of praise to Ruti, whose courage unfolded as the night wore on.

When the herbs began to work, causing great ripping cramps, Ruti made no sound. When the blood began to flow, clotted and dark, Ruti's lips did not part. As the hours passed, the blood ran and did not stop, and still she said nothing. Rachel packed Ruti's womb with wool many times, until finally it was over.

No man knew what happened that night. No child blurted the secret, because none of the women ever spoke of it, not a word, until Zilpah told me the story. By then it was nothing but an echo from the grave.

My mother told me that after the birth of her twin sons, she decided to finish with childbearing. Her breasts were those of an old woman, her belly was slack, and her back ached every morning. The thought of another pregnancy filled her with dread, and so she took to drinking fennel to keep Jacob's seed from taking root again.

But then it happened that the supply of seeds ran low while Inna was far away in the north. Months passed and still she did not return with her pouches of herbs. Leah tried an old remedy—soaking a lock of wool in old olive oil and placing it at the mouth of her womb before lying with Jacob. But her efforts failed, and for the first time, the knowledge of life within her brought her low.

Leah did not wish to take this trouble to Rachel, whose hunger for her own baby had not diminished. The fertile wife had tried to spare her barren sister's feelings by keeping a respectful distance from her. They divided the duties of a chief wife. Leah had charge of the weaving and cooking, the garden and the children. Rachel—still lovely and slim-waisted—served her husband and waited upon traders who came to the camp. She looked after Jacob's needs and, her skills as a healer growing, saw to the pains and illnesses of men, women, and even beasts.

Births and the new moon brought the two women together inside the red tent. But Leah slept facing the western wall while Rachel hugged the east, and they spoke to each other only by way of their sisters: Leah through Zilpah, Rachel through Bilhah.

Now, Leah had no choice. Inna had not returned and Rachel was the only one who knew the herbs, the prayers, the proper massage. There was no one else to ask.

As Rachel left to attend a birth in a nearby camp, Leah made some excuse about fetching water and rushed her steps until she was at Rachel's side. Leah's cheeks burned and she cast her eyes downward as she asked her sister to help her as she had helped Ruti. Rachel surprised her with the gentleness of her answer.

"Do not do away with your daughter," she said. "You are carrying a girl."

"Then she will die," Leah answered, thinking of Rachel's miscarriages. (Inna had pronounced them all girls.) "And even if she lives, she will not know her mother, because I am nearly dead from bearing."

But Rachel argued for all of the sisters, who had long saved their treasures for a daughter. "We will do everything for you as you carry their girl. Leah," she said, using her sister's name for the first time in either woman's memory. "Please," she asked.

"Do as I say before I tell Zilpah," Rachel threatened

mischievously. "She will make your life a misery of scorned goddesses if she discovers your plans."

Leah laughed and relented, for her wish for a daughter was still strong.

While I slept in my mother's womb, I appeared to her and to each of my aunties in vivid dreams.

Bilhah dreamed of me one night while she lay in Jacob's arms. "I saw you in a white gown of fine linen, covered with a long vest of blue and green beads. Your hair was braided and you carried a fine basket through a pasture greener than any I have ever seen. You walked among queens, but you were alone."

Rachel dreamed of my birth. "You appeared at your mother's womb with your eyes open and your mouth full of perfect little teeth. You spoke as you slithered out from between her legs, saying, 'Hello, mothers. I am here at last. Is there nothing to eat?' That made us laugh. There were hundreds of women attending your birth, some of them dressed in outlandish clothing, shocking colors, shorn heads. We all laughed and laughed. I woke in the middle of the night laughing."

My mother, Leah, said she dreamed of me every night. "You and I whispered to each other like old friends. You were very wise, telling me what to eat to calm my upset stomach, how to settle a quarrel between Reuben and Simon. I told you all about Jacob, your father, and about your aunties. You told me about the other side of the universe, where darkness and light are not separated. You were such good company, I hated to wake up.

"One thing bothered me about those dreams," said my

mother. "I could never see your face. You were always behind me, just beyond my left shoulder. And every time I turned to catch a glimpse of you, you disappeared."

Zilpah's dream was not filled with laughter or companionship. She said she saw me weeping a river of blood that gave rise to flat green monsters that opened mouths filled with rows of sharp teeth. "Even so, you were unafraid," said Zilpah. "You walked upon their backs and tamed their ugliness, and disappeared into the sun."

I was born during a full moon in a springtime remembered for a plenitude of lambs. Zilpah stood on my mother's left side, while Bilhah supported her on the right. Inna was there, to be on hand for the celebration and to catch the afterbirth in her ancient bucket. But Leah had asked Rachel to be midwife and catch me.

It was an easy birth. After all the boys before me, I came quickly and as painlessly as birth can be. I was big—as big as Judah, who had been the biggest. Inna pronounced me "Leah's daughter," in a voice full of satisfaction. As with all of her babies, my mother looked into my eyes first and smiled to see that they were both brown, like Jacob's and those of all her sons.

After Rachel wiped me clean, she handed me to Zilpah, who embraced me, and then to Bilhah, who kissed me as well. I took my mother's breast with an eager mouth, and all the women of the camp clapped their hands for my mother and for me. Bilhah fed my mother honeyed milk and cake. She washed Leah's hair with perfumed water, and she massaged her feet.

While Leah slept, Rachel, Zilpah, and Bilhah took me out into the moonlight and put henna on my feet and hands, as though I were a bride. They spoke a hundred blessings around me, north, south, east, and west, to protect me against Lamashtu and the other baby-stealing demons. They gave me a thousand kisses.

In the morning, my mother began to count out two moon cycles in the red tent. After the birth of a boy, mothers rested from one moon to the next, but the birth of a birth-giver required a longer period of separation from the world of men. "The second month was such a delight," my mother told me. "My sisters treated us both like queens. You were never left lying upon a blanket for a moment. There were always arms to hold you, cuddle you, embrace you. We oiled your skin morning and night. We sang songs into your ears, but we did not coo or babble. We spoke to you with all our words, as though you were a grown sister and not a baby girl. And before you were a year old, you answered us without a trace of a baby's lisp."

As I was passed from my mother to one aunt after another, they debated my name. This conversation never ceased, and each woman argued for a favorite she had long hoped to give to a daughter of her own womb.

Bilhah offered Adahni, in memory of my grandmother Adah, who had loved them all. This led to a long session of sighing and remembering Adah, who would have been so delighted by all of her grandchildren. But Zilpah worried that such a name would confuse the demons, who might think Adah had escaped from the underworld and come after me.

Zilpah liked the name Ishara—which gave homage to the

goddess and was easy to rhyme. She had plans for many songs in my honor. But Bilhah didn't like the sound of it. "It sounds like a sneeze," she said.

Rachel suggested Bentresh, a Hittite name she had heard from a trader's wife. "It sounds like music," she said.

Leah listened to them all, and when her sisters got too heated in their arguments about *her* daughter, threatened to call me Lillu, a name they all hated.

In the second full moon after my birth, Leah rejoined her husband and told Jacob my name. She told me that I picked it myself. "During my sixty days, I whispered every name my sisters suggested into your little ear. Every name I had ever heard, and even some I invented myself. But when I said 'Dinah,' you let the nipple fall from your mouth and looked up at me. So you are Dinah, my last-born. My daughter. My memory."

Joseph was conceived in the days following my birth. Rachel had gone to Jacob with the news that he had finally sired a healthy girl. Her eyes shone as she told him, and Jacob smiled to see how his barren wife took pleasure in Leah's baby. That night, after they had enjoyed each other in the gentle fashion of familiar couples, Rachel dreamed of her first son and woke up smiling.

She told no one when her moon blood failed to come. The many false starts and early losses haunted her, and she guarded her secret closely. She went to the red tent at the new moon and changed the straw as though she had soiled it. She was so slender that the slight thickening of her waist went unnoticed by everyone but Bilhah, who kept her own counsel.

At the fourth month, Rachel went to Inna, who told her

that the signs looked good for this boy, and Rachel began to hope. She showed her swelling belly to her sisters, who danced in a circle around her. She put Jacob's hand on the hillock of her womb. The father of ten sons wept.

Rachel grew swaybacked. Her little breasts grew full and painful. Her perfect ankles swelled. But she found nothing but delight in the complaints of breeding women. She began to sing as she tended the cooking fires and took up her spindle. Her family was surprised at the sweetness of her voice, which they had never heard raised in song. Jacob slept with Rachel every night of her pregnancy, a shocking breach of manners and an incitement to demons. But he would not listen to warning, and Rachel basked in his attentions as she grew large.

In her eighth month, Rachel began to sicken. Her skin paled and her hair fell out. She could barely stand without falling into a faint. Fear swallowed her hope, and she called for Inna, who prescribed strong broths made from the bones of rams and bulls. She told Rachel to rest, and came to visit her friend as often as she could.

Inna came to deliver Rachel. The baby's feet were down and there was bleeding long before he appeared. Inna's efforts to turn the child caused Rachel terrible pain, and she cried out so pitifully that all the children of the camp burst into tears at the sound. Jacob sat on the bamah, staring at the face of the goddess, wondering whether he ought to make some offering to her, even though he had promised to worship his father's god only. He tore at the grass and held his head until he could stand the sounds of her screams no longer, and he went off to the high pasture until Rachel was delivered.

It was two days before Reuben was sent to bring him back. Two terrible days in which Leah and Zilpah and Bilhah each bade Rachel goodbye, it seemed so certain that she would die.

But Inna did not give up. She gave Rachel every herb and every medicine in her pouches. She tried combinations that no herb weaver had used. She muttered secret prayers, though she was not initiated into the mysteries of magic words and incantations.

Rachel did not give up, but fought for a heart's desire denied for fifteen years. She battled like an animal, her eyes rolling, sweat pouring from her. Even after three days and three nights, she did not call for death to release her from the torment. "She was mighty to behold," said Zilpah.

Finally, Inna got the baby to turn. But the effort seemed to break something within Rachel, whose body was seized by a shudder that would not let go. Her eyes rolled up into her head and her neck tightened so that she faced backward. It was as though demons had taken possession of her body. Even Inna gasped.

Then it was over. Rachel's body was released from death's grasp, the baby's head appeared, and Rachel found the last of her strength to push him out.

He was small, with a big thatch of hair. A baby like all babies, wrinkled, homely, and perfect. Best of all, he was Rachel's. The tent fell silent as every woman wept grateful tears. Without a word, Inna cut the cord, and Bilhah caught the afterbirth. Leah cleaned Rachel, and Zilpah washed the baby. They sighed and wiped their eyes. Rachel would live to see her baby grow.

Rachel recovered slowly, but she could not give suck.

Three days after Joseph's birth, her breasts grew hard and hot. Warm compresses eased her pain, but the milk dried up. Leah, who was nursing me at the time, took Joseph to her breast as well. Rachel's old anger at Leah flared at that, but it vanished when she discovered that Joseph was a fretful baby who screamed and squirmed until he lay in his own mother's arms.

PART TWO

My Story

Chapter One

I AM NOT CERTAIN whether my earliest memories are truly mine, because when I bring them to mind, I feel my mothers' breath on every word. But I do remember the taste of the water from our well, bright and cold against my milk teeth. And I'm sure that I was caught up by strong arms every time I stumbled, for I do not recall a time in my early life when I was alone or afraid.

Like every beloved child, I knew that I was the most important person in my mother's world. And most important not only to my mother, Leah, but to my mother-aunties as well. Although they adored their sons, I was the one they dressed up and dandled when the boys were wrestling in the dirt. I was the one who continued going to the red tent with them, long after I was weaned.

As a baby, Joseph was my constant companion, first my milk-brother and later my truest friend. At eight months he stood up and walked over to me in my favorite spot at the front of my mother's tent. Though many months older, I was still unsteady on my feet, probably because my aunties liked to carry me. Joseph held out both his hands to me, and I stood up. My mother said that in return for showing me how to walk, I taught him to speak. Joseph liked to tell people that his first word was "Dinah," though Rachel assured me it was the word for *Mamma*, "Ema."

No one thought Rachel would bear another child after the awful time she had had with Joseph, so he and I received the treatment given to the final fruit of a chief wife. According to the custom of the old days, the youngest child inherited a mother's blessing, and one way or another, fathers usually followed suit. But Joseph and I were petted and spoiled also because we were the babies—our mothers' last-born, and our father's joy. We were also our older brothers' victims.

Age made two separate tribes among the children of Jacob. Reuben, Simon, Levi, and Judah were nearly men by the time I knew their names. They were often gone, tending to the herds with our father, and as a group, they had little use for us small ones. Reuben was, by nature, kind to children, but we avoided Simon and Levi, who laughed at us and teased Tali and Issa, the twins. "How do you know which of you is which?" Levi taunted. Simon was even worse: "If one of you dies, our mother won't mourn since she'll have one exactly the same." That always made Tali cry.

I thought I saw longing in the way Judah watched our games. He was far too old to play with us, but as the youngest of the older brothers he was the least among them and suffered for it. Judah often carried me on his back and called me Ahatti, little sister. I thought of him as my champion among the big boys.

At first, Zebulun was the leader of us younger ones, and

he might have been a bully had we not adored him and obeyed him willingly. Dan was his lieutenant—loyal and sweet as you'd expect of Bilhah's child. Gad and Asher were wild, headstrong, and difficult playmates, but they were such wonderful mimics—mocking Laban's lumbering walk and drink-slurred speech with such wicked accuracy—we forgave them anything in exchange for a performance. Naphtali, who was never called anything but Tali, and Issachar, or Issa, tried to lord it over me and Joseph because they were nearly two years older. They would call us babies, but a minute later they would join us on the ground, tossing a pebble into the air to see how many other stones we could pick up with the same hand. It was our favorite game until I could pick up ten stones to their five. Then my brothers declared it a game fit only for girls and never played again.

By our sixth year, Joseph and I had taken charge of the younger band, because we were the best at making up stories. Our brothers carried us from the well to my mother's tent and bowed low before me, their queen. They would pretend to die when Joseph, their king, pointed a finger at them. We sent them out to do battle with demons, and to bring us great riches. They crowned our heads with garlands of weeds and kissed our hands.

I remember the day that game ended. Tali and Issa were doing my bidding, piling up little stones as an altar in my honor. Dan and Zebulun were fanning us with leaves. Gad and Asher were dancing before us.

Then our older brothers happened by. Reuben and Judah smiled and walked on, but Simon and Levi stopped and laughed. "Look at how the babes lead the bigger boys by the nose! Wait until we tell our father that Zebulun and Dan are donkeys for the bare-behinds. He'll make them wait another two years before letting them come up to the high pasture with us." They did not stop mocking until Joseph and I were alone, abandoned by our playmates, who suddenly saw themselves with their brothers' cold eyes.

After that, Zebulun and Dan refused to do any more spinning for our mothers, and after much begging they were permitted to follow their older brothers into the hills. The two sets of twins—when they weren't pulling weeds from the garden or helping at the loom—played by themselves, and the four of them became a tribe of their own, dedicated to hunting games and wrestling matches.

Joseph and I turned more and more to each other, but it wasn't as much fun with just the two of us. Neither of us bent a knee to the other for the sake of a story, and Joseph had to contend with the taunts of our brothers, who abused him for playing with me at all. There were very few girls in our camp—the women joked that Jacob had poisoned the well against them. I tried to make friends with the few daughters of bondswomen, but I was either too old or too young for their games, and so by the time I could carry a water jar from the well, I started to think of myself as a member of my mother's circle.

Not that children were often left to their games. As soon as we were old enough to carry a few sticks of wood, we were put to work pulling weeds and insects from the garden, carrying water, carding wool, and spinning. I do not remember a time before my hand held a spindle. I remember being scolded for my clumsiness, for getting burrs in my wool, and for the unevenness of my string.

Leah was the best mother but she was not the best

teacher. Skills came to her so easily that she could not understand how even a small child could fail to grasp something so simple as the turning of string. She lost patience with me often. "How is it that a daughter of Leah could have such unlucky fingers?" she said one day, looking at the tangle I had made of my work.

I hated her for those words. For the first time in my life, I hated my mother. My face grew hot as tears came to my eyes, and I threw a whole day's spinning into the dirt. It was a terrible act of waste and disrespect, and I think neither of us could believe that I had done it. In an instant, the sharp slap of her palm against my cheek cracked the air. I was far more shocked than hurt. Although my mother cuffed my brothers from time to time, it was the first time she had ever struck me.

I stood there for a long moment watching her face twist in pain over what she had done. Without a word I turned and ran to find Bilhah's lap, where I wept and moaned about the terrible wrong that had been done to me. I told my aunt everything that lay heavy upon my heart. I wept over my useless fingers, which would never get the wool to twist evenly or the spindle to drop and turn smoothly. I was afraid that I had shamed my mother by being so awkward. And I was ashamed of the hatred I suddenly felt toward the one I loved so completely.

Bilhah stroked my hair until I stopped crying and fed me a piece of bread dipped in sweet wine. "Now I will show you the secret of the spindle," she said, putting a finger to my lips. "This is something your grandmother taught me, and now it is my turn to show you."

Bilhah put me on her lap, for which I was nearly too

large. Her arms were barely long enough to reach around me, but there I sat, a baby once again, embraced in safety while Bilhah whispered the story of Uttu into my ear.

"Once, before women knew how to turn wool into string and string into cloth, people roamed the earth naked. They burned by day and shivered by night, and their babies perished.

"But Uttu heard the weeping mothers, and took pity on them. Uttu was the daughter of Nanna, god of the moon, and of Ninhursag, the mother of the plains. Uttu asked her father if she might teach the women how to spin and weave so their babies would live.

"Nanna scoffed and said that women were too stupid to remember the order of cutting, washing, and combing of wool, the building of looms, the setting of woof and warp. And their fingers were too thick to master the art of spinning. But because Nanna loved his daughter he let her go.

"Uttu went first to the east, to the land of the Green River, but the women there would not put aside their drums and flutes to listen to the goddess.

"Uttu went to the south, but she arrived in the middle of a terrible drought, when the sun had robbed the women of their memories. 'We need nothing but rain,' they said, forgetting the months when their children had died of cold. 'Give us rain or go away.'

"Uttu traveled north, where the fur-clad women were so fierce they tore off a breast to ready themselves for the endless hunt. Those women were too hot-headed for the slow arts of string and loom.

"Uttu went to the east, where the sun rises, but found the men had stolen the women's tongues and they could not answer for themselves.

"Since Uttu did not know how to speak to men, she came to Ur, which is the womb of the world, where she met the woman called Enhenduanna, who wished to learn.

"Uttu took Enhenduanna on her lap and wrapped her great arms around Enhenduanna's small arms, and laid her golden hands around Enhenduanna's clay hands, and guided her left hand and guided her right hand.

"Uttu dropped a spindle made of lapis lazuli, which turned like a great blue ball floating in the golden sky, and spun string made of sunlight. Enhenduanna fell asleep in Uttu's lap.

"As Enhenduanna slept, she spun without seeing or knowing, without effort or fatigue. She spun until there was enough string to fill the entire storehouse of the great god Nanna. He was so pleased that he permitted Uttu to teach Enhenduanna's daughters how to make pottery and bronze, music and wine.

"After that, the people could stop eating grass and drinking water and ate bread and drank beer instead. And their babies, swaddled in wool blankets, no longer died of the cold but grew up to offer up sacrifice to the gods."

While Bilhah told me the story of Uttu, she put her nimble hands around my clumsy ones. I smelled the soft, loamy musk that clung to my youngest auntie and listened to her sweet, liquid voice and forgot all about the ache in my heart. And when her story was over, she showed me that the string on my spindle was as evenly made and strong as Leah's own handiwork.

I kissed Bilhah a hundred kisses and ran to show my mother what I had done. She embraced me as though I had returned from the dead. There was no more slapping after that. I even came to enjoy the task of twisting clouds of unruly wool into the fine, strong threads that became my family's clothing and blankets and trade goods. I learned to love the way that my mind wandered where it would while my hands followed their own course. Even when I was old and my spinning was of linen rather than wool, I recalled my auntie's perfume and the way she pronounced the name of the goddess, Uttu.

I told Joseph the story of Uttu the weaver. I told him the tale of the great goddess Innana's journey to the land of the dead, and of her marriage to the shepherd king, Dumuzi, whose love ensured an abundance of dates and wine and rain. These were stories I heard in the red tent, told and retold by my mothers and the occasional trader's wife who called the gods and goddesses by unfamiliar names and sometimes supplied different endings to ancient tales.

Joseph, in turn, told me the story of Isaac's binding and the miracle of his release, and of our great-grandfather Abram's meetings with messengers from the gods. He told me that our father, Jacob, spoke with the El of his fathers, morning and evening, even when he made no sacrifice. Our father said that the formless, faceless god with no other name than god came to him by night, in his dreams, and by day, in solitude only, and that Jacob was sure that the future of his sons would be blessed by this One.

Joseph described to me the wondrous grove of terebinth trees in Mamre, where our great-grandmother spoke to her gods every evening, and where someday our father would take us to pour a libation in the name of Sarai. Those were the stories Joseph heard from Jacob, sitting among our brothers while the sheep and goats grazed. I thought the women's stories were prettier, but Joseph preferred our father's tales.

Our talk was not usually so lofty. We shared the secret of sex and begetting, and laughed, aghast, to think of our parents behaving like the dogs in the dust. We gossiped endlessly about our brothers, keeping close watch on the rivalry between Simon and Levi, which could flare into blows over something as trivial as the placement of a staff against a tree. There was an ongoing contest, too, between Judah and Zebulun—the two oxen among the brothers—but theirs was a good-natured battle to see which was the stronger, and each would applaud his brother's ability to lift great rocks and carry full-grown ewes across a meadow.

Joseph and I watched as Zilpah's sons became my mother's champions, for Gad and Asher were embarrassed by their own mother's eccentricities. Her inability to make decent bread sent them to Leah's tent. They did not understand or value Zilpah's skill at the loom, and of course they had no way of knowing her talent for storytelling. So they carried their little trophies—flowers, brightly colored stones, the remains of a bird's nest—to my mother's lap. She would tousle their hair and feed them and they would strut like little heroes.

On the other hand, Tali and Issa, the twins of Leah's own womb, were not so fond of her. They hated looking so much alike and blamed their mother for it. They did everything they could to distinguish themselves from each other and were almost never seen together. Issa attached himself to Rachel, who seemed charmed by his attentions and let him carry and fetch for her. Tali became fast friends with Bilhah's Dan, and the two of them liked to sleep side by side in Bilhah's tent, hanging on the words of their big brother Reuben, who was also drawn to the peace and stillness that enveloped my aunt.

Leah tried to bribe Issa and Tali back to her with sweets and extra bread, but she was far too busy with the work of her family to pine for attentions from two of her many sons. And she did not suffer for lack of love. When I caught her watching one of her boys walking toward another mother's tent at nightfall, I would pull at her hand. Then she would lift me up so that our eyes could meet, and kiss me on one cheek and then on the other, and then on the tip of my nose. This always made me laugh, which would in turn always bring a warm smile to my mother's face. One of my great secrets was knowing I had the power to make her smile.

My world was filled with mothers and brothers, work and games, new moons and good food. The hills in the distance held my life in a bowl filled with everything I could possibly want.

*

I was a child when my father led us away from the land of the two rivers, south to the country of his birth. Young as I was, I knew why we were going. I could feel the hot wall of anger between my father and my grandfather. I could almost see the heat between them on the rare occasions they sat together.

Laban resented my father for his accomplishments with the herds, and for his sons who were so plentiful and so much more skillful than his own two boys. Laban hated the fact that he owed his success to the husband of his daughters. His mouth turned sour whenever Jacob's name was mentioned.

As for my father, although he was the one who caused the flocks to multiply, the camp to fill with bondsmen, and the traders to make their way to our tents, he was never more than Laban's servant. His wages were meager, but he was thrifty and clever with his little store of goods, and he had been careful with the breeding of his own small flock of brindled goats and grey sheep.

Jacob hated Laban's sloth and the way he and his sons squandered his own good work. When the older boy, Kemuel, left his post guarding the rutting goats one spring, the best of them died from the battle between the strongest males. When Beor drank too much wine and slept, a hawk made off with a newborn kid Jacob had marked for sacrifice.

The worst was when Laban lost Jacob's two best dogs— his smartest and his best loved. The old man had gone for a three-day trading journey to Carchemish and, without asking, had taken the dogs to tend a herd so small a boy could have managed on his own. While Laban was in town, he sold them both for a pittance, which he then lost in a game of chance.

The loss of his dogs put my father in a rage. The night Laban returned to camp, I heard their shouts and curses even as I fell asleep. Afterward, my father's scowl was impenetrable. His fists did not unclench until he had sought out Leah and poured out the details of this latest grievance.

My mother and aunts had nothing but sympathy for Jacob. Their loyalty to Laban had never been strong, and as the years passed, they piled up reasons to despise him— laziness, deceitfulness, the arrogance of his thick-headed sons, and his treatment of Ruti, which only worsened as the years passed.

A few days after the fight about the dogs, Ruti came to my mother and threw herself on the ground. "I am lost," she cried, a sad puddle of a woman in the dust. Her hair was loose and covered with ashes as though she had just buried her own mother.

Laban had lost more than his coins in that Carchemish game. He had gambled away Ruti as well, and now a trader had arrived to claim her as his slave. Laban sat in his tent and refused to come out and acknowledge what he had done to the mother of his sons, but the trader had his walking staff as a bond, and his overseer as a witness. Ruti put her forehead to the ground and begged Leah for help.

Leah listened and then turned to spit on her father's name. "The backside of a donkey has more merit than Laban," she said. "My father is a snake. He is the putrefied offal of a snake."

She put down the jug of milk she was working into curd, and with heavy steps marched to the near pasture where my father was still brooding about his dogs. My mother was so deep in her thoughts she did not seem to notice that I followed her.

Leah's cheeks turned red as she approached her husband. And then she did something extraordinary. Leah got down on her knees and, taking Jacob's hand, kissed his fingers. Watching my mother submit like this was like seeing a sheep hunting a jackal or a man nursing a baby. My mother, who never wanted for words, nearly stuttered as she spoke.

"Husband, father of my children, beloved friend," she said. "I come to plead a case without merit, for pure pity's sake. Husband," she said, "Jacob," she whispered, "you know I place my life in your keeping only and that my father's name is an abomination to me.

"Even so, I come to ask that you redeem my father's woman from the slavery into which he has sold her. A man from Carchemish has come to claim Ruti, whom Laban staked in his game of chance as though she were an animal from the flock or a stranger among us, and not the mother of his sons.

"I ask you to treat her better than her own husband. I ask you to act as the father."

Jacob frowned at his wife's request, although in his heart he must have been pleased that she addressed him not only as her husband but as leader of her family as well. He stood above Leah, whose head was bowed, and looked down on her tenderly. "Wife," he said, and took her hands to raise her up. "Leah." Their eyes met and she smiled.

I was shocked. I had come to watch Ruti's story unfold, but I discovered something else altogether. I saw the heat between my mother and her husband. I saw that Jacob could cause the glow of assent and happiness that I thought only I could summon from Leah.

My eyes opened for the first time upon the fact that my father was a man. I saw that he was not only tall but also broad-shouldered and narrow in the waist. Although by then he must have passed his fortieth summer, his back was straight and he still had most of his teeth and a clear eye. My father was handsome, I realized. My father was worthy of my mother.

Yet I found no consolation in this discovery. As they moved back to the tents, Leah and Jacob walked side by side, their heads nearly touching as she whispered the ransom that Jacob could collect from among his wives to redeem Ruti: honey and herbs, a stack of copper bangles, a bolt of linen and three of wool. He listened silently, nodding from time to time. There was no room for me between them, no need for me. My mother's eyes were full of Jacob. I did not matter to her the way she mattered to me. I wanted to cry, but I realized that I was too old for that. I would be a woman soon and I would have to learn how to live with a divided heart.

Miserable, I followed as my parents entered the circle of tents. Leah fell silent and resumed her place behind her husband. She fetched a jug of her strongest beer to help Jacob soften the trader's resolve. But the man had seen that though she was worn out and homely, Laban's woman was neither harelipped nor lame, as her price had led him to believe. And he was shrewd enough to notice that his presence had caused a stir. He smelled his advantage, which meant it took all of the women's treasures and one of Jacob's pups before the trader forgave the debt and left without

Ruti. Soon, all the women of the camp knew what had happened, and for weeks afterward, Jacob ate like a prince.

Laban never spoke of how Jacob ransomed his wife. He only became fouler in his use of Ruti, whose eyes seemed permanently blackened after that. Her sons, following their father's pattern, showed their mother no respect. They carried no water for her cooking pot and brought her no game from their hunts. She crept around her men in silent service.

Among the women, Ruti spoke only of my mother's kindness. She became Leah's shadow, kissing her hands and her hem, sitting as close to her savior as she could. The ragged woman's presence did not please Leah, who occasionally lost patience with her. "Go to your tent," she said when Ruti got underfoot. But Leah always regretted rebuking Ruti, who cringed at a single cross word from my mother. After she sent her away, Leah sought her out and sat down beside the poor, wasted soul and let herself be kissed and thanked, again and again.

Chapter Two

IN THE DAYS following Ruti's redemption, Jacob began to plan our departure in earnest. During his nights with Leah and during his nights with Rachel, he spoke of his longing to leave Laban's tents and return to the land of his father. Jacob told Bilhah that his restlessness consumed his peace and that he slept badly. Jacob found Zilpah on a night when sleeplessness chased them both, separately, to the whispering comfort of the great terebinth that stood by the altar. Even on still, airless nights, breezes hid among the broad flat leaves of Zilpah's tree. Jacob told his fourth wife that his god had appeared to him and said that it was time to leave the land of the two rivers. It was time to take his wives and his sons and the wealth that he had built up with his hands.

Jacob told Zilpah that his dreams had become ferocious. Night after night, fiery voices called him back to Canaan, to the land of his father. Fierce as his dreams were, they were joyful, too. Rebecca shone like the sun and Isaac smiled a blessing. Even his brother no longer threatened, but appeared as a huge, ruddy bull that welcomed Jacob to ride

upon his wide back. And it seemed Jacob had no need to
fear his brother anymore, for traders from Canaan had
brought news that Esau had become a prosperous herdsman
with many sons of his own, and a reputation for generosity.

In their day alone in the red tent, Jacob's wives spoke
among themselves about their husband's dreams and plans.
Rachel's eyes shone at the prospect of moving to the south.
She was the most traveled among them, having attended at
births throughout the hills, to Carchemish and once to the
city of Haran itself. "Oh, to see great mountains, and a real
city," she said. "Marketplaces filled with fine goods and
fruits whose names we do not even know! We will meet
faces from the four corners. We will hear the music of silver
timbrels and golden flutes."

Leah was not so eager to discover the new worlds beyond
the valley that had given her life. "I am content with the
faces I see around me here," she said, "but I would dearly
love to be free of Laban's stench. We will go, of course. But
I will leave with regret."

Bilhah nodded. "I will grieve to leave Adah's bones. I
will miss seeing the sun rise on the place where I gave birth
to my son. I will mourn the passing of our youth. But I am
ready. And our sons are wild to be gone from here."

Bilhah gave voice to a truth that had gone unspoken.
There was not enough room for so many sons to make their
way in Haran, where every hillock had been claimed for
many generations. There was no land in the country of their
mothers. If the family did not leave together, the women
would soon break their hearts watching as their sons turned
against each other or disappeared in search of their own
paths.

Zilpah's breath grew louder and more uneven as her sisters turned their faces to the future. "I cannot go," she burst out. "I cannot leave the holy tree, which is the source of my power. Or the bamah, which is soaked in my offerings. How will the gods know where I am if I am not here to serve them? Who will protect me? Sisters, we will be beset by demons."

She was wide-eyed. "This tree, this place, this is where *she* is, my little goddess, Nanshe." The sisters sat up to hear Zilpah speak the name of her own deity, something done only on a deathbed. Their sister felt herself at the end of hope, and her voice was choked with tears as she said, "You too, sisters. All of your named gods abide here. This is the place where we are known, where we know how to serve. It will be death to leave. I know it."

There was silence as the others stared. Bilhah spoke first. "Every place has its holy names, its trees and high places," she said, in the calm voice a mother takes to a frightened child. "There will be gods where we go." But Zilpah would not meet Bilhah's eyes, and only shook her head from side to side. "No," she whispered.

Leah spoke next. "Zilpah, we are your protection. Your family, your sisters, are the only surety against hunger, against cold, against madness. Sometimes I wonder if the gods are dreams and stories to while away cold nights and dark thoughts." Leah grabbed her sister by the shoulders. "Better to put your trust in my hands and Jacob's than in stories made out of wind and fear."

Zilpah shrank under her sister's hands and turned away. "No," she said.

Rachel listened to Leah's sensible blasphemy in wonder

and spoke, picking words for thoughts she discovered only as she gave them voice. "We can never answer your fear with proof, Zilpah. The gods are always silent. I know that women in travail find strength and comfort in the names of their gods. I have seen them struggle beyond all hope at the sound of an incantation. I have seen life spared at the last moment, for no other reason than that hope.

"But I know too that gods do not protect even the kindest, most pious women from heartbreak or death. So Bilhah is right. We will take Nanshe with us," she said, naming Zilpah's beloved goddess of dreams and singers. "We will take Gula, too," naming the goddess of healing, to whom Rachel made offerings. And then, as the idea grew in her mind, Rachel blurted, "We will take all of the teraphim from our tents and carry them into Canaan with our husband and our children.

"They will do us no harm, surely," said Rachel, speaking faster and faster as the plan formed in her mind. "If they are in our keeping, they will do Laban no good," she added slyly. Bilhah and Leah laughed nervously at the idea of Laban stripped of his sacred figures. The old man consulted the statues when he had any choice to make, stroking his favorites absentmindedly, for hours at a time. Leah said they soothed him the way a full breast soothed a cranky baby.

To leave with the teraphim was to incite Laban's wrath. Even so, Rachel had some claim to them. In the old days, when the family had lived in the city of Ur, it was the unquestioned right of the youngest daughter to inherit all the holy things. Those ways were no longer held in universal respect, and Kemuel could claim the teraphim as part of an older son's birthright with just as much authority.

The sisters sat in silence, considering Rachel's bold idea.
Finally Rachel spoke. "I will take the teraphim and they will
be a source of power for us. They will be a sign of our
birthright. Our father will suffer as he has made others
suffer. I will not speak of this again."

Zilpah wiped her eyes. Leah cleared her throat. Bilhah
stood up. It had been decided.

I barely took a breath. I was afraid that if they remembered me, I would be sent out of the tent. I sat still between
my mother's right hand and Bilhah's left hand, amazed at
what I had heard.

Rachel was loyal to Gula, the healer. Bilhah's grain
offerings were made to Uttu, the weaver. Leah had a special
feeling for Ninkasi, the brewer of beer, who used a brewing
vat made of clear lapis lazuli and a ladle made of silver and
gold. I thought of the gods and goddesses as aunts and
uncles who were bigger than my parents and able to live
inside the ground or above the earth as they liked. I imagined them deathless, odorless, forever happy, strong, and
interested in everything that happened to me. I was frightened to hear Leah, the wisest of women, wondering if these
powerful friends might be nothing but stories told to calm
the nightmares of children.

I shuddered. My mother put her hand on my cheek to
feel for fever, but I was cool to her touch. Later that night I
awoke screaming and sweating in a terror of falling, but she
came to me and lay down beside me, and the warmth of her
body comforted me. Secure in the knowledge of her love, I
began to cross over into sleep, then I roused for a moment
thinking I heard Rachel's voice saying, "Remember this
moment, when your mother's body heals every trouble of

your soul." I looked around but my auntie was nowhere nearby.

It must have been a dream.

Three days later, Leah walked to the rocky pasture in the west to tell Jacob that his wives were ready to go with him to the land of his birth. I followed after her, carrying some bread and beer for my father. I was not entirely pleased at being pressed into service on such a warm day.

As I came over the rise that separated our camp from the grazing, I was stopped by a scene of perfect wonder. Many of the ewes were heavy with lambs and barely moved in the gathering heat. The rising sun summoned the clover's scent. Only the bees made a sound under the brazen blue banner of sky.

I stopped as my mother walked ahead. The world seemed so perfect, so complete, and yet so impermanent that I nearly wept. I would have to tell Zilpah about this feeling, and ask if she knew a song for it. But then I realized that something in the universe had shifted. Something important had changed. I searched the horizon; the sky was still clear, the clover still pungent, the bees buzzed.

I noticed that my mother and my father were not alone. Leah stood facing her husband. By her side was Rachel.

The two women had made a kind of peace years earlier. They did not work together or consult with each other. They did not sit next to each other in the red tent, or address each other directly. And they were never in their husband's presence at the same time. Yet now the three stood, in plain sight, talking like old friends. The women had their backs to me.

The conversation ended as I approached. My mother and

aunt turned away from Jacob and, upon seeing me, replaced their solemn expressions with the false smiles that adults show children from whom they wish to hide something. I did not return their smiles. I knew they had been talking of leaving. I placed my father's food and drink at his feet and had turned to follow Leah and Rachel back to the tents when Jacob my father spoke.

"Dinah," he said. It was the first time I remember hearing my name in his mouth. "Thank you, girl. May you always be a comfort to your mothers." I looked into his face, and he smiled a real smile at me. But I did not know how to smile at my father or answer him, so I turned to run after my mother and Rachel, who had already begun the walk back to the tents. I slipped my hand into Leah's and peeked back to look at Jacob once more, but he had already turned away from me.

Jacob began to negotiate for our departure that evening. As night fell, and for many nights afterward, the women lay down on their beds with the sounds of men's voices loud in their ears. Laban was perfectly willing to see Jacob gone with his daughters and the grandsons who ate too much and respected him too little. But the old man hated to think that Jacob might leave a rich man.

During the long nights of shouting, Laban sat between his sons, Kemuel and Beor. The three of them drank beer and wine and yawned into Jacob's face, and ended their conversations before anything could be settled.

Jacob sat between his oldest sons, Reuben and Simon, and touched no drink stronger than barley beer. Behind him

stood Levi and Judah. The seven younger boys stood outside the tent, straining to hear what was said. Joseph told
me what he overheard, and I repeated everything to my
mothers. But I did not tell Joseph about the whispered
conversations among the women. I did not report their
hoarding of hard bread, or how they had taken to sewing
herbs into the hems of their garments. I knew better than to
breathe of Rachel's plan to carry off the teraphim.

Night after night, Laban argued that he owed Jacob
nothing more than the meager dowries he'd bestowed upon
Leah and Rachel, which would have left my father without
so much as the tents over our heads. Then, in a great show
of generosity, he offered twenty head of sheep, and twenty
goats—one of each kind for every year of Jacob's service,
which had enriched Laban beyond his dreams.

Jacob, for his part, claimed the right of any overseer,
which would have given him a tenth of the herds, and the
pick of them, too. He demanded his wives' personal property, which amounted to a good pile of grindstones and
spindles, looms and jugs, jewelry and cheeses. He reminded
Laban that his tents, his flocks, and the bondsmen in his
debt had come to him through the work of Jacob's hands.
He threatened to seek justice from the tribunal at Haran,
but that only made Laban sneer. He had gambled and drunk
deeply with the town fathers for many years and had no
doubt whose side they would take.

Late one night, after weeks of fruitless talk, Jacob found
the words that moved Laban's heart. The husband of Leah
and Rachel, the father of the sons of Zilpah and Bilhah,
fixed Laban with his eye and threatened that the god of his
fathers would not look kindly on one who swindled the

anointed of his tribe. Jacob said that his god had come to him in a dream and spoken to him and told him to go with his wives and his sons and his flocks in abundance. Jacob's god had said that anyone who tried to thwart him would suffer in his body, in his flocks, and in his sons.

This troubled the old man, who shivered before the power of any god. When Jacob invoked the god of his fathers, the smirk dropped from Laban's lips. Jacob's success with the flocks, the health of his eleven sons, the loyalty of the bondsmen to him, and even the prowess of his dogs—all this signaled that Jacob was blessed by heaven. Laban remembered all the years of excellent sacrifice that Jacob had made to his god, and the old man reckoned that El must be well pleased by so much devotion.

The next day, Laban shut himself up with his household gods and was not seen until evening, when he called for Jacob. From the moment Jacob faced his father-in-law, he could see that the advantage had shifted. He began to bargain in earnest.

"My father," he said, false honey on his tongue, "because you have been good to me, I wish to take only the animals that are brindled and spotted—the ones whose wool and hides will bring me less at market. You will maintain the purebloods of the herds. I will go out from your house poor but grateful."

Laban sensed a trick in Jacob's offer but he couldn't divine the benefit. Everyone knew that the darker animals did not produce wool that spun white, or skins that tanned evenly. What Laban did not know was that the "poorer" beasts were hardier and healthier than the animals that yielded the fancy wool and the pretty skins. The brindled ewes dropped twins more often than not, and most of their offspring were females, which meant more cheese. The hair of his mottled goats was especially oily, which made for a stronger rope. But these were Jacob's secrets, which he had learned during his years with the herds. This was knowledge that Laban's laziness had cost him.

Laban said, "So be it," and the men drank wine to seal the agreement. Jacob would go with his wives and his sons, and with the brindled and spotted flocks, which numbered no more than sixty goats and sixty sheep. There would have been more livestock, but Jacob traded for two of the bondsmen and their women. In exchange for a donkey and an ancient ox, Jacob agreed to leave two of his dogs, including the best of the herders.

All of the household goods of Leah and Rachel were Jacob's to take, as well as the clothing and jewelry worn by Zilpah and Bilhah. Jacob claimed his sons' cloaks and spears, two looms and twenty-four minas of wool, six baskets of grain, twelve jugs of oil, ten skins of wine, and water skins, one for each person. But that was only the official reckoning, which did not take into account my mothers' cleverness.

They decided upon a date for our departure, in three months' time. While that seemed an eternity when it was first announced, the weeks passed quickly. My mothers set about collecting, discarding, packing, sorting, trading, washing. They devised sandals for the journey and baked loaves of hard bread. They hid their best jewelry deep inside the grain baskets, in case thieves accosted us on the road. They scoured the hills for herbs to fill up their pouches.

Had they chosen to, my mothers could have stripped the garden bare. They could have taken every onion bulb, dug up every buried store of grain, and emptied every beehive within walking distance. But they took only what they considered rightly theirs and nothing more. They did this not out of respect for Laban, but for the bondswomen and their children who would be left behind.

Sent to fetch and carry, I worked hard too. No one petted me or fussed over my hair. No one smiled into my face or praised my spinning. I felt misused and ignored, but no one noticed when I brooded, so I stopped feeling sorry for myself and did as I was told.

It might have been a joyous time had it not been for Ruti, who, in the last weeks of our preparations, lost all heart. She took to sitting in the dust before Leah's tent, a graven image of despair forcing everyone to step around her. Leah crouched down and tried to persuade Ruti to move, to come inside her tent and eat something, to take comfort. But Ruti was past comfort. Leah suffered for the poor woman, who was no older than she, yet whose teeth were gone and who shuffled like a crone. But there was nothing to be done, and after several attempts at coaxing her out of her misery, my mother stood up and moved on.

On the night before the last new moon we spent in the land of the two rivers, the wives of Jacob gathered quietly in the red tent. The sisters sat, letting the three-cornered cakes sit untouched in the basket before them. Bilhah said, "Ruti will die now." Her words hung in the air, unchallenged and true. "One day, Laban will hit her too hard or she will simply waste away from sorrow."

Zilpah sighed into the silence and Leah wiped her eyes. Rachel stared at her hands. My mother pulled me onto her lap, a place that I had outgrown. But I sat there and let her baby me, and enjoyed her thoughtless caresses.

The women burned a portion of their lunar cake in offering as they did for every new moon, as they did every seventh day. But they sang no songs of thanksgiving, nor did they dance.

The next day, the bondswomen joined Jacob's wives for the moon days, but it was more like a funeral than a feast. No one asked the pregnant woman to recount her symptoms. No one spoke of the exploits of her son. The women did not braid one another's hair or rub one another's feet with oil. The sweet cakes went untouched except by babies who wandered in and out, seeking their mothers' breasts and laps.

Of all the bondswomen, only Zibatu and Uzna would be going to Canaan with my mothers. The others would stay behind with their husbands. It was the end of a long sisterhood. They had held one another's legs in childbirth and suckled one another's babies. They had laughed in the garden and sung harmonies for the new moon. But those days were ending and each woman sat with her own memories, her own loss. For the first time, the red tent became a sad place, and I sat outside until I was tired enough to sleep.

Ruti did not appear in the tent. Morning came, and evening, and still she did not come. As the sun rose on the second day, my mother sent me to look for her. I asked Joseph if our grandfather's wife had made bread that morning. I asked Judah if Ruti was anywhere to be found. I asked my brothers and the daughters of the bondswomen, but no one could remember seeing Ruti. No one could recall. By then misery had made her nearly invisible.

I went to the top of the hill where I had been so happy a few months ago, but now the sky was dull and the land appeared gray. I scanned the horizon and saw no one. I walked to the well but I was alone. I climbed the low branches of a tree at the far edge of the near pasture, but I did not see Ruti.

On the way back to tell my mother that she was nowhere to be found, I came upon her. She was lying in the side of a dry wadi, a desolate place where stray lambs sometimes wandered and broke their legs. At first I thought Ruti was asleep on her back, lying against the steep slope. As I walked closer I could see that her eyes were open, so I called out to her, but she made no move to answer me.

That was when I saw that her mouth was slack and that there were flies at the corners of her eyes and on her wrist, which was black with blood. Carrion birds circled above.

I had never seen a corpse before. My eyes filled with Ruti's face, which was no longer Ruti's face but a piece of blue slate bearing traces of a face I remembered. She did not look sad. She did not look pained. She looked nothing but empty. I stared, trying to understand where Ruti had gone. And although I didn't realize it, I was holding my breath.

I might never have moved from that spot had Joseph not appeared behind me. Rachel had sent him out looking for Ruti, too. He walked past me and crouched down beside the body. He blew gently into her fixed eyes, touched her cheek with his finger, and then placed his right hand upon her eyes to close them. I was amazed at my brother's courage and calm.

But then Joseph shuddered and jumped back as though he'd been bitten by a snake. He ran to the bottom of the wadi, down to where water had once flowed and where flowers must have blossomed. Falling to his knees, Joseph retched into the dry bed. With great sobs, he knelt and heaved and coughed. When I walked over to him, he lurched to his feet and motioned me to keep away.

"Go back and tell them," I whispered. "I'll stay here and keep the vultures away." I regretted my words the moment they were out of my mouth. Joseph didn't bother to answer, but bolted as though a wolf were pursuing him.

I turned away from the body, but I could not shut out the sound of the flies at her wrist and the bloody knife that lay by her side. The vultures flapped and squawked. The wind cut through my tunic, and I shivered.

I walked to the top of the wadi and tried to think kind thoughts about Ruti. But all I could remember was the fear in her eyes, the dirt in her hair, the sour smell of her body, the defeated crouch. She had been a woman just as my mother was a woman, and yet she was a creature totally unlike my mother. I did not understand Leah's kindness to Ruti. In my heart, I shared her sons' disdain for her. Why did she submit to Laban? Why did she not demand her sons' respect? How could she find the courage to kill herself when she had no courage for life? I was ashamed of my heart's coldness, for I knew that Bilhah would have cried to see Ruti lying here, and that Leah would pour ashes on her own hair when she learned what had happened.

But the longer I stood there, the more I hated Ruti for her weakness and for making me keep watch. It seemed no one would come for me, and I began to tremble. Perhaps Ruti would rise up and take her knife to me as punishment for my cruel thoughts. Perhaps the gods of the underworld would come for her and take me as well. I started to weep for my mother to come and rescue me. I called the name of each aunt. I called Joseph and Reuben and Judah. But it seemed they had forgotten me.

By the time I saw the shape of two people moving across the meadow, I was sick with worry. But there was no one to comfort me. The women had remained in the tent. Only Ruti's horrible sons had come. They threw a blanket over their mother's face without so much as a sigh. Beor threw the little bundle that was Ruti over his shoulders, as if he were carrying a stray kid. I followed him alone. Kemuel paid no attention to his poor dead mother and hunted a rabbit on the way back. "Ha ha!" he shouted, when his arrow found its mark.

Only when I saw the red tent on the edge of the camp did the tears begin to run down my cheeks again, and I ran to my mothers. Leah searched my face and covered it with kisses. Rachel hugged me close, and laid me down on her fragrant bed. Zilpah sang me a lullaby about abundant rains and luxuriant harvests while Bilhah rubbed my feet until I fell asleep. I did not wake up until the next evening, and by then Ruti was under the ground. We left a few days later.

My father and older brothers, all the bondsmen, and Laban's sons went off to the far pastures to separate the brindled and spotted livestock that now belonged to Jacob. Of all the men, only Laban remained in camp, counting up jugs as they were filled, making messes of neatly piled woolens to check that we took nothing he had not agreed to. "It is my right," he barked without apology.

Eventually Laban grew tired of spying on his daughters' labors and decided to go to Haran "on business." Leah sneered at the announcement. "The old man is going to gamble and drink and boast to the other lazy clods that he is finally rid of his greedy son-in-law and his ungrateful daughters," she told me as we cooked a meal for him to take on his journey. Beor accompanied Laban, who made a great show of leaving Kemuel in command.

"He has my authority in all things," said Laban to the wives and younger sons of Jacob, whom he assembled for his departure. No sooner had Laban disappeared over the hill than Kemuel demanded that Rachel herself bring him strong wine. "Send me no ugly serving girls," he bellowed. "I want my sister."

Rachel made no objection to serving him, as it gave her the opportunity to pour an herb that hastens sleep into his cup. "Drink well, brother," she said sweetly as he swallowed the first cup. "Have another."

He was snoring within an hour of Laban's departure. Every time he roused, Rachel went to his tent with her brew and sat with him, feigning interest in his crude attempts at seduction and filling his cup so full and so often that he lost the whole day and the next one, too.

While Kemuel snored, the men returned, bringing the flocks into the near pasture just over the rise from the tents, so the final hours of our preparation were filled with bleating, dust, and animal smells. They were filled too with the unaccustomed noise and tension of so many men in our midst.

On ordinary days, the tents were populated only by women and children. A sick or feeble man might lie on his bed or sit in the sun while the work of wool and bread and beer progressed about him, but such a man knew enough to be embarrassed and kept to himself.

We had a whole crowd of healthy men with little to do. "What a nuisance," said my mother, of the relentless presence of her sons.

"They're always hungry," grumbled Bilhah, who never grumbled, after sending Reuben away for the second time that morning with a bowl of lentils and onions. Every few minutes, Bilhah or Leah had to stop what they were doing to heat the bread stones.

The presence of the men presented a more subtle difficulty, as well. The tents were Leah's domain, and although she was the one who knew what needed to be done, she would not give orders with her husband by her side. So she stood behind Jacob and softly asked, "Is my husband ready to dismantle the big loom and lay it into the cart?" and he would direct his sons to do what was needed. And so it went, until everything was ready.

Throughout the weeks of preparation, and especially after Laban departed for Haran, I kept close to my aunt Rachel. I found reasons to follow her from one task to the next, offering to carry for her, asking her for advice on my duties. I stayed by her side until nightfall, even falling asleep upon her blankets, and woke in the morning to find myself covered by her sweet-scented cloak. I tried to be careful, but she knew that I was watching her.

On the night before we left, Rachel caught my eye, which was fixed upon her every move. At first she glared, but then she stared back in a way that told me I had triumphed: I could follow her. We went to the bamah, where Zilpah was lying facedown beside the altar, whispering to the gods and goddesses we were about to abandon. She looked up as we sat down among the roots of the great tree there, but I'm not even sure that Zilpah saw me sitting between Rachel's knees. As we waited, my aunt braided my hair and told me about the healing properties of common herbs (coriander seeds for bellyache, cumin for wounds). She had long ago decided that I should learn what Inna had taught her.

We stayed there, in the lap of the tree, until Zilpah rose, sighed, and left. We sat until the sounds from the tents quieted and the last lamps were extinguished. We stayed until the moon, halfway to fullness, was high in the branches above us, and the only sound was the occasional bleating of a sheep.

Then Rachel rose and I followed as she walked softly to Laban's tent. My aunt made no acknowledgment of my presence, and I was not sure she knew I was behind her until she held the tent flap open for me, to a place I had never been nor wished to go.

It was dark as a dry well in my grandfather's tent, and the air was fetid and stale. Rachel, who had been here to ply Kemuel with drink, walked past his snoring body directly to the corner of the tent where a rough wooden bench served as Laban's altar. The teraphim were arrayed in two rows. Rachel reached out for them without hesitation and dropped them, one by one, into the cloth tied around her waist, as though she were harvesting onions. When the last of the idols fell into her apron, she turned, walked across the tent without a glance at Kemuel, who moaned in his sleep as she passed him, and soundlessly held the tent flap open for me.

We walked out into stillness. My heart pounded in my ears and I drew a breath to rid myself of the tent's stink, but Rachel did not pause. She walked quickly to her tent, where Bilhah slept. I heard my aunt rustling among the blankets, but it was too dark to see where she hid the idols. Then Rachel lay down and I heard nothing more.

I wanted to shake her and demand that she show me the treasures. I wanted her to hug me and tell me how well I had done in keeping still. But I remained quiet. I lay down to the pounding of my heart, thinking that Kemuel would rush into the tent and kill us all. I wondered if the teraphim would come to life and cast terrible spells on us for disturbing them. I was sure that morning would never come, and I shivered into my blanket, though the night was not cold. Finally, my eyes closed to a dreamless sleep.

I awoke to a great noise of voices outside the tent. Rachel and Bilhah were already gone, and I was alone with two piles of neatly folded blankets. She had taken them with her, I realized. Rachel had moved the idols without me. After all my careful watching and following, I had missed it. I rushed outside to see my brothers rolling up the goatskins that had been my father's tent. All around me, tents were on the ground, the poles collected, the ropes coiled. My home had been dismantled. We were going.

Jacob had risen at dawn and made a sacrifice of grain and wine and oil for the journey. The herds, sensing a change, were bleating and kicking up dust. The dogs would not stop barking. Half of the tents were down, leaving the camp looking lopsided and desolate, as though a great wind had blown away half the world.

We ate a morning meal salted by the tears of those who

would not accompany us. The women put away the last of the bowls and stood with empty hands. There was nothing left for us to do, but Jacob gave no sign for us to leave. Laban had not returned from Haran as he had promised.

The sun began to rise higher, and we should have been long gone, but Jacob stood alone at the top of the ridge that faced the road to Haran, squinting for a sign of Laban. Jacob's sons muttered among themselves. Zilpah walked to the bamah, where she ripped her tunic and placed ashes on her hair. It grew hot and still, and even the herds quieted down.

Then Rachel walked past Reuben and Simon, Levi and Judah, who stood at the bottom of the hill where Jacob watched, and she approached her husband and said, "Let us go. Kemuel told me his father will return with spears and riders and prevent us from leaving. He is gone to tell the judges in Haran that you are a thief. We must not wait."

Jacob listened and then replied, "Your father fears my god too much to act so boldly. And Kemuel is a fool."

Rachel bowed her head and said, "My husband may know better, but the herds are ready and the goods are packed. Our feet are shod and we stand with nothing to do. We do not steal away in the dark of night. We take nothing but what is our own. The season is right. If we wait much longer the moon will begin to wane, and a darkening moon is no time to embark upon a journey."

Rachel spoke nothing but the truth, and Jacob had no wish to see Laban again. Indeed, he was furious with the old man for making him wait, for making him leave like a thief, without giving proper farewell to the grandfather of his sons.

Rachel's words spoke to Jacob's own purpose, and after she left him, he gave the order to go. Impatient to be underway, the sons of Jacob shouted with happiness, but a wail went up from the women who were staying behind.

My father signaled us to follow him. He led us first to the bamah, where each of us placed a pebble by the altar. The men picked up any small rock that lay at their feet to leave in farewell. Leah and Rachel sought out stones from around the foot of the nearby terebinth, which had given them years of shade and comfort.

No words were spoken. The stones would testify for us, though Bilhah kissed hers before laying it on top of the others.

Zilpah and I alone were prepared for this moment. Weeks earlier, my grieving aunt had taken me to the wadi where Ruti had died and showed me a place at the bottom of the ravine filled with smooth, oval-shaped stones. She chose a tiny white one, the size of her thumbnail. I took a red one, streaked with black, nearly as big as my fist. She kept it for me and placed it in my palm as we walked for the last time to the holy place of my family.

Then Jacob led his family over the hill, to where the bondsmen waited with the herd. My mothers did not look back, not even Zilpah, whose eyes were red but dry.

Chapter Three

MY FATHER ARRANGED his family, his flocks, and all of his household for the journey. Jacob led, holding a great olive staff in his hand, flanked by Levi and Simon, who strutted with importance. Behind them walked the women and children too young to be tending the herds, so Uzna's little son and daughter stayed near their mother's legs, and Zibatu carried her baby girl in a hip sling. I started out near Zilpah, hoping to lighten the sadness that clung to her, but her sorrow finally chased me to my mother and Bilhah, who were engrossed in planning meals and paid no attention to me. So I found my way to Rachel, whose smile did not fade even as the sun began to beat down on us in earnest. The bundle on her back was more than large enough for the teraphim, and I was sure that was where they were hidden.

Joseph, Tali, and Issa were told to stay with the pack animals, near the women, which made them sulk and kick at the dirt and mutter about how they were old enough to be trusted with more important work than tending a tame donkey and the ox who drew the heavy cart.

Directly behind us and the beasts of burden, Reuben had charge of the herd and the shepherds, who included Zebulun and Dan, Gad and Asher, and the bondsmen, Nomir, husband of Zibatu, and Zimri, father of Uzna's children. The four dogs ran around the perimeter of the flocks, their ears flattened to their heads as they worked. They lifted their brown eyes from the goats and sheep only when Jacob approached, and bounded to their master's side to bask for a moment in the touch of his hand and the sound of his voice.

Judah, our rear guard, walked behind the herds, watching out for stragglers. I would have been lonely there with no one to talk to, but my brother seemed to enjoy his solitude.

I was in awe of our numbers and what seemed our great wealth. Joseph told me that we were a small party by any measure, with only two pack animals to carry our belongings, but I remained proud of my father's holdings and I thought my mother carried herself like a queen.

We had walked for only a little while when Levi pointed out a figure ahead, sitting by the side of the path. As we came closer, Rachel shouted, "Inna!" and ran ahead to greet her friend and teacher. The midwife was arrayed for travel, a donkey laden with blankets and baskets by her side. The caravan did not stop at the unexpected sight of the lone woman; it would have been pointless to bring the herd to a halt in the absence of water. Instead, Inna approached Jacob, leading her donkey and falling in a step behind him. Inna did not address my father but spoke to Rachel so that he would overhear her words.

The midwife presented her case with fancy phrases that sounded odd coming from a mouth that usually spoke in the plainest and sometimes the coarsest of terms. "Oh, my friend," she said, "I cannot bear to see you part. My life would be desolate in your absence, and I am too old to take another apprentice. I wish only to join with your family and be among you for the rest of my days. I would give your husband all of my possessions in exchange for his protection and a place among the women of his tents. I would accompany you as your bondswoman or as your maidservant, to practice my craft in the south, and learn what they have to teach there. I would minister to your family, setting the bricks for your women, healing the wounds of your men, offering service to Gula, the healer, in Jacob's name," Inna said.

She flattered my father, whom she called wise as well as kind. She declared herself his servant.

I was one of many witnesses to Inna's speech. Levi and Simon stayed close, curious to learn what the midwife wanted. Leah and Bilhah had quickened their pace to discover why their friend had appeared among them. Even Zilpah roused herself and drew near.

Rachel turned her face to Jacob, her eyebrows posing the question, her hands clasped at her chest. Her husband smiled into her face. "Your friend is welcome. She will be your maidservant in my eyes. She is yours, as though she were part of your dowry. There is nothing more to say."

Rachel kissed Jacob's hand and placed it for a moment upon her heart. Then she led Inna and her donkey back to our animals, where the women could talk more freely.

"Sister!" Rachel said to the midwife. "What is this about?"

Inna dropped her voice and began by telling a sorry tale

about a deformed stillbirth—a tiny head, twisted limbs—born to a girl made pregnant at her first blood. "Too young," said Inna, with an angry mouth. "Far too young." The father was a stranger, a wild-haired man of many years, who wore only a loincloth and brought his wife to Inna's hut. When the baby and mother both died, he accused the midwife of causing his misfortune by casting spells upon them.

Inna, who had spent three terrible days working to save the mother, could not hold her tongue. Exhausted and sorrowful, she called the man a monster and accused him of being the girl's father as well as her husband. Then she spit in his face.

Enraged, the stranger reached for her throat and would have killed her had it not been for neighbors who were drawn by her screams and pulled him away. Inna showed us the black bruises on her throat. The man demanded restitution from Inna's father, but Inna had no father, nor had she brother or husband. She had lived alone after her mother's death.

Having kept her family's hut, she did not want for shelter, and midwifery kept her in grain and oil and even wool for trade. Since she was a burden to no one, none had troubled about her. But now the angry stranger demanded to know why the townspeople tolerated such an "abomination."

"A woman alone is a danger," he screamed into the faces of Inna's neighbors. "Where are your judges?" he hissed. "Who are your elders?"

At that Inna grew frightened. The most powerful man of her mud village had hated her since she had turned down a marriage offer on behalf of his half-wit son. She feared that he would incite the men against her, and perhaps even enslave her. "Idiots. All of them," she said, and spit into the dust.

"My thoughts turned to you for refuge," she said, addressing all the women of my family, who walked nearby, listening to her every word. "Rachel knows I have always wanted to see more of the world than these dusty hills, and since Jacob treats his wives better than most, I came to see your departure as a gift from the gods," she continued. "And sisters, I must tell you, I am tired of eating my evening meal alone. I wish to see a baby I delivered as he grows into manhood. I wish to celebrate the new moon among friends. I want to know that my bones will be planted well after my death." Looking around at us, she smiled broadly. "So here I am."

The women smiled back at her, happy to have such a healer among them. Although Rachel was skilled, Inna was famous for her golden hands, and beloved for her stories.

Zilpah saw Inna's appearance as a good omen. The midwife's presence lifted her spirits so much that later my aunt began to sing. It was nothing exalted, only a children's song about a fly who bothered a rabbit, who ate the insect but was eaten by a dog, who was in turn eaten by a jackal, who was hunted by a lion, who was killed by a boastful man, who was snatched by An and Enlil, the sky gods, and placed in the heavens to teach him a lesson.

It was a simple song known to every child and thus to every adult who had been a child. By the last verse, all of my mothers and the bondswomen and their children were singing. Even my brothers had joined in, with Simon and Levi making a contest of it, outshouting each other. When the song ended everyone clapped hands and laughed. It was sweet to be free of Laban's shadow. It was sweet to be at the beginning of a new life.

That was the first time I heard women's voices and men's voices raised in song together, and throughout the journey the boundaries between the men's lives and the women's relaxed. We joined the men in the work of watering the herd, they helped us unpack for the evening meal. We listened to them sing herding songs, addressed to the night sky and filled with tales of the constellations. They heard our spinning songs, which we sang as we walked and worked wool with small spindles. We applauded one another and laughed together. It was time out of life. It was like a dream.

Most of the singing took place just before sleep or early in the morning while we were still fresh. By afternoon, everyone was hungry and footsore. It took the women several days to get accustomed to wearing sandals from sunup to sunset—at home we stayed barefoot in and around the tents. Inna relieved our blisters and soothed our aches by massaging our feet with oil perfumed with thyme.

There was nothing wrong with our appetites, though. The long days left everyone ferociously hungry, and it was good that my brothers could supplement the simple bread and porridge of the road with birds and hares they hunted along the way. The meat tasted strange but wonderful the way Inna prepared it, with a bright yellow spice she got in trade.

There was little conversation during the evening meal. The men were in their circle, the women among themselves. By the time the moon rose, everyone was asleep—the women and babies crowded inside one large tent, the men and boys on blankets under the stars. At dawn, after a hurried meal of cold bread, olives, and cheese, we began again. After a few days of this, I could barely remember my old life, rooted in one place.

Every morning brought a new wonder. The first day, Inna joined us. The second day, late in the afternoon, we came upon a great river.

My father had said we would cross the great water, but I had given no thought to the meaning of his words. When we came to the top of a hill overlooking the river valley, I was amazed. I had never seen so much water in one place, nor had any of us except Jacob and Inna. The river was not very wide where we forded it, or "him" as Zilpah would have me say. Even so, it was twenty times wider than the streams I had known. He lay across the valley like a sparkling path, the setting sun catching fire on the way.

We came to a crossing where the bottom was packed with pebbles and the ford was wide. The ground on either bank had been beaten smooth by many caravans, and my father decided we would stop there until morning. The animals were led to water, and we made camp, but before the meal, my father and my mothers gathered by the banks of the Euphrates and poured a libation of wine into the great river.

We were not the only ones at the ford. Up and down the banks, traders had stopped to eat and sleep. My brothers wandered and stared at the new faces and strange clothes. "A camel," Joseph shouted, and our brothers chased after him to get a closer look at the spindly-legged beast. I could not go with them, but I did not regret being left behind. It gave me a chance to go down to the river, which drew me like a storyteller.

I stood by the water's edge until the last trace of daylight had drained from the sky, and later, after the evening meal, I returned to savor the smell of the river, which was as heady to me as incense, heavy and dark and utterly different from the sweet, thin aroma of well water. My mother, Leah, would have said I smelled the rotting grasses of the marsh and the mingled presence of so many animals and men, but I recognized the scent of this water the way I knew the perfume of my mother's body.

I sat by the river even after the others went to sleep. I dangled my feet in the water until they were wrinkled and soft and whiter than I had ever seen them. In the moonlight, I watched as leaves made their way slowly downstream and out of sight. I was lulled by the slow rush of the water against the shallow banks, and was nearly asleep when voices roused me. Turning to look upstream, I saw two shapes moving about in the middle of the river. For a moment I thought they might be river demons or water beasts come to drag me to a watery grave. I had no idea that people could move through the water like that—I had never seen swimming. But soon I realized they were merely men, the Egyptians who owned the camel, speaking to one another in their strange, purring language. Though their laughter was quiet, the water carried the sound as though they were whispering directly in my ears. I did not go to my blanket until they had left the water and returned the river to continue his peaceful journey through the night, undisturbed.

In the morning, my father and my brothers walked into the river without even pausing, lifting their robes to keep dry. My mothers hung their sandals upon their girdles and giggled about showing so much of their legs. Zilpah hummed a river song as we crossed. The twins rushed ahead, splashing each other thoughtlessly.

But I was afraid. Even though I had fallen in love with the river, I could see that at his deepest point, the water lapped against my father's waist. That meant I would be submerged to my neck and I would be swallowed. I thought about taking my mother's hand, like a baby, but she was balancing a bundle on her head. All of my mothers' hands were busy, and I was too proud to ask Joseph for his.

I had no time to be afraid. The pack animals were at my back, forcing me ahead, so I entered the river and felt the water rise to my ankles and calves. The current felt like a caress on my knees and thighs. In an instant, my belly and chest were covered, and I giggled. There was nothing to fear! The water held no threat, only an embrace I had no wish to break. I stood to one side as the ox passed, and then the rest of the animals. I moved my arms through the water, feeling them float on the surface, watching the waves and wake that followed my gesture. Here was magic, I thought. Here was something holy.

I watched the sheep craning their necks high out of the water, the goats, wide-eyed, barely touching the bottom with their hooves. And then came the dogs, who somehow possessed the trick of running through the water—pumping their legs and moving along, snorting, but not suffering. Here was more magic; our dogs could swim as well as Egyptians.

Finally Judah came up alongside me, looking as dubious of the water as I had felt just a few moments earlier. "Sister," he said. "Wake up and walk with me. Here is my hand," he offered. But as I reached out to take it, I lost my footing and fell backward. Judah grabbed me and dragged. I was on my back, the sky above me, and I felt the water holding me up. Aiee. A little shriek escaped from my mouth. A river demon, I thought. A river demon has hold of me. But Judah pulled me out onto the pebbles of the far bank, and I lost the wild lightness in my body.

Later that night, when I lay down to sleep among the women, I told my mothers what I had seen and felt by the side of the river and then in the water, during my crossing. Zilpah pronounced me bewitched by the river god. Leah reached out and squeezed my hand, reassuring us both. But Inna told me, "You are a child of water. Your spirit answered the spirit of the river. You must live by a river someday, Dinah. Only by a river will you be happy."

I loved every moment of the journey to Canaan. As long as I kept my spindle busy, my mothers didn't mind what I did or where I went, so I wandered from the front of the caravan to the back, trying to be everywhere and see everything. I remember little of the land or sky, which must have changed as we traveled. Once, Rachel and Inna brought me with them to gather herbs and flowers up a hill that grew steeper and more rugged as we headed south. I was amazed to see trees growing so thickly that women as slender as Rachel and Inna had to walk in single file to pass among them. I recall their curious needles that left my fingers smelling green all day.

Best of all I liked the sights of the road. There were caravans heading back to Egypt loaded with cedar, lines of slaves headed for Damascus, and traders from Shechem heading for Carchemish, near our old home. So many strange people passed by: men who were clean-shaven as boys and huge, black, bare-chested men. Although there were fewer women on the road, I glimpsed mothers shrouded in black veils, naked slave girls, and a dancer who wore a breastplate made of copper coins.

Joseph was as fascinated by the people as I, and he would sometimes run over to get a closer look at a particularly strange animal or costume. I was too shy to go with him, and my mothers would not have permitted it. My brother described what he saw and we marveled over it all.

I did not share my observations of my own family with Joseph, though. I felt like a thief, spying upon my parents and brothers, but I burned to know more about them—especially my father. Since Jacob walked with us for a little while every day, I watched him and noticed how he treated my mothers. He spoke to Leah about provisions and plans and to Rachel about memories of his trip north to Haran. He was careful not to slight either woman in his attentions.

Zilpah bowed her head when my father approached, and he responded in kind, but they rarely spoke. Jacob smiled at Bilhah as though she were his child. She was the only one he touched, running his hand over her soft black hair whenever he passed. It was an act of familiarity that seemed to express his fondness, but also proved her powerlessness as the least of his wives. Bilhah said nothing, but blushed deeply at these caresses.

I noticed that Reuben's devotion to Bilhah had not faded over time. Most of my brothers, as they grew into their height and sprouted beards, loosened their childhood ties to mothers and aunties. All except Reuben, who liked to linger near the women, especially Bilhah. During the trip, he seemed to know where she was at every moment. When he called for her, she replied, "Yes, brother," even though he was her nephew. She never spoke of him to anyone and I don't think I ever heard her give voice to his name, but I could see their abiding affection, and it made me glad.

Reuben was easy to know, but Judah was restless. He had chosen his position behind the herd, but sometimes he pressed one of the younger brothers to take his post so he could wander. He would climb to the top of a rocky hill and shout down to us, then disappear until nightfall. "He's young for it, but that one's already hungry for a woman," Inna muttered to my mother one evening, when Judah came to the fire later that night, looking for his supper.

I turned to Judah and realized that my brother's body had begun to take the shape of a man, his arms well muscled, his legs showing hair. He was the handsomest of all my brothers. His teeth were perfect, white and small; I remember this because he smiled so rarely they were always a surprise. Years later when I saw pearls for the first time, I thought of Judah's teeth.

Looking at Judah as a man, I had the thought that Reuben was certainly of an age to marry and father children. Indeed, he was not much younger than Nomir, whose daughter was almost ready to walk. Simon and Levi were old enough to have wives, too. And then I understood another reason why we had left Haran—to get my brothers bride-prices without Laban's sticky fingers getting in the way. When I asked my mother about this, she said, "Well, of course," but I was impressed with my own worldliness and insight.

No one spoke of Laban anymore. As the days passed and the moon began to wane, it seemed we were free of my grandfather's grasp. Jacob had all but stopped visiting Judah at the rear of the herd, looking over his shoulder to see whether his father-in-law was coming. Instead, his thoughts turned toward Edom and his meeting with Esau, the brother whom he had not seen for twenty years, since the day he had stolen his father's blessing and fled. The farther we walked from Haran the more Jacob spoke of Esau.

On the day before the new moon, we stopped early in the afternoon to give us time to prepare the red tent and cook for the three days given to the women. Since we would stay in this place for more than one night, my father raised his tent as well. We were near a pretty little stream where wild garlic grew in profusion. The smell of bread soon filled the camp, and great pots of stew were prepared so that the men would have plenty to eat while my mothers retired from their service.

My mothers and Uzna entered the women's tent before the sun set. I stayed outside to help serve the men. I never worked harder in my life. It was no small task feeding fourteen men and boys, and two young children, not to mention the women inside. Much of the serving fell to me, since Zibatu was often nursing her baby. Inna had no patience for my brothers.

I was proud to be feeding my family, doing the work of

a grown woman. When we finally joined my mothers in the tent after dark, I was never so grateful for rest. I slept well and dreamed of wearing a crown and pouring water. Zilpah said these were sure signs that my womanhood was not far off. It was a sweet dream, but it ended the next morning in a nightmare haunted by Laban's voice.

But it was no dream. My grandfather had arrived, demanding justice. "Give me the thief who took my idols," he bellowed. "Where are my teraphim?"

I ran out of the tent just in time to see my father, the olive staff in his hand, stride up to meet Laban. Beor and Kemuel stood behind my grandfather, along with three bondsmen from Haran, who kept their eyes on the ground rather than look into the face of Jacob, whom they loved.

"Whom do you call a thief?" my father demanded. "Whom do you accuse, you old fool? I served you for twenty years without pay, without honor. There was no thief in this place until you broke its peace."

Laban was struck dumb by his son-in-law's tone. "I am the reason for your comfortable old age," Jacob said. "I have been an honest servant. I took nothing that was not mine. I have nothing here except that which you agreed was mine, and it was not fair payment for what I have given you.

"Your daughters are my wives and want none of you. Your grandsons are my sons, and owe you nothing. While I stood on your land, I gave you honor you did not deserve, but now I am not bound by the obligations of guests and hosts."

By then, all my brothers had gathered behind Jacob, and

together they looked like an army. Even Joseph held a staff in his hands. The air was brittle with hatred.

Laban took a step back. "My son! Why do you rebuke me?" he wheedled, his voice suddenly old and soft. "I am here only to say farewell to my beloved family, my daughters and my grandsons. We are kinsmen, you and I. You are my nephew, and I love you as a son. You misunderstood my words. I wish only to kiss my family and give you my blessing," he said, stretching his fingers wide, bowing his head like a dog showing submission. "Is not the god of Abram also the god of my fathers? He is great, to be sure. But my son," Laban said, looking up into Jacob's face, "what of my other gods? What have you done with them?"

"What do you mean?" my father said.

Laban narrowed his eyes and answered, "My household gods have been stolen, and they disappeared upon your departure. I come to claim them for me and for my sons.

"Why do you wish to strip me of their protection? Do you fear their wrath, even though you worship the faceless one only?"

My father spat at Laban's feet. "I took nothing. There is nothing in my household that belongs to you. There is no place for thieves under my tents."

But Laban stood firm. "My teraphim are precious to me, nephew. I do not leave this place without them."

At this, Jacob shrugged. "They are not here," he said. "See for yourself." And with that he turned his back on Laban and walked away, into the woods and out of sight.

Laban began his search. My brothers stood, their arms crossed against their chests, and watched as the old man untied every bundle, unfurled every rolled-up tent, sifted his fingers through every sack of grain, squeezed every wine-skin. When he moved toward Jacob's tent, Simon and Levi tried to block his way, but Reuben motioned them aside. They followed Laban and watched as he rummaged through our father's blankets and even lifted the floor mat to kick at the earth, in case a hole had been dug.

The day wore on, and still Laban searched. I ran back and forth from where my grandfather hunted to the red tent, reporting what I saw to my mothers. Their faces stayed blank, but I knew they were worried. I had never seen women's hands working during the new moon, yet here every one of them was busy with her spindle.

After Laban had ransacked my father's tent, there was nowhere left for him to search except the red tent. His eyes fixed upon the women's tent on the edge of the camp. It was unthinkable that a healthy man would walk of his own will inside that place during the head of the month. The men and boys stared to see if he would place himself among bleeding women—even worse, his own daughters.

Laban muttered to himself as he approached the women's tent. At the door, he stopped and looked over his shoulder. He glared at his sons and grandsons, and then Laban opened the flap and walked in.

Laban's hoarse breath was the only sound. He glanced around the tent nervously, not meeting any of the women's eyes. No one moved or spoke. Finally and with great contempt he said, "Bah," and moved toward a pile of blankets.

Rachel stood up from her place on the straw. She did not drop her eyes as she addressed her father. Indeed, she stared straight into his face, and without anger or fear or any apparent emotion she said, "I took them, Father. I have all of the teraphim. All of your gods. They are here.

"I sit upon them. The teraphim of our family now bathe in my monthly blood, by which your household gods are polluted beyond redemption. You can have them if you wish," Rachel continued calmly, as though she were speaking of trifling things. "I will dig them out and even wipe them off for you if you like, father. But their magic has been turned against you. You are without their protection from this time forward."

No one drew breath as Rachel spoke. Laban's eyes widened, and he began to tremble. He stared at his beautiful daughter, who seemed to glow in the rosy light that filtered through the tent. It was a long and terrible moment that ended when Laban turned and shuffled out of our sight. Outside in the light, he found himself facing Jacob, who had returned.

"You found nothing," my father said, with supreme confidence. When Laban made no reply, Jacob continued, "There are no thieves in my tents. This will be our last meeting, old man. We are finished."

Laban said nothing, but opened his palms wide and bowed his head in acquiescence. "Come," he said. "We will settle our case." My grandfather motioned for Jacob to follow him up the hill to his camp. My brothers followed to give witness.

Laban and Jacob each selected ten stones and layered them one upon another until they had created a cairn to mark the boundaries between them. Laban poured wine over it. Jacob poured oil upon it. Each man swore peace to the other, touching the other's thigh. Then Jacob turned and walked down the hill. It was the last time any of us saw Laban, which we counted as a blessing.

Jacob was eager to be gone from the place, so the red tent was dismantled the next morning and we continued our journey toward the land my father called home.

My father was consumed with memories of Esau. Though it had been twenty years, Jacob could still see his brother's face when Esau finally understood the full meaning of what had befallen him. Not only had Jacob betrayed him by stealing his beloved father's blessing, it was clear that Rebecca had been behind it—the last of many proofs of her preference for her younger son.

Jacob had watched his brother's face as Esau pieced together the family treason, and my father was ashamed. Jacob understood the pain in Esau's belly and knew if he had been in his brother's place, he, too, would have given chase with a drawn dagger.

Jacob dwelt upon a vision of his terrible avenging brother, describing him daily to his sons, and to Leah, Rachel, and Bilhah during his nights with them, for now he raised his own tent so he could be comforted by a woman until morning. Jacob's fear was so great that it had erased all memory of his brother's love, which had always been stronger than his short-lived rages. He forgot the times Esau had fed him and protected him, laughed with him, and praised him.

My father's fear made Esau into a demon of revenge, whom I imagined red as a fox with arms like tree trunks.

This uncle haunted my dreams and turned the journey that I had loved into a forced march toward certain death.

I was not the only one who walked in fear. There was no more singing on the road or in camp after my father began to tell his Esau stories. The journey was quiet in the days after we took final leave of Laban, and even Judah no longer wished to walk alone at the back of the herd.

Soon there was another river to be crossed, and Esau was banished from my thoughts. I rejoiced to see flowing water again and ran up to the riverbank to put my face near the delicious smell and sound.

My father, too, seemed refreshed by the sight of the river and by the task at hand. He declared we would make camp on the far side that night and gathered his oldest sons around him to assign them their duties.

Although the water was nowhere near as wide as it had been at the great river to the north, this river was deeper in the center and much faster. Leaves did not meander downstream, but rushed away as though chasing after swift prey. Our crossing had to be quick, as the sun was already beginning its descent.

Inna and Zilpah poured an offering to the river god as the first of the animals were herded into the water and guided across. The smaller animals had to be taken two by two and by the scruff of the neck, with a man on either side. The dogs worked until they were exhausted. We nearly lost one of them in the current, but Joseph grabbed him and became a momentary hero among his brothers.

All of the men grew weary. Even Judah staggered from the effort of guiding frightened animals while withstanding a current that dragged at him. The river was generous, and none of the animals was lost. By the time the sun was resting on the tops of the trees, only the ox, donkeys, women, and babies remained.

Reuben and Judah struggled with the terrified ox, who bellowed like an animal headed for slaughter. It took a long while for them to drag the beast across, and by then it was dusk. My mother and I were the last to be taken across, my hand in hers this time so that I would not be stolen by the current. When we reached the far shore, it was dark and only my father was left behind.

Jacob called across the water. "Reuben," he said.

And my brother replied, "I am here."

"See to the animals," my father said. "Don't bother with a tent. The night is warm enough. I will cross with the first light. Be ready to leave."

My mother was not pleased by Jacob's plan and told Reuben to call back to our father and offer to cross the river and spend the night with him. He would not permit it. "Tell your mother to sit on her fears. I am neither a child nor a doddering elder. I will sleep by myself under the sky, as I did in my youth when I traveled north. Be ready to leave in the morning," said Jacob, and spoke no more.

The moon was still new, so the night was dark. The water would have sweetened the air had not the wet coats of the animals muddied its perfume with musk. They bleated in their sleep, unused to being wet in the chill of the night. I tried to stay awake to listen to the music of the rushing water, but this time the splashing lulled me into a deep sleep. Everyone slept heavily. If my father cried out, no one heard him.

*

Reuben was at the riverbank with Leah before sunrise to greet Jacob, but my father did not appear. The birds' greeting of the day had stilled and the sun had begun to dry the dew, but there was no sign of him. At Leah's signal, Reuben, Simon, and Judah plunged into the water to seek their father. They found him beaten and naked in the middle of a brushy clearing where the grass and bushes had been crushed and broken in a wide circle around him. Reuben ran back to us shouting for a robe to cover our father, and then he carried him back across the stream.

Uproar gave way to silence when Jacob was brought, senseless, lying in his son's arms, his left leg hanging at an awkward angle as though it were no longer attached to his body. Inna rushed forward and ordered my father's tent raised. Bilhah built a fire. The men stood by with empty hands. Reuben had no answers to their questions, and they fell silent.

Inna walked out of the tent and said, "Fever." Rachel ran for her herb kit. Inna gestured for Reuben to follow her back inside, and a few moments later we heard the terrible, animal scream as he guided our father's leg back into its place. The whimpering that followed was even worse.

Unnoticed and unneeded, I sat outside the tent, watching Inna's resolute face and Rachel's flushed cheeks as they walked in and out. I saw my mother's lips press into a thin line as she bent her head to hear their reports. I listened through the walls of the tent while my father screamed at a blue river demon and marshaled an army of angels to fight against a mighty enemy that rose from the waters. Zilpah muttered incantations to Gula, and Inna sang of ancient gods whose names I had never heard, Nintinugga, Ninisinna, Baba.

I heard my father weep and beg for mercy from his brother. I heard Jacob, the father of eleven sons, call out for his mother, "Ema, Ema," like a lost child. I heard Inna hush him and encourage him to drink, as though he were a swaddling baby.

On that endless day, no one ate or worked. In the evening, I fell asleep in my place by the tent, my dreams shaped by my father's cries and my mothers' murmurs.

At dawn, I started awake and was greeted by the stillness. I jumped to my feet in terror, certain that my father was dead. Surely we would be captured by Esau and made into slaves. But as I began crying, Bilhah found me and held me.

"No, little one," she said, stroking my matted hair. "He is well. He has recovered his sense, and he sleeps calmly now. Your mothers are sleeping, too, they are so weary from their labors."

By dusk of the second night after his ordeal, my father was well enough to sit by the door of his tent for the evening meal. His leg was still painful and he could barely walk, but his eyes were clear and his hands were steady. I slept without fear again.

We stayed for two months by the river Jabbok, so that Jacob could heal. The women's tents were set up, and the bondsmen's too. Days took on an orderliness, with the men tending the herds while the women cooked. We built an oven with clay from the river, and it was good to have fresh bread again, moist and warm, instead of the dried stuff we had eaten on the road, which always tasted of dust. During the first days of Jacob's illness, two sheep were slaughtered to make strengthening broths from their bones, so there was meat for a while. The rare treat made it seem like a festival.

But as my father recovered his health, his fear returned even greater than before and changed him. Jacob could speak of nothing else but his brother's revenge, and he saw the nighttime attack and his struggle with the army of angels as portents of the battle to come. He grew suspicious of any attempt to calm him and sent gentle Reuben away. Instead, he came to depend upon Levi, who let Jacob number his worries endlessly and nodded grimly at our father's direst predictions.

Among themselves, my mothers pondered the meaning of Jacob's latest dream, so powerful that it had crossed over into this world. They debated Jacob's worries and plans. Should he attack? Was it a mistake to send a messenger to Esau? Would it not have been wiser to appeal to his father, Isaac, for help? Perhaps the women should send a messenger to Rebecca, who was not only their mother-in-law, but their aunt as well? But they made no mention of the change in their husband's manner. The confident man had become tentative and cautious. The affectionate father had turned demanding and even cold. Perhaps they thought it a symptom of his illness, or perhaps they simply did not see what I saw.

I grew to hate every mention of Esau, though after a time my fear gave way to boredom. My mothers did not even notice when I started avoiding their tents. They were too caught up in my father's unfolding story and speculations about what lay ahead, and there was little for me to do. All our wool was spun, and the looms would not be unpacked, so my hands were often idle. No one called for me to fetch water or carry wool, and there was no garden to weed. I was near the end of childhood, and I was freer than I had ever been or would be again.

Joseph and I took to exploring the river. We walked its banks and watched the tiny fish that swarmed in its eddies. We hunted frogs, vivid green ones unlike any we'd ever seen. I picked wild herbs and salads. Joseph trapped grass-hoppers to dip in honey. We bathed our feet in the cool, swift waters, and splashed each other until we were drip-ping. We dried ourselves in the sun, and our clothes smelled like the breeze and the water of the Jabbok.

One day we walked upstream and discovered a natural bridge over the river—a path of flat stones that made for an easy crossing. With no one to forbid it, we crossed to the far side, and we soon realized that we had found the very place where our father had been wounded. We recognized the clearing he had described—the circle of eighteen trees, the beaten-down grass, and the broken and bent bushes. We found a scorched place on the ground where a great fire had burned.

The hairs on my neck stood on end, and Joseph took my hand in his, which was damp with fear. Looking up, we heard nothing—no birdsong or whispering of leaves in the wind. The charred place gave off no smell, and even the sunlight seemed muted around us. The air seemed as dead as Ruti lying in the wadi.

I wanted to leave, but I could not move. Joseph told me later that he would have fled, too. But his feet were rooted in the earth. We lifted our eyes to the sky, wondering if our father's fearful angels would return, but the heavens remained empty. We stood like stones, waiting for something to happen.

A loud crash from the circle of trees broke like thunder, and we shrieked, or at least we tried to cry out, but no sounds issued from our open mouths as a black boar ran out of the forest. He ran straight for us across the battered meadow. We screamed our silent scream again, nor was there any noise from the hooves of the beast, which moved at us with the speed of a gazelle. I thought we were about to die, and my eyes filled with pity for our mothers and I heard Leah sobbing behind me.

When I turned to find her, she was not there. Still, the spell had broken. My feet were free and I ran back toward the river, pulling Joseph with a strength greater than my own. Perhaps there were angels on my side, too, I thought as I reached the foot stones and found my way over. Joseph slipped off the first rock and cut his foot. This time his voice rang out in pain. The sound of his cry seemed to stop the boar in his tracks, and the animal fell, as though struck by a spear.

Joseph recovered his footing and scrambled back to the far shore, where I held out my hands to him, and we embraced, trembling, amid the sounds of the water, the rustling of leaves, and the terrified beating of our own hearts.

"What was that place?" my brother asked, but I could only shake my head. We looked back to the boar and the clearing and the ring of trees, but the beast had vanished and the scene now seemed ordinary and even beautiful: a bird flew across the horizon, chirping, and the trees swayed with the wind. I shuddered, and Joseph squeezed my hand. Without a word, we swore the day to secrecy.

But my brother was never the same. From that night forward, he began to dream with the power of our father's dreams. At first, he spoke of his wondrous encounters with angels and demons, with dancing stars and talking beasts, to me only. Soon, his dreams were too big for my ears alone.

Chapter Four

JOSEPH AND I returned to camp, afraid we would be questioned about our absence and worried about trying to keep what had happened from our keen-eyed mothers. But no one saw us come. All eyes were fixed upon a stranger who stood before Jacob. The man spoke in the clipped accents of the south, and the first words I heard from his mouth were "my father." As I crept around to see the face of the messenger, I saw someone who could only be a kinsman.

It was Eliphaz, Esau's oldest son and my cousin, who looked so much like Judah that I clapped my hand over my mouth to keep from blurting it out loud. He was as ruddy and handsome as Judah, though taller—as tall as Reuben, in fact. He spoke with Reuben's gestures, his head tilted to one side, his left arm wrapped around his waist, his right hand clenching and unclenching, as he brought us the news we had dreaded for so long.

"My father arrives before dusk," said Eliphaz. "He comes with my brothers and with bondsmen and slaves, forty in all, including the women. My mother is among them," he added, nodding toward my mothers, who smiled at the courtesy, in spite of themselves.

While Eliphaz spoke, my father's face was a mask— unchanging and impassive. In his heart, however, he railed and wept. Shattered now were his careful plans for dividing our numbers so Esau could not destroy us in one attack. Useless, all those evenings spent directing my brothers as to which animals would be given as a peace offering and which animals should be hidden from Esau's grasp. My mothers had not even begun to separate and prepare the goods my father wanted to present to his older brother in hopes of appeasing his terrible anger.

But now he was trapped, and he cursed himself for occupying his thoughts for too long with demons and angels, and clouding his purpose, for now our tents were in an indefensible position, with the river blocking escape behind us.

Jacob betrayed none of this to his nephew, however. He greeted Eliphaz with equal courtesy and thanked him for his message. He led him to his own tent, bade him rest, and called for food and drink. Leah went to prepare the meal. Rachel brought him barley beer, but the women did not rush so that Jacob could have time to think.

While Eliphaz rested, Jacob found my mother and told her to get the women dressed in their finest robes and to prepare offerings. He had Reuben gather his brothers, also in their finest attire, but he directed that they gird themselves with hidden daggers so that Esau could not massacre them without some cost to himself. All of this was done swiftly, so that when Eliphaz arose from his meal, we were all arrayed and ready to leave.

"It is not necessary, uncle," Eliphaz said. "My father comes to you. Why not receive him here in comfort?"

But Jacob said no. "I must greet my brother in a manner fit for a man of his station. We go out to give him welcome."

Leaving only the bondsmen and their wives behind, Jacob led us. Eliphaz walked at his side, followed by the animal offering—twelve strong goats and eighteen healthy sheep— shepherded by my brothers. I saw Leah look back over her shoulder, and sadness and fear crossed her face like clouds across the sun, but she put away her sorrow quickly, and remade her countenance into a picture of serenity.

We walked for only a short time—not even long enough for our long robes to grow dusty—before my father put down his staff. Esau was in sight on the far side of a gently sloping valley. Jacob walked out alone to greet his brother, and Esau did the same, as their retinues of grown sons followed at a little distance. From the hillside, I watched in terror as the two men came face to face. In an instant, my father was on the ground before his brother. For one awful moment I thought he had been felled by an unseen arrow or spear. But then he rose to his knees and bowed low, prostrating himself in the dust, again and again, seven times in all. It was the greeting of a slave to a master. My mother looked away in shame.

Apparently my uncle was also distressed by his brother's display, for he leaned down and took Jacob by the arm, shaking his head from side to side. I was too far away to hear words, but we could see the two men talking to each other, first crouching near the ground, then standing.

And then the unthinkable happened. Esau threw his arms around my father. My brothers immediately put their hands on the daggers hidden in their girdles. But Esau had moved not to harm his brother but to kiss him. He gathered our father to his bosom in a long embrace, and when at last they let go of each other, Esau pushed Jacob on the shoulder, a gesture of boys at play. Then he ran his hand through our father's hair, and at that, both men laughed the same hearty laugh that proved they had shared their mother's womb, even though one was dark and one was fair, one was slender and one was stocky.

My father said something to his brother, and again Esau held him to his chest, but this time when they parted, there was no laughter. Reuben later said that their cheeks were wet with tears as they turned to walk back toward us, their arms hung around each other's shoulders.

I was amazed. Esau, the red-faced bloodthirsty avenger, weeping in my father's arms? How could this man be the monster who haunted my dreams and chased the song from my brothers' lips?

My mothers exchanged glances of disbelief, but Inna's shoulders shook with silent laughter. "Your father was such a fool," she said weeks later in Succoth as we retold the story of that day. "To fear such a baby-faced sweetling? To give us all nightmares over such a lamb as that?"

My father led Esau back to where we stood, and Jacob presented gifts to his brother. Our uncle dutifully declined them three times, and then dutifully accepted his brother's offerings, praising each one in the most flattering terms. The ceremony of the gifts took a long time, and I wanted only to get a closer look at the cousins who stood behind Esau, especially at the women, who wore necklaces and dozens of bracelets on their arms and ankles.

After he had accepted the animals, the wool, the food-stuffs, and Jacob's second-best herding dog, Esau turned to his brother and asked, in what sounded like my father's own voice, "Who are these fine men?"

So Jacob presented his sons, who bowed low before their uncle, as they had been instructed. "Here is Reuben, my firstborn, son of Leah, who stands there." My mother bowed her head very low, less to show respect I think than to keep Esau from noticing her mismatched eyes before he had counted all of her sons.

"And here are more of Leah's children: Simon and Levi. This is Judah," my father said, clapping his fourth son on the shoulder. "You can see how your image was never far from my mind." Judah and Esau smiled at each other with the same smile.

"Zebulun is also Leah's son, and there are her twins Naphtali and Issachar."

Esau bowed to my mother and said, "Leah is the mother of myriads." And Leah blushed with pride.

Next, my father presented Joseph. "This is the youngest, the only son of my Rachel," he said, flaunting his fondness for my aunt. Esau nodded and looked at the favorite son and stared at Rachel's undiminished beauty. She stared back at him, still thunderstruck by the events of the day.

Next Jacob called out the name of Dan. "This is the son of Rachel's handmaid Bilhah. And here are Gad and Asher, borne to me by Leah's girl, Zilpah."

It was the first time I had heard the distinctions between my brothers, or my aunties, made so clear or public. I saw the sons of the lesser wives whom the world called "hand-maids," and I saw how their heads dropped to be so named.

But Esau knew what it was to be second, and he approached the lesser sons just as he had my other brothers, going to Dan, Gad, and Asher, taking their hands in greeting. The sons of Bilhah and Zilpah stood taller, and I was proud to have such an uncle.

Now it was my father's turn to ask about the sons of Esau, who named them each with pride: "You have met Eliphaz already, my firstborn by Adath, who stands there," he said, pointing to a small, plump woman who wore a head covering made of hammered copper disks.

"And here is Reuel," said Esau, putting his arm around a thin, dark man with a full beard. "He is the son of Basemath," nodding at a sweet-faced woman who held a baby on her hip.

"My little boys are Jeush, Jalam, and Korah. They stand with Basemath there, but they are the sons of Oholibama, my youngest wife," Esau said. "She died last spring, in childbirth."

There was much craning of necks as introductions were made, but soon we were able to get a closer look as everyone began the short walk back to Jacob's riverside camp. My older brothers eyed their grown cousins, but did not speak. The women drew together and began the slow process of acquaintance. We found Esau's daughters among them, including Adath's two youngest. Indeed, Adath had borne many girls, some of whom were grown and mothers themselves, but Libbe and Amat were still with her. They were not much older than I, but they ignored me because I still wore a child's dress, and they were women.

Basemath was a kind stepmother to all of Oholibama's children, and especially to the baby girl, Iti, who had cost

Oholibama her life. Basemath had lost so many babies, both boys and girls, she could barely number them. She had only the one son, Reuel, and one living daughter, Tabea, who was just my height. Tabea and I fell into step beside each other but kept quiet, not daring to disturb the solemn silence that fell upon the procession.

It was late in the afternoon when we reached our tents. A messenger had been sent to tell the bondswomen to begin the evening meal, and we were greeted by the smell of baking bread and cooking meat. Still, there was much to be done before we could have the kind of feast called for by an occasion as great as the reconciliation of the sons of Isaac.

The women fell to work, and Tabea was sent to help me collect wild onions along the river. We nodded our heads like dutiful daughters, but as soon as we faced away from our elders, I nearly laughed out loud. A wish had been granted. We could be alone.

Tabea and I walked with great purpose toward the onion patch that I had picked bare the first day we had come to the Jabbok, and we found enough new shoots to fill her basket. But we decided that our mothers did not need to know how quickly we had finished, and we took advantage of our freedom, putting our feet into the water and pouring out the handful of stories that compose the memory of childhood.

When I admired the copper bangles on her wrist, she told me her mother's life story. How Esau had been smitten by the lovely young Basemath when he saw her in the market-place near Mamre, where our grandmother Rebecca lived. For a bride-price, he had offered Basemath's father, in addition to the usual number of sheep and goats, no fewer than forty copper bangles, "so that her wrists and ankles should announce her beauty," he said. Esau loved Basemath, but she suffered at the hands of his first wife, Adath, who was jealous. Not even the stillbirths of Basemath's babies had softened Adath's heart. When I asked how they could celebrate the new moon together with so much anger in the house, Tabea said the women of her family did not mark the moon's death and rebirth together. "That's another thing the Grandmother hates about the wives of Esau," Tabea said.

"You know our grandmother?" I asked. "You know Rebecca?"

"Yes," said my cousin. "I saw her twice, at barley harvests. The Grandmother smiles at me, though she does not speak to my mother, nor Adath, nor did she take notice of Oholibama when she was alive.

"The Grandmother says hateful things about my mother, and that is wrong." My cousin knit her brow and her eyes filled with tears. "But I love the Grandmother's tent. It is so beautiful there, and even though she is the oldest woman I ever saw, her beauty is not erased." Tabea giggled and said, "The Grandmother tells me that I look like her, even though it is clear that I resemble my mother in every way."

Tabea did seem a copy of Basemath, with her thin nose and glossy, dark hair, her fragile wrists and ankles. But when I met Rebecca, I remembered my cousin's words and saw what the Grandmother meant. It was Tabea's eyes that Rebecca could claim as her own, for my cousin's eyes were black and direct as arrows, where Basemath's were brown and always downcast.

I told Tabea about the red tent and how my mothers

celebrated the new moon with cakes and songs and stories, leaving ill will outside for the duration of the darkness. And how I, the only daughter, had been permitted inside with them throughout my childhood, although it was against custom for anyone past weaning and not yet a woman to enter. At this, we both looked down upon our chests and pulled our tunics tight to compare what was happening to our bodies. Although neither of us was ready to suckle, it seemed that I would reach womanhood first. Tabea sighed and I shrugged and then we laughed until our eyes filled with tears, which made us laugh even more until we were rolling on the ground.

When we caught our breath, we spoke of our brothers. Tabea said she did not know Eliphaz well, but that Reuel was kind. Of the little boys, she hated Jeush, who pulled her hair at every turn and kicked her shins whenever he was sent to help her in the garden. I told her how Simon and Levi made Joseph and my other brothers abandon our games, and how they treated me like their personal servant whose only duty it was to keep their wine cups filled. I even told her how I spit into their cups when I had the chance. I spoke of Reuben's kindness, and Judah's beauty, and how Joseph and I had been nursed together.

I was shocked when Tabea said she wanted no children. "I have seen my mother cradle too many dead babes," she said. "And I heard Oholibama scream for three days before she gave up her life for Iti. I am not willing to suffer like that." Tabea said she wanted no part of marriage but would rather serve at Mamre and change her name to Deborah. Or else, she said, she would sing at the altar of a great temple like the one in Shechem. "There I would become one of the consecrated women who weave for the gods and wear clean robes always. Then I will sleep alone unless I choose to take a consort at the barley festival."

I did not understand her desires. Indeed, I did not fully understand her words, since I knew nothing about temples or the women who serve there. For my part, I told Tabea I hoped for ten strong children like those my mother had borne, though I wanted five girls at least. It was the first time I had said these things aloud, and perhaps the first time I had even given them thought. But I spoke from my heart.

"You have no fear of childbirth?" asked my cousin. "What of the pain? What if the baby dies?"

I shook my head. "Midwives do not fear life," I said, and I realized that I had come to think of myself as Rachel's apprentice and Inna's granddaughter.

Tabea and I stared into the water and our words ebbed. We pondered the difference between us and wondered if our hopes would be fulfilled, and whether we would ever learn what happened to the other after our fathers took their leave. My thoughts flew back and forth, like the shuttle on a great loom, so that when I finally heard my name in my mother's mouth, there was some anger in it. We had tarried too long. Tabea and I walked quickly, hand in hand, back to the cooking fires.

My cousin and I did our best to stay together after that, watching our mothers circle one another with thinly veiled curiosity. They studied one another's clothes and recipes, politely asking one another to repeat their names, just one more time, if you please, to get the pronunciation right. I could see my mother's eyebrows rise at the Canaanite women's use of salt, and I noticed Adath stiffen at the sight of Bilhah adding a handful of fresh onions to her dried-goat stew. But all judgments were masked under thin smiles amid the rush to prepare the feast.

While the women readied the meal, Esau and Jacob disappeared within my father's tent. After the sons of Esau put up their tents for the night, they gathered near my father's door, where my brothers also stood. Reuben and Eliphaz exchanged pleasantries about their fathers' flocks, subtly comparing the number and health of each herd, sizing up each other's approach to pasturage and skills with dogs. Eliphaz seemed surprised that neither Reuben nor any of his brothers had yet married or sired children, but this was not a subject that Reuben would discuss with the son of Esau. There were long lulls in the conversation between the cousins, who kicked at the dirt and clenched and unclenched their fists in boredom.

Finally, the flap to the tent opened and my father and Esau walked out, rubbing their eyes at the lingering brightness of the day, calling for wine and for the meal to begin. The two brothers sat on a blanket that Jacob himself spread. Their sons arranged themselves in self-conscious order of rank, Eliphaz and Reuben standing behind their fathers, Joseph and Korah sitting at their sides. As I ran back and forth, keeping the wine cups filled, I noticed how my brothers outnumbered Tabea's, and that they were much more handsome than the sons of Esau. Tabea served bread, while our mothers and their servants filled the men's plates until they could eat no more.

Every woman noticed who had taken the most of her stew, her bread, her beer, and each man took pains to compliment the food served by his brother's wives. Esau drank deeply of my mother's beer and favored Bilhah's oniony goat dish. Jacob ate little, but did his best to honor the food brought him by Basemath and Adath.

When the men were done, the women and girls sat down, but as happens with great meals, there was little appetite after the hours of stirring and tasting. The mothers were served by the slaves of Esau—two strong girls wearing small silver rings through holes in their upper ears. One of them was pregnant; Tabea whispered that it was Esau's seed, and if she bore a son, the girl would remove the upper earring and become a lesser wife. I stared at the strapping slave girl, her ankles as thick as Judah's, and then glanced at the slender Basemath, and told Tabea that Esau's taste in wives was as generous as his other appetites. She started to giggle, but a glare from Adath stifled us.

The light was starting to fade when Jacob and Esau began to tell stories. Our bondswomen brought lamps and Esau's slaves kept them filled with oil, so the light from the flames danced upon the faces of my family, suddenly grown numerous. Tabea and I sat knee to knee, listening to the story of our great-grandfather Abram, who had left the ancient home in Ur where the moon was worshiped in the name of Nanna and Ningal, and gone to Haran where the voice of El had come to him and directed him to Canaan. In the south, Abram had done great deeds—killing a thousand men with a single blow because El-Abram had given him the power of ten thousand.

Jacob spoke of the beauty of Sarai, Abram's wife and a servant of Innana, the daughter of Nanna and Ningal. Innana loved Sarai so well that the goddess came to her in the terebinth grove at Mamre and gave her a healthy son in the extremity of her life. That son was our grandfather Isaac, the husband of Rebecca, who was the niece of Sarai the priestess. It was Rebecca, my grandmother, who divined for the people now at Sarai's holy grove in Mamre.

Having recalled the family history in the proper fashion, my father and my uncle moved on to childhood stories, slapping each other on the back as they recalled the times they had slipped away from their mother's garden to play with the baby lambs, helping one another remember the names of their favorite dogs—the Black, the Dappled, and especially the Three-Legged Wonder, a miraculous bitch that survived a jackal's attack and still herded with the best.

It was wonderful to see my father's face as these stories spilled out. I could see him as a boy again—carefree, strong, willful. His reserve melted as Esau reminded him of a day they had fallen into a wadi and entered their mother's tent covered in thick grey mud. He laughed at the story about a time the brothers stole a whole day's worth of baking, ate themselves sick, and suffered a beating for it.

After many stories, a satisfied hush fell over the company. We listened to the rustling of the herds and the Jabbok's whispers. And then Esau began a song. My father broke into a wide grin and joined in, giving loud and lusty voice to the words of an unfamiliar herding song all about the power of a certain ram. The women pinched their lips together as the verses continued, each one randier and bolder than the last. To my amazement, my brothers and our cousins knew every word and joined in, making a great shout of their voices, and finishing with a whoop and then laughter.

When the men were finished, Esau nodded to his first

wife, who gave a sign that opened the mouths of his wives and daughters, his bondswomen and slave girls. It was a hymn to Anat, a name the Canaanite women used for Innana, and it praised the goddess's prowess in war and her power in love.

Their song was unlike anything I'd ever heard, and the hair on the back of my neck stood on end, as though Joseph were tickling me with a stalk of grass. But when I turned to rebuke him, I saw that he sat by our father's side, his eyes shining and fixed upon the singers. They sang the words in unison, yet somehow created a web of sound with their voices. It was like hearing a piece of fabric woven with all the colors of a rainbow. I did not know that such beauty could be formed by the human mouth. I had never heard harmony before.

When they finished, I discovered tears in my eyes and saw that Zilpah's cheeks were wet, too. Bilhah's lips were parted in admiration, and Rachel's eyes were closed to listen with perfect attention.

The men applauded and asked for more, so Basemath began anew with a song about the harvest and the fullness of the earth. Tabea joined with them, and I was dazzled to think that my friend could perform such a miracle with her mothers. I closed my eyes. The women sang like birds, only more sweetly. They sounded like the wind in the trees, but louder. Their voices were like the rush of the river's water, but with meaning. Then their words ceased and they began to sing with sound that meant nothing at all, yet gave new voice to joy, to pleasure, to longing, to peace. "Lu, lu, lu," they sang.

When they finished, Reuben applauded the music of our

kinswomen and bowed low to them. Joseph and Judah and Dan also rose and bowed in thanks, and I thought, "These four are my favorites, and the best of my brothers."

There were more songs and a few more stories, and we sat by the light of the lamps. Only when the moon began to set did the women clear the last of the cups. With sleeping children in their arms, the young mothers moved toward their own beds, and the men began taking their leave too. Finally, only Jacob and Esau sat, staring silently at the sputtering wick of the last lamp.

Tabea and I slipped away and walked down to the river, our arms around each other's waists. I was perfectly happy. I could have stood there until dawn, but my mother came to find me, and though she smiled at Tabea, she took my hand and pulled me away from my friend.

I woke the next morning to the sounds of Esau's tribe making ready to leave. During their late-night conversation, my father told his brother that he would not follow him back to Seir. As fondly as the brothers had met, their fortunes could not be married. My uncle's lands were vast and his position secure. Had we joined him, Jacob's worth would be judged puny in comparison. My brothers, too, would have been at a disadvantage, since Esau's sons already had flocks and lands of their own. And for all the fellowship of the night before, the sons of Isaac were not entirely reconciled, nor could they ever be. The scars they had borne for twenty years could not be erased with a single meeting, and the habits of those years, lived in such different worlds, were bound to come between them.

Nevertheless, the brothers embraced with declarations of love and promises to visit. Reuben and Eliphaz clasped each other by the shoulder, the women nodded goodbye. Tabea showed her boldness by running from her mother's side to hug me, and we tasted each other's tears. While we held each other she whispered, "Take heart. We will be together again soon at the Grandmother's tent. I heard my mother say we would surely meet you there at the barley festival. Remember everything that happens from now until then, so you can tell me." With that, she kissed me and ran back to her mother's side. She waved her hand until she was out of my sight. As soon as they departed, my father instructed Reuben and my mother to prepare for our own leave-taking.

I did my part with a happy heart, glad to take up our travels free of the fear of Esau, eager to see my friend again and to meet the Grandmother, who had already begun to live in my imagination. I was certain that Rebecca would love my mothers; after all, they were her nieces as well as her daughters-in-law. And I imagined myself her pet, her favorite. Why shouldn't I be, I thought. After all, I was the female heir of her favored son.

The next morning we departed, but we did not travel far. On the second day, my father plunged his staff into the earth near a small stream beneath a young oak tree and announced his intention to stay. We were near a village called Succoth, he said, a place that had been kind to him on his journey north. My brothers had scouted the land before and secured a site for us, and within a few days there were pens and stalls for the animals and a fine clay oven, large enough to bake both bread and cakes. We dwelt there for two years.

The journey from the house of Laban had given me a taste for change, and the daily routines of settled life in Succoth bored me at first. But my days were filled from sunrise to dusk, and soon I learned to enjoy the alchemy of turning flour into bread, meat into stew, water into beer. I also moved from spinning to weaving, which was far more difficult than I had ever imagined, and a skill I never mastered like Zilpah and Bilhah, for whom the warp never broke.

As the oldest girl, I was often given charge of the bonds-women's children, and learned both to love and resent the runny-nosed monsters. I was needed so much within the world of women that I barely noticed how little I had to do with my brothers or how things changed among them. For those were the days when Levi and Simon replaced Reuben at my father's right hand, and became his closest advisers.

Succoth was a fertile place for my family. Zibatu had a new baby, and so did Uzna—both of them sons whom my father took to his altar under the oak tree. He circumcised them and declared them free of their fathers' indenture, full members of the tribe of El-Abram, and the tribe of Jacob grew.

Bilhah conceived in Succoth, but she miscarried before the baby moved in her womb. Rachel was bereaved in this manner as well, and for nearly a month after would not let Joseph out of her sight. My mother, too, lost a child, who came from the womb months too soon. The women looked away from the tiny doomed girl, but I saw only her perfect beauty. Her eyelids were veined like a butterfly's wing, her toes curled like the petals of a flower.

I held my sister, who was never given a name, and who never opened her eyes, and who died in my arms.

I was not afraid to hold that small death. Her face was peaceful, her hands perfectly clean. It seemed she would wake at any moment. The tears from my eyes fell upon her alabaster cheek, and it appeared that she mourned the passing of her own life. My mother came to take my sister from me, but seeing my sorrow, permitted me to carry her to burial. She was shrouded in a scrap of fine cloth and laid beneath the strongest, oldest tree within sight of my mother's tent. No offerings were made, but as the bundle was covered with earth the sighs that poured from my mothers' mouths were as eloquent as any psalm.

As we walked away from the baby's death, Zilpah muttered that the gods of the place were arrayed against life, but as usual, my auntie misread the signs. For the bondswomen grew great with child as quickly as their babies were weaned. Every ewe and goat bore twins, and all of them survived. The flocks grew quickly and made my father a prosperous man, which meant my brothers could wed.

Three of them married in Succoth. Judah married Shua, the daughter of a trader. She conceived during their nuptial week and bore him Er, the first of his sons and the first of my father's grandsons. I liked Shua, who was plump and good-natured. She brought the Canaanite gift of song into our tents and taught us harmonies. Simon and Levi took two sisters to wife—Ialutu and Inbu, daughters of a potter.

It fell to me to stay with the babies and mind the fires while the wives of Jacob attended the festivities. I was furious about being left behind, but in the weeks after the nuptials, I heard my mothers talk over every detail of the weddings so much that I felt I had been there myself.

"Surely you must admit the singing was wonderful," said Zilpah, who returned from each one humming a new melody, slapping the rhythm with her hand against a bony thigh.

"Well, of course," said my mother, in an offhand way. "They learn this from their mothers and grandmothers."

Rachel grinned, and leaned over to Leah: "Too bad their grandmothers could not cook, eh?"

Leah smirked in agreement. "When it is Dinah's turn to enter the bridal tent, I will show them all how a wedding feast should be arrayed," she said, running her hand over my head.

Only Bilhah seemed to enjoy her nephews' weddings. "Oh, sister," she said to Leah, "didn't you think the veil was pretty, shot through with golden threads and hung with the dowry coins? I thought she was arrayed like a goddess."

Leah would have none of it. "Are you going to tell me that your belly was full after the meal?" she said.

But Leah was not unhappy in the brides her sons brought her. They were all healthy and respectful, though Shua quickly became the favorite. The two sisters never fully entered my mothers' circle, and they lived with their husbands at a short distance from the rest of us, closer to the herds, my brothers said. I think Simon and Levi moved because Ialutu and Inbu wanted to keep their distance. I did not miss their company at all. They treated me with the same disdain as their husbands, and besides, my mother was right; neither of them could cook.

Of Jacob's older sons, only Reuben remained unmarried. My eldest brother seemed content to serve his mother and to do kindness to Bilhah, whose only son was still too young to hunt.

Early one morning while everyone slept, a woman's voice called, "Where are the daughters of Sarai? Where are the wives of Jacob?"

It was a soft voice, and yet it woke me from a deep sleep where I lay at my mother's feet. Like me, Leah sat up at the sound and hurried outside, arriving at the same moment as Rachel. Within a heartbeat, Bilhah and Zilpah were there as well, the five of us staring at the messenger from Mamre, whose dress shimmered silver in the blue glow that heralds the dawn.

Her speech was formal, in the manner of all messengers. "Rebecca, the oracle at Mamre, the mother of Jacob and Esau, the grandmother of hundreds of myriads, calls you to the canopy of terebinths for the barley festival.

"Let Jacob be told and know."

Silence greeted the declaration of this visitor, who spoke in strange accents that bent every word in three places. It was as though we were all sharing a dream, for none of us had ever seen red hair before, nor had we ever seen a woman carry the messenger's striped bag. And yet it was no dream, as the morning chill made us shiver.

Finally Leah caught her breath and gave welcome, offering the stranger a place to sit and bread to eat. But as soon as we were assembled around our guest, my aunties and I again fell still and stared in plain amazement. The messenger looked around her and broke into a smile that showed a row of small, yellow teeth between a pair of oddly dappled lips. Speaking now in an ordinary voice and with a lightness that set everyone at ease, she said, "I see you number few redheads among you. Where I come from, it is said that redheaded women are begotten during their mother's periods. Such is the ignorance of the lands to the north."

Bilhah laughed out loud to hear such boldness from a stranger. This seemed to please our guest, who turned to my aunt and presented herself. "My name is Werenro and I serve the Grandmother." At that, she pulled her hair back to show her ear, pierced high with the plain bronze stud, and added, "I am the world's happiest slave." Again, Bilhah laughed aloud at such plainspokenness. I giggled, too.

As soon as the men were fed, Leah sent for Jacob and presented the messenger, who by then had covered the fire of her hair and lowered her eyes. "She comes from your mother," Leah said. "Rebecca bids us attend her barley festival. The messenger awaits your reply."

Jacob seemed startled by the newcomer's presence but composed himself quickly and told Leah that they would obey Rebecca in everything, and that he would come to her at harvest time, he and his wives, with his sons and his daughters.

Werenro then withdrew to my mother's tent and slept. I worked nearby all day, hoping to catch a glimpse of her. I tried to think of some reason to enter the tent. I wanted to see that hair again, and my fingers longed to touch the robes that moved like weeds in flowing water. Inna told me

Werenro's clothes were made of silk, a kind of cloth that was woven by worms on their own tiny looms. I raised my eyebrow—doing my best to copy my mother's most disdainful gesture—to show that I was too old to be taken in by such nonsense. Inna laughed at me and wasted no further breath on my disbelief.

Werenro rested undisturbed late into the evening, until after the men had eaten and the bowls of the women's evening meal were cleared. My mothers had gathered by their fire, hoping the stranger would appear in time to give us a story.

The messenger walked out of the tent, and seeing us arrayed around her, she bowed deeply, with her fingers stretched wide, in an unfamiliar gesture of obeisance. Then she straightened her back, looked into our faces one by one, and grinned like a little child who has stolen a fig. Werenro was unlike anyone or anything else in the world. I was enchanted.

She bowed her head at my mothers in thanks for the bowl of olives, cheese, and fresh bread that had been left for her. Before eating, she recited a short prayer in a language that sounded like a buzzard's cry. I laughed at the noise, thinking she was making another joke, but the redheaded stranger shot me a look of withering anger. I felt as though my face had been slapped, and my cheeks grew hot and as crimson as her hair, which was once again visible and as improbably red as I remembered. But in the next moment, she smiled forgiveness at me, and patting the ground by her side, welcomed me to a place of honor.

After she put aside the last of her meal, with compliments for the bread and extravagant praise for the beer, Werenro began a chant. There were many strange names in her story, and a melody that was sadder than anything I'd ever heard. She held us all rapt, like a baby on a lap.

It was a story of the beginning of the world, of Tree and Hawk, who gave birth to Red Wolf, who populated the world with a womb that gave birth to all red-blooded life, save woman and man. It was a very long story, mysterious and filled with names of unfamiliar trees and animals. It was set in a place of terrible cold, where the wind screamed in pain. It was frightening and thrilling, and lonely.

When Werenro stopped, the fire was out and only one lamp sputtered a dim light. The little ones were asleep in their mothers' laps and even a few of the women dozed, their heads dropping on their chests.

I looked into the face of the messenger, but she did not see me. Her eyes were closed above smiling lips. She was far away in the land of her story, a cold land of strange myths, where her own mother was buried. I felt the messenger's loneliness, so far from home. I understood Werenro's heart the way I understood the sun when it warmed my face. I reached out my hand and placed it on her shoulder, and Werenro turned to me, opened eyes that glistened with tears, and kissed me on the lips. "Thank you," she said, and stood.

She walked into my mother's tent and left before dawn without telling me how the red wolf in her story gave rise to man and woman. But this did not worry me, for I knew that I would hear the rest of it at Mamre, when we went to see the Grandmother at last.

Chapter Five

PREPARATIONS FOR THE journey began a month before the barley harvest. My father decided that he would bring all of his wives to Mamre and most of his sons. Simon and Levi were told to remain behind with the flocks, and since both of their wives were pregnant for the first time, they did not object. Although Shua was not with child, Judah asked to be left back as well, and the women all knew why; the whooping sounds of their nightly pleasure were a source of jokes and smirking.

My brothers and I were summoned to our mothers, who examined our best clothes and found them wanting. A flurry of washing, mending, and sewing followed. Rachel decided to make a new tunic for her only son. Joseph's robe, decorated with bands of red and yellow, earned him some awful teasing from his brothers. He ignored their taunts and swore he preferred the garment his mother had made for him over the dull stuff that men were given to wear. I couldn't tell if he was putting on a brave front or really liked his finery.

I was given bracelets for my wrists—my first jewelry.

They were only copper, but I loved them, especially the womanly sound they made. Indeed, I spent so much time admiring the way the three bands gathered on my wrists that I paid no attention to my feet and, on the first day I wore them, tripped and scraped my chin raw. I was horrified at the thought that I would meet the Grandmother looking like a scabby child. Every day until we left I studied my face in Rachel's mirror, begged Inna for salve, and picked at the enormous red crust.

The day we left for Mamre, I was beside myself with excitement and ignored every request made of me. My mother, who was everywhere at once, making sure that the oil and wine jars were securely sealed, that the brothers had combed their beards, that everything was ready, finally lost patience with me. It was one of the few times she ever raised her voice to me. "Either you help me, or I will leave you behind to wait upon your brothers' wives," she said. She didn't have to say another word.

The journey took only a few days, and it was a joyful trip. We sang as we walked, preening in our finery and proud of our beautiful flock, for only the best of the animals had been culled for gifts to the Grandmother.

Jacob walked beside Rachel early in the morning, inhaling her perfume, smiling, saying little. Then he took his place beside Leah to discuss the animals, the crops, and the proper etiquette for greeting his parents. Late in the afternoon, Jacob found his way to Bilhah, displacing Reuben, her shadow. My father walked with his hand upon her little shoulder, as though he needed her support.

I was perfectly happy. Joseph stayed beside me and even forgot himself enough to hold my hand from time to time.

At night, I settled in beside Zilpah, who fed my awe of the Grandmother with tales about Rebecca's reputation as a diviner, healer, and prophet, so that I could barely fall asleep. I could barely keep myself from running, for I was going to see Tabea again. Werenro would smile at me and tell more of her story. And I would meet the Grandmother, who I imagined would understand me instantly and adore me above any of my brothers.

Midmorning on the third day, we caught sight of Rebecca's tent. Even from a distance it was a marvel, though at first I didn't really understand what shimmered on the far side of the valley before me. It was enormous—far bigger than any tent I had ever seen, and utterly unlike our dull goat-hair dwellings. This was an earthbound rainbow—red, yellow, and blue—billowing upon the high ground under a stand of great old trees whose branches implored a cloudless heaven.

As we came closer, it became clear that this was less a home than a canopy, open on all sides to welcome travelers from every direction. Inside, we caught glimpses of vivid hangings in patterns that were both delicate and bold, with scenes of dancing women and flying fish, stars, crescents, suns, birds. It was more beautiful than any handmade thing I had seen.

When we could almost feel the shade of the sacred grove, the Grandmother came into view. She did not come out to meet us, nor did she send any of her women out, but waited in the shade of the wonderful tent, arms crossed, watching. I could not take my eyes off her.

I do not remember my father's formal greeting or the ceremony to present my brothers, one by one, and then the gifts, and finally my mothers and me. I saw only her. The Grandmother—my grandmother. She was the oldest person I had ever seen. Her years proclaimed themselves in the deep furrows on her brow and around her mouth, but the beauty of youth still clung to her. She stood as erect as Reuben and nearly as tall. Her black eyes were clear and sharp, painted in the Egyptian style—a pattern of heavy black kohl that made her appear all-seeing. Her robes were purple—the color of royalty and holiness and wealth. Her head covering was long and black, shot through with gold threads, providing the illusion of luxurious hair, where in fact only a few grey strands were left to her.

Rebecca did not notice while I stared. The eyes of the Grandmother were fixed upon the son she had not seen since he was a smooth-cheeked boy, now a man with grown sons and a grandfather. She showed no emotion as Jacob presented his children, his wives, and the gifts he had brought. She nodded, accepting everything, saying nothing.

I thought she was magnificent—aloof as a queen. But I saw my mother's mouth purse in displeasure. She had anticipated a show of maternal love for the favored son. I could not see my father's face to measure his reaction.

After the official welcome, the Grandmother turned away from us and we were taken to the west side of the hill, to set up our tents and prepare for the evening meal. That's where I learned that Tabea had not yet arrived and that Werenro had been sent to Tyre, to trade for the rare purple dye that the Grandmother favored.

No men lived at the grove. Rebecca was attended by ten women, who also saw to the pilgrims who came seeking advice and prophecy from her they called "Oracle." When I asked about my father's father, one of the Grandmother's attendants told me that Isaac dwelt a short distance away, in the village of Arba in a snug hut that was kinder than an open tent to his old bones. "He will come for the meal tonight," said the woman, whose only name was Deborah. The Grandmother called all of her acolytes Deborah, in honor of the woman who had been her childhood nurse and lifelong retainer, and whose bones lay buried beneath the trees of Mamre.

The Grandmother's women spoke in shy whispers and dressed in the same plain white tunic. They were uniformly kind but distant, and I quickly stopped trying to see them as individuals and began to think of them all as the Deborahs.

The afternoon passed quickly in preparation for the evening meal. Just as the first bread was coming off the fire, word came that Isaac had arrived. I raced around to watch as my grandfather approached the grove. Rebecca came to watch, too, and she raised her hand in a brief greeting. My father walked out to greet him, his step growing faster and faster until he was actually running toward his father.

Isaac did not respond to his wife's salute or his son's excitement. He continued, seemingly serene in his cushioned seat upon a donkey being led by a woman wearing the white robes of my grandmother's entourage—though this one wore a veil that covered everything but her eyes. It was only when he came close that I saw that my grandfather was blind, his eyes closed in a tight squint that soured the whole of his face into a permanent scowl. He was small-boned and thin, and would have seemed frail except that his hair was as thick and dark as a younger man's.

The Grandmother watched as the serving woman helped Isaac descend and walked him to his blanket on the east side of Mamre. But before the servant released his elbow, Isaac took her hand in his and brought it to his lips. He kissed her palm and placed it upon his cheek. Isaac's face relaxed into a smile so that anyone who cared to see would know that the veiled one was the companion of my grandfather's heart.

My father stood before Isaac and said, "Father?" in a voice overflowing with tears. Isaac turned his face toward Jacob and opened his arms. My father embraced the old man, and both of them wept. They spoke in whispers as my brothers stood and waited to be introduced. My mothers held back, exchanging glances of concern over the food, which would be dry and tasteless if it wasn't served soon.

But the men would not be rushed. Isaac pulled his son to a seat by his side as Jacob introduced each of his sons. Isaac ran his hands over the faces of my brothers Reuben and Zebulun, Dan, Gad, and Asher, Naphtali and Issachar. When Joseph was finally named as the youngest son, the Grandfather pulled him down into his lap, as though he were a baby and not a boy nearing manhood. Isaac tenderly ran his fingers over the contours of Joseph's face and over the sinews of his arms. A breeze rose up and lifted the silken tent high above them, embracing the Grandfather and his grandson in its wonderful rainbow. It was a grand sight and it took my breath away. And that is precisely when Rebecca, who had kept her distance until then, finally broke her majestic silence.

"You must be hungry and thirsty, Isaac," she said, offering hospitality in an ungracious voice. "Your children are parched from their journey. Let your Deborah bring you inside. Let your daughters-in-law show me whether they can cook."

A flurry of white garments laid out the meal, and the feast began. My grandfather ate well, taking his mouthfuls from the fingers of the veiled woman. He asked whether his grandsons had eaten enough and reached out from time to time to find his son—placing a doting hand on his shoulder or his cheek, leaving smears of oil that my father did not wipe away. I watched this from behind a tree, for with all those servants there was no need of my carrying food or drink.

My brothers were hungry and finished quickly, and soon Zilpah fetched me back to our side of the great tent, where the women were gathered. The Grandmother sat down, and we watched as she had a single taste of everything before her. She said nothing about the stews or the breads or the sweets. She did not praise the cheese or the giant olives my mothers had collected. She did not acknowledge my mother's beer.

But already, I was not surprised by Rebecca's silence. I had stopped thinking of her as a woman like my mothers, or like any other woman for that matter. In the space of an afternoon, she had become a force of the gods, like a rainstorm or a brushfire.

Because the Grandmother ate little and said nothing, our meal was more somber than festive. There was no passing of bowls for a second taste, no compliments, no questions, no conversation at all. The great feast was done in a few minutes, and the Deborahs cleared the last cups before there was time to think of refilling them.

The Grandmother rose to her feet and walked to the western edge of her tent, where the sun was setting in a blaze of orange and gold. Her attendants followed. Rebecca reached her hands to the sun, as if to touch its last rays.

When she dropped her hands, the attendants began singing a song inviting the barley-harvest moon. The verses repeated an ancient prophecy. When every stalk of every barley field numbered twenty-seven seeds, the end of days would arrive and there would be rest for the weary and evil would vanish from the earth like starlight at sunrise. The last chorus ended just as darkness swallowed the camp.

Lamps were lit among the men and lamps were lit among the women. The Grandmother came with us, and I feared we would sit in silent attendance for the whole of the evening, but my fear was ungrounded, for as soon as the lights were kindled, she began to speak.

"This is the story of the day I came to the tent of Mamre, to the grove of sacred trees, to the navel of the world," said the Grandmother, Rebecca, in tones that could have been heard by the men, had they been listening.

"It was in the weeks after the death of Sarai the Prophet, beloved of Abram, mother of Isaac. She who gave birth when she was too old to carry water, much less carry a child. Sarai, cherished mother.

"On the morning I entered this grove, a cloud descended over the tent of Sarai. A golden cloud that bore no rain, nor did it cover the sun. It was a cloud that is seen only upon great rivers and upon the sea, but never before in a place so high. And yet the cloud hovered above the tent of Sarai while Isaac knew me and I became his wife. We spent our first seven days as husband and wife under that cloud, in which the gods were surely present.

"And there was never a harvest richer in wine and grain and oil than that spring, my daughters," she said, in a whisper that was at once proud and defeated. "Ah, but for me, so many daughters born dead. So many sons, dead in the womb. Only two survive. Who can explain this mystery?"

The Grandmother fell silent, and her dark mood covered her listeners and our shoulders sagged. Even I, who had lost no children, felt a mother's bereavement. After a moment, my grandmother rose and pointed to Leah, that she should follow her into an inner chamber of the great tent, where the lamps were lit with scented oil and the tapestries glowed. The rest of us sat for a while before we realized that we had been dismissed.

My mother's interview with the Grandmother went on late into the night. First, Rebecca took a long look at her daughter-in-law, betraying her shortsightedness by getting very close and peering into her face. Then she began the close interrogation into every detail of Leah's life.

"Why did they not put you out to die at birth, with eyes such as yours? What is your mother's burial place? How do you prepare wool for dying? Where did you learn to make that beer? What kind of father is Jacob, my son? Which of your sons is your favorite? Which of your sons do you fear? How many lambs does my son sacrifice to El at the spring festival? What is your practice at the new moon? How many babies have you lost in childbearing? What plans do you make for your daughter's coming-of-age? How many epahs of barley do you grow in Succoth, and how many of wheat?"

My mother could not even remember all of the questions put to her that night, but she answered them fully and without taking her eyes from the Grandmother's face. This startled the older woman, who was used to unnerving people, but Leah was not cowed. The two of them glared at each other.

Finally, when the Grandmother could think of nothing else to ask, she nodded and made a wordless sound, a grunt of grudging approval. "Very well, Leah, mother of many sons. Very well." With a wave of her hand, my mother was sent away. She found her way to her blanket and fell asleep, exhausted.

Over the next two days, my aunties were called to the Grandmother's inner chamber, one by one.

Rachel was greeted with kisses and caresses. Girlish laughter rang out as the two of them passed an afternoon together. The Grandmother patted my lovely aunt's cheeks and gently pinched her arms. Rebecca, who had been the beauty of her generation, took out her makeup box—a large, black, lacquered thing with many compartments, each one filled with a potion or unguent, perfume or paint. Rachel left the Grandmother's presence smiling and smelling of lotus oil, her eyelids green and her eyes ringed with a shiny black kohl that made her look formidable instead of merely beautiful.

When Zilpah was sent for, my auntie fell upon her face before the Grandmother, and was rewarded with a short poem about the great Asherah, consort of El and goddess of the sea. The Grandmother looked briefly into Zilpah's face, closed her black eyes, and foretold the time and place of my auntie's death. This news, which she never revealed to a soul, did not disturb Zilpah. If anything, it gave her a kind of peace that lasted the rest of her life. From that day forward, Zilpah smiled while she worked at the loom—not a wistful little grin at all, but a big, tooth-showing smile, as though she were remembering a good joke.

Bilhah dreaded her interview with the Grandmother and stumbled as she approached the old woman. The Grandmother frowned and sighed while Bilhah kept her eyes on her hands. The silence grew heavy, and after a short time, Rebecca turned and walked out, leaving Bilhah alone with the beautiful tapestries that seemed to mock her.

These meetings meant little to me. For three days my eyes were on the horizon, watching for Tabea. She finally arrived on the day of the festival itself, with Esau and his first wife, Adath. The sight of my best friend was more than I could stand, and I ran to her. She threw her arms around me.

When we stood apart, I saw how much she had changed in the few months we had been apart. She was taller than I by a good half head, and there was no need to pull her garments tightly against her chest to see her breasts. But when I saw the belt that declared her a woman, my mouth dropped. She had entered the red tent! She was no longer a child but a woman. I felt my cheeks grow warm with envy as hers grew pink with pride. I had a thousand questions to ask her about what it was like and about her ceremony, and whether the world was a different place now that her place in it was different.

But I had no time to ask my cousin anything. The Grandmother had already taken note of Tabea's apron and approached my coin-covered aunt. Within a few moments, she was screaming at Adath with a fury I thought reserved for gods who had thunder and lightning at their disposal.

Rebecca's anger was terrible. "You mean to tell me that her blood was wasted? You shut her up alone, like some animal?"

Adath cringed and made as if to answer when the Grandmother raised her fists. "Don't dare to defend yourself, you ignorant nothing," she hissed. "You baboon! I told you what to do and you disobeyed me, and now there is nothing to be done. The best of his girls, the only one of his seed with even a trace of intelligence or feeling, and you treated her like a ... like a ... Pah!" Rebecca spit at her daughter-in-law's feet. "I have no words for this abomination."

Her voice grew icy and hushed. "Enough. You are not fit to be in my tent. Get out of here. Be cursed and leave this place and never let me see you again."

The Grandmother drew herself up to her full height and slapped Adath with all her strength. The poor woman crumpled to the ground, whimpering in fear that a spell had been cast on her. The men, who had rushed over to discover the reason for the Grandmother's displeasure, recoiled at the sight of the Oracle's curse and quickly turned away from what was clearly women's business.

Adath crawled away, but now Tabea was on the ground at Rebecca's feet, sobbing, "No, no, no." My cousin's face had turned ashen and her eyes were wide with terror. "Take my name and call me Deborah, too. Make me the least of your servants, but do not banish me. Oh please, Grandmother. Please. I beg you, I beg you."

But Rebecca did not look at the creature suffering at her feet. She did not see Tabea tear at her face until there were bloody streaks down her cheeks. She did not see her rip her robe into shreds or swallow handfuls of dust. The Grandmother turned and walked away from the death throes of Tabea's hope, wrapping her cloak tightly around her body, as if to protect herself against the misery before her. Finally, Tabea was lifted from the ground by the Grandmother's followers and carried back to the tents of Esau's wives.

I did not really understand what had happened, but I knew that my dear friend had suffered an injustice. My ears rang and my heart pounded. I could not believe the Grandmother's cruelty. My beloved cousin, who cared more for Rebecca than for her own mother, had been treated worse than the lepers who came seeking miracle cures. I hated Rebecca as I had never hated anyone.

My mother took my hand, led me to her tent, and gave me a cup of sweet wine. Stroking my hair, she answered my question even before I asked. Leah, my mother, said:

"The girl will suffer for the rest of her days, and your compassion is well placed. But your hatred is undeserved, daughter.

"It was not her intention to harm Tabea. I think she loved her well enough, but she had no choice. She was defending her mother and herself, me and your aunties, you and your daughters after you. She was defending the ways of our mothers and their mothers, and the great mother, who goes by many names, but who is in danger of being forgotten.

"This is not easy to explain, but I will tell you. Because you are my only daughter and because we lived for so long in such isolation, you already know much more than you should. You have spent time with us in the red tent. You have even attended a birth, which is something you must never tell the Grandmother. I know that you will not reveal what I tell you now."

I nodded my promise, and my mother sighed from her heart. She looked down at her hands, brown from the sun, wise with use, and rarely in repose as they were now. She placed her palms face up upon her knees and closed her eyes. Half singing, half whispering, Leah said:

"The great mother whom we call Innana is a fierce warrior and Death's bridesmaid. The great mother whom we call Innana is the center of pleasure, the one who makes women and men turn to one another in the night. The great mother whom we call Innana is the queen of the ocean and the patron of the rain.

"This is known to all—to the women and to the men. To the suckling babes and to the failing grandfathers."

Here she stopped and broke into a big, girlish grin. "Zilpah would be so amused at the sight of me speaking legend," she said, looking straight at me for a moment, and I smiled back at her, sharing the joke. But after a moment my mother resumed her formal pose and continued:

"The great mother whom we call Innana gave a gift to woman that is not known among men, and this is the secret of blood. The flow at the dark of the moon, the healing blood of the moon's birth—to men, this is flux and distemper, bother and pain. They imagine we suffer and consider themselves lucky. We do not disabuse them.

"In the red tent, the truth is known. In the red tent, where days pass like a gentle stream, as the gift of Innana courses through us, cleansing the body of last month's death, preparing the body to receive the new month's life, women give thanks—for repose and restoration, for the knowledge that life comes from between our legs, and that life costs blood."

Then she took my hand and told me, "I say this before the proper time, daughter mine, though it will not be long before you enter the tent to celebrate with me and your aunties. You will become a woman surrounded by loving hands to carry you and to catch your first blood and to make sure it goes back to the womb of Innana, to the dust that formed the first man and the first woman. The dust that was mixed with her moon blood.

"Alas, many of her daughters have forgotten the secret of Innana's gift, and turned their backs on the red tent. Esau's wives, the daughters of Edom, whom Rebecca despises, give no lesson or welcome to their young women when they come of age. They treat them like beasts—setting them out, alone and afraid, shut up in the dark days of the new moon, without wine and without the counsel of their mothers. They do not celebrate the first blood of those who will bear life, nor do they return it to the earth. They have set aside the Opening, which is the sacred business of women, and permit men to display their daughters' bloody sheets, as though even the pettiest baal would require such a degradation in tribute."

My mother saw my confusion. "You cannot understand all of this yet, Dinah," she said. "But soon you will know, and I will make sure that you are welcomed into the woman's life with ceremony and tenderness. Fear not."

It was dark when my mother uttered the last of these words. The songs of the barley festival reached our ears, and my mother rose, offering me her hand. We walked out into the night, to watch the offerings, burnt on an altar beside the tallest tree. Wonderful music was sung, harmonies of many parts. The Deborahs danced in a circle to the sound of their own clapping. They spun and crouched, leaped and swayed as though sharing a single mind, a single body, and I understood Tabea's wish to join their dance.

Adath disappeared during the night, taking my friend with her, strapped onto the back of a donkey, like an offering not yet dead, with a rag stuffed in her mouth to muffle the cries.

In the few days before our departure, I avoided the Grandmother and stayed near my mothers. I wished only to leave the place, but as we prepared to return to Succoth, Leah came to me with a grim face. "The Grandmother says that you are to stay here at Mamre for three months," she said. "Rebecca spoke to your father, and it has been arranged without my . . ." She stopped at the sight of my stricken face. "I wish I could stay or leave Zilpah with you, but the Grandmother will have none of it. She wants you only."

There was a long pause before she said, "It is an honor." She cupped my chin between her two hands and added tenderly, "We will be together again when the wheat is ripe."

I did not cry. I was frightened and angry, but I was determined not to weep, so I kept my mouth closed, breathed through my nose, and kept my eyes from blinking. That was how I survived as I watched my mother's form grow smaller and smaller and then disappear into the horizon. I had never imagined the loneliness of being without her or my aunts or even one of my brothers. I felt like a baby left outside to die, but I did not cry. I turned back to the Deborahs who watched me anxiously, but I did not cry.

Only at night, alone on my blanket, I turned my face to the ground and wept until I choked. Every morning I arose, groggy and confused until I remembered that I was alone in my grandmother's tent.

My memories from those months in Mamre seem pale and scattered. When I returned to my mothers, they were disappointed that I could not say more of wonders I had seen or secrets I had learned. It was as though I had walked through a cave filled with jewels and picked up only a handful of grey pebbles.

This is what I do remember.

I recall that once in every seven days, the Grandmother made a great show of baking. The rest of the week she did not soil her hands with the work of women, much less the kneading and handing of dough. But on the seventh day, she took flour and water and honey, turned them and shaped them, and sacrificed a corner from a three-sided cake, "for the Queen of Heaven," she whispered to the dough before consigning it to flame.

I doubted that the Queen would much care for the dry, tasteless things Rebecca offered. "Aren't they good?" she demanded when they came out of the oven. I nodded dutifully, washing my portion down with water, which was all I was given to drink. Luckily, her servants were far better bakers, and their cakes were sweet and moist enough for any queen. Still, when my grandmother whispered over her small domestic offering, it was the only time I saw her smile with her eyes.

It was my job to go to Rebecca early in the morning to assist her morning ablutions in preparation for the pilgrims who arrived at the grove daily. I carried her elaborate cosmetic box, which contained different scents for forehead, wrists, armpits, and ankles, a potion for the skin beneath the eyes, and a sour-smelling concoction for the throat. After the perfumes and creams, she began the careful application of color to lips, eyes, and cheeks. She said that the most important beauty treatment of all was to smell sweet, and her breath was always scented with mint, which she chewed morning and night.

The Grandmother seemed to burn with some kind of fire. She ate little and rarely sat down. She looked down upon anyone who required rest. Indeed, she criticized everyone except her sons, and although she favored Jacob, praising his good looks and his fine sons, it was clear that she depended on my uncle for everything. Messengers came and went from Seir every other day. Esau was called upon to deliver an extra epah of barley or to find meat worthy of the Grandmother's table. I saw him every fortnight at least, his arms full of gifts.

My uncle was a good man and a fine son. He made sure that wealthy pilgrims visited the grove and brought rich offerings. He found Isaac the stone hut that afforded Rebecca the luxury of living like a priestess, without a man to serve. The Grandmother patted Esau's cheek whenever he left her tent, and he would glow as though she had praised him to heaven. Which she never did.

My grandmother never spoke ill of Esau, nor did she say anything good about him. His wives, however, she detested in detail. Although they were dutiful women who, at one time, sent fine gifts in hopes of winning her approval, she dismissed them all as slovenly idiots. For years she had sneered at them openly, so they visited only when Esau insisted.

She was not much kinder about my mothers. She considered Rachel lazy—beautiful, but lazy. She called Bilhah ugly and Zilpah a superstitious stick. She grudgingly admitted that Leah was a good worker and clearly blessed to have delivered so many healthy sons. But even Leah was not good enough for Jacob, who deserved a perfect mate. Not a giantess with mismatched eyes.

She actually said such things in my presence! As though I were not my mother's daughter, as if my aunts were not my beloved mothers, too. But I did not defend them. When the Oracle spoke, no contradictions were permitted. I was not as bold as Leah, and my nighttime tears often tasted of shame as well as loneliness.

Rebecca saved the worst of her tongue for her husband, though. Isaac had grown foolish with old age, she said, and he smelled—something she could not abide. He had forgotten what he owed her, for hadn't she been right to make him give the blessing to Jacob? She spoke incessantly about Isaac's ingratitude, and her suffering at his hands. But it was not clear to me what my grandfather had done. He seemed gentle and harmless when he came on hot days, to enjoy the breezes beneath the great terebinths. I was glad that Isaac had no need of Rebecca's care. He was well served by his veiled Deborah. It was rumored that her covering hid a harelip, though it was unthinkable that such a one would not have been killed in infancy.

When Esau came to Mamre, he visited his mother first and saw to her needs. He was polite and even fond, but as soon as he could, he turned to the Grandfather and accompanied him back to Arba, where the two men enjoyed their evening wine. They stayed up very late, talking and laughing, served by the veiled Deborah.

I learned this from the other ones who wore white. They were kind to me. They patted my shoulder when they gave me my dinner, brushed my hair, and let me work with their beautiful ivory spindles. But they did not tell stories in the evenings, and I never learned the names their own mothers had given them, or how they had come to Mamre, or if they missed the company of men. They seemed mild and content, but as colorless as their robes. I did not envy them their life with the Oracle.

At the new moon, Rebecca did not permit me to enter the red tent with the women who bled; she was strict about this observance. She who was past childbearing did not enter, nor could I, who was still unripe. One of the other Deborahs stayed outside with us as well. She explained that her periods had never come, but did not complain about her lack of rest. She and I cooked and served the celebrants, whose quiet laughter made me long for my mothers' tent.

When the women emerged, rested and smiling, on the morning after the third day, I was permitted to follow them as they stood at the highest point of the hill to watch the sun rise. The Grandmother herself poured out a libation of wine, while the women sang a wordless song of quiet rejoicing. In the deep silence that followed, it seemed to me that the Queen of Heaven was in the trees above us. That memory returns to me at every new moon.

I never learned to love my grandmother. I could not forget or forgive what she had done to Tabea. Nevertheless, the day came when I honored her.

The doors to the Oracle's tent were always open, and from every direction the stranger was made welcome. This had been the decree of Sarai and Abram, who, it was said, gave an equal welcome to princes and beggars. And so, every morning, Rebecca would receive pilgrims inside the beautiful tent. She saw all who came—wretched or resplendent—nor did she hurry with the poor.

I stood with her women as she greeted the guests. First, a childless woman approached and begged for a son. The Oracle gave her a red cord to tie around one of the trees at Mamre, whispered a blessing in the barren one's ear, and bid her go with the Deborah skilled in herbs.

Next there was a trader seeking a charm for his caravan. "It has been a bad season for me," he began. "I am nearly destitute, but I have heard of your powers," he said, with a bit of a dare creeping into his voice. "I've come to see for myself."

The Grandmother moved close to him and looked into his face until he turned away from her gaze. "*You* must make restitution," she said in a way that sounded like a warning.

His shoulders sagged and his swaggering manner melted.

"I don't have the goods to make restitution, Grandmother," he said.

"There is no other way," said the Oracle, in a loud, formal voice. She dismissed him with a wave of her hand, and he backed meekly out of her presence and ran down the hillside as though an army were chasing him.

Rebecca saw my open mouth and explained with a shrug, "Only thieves come looking for business miracles."

The last pilgrim that morning was a mother carrying a child who was old enough to walk—three years, maybe four. But when the woman unwrapped him, we could see why he was still in her arms. His legs were withered and his feet were covered with sores, raw and oozing, and painful to see. From the look in his eyes, it was clear that he was nearly dead with suffering. The Grandmother took the boy from his mother's arms. She carried him to her cushion, her lips pressed against his forehead, and sat with him in her lap. She called for an unguent used for burns, something that soothes but cannot heal. Then, with her own hands, without flinching or drawing back, she rubbed the stuff into his wounds. When Rebecca was done, she wrapped her perfumed hands around his diseased feet, and held them as though they were precious, delicate, and clean. The mother gaped, but the little boy had no awe of his healer. With the pain eased for the moment, he rested his head upon her shallow breast and fell asleep.

No one moved or spoke. I don't know how long we stood as he dozed, but my back ached before the child opened his eyes. He wrapped his arms around the Grandmother's neck and kissed her. She embraced him in return, and then carried him back to his mother, who wept to see the smile on her boy's face, and who wept again to see the sadness upon the Oracle's face, which showed there was nothing she could do to keep this one alive.

I could not hate Rebecca after that. Although I never saw her show such tenderness to anyone else, I could not forget the way she took that little boy's pain into her own hands and gave comfort to him and peace to his mother.

I never spoke about Tabea to my grandmother. I did not dare. In silence, I mourned the loss of my best friend as sorrowfully as if I had wrapped her in a shroud.

But it was Werenro we put into the ground.

I had been anxious to see the messenger again, as were the others at Mamre. She was a favorite among the Deborahs, who smiled when I asked about her return. "Surely she will come soon," said the one who liked to brush my hair. "And then we will have stories in the evening and you will not be so sad."

But word came with a trader on his way from Tyre that Werenro, messenger to Rebecca of Mamre, had been murdered. The remains of her body were found on the edge of the city, the tongue cut out, red hair scattered all around. A trader who had visited the shrine years before remembered the strange-looking woman who served the Oracle and recognized her bag. He gathered what was left of her, to bring her bones back to the Grandmother, who betrayed no emotion at the terrible news.

The sack he carried was pitifully small, and we buried it deep in the earth in a plain earthenware jar. I heard the Deborahs weep that night, and added another layer of salt to my own blanket. But when I dreamed of Werenro, she

was smiling her dappled smile from a seat in a great tree, a
large bird perched on her shoulder.

The day after Werenro was buried, I went to Rebecca in
the morning as usual, but she was already dressed, scented,
and painted for the day. She sat on her cushions, silent and
withdrawn. I was not even certain she noticed that I had
entered. I coughed. She did not look up at me, but after a
time she spoke, and I knew why pilgrims came to Mamre.

"I know you are here, Dinah," she said.

"I know that you hate me on behalf of Esau's girl. It was
a pity. She was the best of them, and of course it was not
her fault. It was the poor stupid mother, who did not do
what I told her but what her own stupid mother taught her.
I should have taken her as a baby. The girl had no chance."

My grandmother said this without looking at me, as
though she were airing her own thoughts. But then she
turned her eyes upon me and fixed me in her gaze.

"You are safe from that fate," she said. "Your mother
will not let them turn your maidenhood into a prize. She
will not permit your blood to be anything but an offering
into the womb of the great mother. You are safe in that
way.

"Some other unhappiness awaits you, though," she said,
peering at me intently, trying to discern my future. "Something I cannot fathom. Just as I could not foresee the end of
Werenro. Perhaps your sorrow will be nothing worse than
a lost baby or two, or maybe an early widowhood, for your
life will be very long. But there's no use in frightening
children with the price of life."

There was silence for a time, and when Rebecca next
spoke, although her words were about me, it was as though

I were no longer there. "Dinah is not the heir, either. I see now that there will be none. Mamre will be forgotten. The tent will not stand after me." She shrugged, as though it was of no great matter.

"The great ones need nothing from us, truly. Our libations and prayers are of no more importance than birdsong or bee song. At least their praises are assured."

She rose and walked toward me, until our noses nearly touched. "I forgive you for hating me," she said, and waved me out of the tent.

Reuben came a few days later, and I left Mamre without so much as a nod from the Grandmother. Glad as I was to be returning to my mother's tent, my eyes stung with tears as we walked away. I returned empty-handed. I had merited little of Rebecca's attention. I had failed to please her.

Chapter Six

ALTHOUGH I HAD longed for home every moment of my absence, I was shocked by it when I arrived. Nothing was as I remembered it. My brothers, my father, and all of the other men had become impossibly crude and brutish. They grunted rather than spoke, scratched themselves and picked their noses, and even relieved themselves in plain sight of the women. And the stink!

The noise of the camp was overwhelming, too. Barking dogs, bleating sheep, crying babies, and screaming women. How was it that I had never noticed the way they all shrieked at each other and at the children? Even my own mother was changed. Every word out of her mouth was critical, demanding, and imperious. Everything had to be done her way, and nothing I did was good enough. I heard only scorn and anger in her voice when she told me to fetch water, or mind one of the babies, or help Zilpah with the weaving.

Whenever she spoke to me, my eyes stung with tears, my throat closed in shame and anger, and I kicked at the dirt. "What is the matter?" she asked, three times a day. "What is wrong with you?"

There was nothing wrong with me, I thought. It was Leah who had become short-tempered and sour and impossible. Somehow she had aged years in the months I had been gone. The deep lines of her forehead were often caked with dust, and the grime under her fingernails disgusted me.

Of course, I could never voice such disrespect, so I avoided my mother and escaped to the calm of Zilpah's loom and the gentleness of Bilhah's voice. I even took to sleeping in Rachel's tent, which must have caused Leah some pain. Inna, who I now realized was at least as old as the Grandmother herself, scolded me for causing my mother such sorrow. But I was too young to understand that the changes were mine, not my mother's.

After a few weeks, I grew accustomed once more to the daily sound and smell of men again, and found myself fascinated by them. I stared at the tiny buds on the baby boys who ran about naked, and I spied upon mating dogs. I tossed and turned on my blanket and let my hands wander over my chest and between my legs, and wondered.

One night, Inna caught me by the side of Judah's tent, where he and Shua were making another baby. The midwife grabbed my ear and led me away. "It won't be long now, my girl," she told me, with a leer. "Your time is coming." I was mortified and horrified to think that Inna might tell my mother where she had found me. Even so, I could not stop thinking about the mystery of men and women.

On the nights I was consumed with curiosity and longing, my father and his sons were deep in conversation. The herds would soon be too numerous for the lands at our disposal, and my brothers wanted greater prospects for themselves, and their sons. Jacob had begun to dream again, this time about a walled city and a familiar valley in the shoulder between two mountains. In his dreams, we were already in Shechem, where his grandfather had poured wine over a pile of stones and called it a holy altar. My brothers liked this dream. They did business in the city and returned to the tents full of stories about the marketplace, where wool and livestock got good prices. Shechem's king, Hamor, was peaceful and welcomed tribes who wished to make the land blossom. Simon and Levi spoke to Hamor's vizier in my father's name and returned to Jacob, all puffed up with themselves over their agreement for a good-sized parcel of land with a well on it.

So the tents were taken down and the herds gathered and we traveled the short distance to the place that the king said could be ours. My mothers declared themselves pleased with the valley.

"Mountains are where heaven meets earth," said Zilpah, satisfied that she would find inspiration.

"The mountains will protect us against bad winds," said Leah, with reason.

"I must find a local herb-woman to show us what these hills have to offer," Rachel said to Inna.

Only Bilhah seemed unhappy in the shadow of Ebal, which was the name of the mountain on whose side we raised our tents. "It is so big here," she sighed. "I feel lost."

We built ovens and planted seed. The herds multiplied, and three more of my brothers took wives, young girls who provoked no objections from my mothers. They were of Canaan and knew nothing of the customs of Haran, where mothers are honored for strength as well as beauty. And while my new sisters entered the red tent to please Leah, they never laughed with us. They watched our sacrifice to the Queen of Heaven without interest and refused to learn what to do. "Sacrifices are for men," they said, and ate their sweets. Still, my brothers' brides were hard workers and fertile. I acquired many nieces and nephews in Shechem, and the family of Jacob prospered.

There was peace in our tents except for Simon and Levi, who dwelt in the ever-widening margins of their own discontent. The well, which had made the land seem such a prize, turned out to be an ancient, crumbling pile of stones that dried out soon after we arrived. My brothers dug another, a backbreaking job that failed in the first place they tried. Simon and Levi were certain that Hamor had purposefully swindled them, and they fed on each other's anger about what they called their humiliation. By the time the second well was giving water, their resentment was as much a part of them as their own names. I was grateful that my path rarely brought me in contact with them. They frightened me with their black looks and the long knives that always hung from their belts.

When the air was sweet with spring and the ewes heavy with lambs, my month arrived. As evening gathered on the first night of darkness, I was squatting to relieve myself when I noticed the smear on my thigh. It took me several moments before I understood what I saw. It was brown rather than red. Wasn't it supposed to be red? Shouldn't I feel some ache in my belly? Perhaps I was mistaken and bled from my leg, yet I could find no scrape or scratch.

It seemed I had been waiting forever for womanhood, and yet I did not jump up to tell my mothers. I stayed where I was, on my haunches, hidden by branches, thinking: My childhood is over. I will wear an apron and cover my head. I will not have to carry and fetch during the new moon anymore, but will sit with the rest of the women until I am pregnant. I will idle with my mothers and my sisters in the ruddy shade of the red tent for three days and three nights, until first sight of the crescent goddess. My blood will flow into the fresh straw, filling the air with the salt smell of women.

For a moment I weighed the idea of keeping my secret and remaining a girl, but the thought passed quickly. I could only be what I was. And I was a woman.

I raised myself up, my fingers stained with the first signs of my maturity, and realized that there was indeed a dull ache in my bowels. With new pride, I carried myself into the tent, knowing that my swelling breasts would no longer be a joke among the women. Now I would be welcome inside any tent when Rachel and Inna attended at a birth. Now I could pour out the wine and make bread offerings at the new moon, and soon I would learn the secrets that pass between men and women.

I walked into the red tent without the water I'd been sent for. But before my mother could open her mouth to scold me, I held up my soiled fingers. "I am not permitted to carry anything either, Mother."

"Oh, oh, oh!" said Leah, who for once had no words.

She kissed me on both cheeks, and my aunts gathered around and took turns greeting me with more kisses. My sisters-in-law clapped their hands and everyone began talking at once. Inna ran in to find out what the noise was about, and I was surrounded by smiling faces.

It was nearly dark, and my ceremony began almost before I realized what was happening. Inna brought a polished metal cup filled with fortified wine, so dark and sweet I barely tasted its power. But my head soon floated while my mothers prepared me with henna on the bottoms of my feet and on my palms. Unlike a bride, they painted a line of red from my feet up to my sex, and from my hands they made a pattern of spots that led to my navel.

They put kohl on my eyes ("So you will be far-seeing," said Leah) and perfumed my forehead and my armpits ("So you will walk among flowers," said Rachel). They removed my bracelets and took my robe from me. It must have been the wine that prevented me from asking why they took such care with paint and scent yet dressed me in the rough homespun gown used for women in childbirth and as a shroud for the afterbirth after the baby came.

They were so kind to me, so funny, so sweet. They would not let me feed myself but used their fingers to fill my mouth with the choicest morsels. They massaged my neck and back until I was as supple as a cat. They sang every song known among us. My mother kept my wine cup filled and brought it to my lips so often that soon I found it difficult to speak, and the voices around me melted into a loud happy hum.

Zebulun's wife, Ahavah, danced with her pregnant belly

to the clapping of hands. I laughed until my sides ached. I smiled until my face hurt. It was good to be a woman!

Then Rachel brought out the teraphim, and everyone fell silent. The household gods had remained hidden until that moment. Although I had been a little girl when I'd seen them last, I remembered them like old friends: the pregnant mother, the goddess wearing snakes in her hair, the one that was both male and female, the stern little ram. Rachel laid them out carefully and chose the goddess wearing the shape of a grinning frog. Her wide mouth held her own eggs for safekeeping, while her legs were splayed in a dagger-shaped triangle, ready to lay a thousand more. Rachel rubbed the obsidian figure with oil until the creature gleamed and dripped in the light of the lamps. I stared at the frog's silly face and giggled, but no one laughed with me.

In the next moment, I found myself outside with my mother and my aunts. We were in the wheat patch in the heart of the garden—a hidden place where grain dedicated to sacrifice was grown. The soil had been tilled in preparation for planting after the moon's return, and I was naked, lying facedown on the cool soil. I shivered. My mother put my cheek to the ground and loosened my hair around me. She arranged my arms wide, "to embrace the earth," she whispered. She bent my knees and pulled the soles of my feet together until they touched, "to give the first blood back to the land," said Leah. I could feel the night air on my sex, and it was strange and wonderful to be so open under the sky.

My mothers gathered around: Leah above me, Bilhah at my left hand, Zilpah's hand on the back of my legs. I was grinning like the frog, half asleep, in love with them all. Rachel's voice behind me broke the silence. "Mother! Innana! Queen of the Night! Accept the blood offering of your daughter, in her mother's name, in your name. In her 7blood may she live, in her blood may she give life."

It did not hurt. The oil eased the entry, and the narrow triangle fit perfectly as it entered me. I faced the west while the little goddess faced east as she broke the lock on my womb. When I cried out, it was not so much pain but surprise and perhaps even pleasure, for it seemed to me that the Queen herself was lying on top of me, with Dumuzi her consort beneath me. I was like a slip of cloth, caught between their lovemaking, warmed by the great passion.

My mothers moaned softly in sympathy. If I could have spoken I would have reassured them that I was perfectly happy. For all the stars of the night sky had entered my womb behind the legs of the smiling little frog goddess. On the softest, wildest night since the separation of land and water, earth and sky, I lay panting like a dog and felt myself spinning through the heavens. And when I began to fall, I had no fear.

The sky was pink when I opened my eyes. Inna was crouched beside me, watching my face. I was lying on my back, my arms and legs wide like the spokes of the wheel, my nakedness covered by my mother's best blanket. The midwife helped me to my feet and led me back to a soft corner in the red tent, where the other women still slept. "Did you dream?" she asked me. When I nodded that I had, she drew close and said, "What shape did she take?"

Oddly, I knew what she wanted to know, but I didn't know what to call the creature that had smiled at me. I had never seen anything like her—huge, black, a toothy grin, skin like leather. I tried to describe the animal to Inna, who seemed puzzled. Then she asked, "Was she in the water?"

I said yes and Inna smiled. "I told you that water was your destiny. That is a very old one, Taweret, an Egyptian goddess who lives in the river and laughs with a great mouth. She gives mothers their milk and protects all children." My old friend kissed my cheeks and then pinched them gently. "That is all I know of Taweret, but in all my years, I never knew a woman who dreamed of her. It must be a sign of luck, little one. Now sleep."

My eyes did not open until evening, and I dreamed all day about a golden moon growing between my legs. And in the morning, I was given the honor of being the first one outside, to greet the first daylight of the new moon.

When Leah went to tell Jacob that his daughter had come of age, she found that he already knew. Inbu had spoken of it to Levi, who whispered to his father of "abominations."

The Canaanite woman had been shocked by the ritual that had brought me into the ancient covenant of earth, blood, and the sky. Inbu's family knew nothing of the ceremony for opening the womb. Indeed, when she married my brother, her mother had run into the tent to snatch the bloodstained blanket of her wedding night, just in case Jacob—who had paid the full bride-price—wanted proof of her virginity. As though my father would wish to look upon a woman's blood.

But now Inbu had told Levi of the sacrifice in the garden—or at least what she guessed of it—and he went to our father, Jacob. Men knew nothing of the red tent or its ceremonies and sacrifices. Jacob was not pleased to learn of them. His wives fulfilled their obligations to him and to his god; he had no quarrels with them or their goddesses. But he could no longer pretend that Laban's teraphim were not in his house, and he could not abide the presence of goods he had forsworn.

So Jacob called Rachel before him and ordered her to bring the household gods she had taken from Laban. He took them all to an unknown place and shattered them, one by one, with a rock. Then he buried them in secret, so no one could pour libations over them.

Ahavah miscarried the next week, which Zilpah called a punishment and a portent of worse to come. Leah was not so concerned about the teraphim. "They were hidden in a basket for years and that did us no harm. The problem is with the wives of my sons, who do not follow our ways. We must teach them better. We must make them our own daughters." And so my mother took Ahavah into her heart, and Judah's Shua. In the following years, she also tried to teach Issachar's bride, Hesia, and Gad's Oreet. But they could not abandon their own mothers' ways.

Inbu's treason left a deep breach in its wake, and a division that never healed. The wives of Levi and Simon never came to the red tent again, but stayed under their own roofs at the new moon and kept their daughters with them. And Jacob began to frown at the red tent.

With every new moon, I took my place in the red tent and learned from my mothers how to keep my feet from touching the bare earth and how to sit comfortably on a rag over straw. My days took shape in relation to the waxing and waning of the moon. Time wrapped itself around the gathering within my body, the swelling of my breasts, the aching anticipation of release, the three quiet days of separation and pause.

Although I had stopped worshiping my mothers as perfect creatures, I looked forward to those days with them and the other women who bled. Once, when it happened that only my mothers and I sat in the tent, Rachel remarked that it was like the old days in Haran. But Leah said, "It is not the same at all. Now there are many to serve us and my daughter sits on the straw with us." Bilhah saw that my mother's words bruised Rachel's heart, for she still longed for a daughter and had not given up hope. My gentle aunt said, "Ah, but Leah, it truly is pleasant with the five of us again. How Adah would have smiled." My grandmother's name worked its usual charm, and the sisters relaxed in memory of her. But the damage had been done, and the old chill between Leah and Rachel returned to the women's quarters.

Not long after we settled in the shadow of Ebal, Inna and Rachel delivered a large breech baby boy to one of our bondswomen. The mother lived, something rarely seen with foot-first babies in that place. Soon women from the hillsides and even from far down in the valley began to send for them at the first sign of a difficult birth. It was rumored that Inna and Rachel—but especially Rachel, who was blood kin to the line of Mamre—possessed powers to appease Lamashtu and Lillake, ancient demons said to thirst after newborn blood, and much feared by the local people.

Many times I walked out with my aunt and the old midwife, who found it easier to lean on her walking staff without a bag on her shoulder. The hill folk were shocked that they took an unwed girl like me to visit birthing women. But in the valley they did not seem to care, and the first-time mothers, some younger than I, asked that I be the one to hold their hands and look into their eyes when the pains bore down hard.

Though I was certain my teachers knew everything about delivering babies, Rachel and Inna tried to learn what they might from women wherever they went. They were pleased to discover an especially sweet mint that grew in the hills. It settled the stomach quickly and was a blessing for those who suffered from bloating and vomiting during pregnancy. But when Inna saw how some of the hill women painted the mother's body with yellow spirals "to fool the demons," she curled her lip and muttered that it did nothing but irritate the skin.

There was one great gift that my teachers learned from the women of Shechem's valley. It was not an herb or a tool, but a birth song, and the most soothing balm that Inna or Rachel had ever used. It made laboring women breathe easier and caused the skin to stretch rather than tear. It eased the worst pains. Those who died—for even with a midwife as skillful as Inna some of them died—even they smiled as they closed their eyes forever, unafraid.

We sang:

> "*Fear not, the time is coming*
> *Fear not, your bones are strong*
> *Fear not, help is nearby*

Fear not, Gula is near
Fear not, the baby is at the door
Fear not, he will live to bring you honor
Fear not, the hands of the midwife are clever
Fear not, the earth is beneath you
Fear not, we have water and salt
Fear not, little mother
Fear not, mother of us all."

Inna loved that song, especially when the women of the house could add harmonies and make the magic even greater. She was delighted to have learned something so powerful so late in her life. "Even the oldest of us," she said, shaking a bony finger at me, "even we crones can pick up new tricks here and there."

Our beloved friend was aging, and the time came when Inna was too stiff to walk out in the night or to manage steep paths, so Rachel took me with her and I began to learn with my hands as well as with my eyes.

Once when we were called to help a young mother deliver her second son—an easy birth from a sweet woman who smiled even as she labored—my aunt let me place the bricks and tie the cord. On the way home Rachel patted my shoulder and told me I would be a good midwife. When she added that my voice suited the song of the fearless mother, I was never so proud.

Chapter Seven

SOMETIMES WE WERE called to assist a laboring mother who lived within sight of the city. Those trips were my special delight. The walls of Shechem awed me more than the misty mountains that inspired sacrifices from Jacob and Zilpah. The minds that had conceived such a great project made me feel wise, and the force of the sinews that had built the fortress made me feel strong. Whenever I caught sight of the walls, I could not look away.

I longed to go inside, to see the temple square and the narrow streets and crowded houses. I knew a little about the shape of the place from Joseph, who had been to Shechem with our brothers. Joseph said that the palace where Hamor the king lived in splendor with his Egyptian wife and fifteen concubines contained more rooms than I had brothers. Joseph said that Hamor had more servants than we had sheep. Not that a dusty shepherd like my brother could even hope for a peek inside such a grand house. Still, I liked his tall stories. Even lies about the place thrilled me, and I fancied that I could smell the perfume of courtesans on my brother's tunic when he returned from the market.

My mother decided she wanted to see the place for herself. Leah was certain that she could drive a better bargain for our wool than Reuben, who was too generous to be trusted with such transactions. I nearly kissed her hands when she said I would go to help her. Reuben settled us into a good spot just outside the gate, but he stood at a distance from us when our mother began calling out to every passing stranger and haggled like a camel trader with those who approached.

There was little for me to do but watch, which I did happily. That day at the eastern gate was a marvel. I saw my first jugglers. I ate my first pomegranate. I saw black faces and brown faces, goats with impossibly curly coats, women covered in black robes and slave girls who wore nothing at all. It was like being on the highway again, but without sore feet. I saw a dwarf hobbling alongside a donkey as white as the moon, and watched a caftaned high priest buy olives. Then I saw Tabea.

Or at least I thought I saw her. A girl of her height and coloring walked toward our display. She was dressed in the white robes of the temple, head shaven, both ears pierced. I stood and called out to her, but she turned on her heels and rushed away. Without thinking and before my mother could stop me, I ran after her, as though I were a child and not a young woman. "Tabea!" I called out. "Cousin!" But she did not hear me, or if she did, she did not stop, and the white robes disappeared through a doorway.

Reuben caught up with me. "What were you doing?" he asked.

"I thought it was Tabea," I said, near tears. "But I was mistaken."

"Tabea?" he asked.

"A cousin from Esau. You do not know her," I said. "I'm sorry I made you chase me. Is Mother angry?"

He laughed at the foolishness of my question, and I laughed too. She was furious, and I had to sit facing the wall the rest of the afternoon. But by then, my light heart had gone out of me, and I was content just listening to the sounds of the marketplace, nursing memories of my lost friend.

After our return from that trip, a messenger arrived from the city. She wore a linen robe and beautiful sandals and would speak only to Rachel. "One of the women in the king's household is about to deliver," she said to my aunt. "Hamor's queen calls for the midwives from Jacob's house to attend her."

Leah was not pleased when I began to prepare my kit for the journey. She went to Rachel and asked, "Why not take Inna to the queen with you? Why do you insist on taking Dinah away from me, just when there are olives to harvest?"

My aunt shrugged. "You know that Inna cannot walk as far as the city any longer. If you wish me to take a slave, I will. But the queen expects two of us, and she will not be so disposed to buy your woolens if I walk into the palace without skilled assistance."

Leah glared at her sister's smooth words, and I dropped my eyes to the ground so that my mother could not see how much I longed to go. I held my breath as my mother decided. "Pah," she said, throwing up her hands and walking away. I clapped my hands over my mouth to keep from crowing, and Rachel grinned at me like a child who had outfoxed her elders.

We finished our preparations and dressed in festival robes, but Rachel stopped me before we walked out, and braided my hair into smooth ropes. "Egyptian-style," she whispered. Bilhah and Zilpah waved us off, but Leah was nowhere to be seen as we headed into the valley with the messenger.

Walking through the gates of the city that first time, I was sorely disappointed. The streets were smaller and dustier than I had imagined. The smell was an awful mixture of rotten fruit and human waste. We moved too quickly to see inside the dark hovels, but I could hear and smell that the goats lived with their owners, and I finally understood my father's disdain for city dwelling.

Once we crossed the threshold of the palace, we entered a different world. The walls were thick enough to block out the sounds and smells of the street, and the courtyard in which we stood was spacious and bright.

A naked slave approached and motioned for us to follow her through one of the doorways into the women's quarters, and then into the room where the mother-to-be panted on the floor. She was about my age and by the look of her, early in her labor. Rachel touched her belly and examined the womb and rolled her eyes at me. We had been summoned for the most straightforward of births. Not that either of us minded; a trip to the palace was an adventure for which we were grateful.

Soon after we met the mother, Hamor's queen walked into the room, curious to see the hill-bred midwives. The queen, who was called Re-nefer, wore a gossamer linen sheath covered by a tunic of turquoise beads—the most elegant clothing I had ever seen. Even so, my aunt was not outshone by the lady. Old as Rachel was, lined by sun and work, crouched on the floor with her hand between the legs of a woman in travail—even so, my aunt glowed her golden light. Her hair was still lustrous and her black eyes sparkled. The women looked each other over with approval and nodded their greeting.

Re-nefer raised her gown above her knees and squatted on the other side of Ashnan, for that was the name of the young mother who huffed and moaned more in fear than pain. The two older women began to talk about oils that might ease the baby's head, and I was impressed both at how much the noblewoman knew of birthing and at Rachel's ease in conversing with a queen.

Ashnan, it turned out, was the daughter of the queen's nursemaid. The woman on the bricks had been a playmate of her own son's infancy and his milk-sister—just like Joseph and me. The nursemaid had died when the children were still babies, and Re-nefer had been tender toward the girl ever since and was even more so now that she was pregnant by Hamor. Ashnan was his newest concubine.

All this we learned from Re-nefer, who stayed beside Ashnan from noon until nearly sunset. The mother was strong and all the signs were good, but the birth went slowly. Strong pangs were followed by long pauses, and when Ashnan fell asleep late in the afternoon, exhausted by her labors, Re-nefer took Rachel to her own chamber for refreshment and I was left to watch the mother.

I was nearly asleep myself when I heard a man's voice in

the antechamber. I should have sent word through the slave girl, but I didn't think of it. I was bored and stiff from sitting so many hours, so I rose and went myself.

His name was Shalem. He was a firstborn son, the handsomest and quickest of the king's children, well liked by the people of Shechem. He was golden and beautiful as a sunset.

I dropped my eyes to the ground to keep from staring—as though he were a two-headed goat or something else that defied the order of things. And yet, he did defy nature. He was perfect.

To avoid looking up into his face, I noticed that his fingernails were clean and that his hands were smooth. His arms were not black from the sun like my brothers', though neither were they sickly. He wore only a skirt, and his chest was naked, hairless, well muscled.

He was looking at me, too, and I shuddered at the stains on my apron. Even my festival tunic seemed shabby and drab compared to the gleaming homespun of the simple garment he wore at home. My hair was awry and uncovered. My feet were dirty. I began to hear the sound of breathing, without knowing if it was my own or his.

Finally, I could not help myself and lifted my eyes to his. He stood taller than me by a handbreadth. His hair was black and shining, his teeth straight and white. His eyes were golden or green or brown. In truth, I did not look there long enough to discern their color because I had never been greeted with such a look. His mouth smiled politely, but his eyes sought the answer to a question I did not fully understand.

My ears rang. I wanted to run, and yet I did not wish to end this strange agony of confusion and need that came upon me. I said nothing.

He was disconcerted, too. He coughed into his fist, glanced toward the doorway where Ashnan lay, and stared at me. Finally, he stuttered a question about his milk-sister. I must have said something, though I have no memory of my words. All I remember is the ache in the moment when we met in that bare little hallway.

It amazes me to think of all that happened in the space of a silent breath or two. All the while I scolded myself, thinking, Foolish! Childish! Foolish! Mother will laugh when I tell her.

But I knew I would not be telling this to my mother. And that thought made me blush. Not the warmth of my feeling for this Shalem, whose name I had not even learned, whose presence made me dumb and weak. What caused my cheeks to color was the understanding that I would not speak of the fullness and fire in my heart to Leah.

He saw me color and his smile widened. My awkwardness vanished and I smiled back. And it was as though the bride-price had been paid and the dowry agreed to. It was as though we were alone in our bridal tent. The question had been answered.

It sounds comical to me now, and if a child of mine confessed such things to me, I would laugh out loud or scold her. But on that day I was a girl who was ready for a man.

As we grinned at each other, I remembered the sounds from Judah's tent and I understood my own fevered nights. Shalem, who was a few years older than I, recognized his own longing and yet he felt more than the simple stirring of desire, or that is what he said after we had redeemed our promise and lay in each other's arms. He said he was smitten and shy in the antechamber of the women's quarters. He said he had been enchanted, struck dumb, and thrilled. Like me.

I do not think we spoke another word before Rachel and the queen swept into the room and pulled me back into the birth chamber. I did not have time to think of Shalem then, for Ashnan's water broke and she delivered a big healthy boy who barely ripped her flesh. "You will heal in a week," Rachel told the girl, who sobbed with relief that it was done.

We slept in the palace that night, though I hardly closed my eyes with excitement. Leaving the next morning was like dying. I thought I might never see him again. I thought perhaps it had been a mistake on my part—the fantasy of a raw country girl in the presence of a prince. But my heart rebelled at the idea and I twisted my neck looking back as we departed, thinking he might come to claim me. But Shalem did not appear, and I bit my lips to keep from weeping as we climbed the hills back to my father's tents.

Nobody knew! I thought they would all see it in me. I thought that Rachel would guess at my secret and pry the story from me as we walked home. But my aunt wanted only to talk about Re-nefer, who had praised her skills and given her a necklace of onyx beads.

When we returned to camp, my mother hugged me without sensing the new heat in my body and sent me to the olive grove, where the harvest was busy. Zilpah was there overseeing the press and barely answered my greeting. Even Bilhah of the discerning heart was preoccupied with a batch of oil jars that had cracked, and she saw nothing.

Their inattention was a revelation to me. Before my trip to Shechem, I had supposed that my mothers could see my thoughts and look directly into my heart. But now I discovered that I was separate, opaque, and drawn into an orbit of which they had no knowledge.

I delighted in the discovery of my solitude and protected it, keeping myself busy at the far end of the orchard and even sleeping in the makeshift tent near the edge of the harvest with my brothers' wives. I was happy to be alone, thinking only of my beloved, numbering his qualities, imagining his virtues. I stared at my hands and wondered what it would be like to touch his gleaming shoulders, his beautiful arms. In my dreams I saw sunlight sparkling on water and I awoke smiling.

After three days of drunken happiness, my hopes began to sour. Would he come for me? Were these callused hands too rough to delight a prince? I chewed on my fingernails and forgot to eat. At night, I lay sleepless on my blanket, turning our meeting over and over in my mind. I could think of nothing but him, yet I began to doubt my memories. Perhaps his smile had been one of indulgence rather than of recognition. Perhaps I was a fool.

But just as I began to fear that I would betray myself to my mothers in a flood of tears, I was saved. The king himself sent for me. Hamor would deny his young consort nothing, and when Ashnan asked if Jacob's kind young daughter could be brought to distract her during her confinement, a messenger was dispatched. The king's man even brought a slave to take my place in the harvest. My mother found the gesture thoughtful and generous. "Let her go," she said to my father. Jacob did not object, and sent Levi to accompany me to the door of the women's quarters in Hamor's palace.

Waving to my mothers, I could see Bilhah and Rachel peering after me. Either my haste or my pleasure at the king's bidding alerted them to something, but by then it was too late to ask. They waved back as I descended into the valley, but I could feel their questions at my back. A hawk circled high above us all the way down into the valley. Levi said it was a good sign, but the messenger spit on the ground every time the bird's shadow crossed our path.

My brother left me at the door of Hamor's palace, charging me in a loud, pompous voice for the benefit of the messenger "to behave as befits one of the daughters of Jacob." Since I was Jacob's only surviving daughter, I smiled. I had been told to behave as myself, and I had every intention of doing that.

In the next three weeks, I met the daughters of Shechem. The wives of all the important men came to visit Ashnan and her little boy, who would not be publicly named until he reached three months, according to the custom of Egypt. "So the demons will not know how to find him," Ashnan whispered, fearing the presence of evil even within the safety of her comfortable rooms.

Ashnan was rather a silly girl with fine teeth and big breasts, which regained their shape and beauty quickly after the baby was given to a nurse. I had never heard of a healthy woman giving an infant to another woman's breast; in my world, a wet nurse was used only when the mother was dead or dying. But then, what did I know of the lives of royal women? Indeed, I was amazed by almost everything I saw at first.

I did not much care for being Ashnan's servant, for that is how she treated me. I brought her food and fed it to her. I bathed her feet and her face. She wanted massage, and so I learned the art from an old woman of the house. She wanted paints as well, and chattered away as she taught me how to apply kohl around my own eyes, and a ground green powder to my lids. "Not only does it make you look beautiful," said Ashnan, "it keeps the gnats away."

Ashnan also taught me boredom, which is a dreadful calamity visited upon women in palaces. There was one afternoon I actually shed tears at the monotony of having to sit still as Ashnan slept. All I had to occupy myself with was worry over whether Shalem was aware of my presence under his father's roof. I began to doubt that he remembered the unkempt assistant to his milk-sister's midwife. I was trapped without answers, for the walls between the women's world and men's quarters were thick, and in the world of the palace there was no work to create a crossing of paths.

After many days, Re-nefer looked in upon Ashnan and I tried to find the courage to speak to her about her son. But all I could do was stammer in her presence and blush. "Do you miss your mother, child?" she kindly asked. I shook my head, but looked so miserable that the queen took my hand and said, "You need some distraction, I think. A girl like you who lives under the sun must feel like a trapped bird within these walls."

I smiled at Re-nefer and she squeezed my fingers. "You will go out into the marketplace with my maid," she said.

"Help her pick the best of the pomegranates, and see if you can hunt up some fine figs for my son. Shalem likes figs."

The next morning I walked out of the palace and into the babble of the city, where I stared to my heart's content. The servant by my side seemed in no hurry and let me wander where I would. I stopped at almost every stall and blanket, wonder-struck at the variety and quantity of lamps, fruits, woven goods, cheeses, dyes, tools, livestock, baskets, jewelry, flutes, herbs, everything.

But there were no figs to be had that day. We searched for them until I was nearly dizzy from heat and thirst, but I hated to return to the palace without satisfying the queen's request, without bringing fruit to my beloved. Finally, when we had looked in every corner, there was nothing to do but turn back.

At the moment we set our path for the palace, I spied the oldest face I had ever seen — an herb seller whose black skin was lined deep as a dry wadi. I stood by her blanket and listened to her rattle on about some liniment "good for the backache." But when I leaned down to finger a root I had never seen, she grabbed my wrist and stared up into my face. "Ah, the young lady wants something for her lover! Something magic that will bring her young man to bed, so she may be rid of her tiresome virginity."

I pulled my arm away, horrified that the conjurer had seen so far into my heart. It was probably only a speech she made to every young girl who approached, but Re-nefer's maid saw my confusion and laughed. I was mortified, and rushed away from the old one.

I did not see Shalem approach, but he stood before me, the afternoon sunlight filling the sky around his head like a glowing crown. I looked into his face and gasped. "Are you well, my lady?" he asked, in the sweet, reedy voice that I remembered. I was mute.

He looked at me with the same hunger I felt, and put a warm hand on my elbow to squire me back to the palace, the queen's woman following us, wearing a big grin. Her mistress had been right; there was a light between the prince and the granddaughter of Mamre.

Unlike me, Re-nefer's son had not been able to hide his heart from his mother. Re-nefer had despised the women of the city since she arrived in Shechem as a young bride. "Stupid and empty," she branded them all. "They spin badly, weave atrociously, dress like men, and know nothing of herbs. They will bear you stupid children," Re-nefer had told her son. "We will do better for you."

Re-nefer had been impressed by the bearing of the mid-wife from the hills, and she had liked the looks of the girl carrying her bag, too. She approved of my height and the strength of my arms, my coloring and the way I carried my head. The fact that one as young as I was already walking in a midwife's path told her I was no fool. When Rachel had gone with the queen for refreshment during Ashnan's labor, Re-nefer had gotten more information about me so discreetly that Rachel did not suspect her purpose as she was quizzed about my age, my mother's status, my skill at hearth and loom.

When Re-nefer and Rachel surprised me and Shalem in the anteroom, she discerned at once that the seed of her idea had already sprouted on its own. She did what she could to nurture its growth.

Re-nefer told Ashnan to send for me from my father's house, and she told her son to go out to seek me in the market that morning. "I'm afraid that the little girl from the hills will be lost," she said to Shalem. "You know that my servant is fool enough to let her out of her sight. But maybe you do not remember the looks of the one called Dinah?" she asked her son. "She was the dark-eyed girl with the curly hair and the fine hands who came with the midwife. You spoke to her in the antechamber when Ashnan was in travail." Shalem agreed to do his mother's bidding with such speed that Re-nefer had trouble stifling a laugh.

When the prince and I returned to the palace, we found the courtyard deserted, as Re-nefer had instructed. The servant disappeared. We stood in silence for only a moment and then Shalem drew me into the shadow of a corner and put his hands on my shoulders and covered my mouth with his mouth and pressed his body against mine. And I, who had never been touched or kissed by any man, was unafraid. He did not hurry or push, and I put my hands on his back and pressed into his chest and melted into his hands and his mouth.

When his lips found my throat, I groaned and Shalem stopped. He looked into my face to discover my meaning, and seeing only yes, he took my hand and led me down an unfamiliar corridor into a room with a polished floor and a bed that stood on legs carved like the claws of a hawk. We lay down upon sweet-smelling black fleece and found one another.

I did not cry out when he took me, because, though he was young, my lover did not rush. Afterward, when Shalem lay still at last and discovered that my cheeks were wet, he said, "Oh, little wife. Do not let me hurt you again." But I told him that my tears had nothing of pain in them. They were the first tears of happiness in my life. "Taste them," I said to my beloved, and he found they were sweet. And he wept as well. We clung to each other until Shalem's desire was renewed, and I did not hold my breath when he entered me, so I began to feel what was happening to my body, and to understand the pleasures of love.

No one disturbed us. Night fell and food was left at the doorway—wonderful fruit and golden wine, fresh bread and olives and cakes dripping in honey. We ate every morsel like famished dogs.

After we ate, he washed me in a large tub of warm water that appeared as mysteriously as the food. He told me of Egypt and of the great river where he would take me to bask and swim.

"I cannot swim," I told Shalem.

"Good," he replied. "Then I can be the one to teach you."

He put his hands into my hair until they were tangled in knots and it took us long moments to free him. "I love these shackles," he said, when he could not free himself, and he grew large and our coupling was exquisitely slow. His hands caressed my face, and we cried out in pleasure together.

Whenever we were not kissing or coupling or sleeping, Shalem and I traded stories. I told him of my father and my mothers and described my brothers, one by one. He was delighted by their names and learned each one, in the order of his birth, and knew which one came from the womb of which mother. I'm not sure my own father could have listed them so well.

He told me of his tutor, a cripple with a wonderful voice, who taught him to sing and to read. Shalem told me of his mother's devotion and his five half brothers, none of whom had learned the arts of Egypt. He told me of his trip to the priestess, who initiated him in the art of love in the name of heaven. "I never saw her face," he said. "The rites take place in the innermost chamber, where there is no light. It was like a dream locked inside a dream." He told me of three times he had slept with a slave girl, who giggled in his embrace and asked for payment afterward.

But by the end of our second day together, our embraces outnumbered his experiences with other women. "I have forgotten them all," he said.

"Then I will forgive you them all," I said.

We made love again and again. We slept and awoke with our hands on each other. We kissed each other everywhere, and I learned the flavor of my lover's toes, the smell of his sex before and after coupling, the dampness of his neck.

We were together as bride and groom for three days before I began to wonder why I had not been fetched to go and wash Ashnan's feet or rub her back. Shalem, too, forgot his obligatory evening meals with his father. But Re-nefer took care that we should know nothing of the world and that the world should give us peace. She sent choice foods at all hours of the day and night and instructed the servants to fill Shalem's bath with fresh scented water whenever we slept.

I had no worries for the future. Shalem said our lovemaking sealed our marriage. He teased me about the bride-price he would bring to my father: buckets of gold coins, camels laden with lapis and linen, a caravan of slaves, a herd of sheep so fine their wool never needed washing. "You deserve a queen's ransom," he whispered, as we drifted back to our shared dreams.

"I will build you a tomb of surpassing beauty," Shalem said. "The world will never forget the name of Dinah, who judged my heart worthy."

I wish I had been as bold with my words. Not that I was shy. Shalem knew of my delight in him, my gratitude for him, my lust for him. I gave him everything. I abandoned myself to him and in him. It was only that I could not find a voice for the flood of my happiness.

While I lay in Shalem's first embrace, Levi was storming out of Hamor's palace, furious that he had not been given the audience with the king that he considered his due. My brother had been dispatched to see when I would be sent home, and had he been given a fine meal and a bed for the night, my life might have had a different telling.

Later, I wondered what might have happened had Reuben or Judah come for me. Hamor was not eager to meet with that particular son of Jacob, the quarrelsome one who had accused him of swindling the family. Why should the king suffer through another round of accusations by some whining son of a shepherd?

If it had been Reuben, Hamor would have welcomed him to dine and spend the night. Indeed, if it had been any of the others, even Joseph, he would have received a fine welcome. Hamor approved of Jacob nearly as much as his queen liked Jacob's wives. The king knew that my father tended his flocks with such skill that he had quickly become the richest shepherd in the valley. Jacob's wool was the softest, his wives skilled, and his sons loyal. He caused no feuds among neighbors. He had enriched the valley, and Hamor was eager for good relations with him. Marriages between their two houses were much to be desired, so Hamor was pleased when Re-nefer whispered that his son favored Jacob's daughter. Indeed, as soon as the king heard that Shalem was lying with me, he began to count out a handsome bride-price.

When Hamor heard from the servants that the young couple were well matched, adoring, and busy producing his grandson, the news aroused him so much that he called Ashnan to his bed a full week before her confinement was due to end. When Re-nefer discovered them, she barely scolded her husband and the girl, so great was her joy at her son's match.

On the fourth day of our happiness, Shalem arose from our bath, dressed, and told me he was going to speak to his father. "It is time for Hamor to arrange for the bride-price." He looked so handsome in his tunic and sandals that my eyes filled with tears again. "No more weeping, not even for happiness," he said, and lifted me, still wet from the water, and kissed my nose and my mouth and put me on the bed and said, "Wait for me, beloved. Do not dress. Only lie here so I may think of you like this. I won't be long."

I covered his face with kisses and told him to hurry back. I was asleep when he slipped beside me, smelling of the world beyond our bed for the first time in days.

Hamor departed for Jacob's camp early the next morning, a laden wagon behind him. He did not bring a tent or servants for a night's stay. He did not expect to stay or to haggle. How could he have imagined any objection to his good news and generous gift?

The news about Shalem and Jacob's daughter was widespread in the city, but unknown in Jacob's tents. When he heard that I had been taken as wife by the prince of the city, he said nothing and made no reply to Hamor's offer. He stood like a stone, staring at the man of whom his sons Levi and Simon had spoken with such venom—a man of his own years, it turned out, but richly dressed, smooth spoken, and fat. The king waved at a cart laden with goods and trailing sheep and goats. He declared them kin, soon to share a grandchild.

Jacob hooded his eyes and covered his mouth with his hand so Hamor would not see his discomfort or surprise. He nodded as Hamor praised his daughter's beauty. Jacob had given no thought to a marriage for his daughter, although his wife had begun to speak of it. She was of age, to be sure. But Jacob was uneasy about this match, although he could not say why, and he felt his neck stiffen at Hamor's expectation that he would do as he was told.

He searched his mind for a way to postpone a decision, a way to regain the upper hand. "I will discuss this with my sons," he told the king, with more force than he meant.

Hamor was stung. "Your daughter is no virgin, Jacob," the king pressed. "Yet here is a bride-price fit for a virgin princess of Egypt—more than my own father gave for my wife. Not that your daughter is unworthy of this and more.

Name what you wish and it is yours, for my son loves the girl. And I hear she is willing, too," and here Hamor smiled a bit too broadly for Jacob's taste. He did not like to hear his daughter spoken of so crudely, even though he could not quite conjure up the image of Dinah's face. All he could recall clearly was the sight of hair, unruly and wild, as she chased after Joseph. The memory came from long ago.

"I will wait for my sons," said Jacob, and he turned away from the king, as though the lord of Shechem were no more than a shepherd, and left it to his wives to welcome the king with drink and food. But Hamor saw no reason to stay and headed back to his palace, trailing his gifts behind him.

Jacob called for Leah and spoke to her in the hardest words he had ever used with a wife. "Your daughter is no longer a girl," he said. "You were insolent to keep this from me. You have overreached before, but never to shame me. And now this."

My mother was as surprised as her husband and pressed Jacob for news of her daughter. "The prince of Shechem has claimed her. His father comes to pay the full bride-price of a virgin. And so I assume that she was until she went within the walls of that dung heap of a city." Jacob was bitter. "She is of Shechem now, I suppose, and of no use to me."

Leah was furious. "Go seek out your wife, my sister," she said. "It was Rachel who took her there. Rachel is the one with eyes for the city, not me, husband. Ask your wife." And the smell of bile rose from my mother's words.

I wonder if she thought of me at all then, if she suffered over whether I had consented or cried out, if her heart reached out to discover whether I wept or rejoiced. But her words spoke only of the loss of a daughter, gone to the city where she would reside with foreign women, learn their ways, and forget her mother.

My father called for Rachel next. "Husband!" cried Rachel, smiling as she approached him. "I hear there are happy tidings."

But Jacob did not smile. "I do not like the city or its king," he said. "But I like even less an untrustworthy daughter and a lying wife."

"Say nothing you will regret," replied Rachel. "My sister sets you against me and against your only daughter, who is beloved of your mother at Mamre. This is a good match. The king says they are fond, does he not? Have you forgotten your own fire, husband? Have you grown so old that you do not remember that longing?"

Jacob's face betrayed nothing. He looked long at Rachel, and she returned his gaze. "Give them your blessing, husband," Rachel said. "Take the wagons laden with silver and linen and give Hamor the welcome due a king. You are the master here. There is no need to wait."

But Jacob stiffened at Rachel's insistence. "When my sons return from their travels, I will decide."

Hamor could not recall ever being treated so badly. Even so, he was well disposed toward Jacob. "A good ally, I think," he told Shalem the next day. "But an enemy to avoid. He is a proud man," Hamor said. "He does not like to lose control of his family's fate. Odd that he should not yet know how children stop serving their parents once they are grown. Even daughters."

But Shalem pressed his father to return as soon as possible. "I love the girl," he said.

Hamor grinned. "Fear not. The girl is yours. No father would want her back as she is now. Go back to your wife, and let me worry about the father."

Another week passed, and my husband and I grew to love each other in subtler ways, with caresses and endearments. My feet did not touch ground. My face ached from smiling.

And then I received a special wedding gift: Bilhah came to see me. My aunt appeared at the palace gate asking for Dinah, wife of Shalem. She was taken first to Re-nefer, who plied her with questions about Jacob's hesitancy over her husband's offer. The queen asked about Leah and Rachel as well, and told Bilhah not to leave the palace without gifts for her daughter-in-law's family. And then Re-nefer herself brought my aunt to me.

My hug lifted my little aunt off the ground, and I covered her dark face with a dozen kisses. "You are glowing," she said, when she stood back, holding my hands in hers. "You are happy." She smiled. "It is wonderful that you should find such happiness. I will tell Leah and she will be reconciled."

"Is my mother angry?" I asked, bewildered.

"Leah believes Rachel sold you into the hands of evil. She is like your father in her distrust of the city, and she is not pleased that you will make your bed within walls. Mostly, I think, she misses you. But I will tell her of the light in your eyes, of the smile on your lips, and of your womanly bearing now that you are a wife.

"He is good to you, yes?" Bilhah asked, giving me the chance to praise my Shalem. I found myself bursting to tell someone the details of my happiness, and I spilled everything into Bilhah's willing ear. She clapped her hands to hear me speak like a bride. "Oh, to love and be loved like this," she sighed.

Bilhah ate with me and peeked at Shalem. She agreed that he was beautiful but refused to meet him. "I cannot speak to him before my husband does," she demurred. "But I have seen enough to bring back a good report of our daughter."

In the morning, she embraced me and left with Reuben, who had brought her. She carried the word of my happiness into my father's tents, but her voice was drowned out by the shouts of my brothers, who called me harlot. And Jacob did nothing to stop their foul mouths.

Simon and Levi had returned to our father after several days, defeated in a secret purpose. They had been in Ashkelon seeking trade not merely for the family's goats and sheep, wool, and oil, but to speak with slave traders, whose business could yield far greater wealth than any hard-earned harvest of the earth. Simon and Levi wanted wealth and the power it would bring them, but they had no hope of inheriting those from Jacob. It was clear that Reuben would get their father's birthright and the blessing would go to Joseph, so they were determined to carve out their own glory, however they could.

But Levi and Simon discovered that the slavers wanted nothing but children. Business was bad. Too many traders had weakened the market, and now they were assured of a good price only for healthy youngsters. My brothers could get nothing at all in trade for the two old serving women they had from their wives' dowries. They returned home thwarted and bitter.

When they heard that Hamor had offered my father a

king's bride-price for me, they raised their voices against the marriage, sensing that their own positions would be diminished by such an alliance. Jacob's house would be swallowed up in the dynasties of Shechem, and while Reuben might expect to become a prince, they and their sons would remain shepherds, poor cousins, nobodies. "We will be lower than Esau," they muttered to each other and to the brothers over whom they still held sway: Zebulun, Issachar, and Naphtali, of Leah's womb, and Zilpah's Gad and Asher.

When Jacob called all his sons to his tent to consider Hamor's offer, Simon raised his fist and cried, "Revenge! My sister has been ravaged by an Egyptian dog!"

Reuben spoke on behalf of Shalem. "Our sister did not cry out," he said, "nor does the prince cast her aside."

Judah agreed. "The size of the bride-price is a compliment to our sister, to our father, and to all the house of Jacob. We will become princes ourselves. We would be fools not to take the gifts that the gods give us. What kind of idiot mistakes a blessing for a curse?"

But Levi ripped his clothing as though mourning my death, and Simon warned, "This is a trap for the sons of Jacob. If we permit this marriage, the fleshpots of the city will consume my sons and my brothers' sons. This marriage displeases the god of our father," he said, challenging Jacob to disagree.

Their voices grew loud and my brothers glared at one another across the lamps, but Jacob did not let his own thoughts be known. "The uncircumcised dog rapes my sister every day," Simon thundered. "Am I to permit this desecration of our only sister, my own mother's daughter?"

At this, Joseph pulled a skeptical face and half-whispered

to Reuben, "If my brother is so concerned about the shape of our brother-in-law's penis, let our father demand his foreskin for a bride-price. Indeed, let all the men of Shechem become like us. Let them pile up their membranes as high as my father's tent pole, so that their sons and ours will piss the same, and rut the same, and none will be able to tell us apart. And thus will the tribe of Jacob grow not merely in generations to come, but even tomorrow."

Jacob seized upon Joseph's words, which had been spoken only in mockery of the brothers who had tortured him since infancy. But Jacob did not hear the edge in his son's words. He said, "Abram took up the knife for those of his household who were not of his covenant. If the men of Shechem agree to this, none could say that our daughter was injured. If the men of the city make such sacrifice to the god of my fathers, we shall be remembered as makers of souls, as gatherers of men. Like the stars in the heavens, as it was told to our father Abram. Like the sands of the sea, was it foretold by my mother Rebecca. And now I will make it come to pass. I will do what Joseph says, for he has my heart." Jacob spoke with such passion that there was no use in further speech.

Levi's face twisted in anger at Jacob's decision, but Simon placed a hand on his brother's arm and pulled him away into the night, far from the light of lamps and the ears of their brothers.

When Hamor journeyed to Jacob's tent the second time, Shalem accompanied him. Determined not to return to the city without my father's blessing, he brought two donkeys laden with still more gifts. My beloved was confident as he left, but when he reached my father's tent, the king's party was again met with crossed arms, and not so much as a ladle of water was offered before the men began discussing terms.

My father spoke first, and without ceremony. "You come for our daughter," he said. "We will agree to the marriage, but I doubt if our terms will suit you, for they are severe."

Hamor replied, his earlier warmth for the man blasted by the insulting lack of hospitality. "My son loves the girl," the king said. "He will do anything for her, and I will do what my son wishes. Name your terms, Jacob. Shechem will fulfill them so that your children and my children will bring forth new generations upon the land."

But when Jacob named the price for his daughter, Hamor paled. "What form of barbarity is this?" he asked. "Who do you think you are, shepherd, to demand the blood of my son's manhood, and mine, and that of my kinsmen and subjects? You are mad from too much sun, too many years in the wilderness. Do you want the girl back, such as she is? You must think very little of this daughter to make such sport of her future."

But Shalem stepped forward and put his hand on his father's arm. "I agree to the demands," he said to Jacob's face. "Here and now, if you like. I will honor the custom of my wife's family, and I will order my slaves and their sons to follow me. I know my father speaks out of fear for me and in loyalty to his men, who would suffer. But for me, there is no question. I hear and obey."

Hamor would have argued against his son's offer, and Levi and Simon were poised to spit in his face. The air smelled like lightning, and daggers might have been drawn had Bilhah not appeared, with water and wine. Women with bread and oil followed, and Jacob nodded for them to serve. They ate a few mouthfuls in silence.

The terms were agreed to that evening. Jacob accepted four laden donkeys for a bride-price. Shalem and Hamor would go under the knife in three days, as would the men of Shechem, noble and slave alike. All of the healthy men found within the walls of the city on that same morning would also accept the mark of Jacob upon them, and Hamor promised that every son born within the city from that time forth would be circumcised on the eighth day, as was the custom among the sons of Abram. Hamor also pledged that the god of Jacob would be worshiped in his temple, and the king went so far as to call him Elohim, the one god of the many gods.

My father made me a handsome dowry. Eighteen sheep and eighteen goats, all of my clothing and jewelry, my spindle and grindstone, ten jars of new oil and six great bolts of wool. Jacob agreed to permit marriages between his children and those of Shechem, from that time forth.

Hamor put his hand under Jacob's thigh and Jacob touched the king as well, and my betrothal was sealed without a smile or satisfaction.

That same night, Shalem slipped away from his father's tent and back into our bed with the news. "You are a married woman now and not merely a ruined girl," he whispered, waking me before the first light of morning.

I kissed him and pushed him away. "Well then, now that I am wed and you may not put me aside, I may tell you that my head aches and I cannot receive my lord at this moment," I said, gathering my robe about my shoulders,

and feigning a great yawn even as I slipped my hand
between my husband's legs. "You know, my lord, that
women only submit to the caresses of their husbands—they
do not enjoy the rough use of their bodies."

Shalem laughed and pulled me down on the bed, and we
made love with great tenderness that morning. It was a
reunion after what had been our longest parting since that
day he found me in the market and led me to his bed, which
we had made ours.

We slept late into the day, and only after we had eaten
did he tell me my father's demand. I grew cold and my
stomach turned. In my mind's eye, I saw my beloved in
agonies of pain, saw the knife cut too deep, the wound
fester, and Shalem dying in my arms. I burst into tears like
a little child.

Shalem made light of it all. "It is nothing," he said. "A
flesh wound. And I hear that afterward, my pleasure of you
will be even greater than it is now. So prepare yourself,
woman. I will be upon you night and day."

But I did not smile. I shivered with a cold that entered
my bones and would not leave.

Re-nefer tried to reassure me, too. She was not displeased
at the bargain her husband had struck. "In Egypt," she said,
"they take boys for circumcision when their voices change.
It is a merry enough time—they chase the boys and catch
them, and afterward, they are petted and fed on every sweet
and savory thing they ask for. Rest assured, they all survive.

"We will have my guard do the deed," she said. "Nehesi
has dispatched many a foreskin. I can care for the pain, and
you will help me, little midwife." She rattled on and on
about how easy it would be, and then whispered, with a

knowing leer, "Do you not find the male member more attractive without its hood?" But I found nothing amusing about Shalem's test, and I did not return my mother-in-law's smile.

The three days passed. I clung to my husband like a wild thing those nights, and tears ran down my face even as I reached greater pleasures than before. My husband licked the water from my cheeks and ran his salty tongue the length of my body. "I will tease you about this when our first son is born," he whispered, as I lay on his chest, still shaking with cold.

The appointed hour arrived. Shalem left me at dawn. I stayed in bed, pretending to sleep, watching him wash and dress through closed eyes. He leaned down to kiss me, but I did not turn my face up to meet his lips.

I lay there alone, counting my hatred. I hated my father for asking such a terrible price. I hated my husband and his father for agreeing to pay it. I hated my mother-in-law for smoothing the way. I hated myself most for being the cause of it all.

I lay on the bed, huddled beneath blankets, shivering with anger and fear and unrecognized foreboding, until he was brought back to me.

It was done in the king's antechamber. Shalem was first, and then his father, Hamor. Nehesi said that neither king nor prince cried out. Ashnan's little son followed, and wailed, but the little one did not suffer long, since he had a full breast to console him. The men of the household and the few poor souls who had not disappeared to the country-side outside the walls were not so lucky. They felt the knife keenly, and many screamed as though they were murdered.

Their cries pierced the air throughout the morning, but ceased by noon.

It turned into an unmercifully hot day. There was no breeze or cloud, and even within the thick walls of the palace the air was damp and heavy. The recovering men sweated through their clothing and soaked the beds where they slept.

Hamor, who uttered no sound when he was cut, fainted in pain, and when he woke put a knife between his teeth to keep from screaming. My Shalem suffered too, though not as badly. He was younger and the salves seemed to ease him, but for him too, the only complete remedy was sleep. I dosed him with a sleeping draft, and whenever he roused, he was thick-headed and weary, slack-jawed and dazed. I bathed my beloved's face as he slept his drugged sleep and washed his sweating back with the softest touch I could muster. I did my best not to weep so my face would be fresh when he awoke, but as the day wore on the tears came in spite of my efforts. By nightfall, I was exhausted, and I slept by my husband's side swathed in blankets against the icy winds of my fears, even as Shalem slept naked in the heat.

In the night, I woke once to feel Shalem caressing my cheek. When he saw my eyes open, he managed a wincing smile and said, "Soon this will be nothing but a dream and our embraces will be sweeter than ever." His eyes closed again, and I heard him snore for the first time. As I drifted into sleep, I thought how I would tease him about the noise he made in his sleep—like an old dog in the sun. To this day I am not sure that Shalem spoke those words to me, or if it was a dream to comfort me.

The rest I know to be true.

First, there was the sound of a woman screaming. Something terrible must have happened to that poor soul, I thought, trying to turn away from the keening, shrieking, shrilling cry, too dreadful for the real world, the noise of a nightmare.

The wild, terrified scream came from a great distance, but its distress was so insistent and disturbing that I could not push it aside, and sought to awaken from my heavy sleep and escape the cries. They grew more and more frightening until I realized that my eyes were open and that the tormented soul I pitied was not dreamed or even distant. The screams were my own screams, the unearthly sound was coming from my twisted mouth.

I was covered in blood. My arms were coated with the thick, warm blood that ran from Shalem's throat and coursed like a river down the bed and onto the floor. His blood coated my cheeks and stung my eyes and salted my lips. His blood soaked through the blankets and burned my breasts, streamed down my legs, coated my toes. I was drowning in my lover's blood. I was screaming loud enough to summon the dead, and yet no one seemed to hear. No guards burst through the door. No servants rushed in. It seemed that I was the last person alive in the world.

I heard no footsteps and had no warning before strong arms seized me, prying me loose from my beloved. They carried me off the bed trailing blood, screaming into the blackness of the night. It was Simon who lifted me and Levi who stopped up my mouth, and the two of them trussed me hand and foot like a sacrificial goat, loaded me on the back of a donkey, and packed me off to my father's tent before I could alarm any poor soul still left alive in the doomed city. My brothers' knives worked until the dawn revealed the abomination wrought by the sons of Jacob. They murdered every man they found alive.

But I knew nothing of that. I knew only that I wanted to die. Nothing but death could stop my horror. Nothing but death could give me peace from the vision of Shalem slashed, bleeding, dead in his startled sleep. Had someone not loosened the gag when I vomited, I would have had my wish. All the way back up the hillside to the tents of Jacob I screamed in silence. Oh gods. Oh heaven. Oh Mother. Why do I still live?

Chapter Eight

I WAS THE first they knew of it. My own mother saw me and shrieked at the sight of my bloodied body. She fell to the ground, keening over her murdered child, and the tents emptied to learn the cause of Leah's grief. But Bilhah unbound me and helped me to stand, while Leah stared—first horrified, then relieved, and finally thunderstruck. She reached out her hands toward me but my face stopped her.

I turned, intending to walk back to Shechem. But my mothers lifted me off my feet, and I was too weak to resist. They stripped off my blankets and robes, black and stiff with the blood of Shalem. They washed me and anointed me with oil and brushed my hair. They put food to my lips, but I would not eat. They laid me down on a blanket, but I did not sleep. For the rest of that day, no one dared speak to me, and I had nothing to say.

When night fell again, I listened to my brothers' return and heard the sound of their booty: weeping women, wailing children, bleating animals, carts creaking under the weight of stolen goods. Simon and Levi shouted hoarse orders. Jacob's voice was nowhere to be heard.

I should have been defeated by grief. I should have been exhausted past seeing. But hatred had stiffened my spine. The journey up the mountain, bound like a sacrifice, had jolted me into a rage that fed upon itself as I lay on the blanket, rigid and alert. The sound of my brothers' voices lifted me off of my bed and I walked out to face them.

Fire shot from my eyes. I might have burned them all to a cinder with a word, a breath, a glance. "Jacob," I cried with the voice of a wounded animal. "Jacob," I howled, summoning him by name, as though I were the father and he the wayward child.

Jacob emerged from his tent, trembling. Later he claimed that he had no knowledge of what had been done in his name. He blamed Simon and Levi and turned his back on them. But I saw full understanding in his clouded eyes as he stood before me. I saw his guilt before he had time to deny it.

"Jacob, your sons have done murder," I said, in a voice I did not recognize as my own. "You have lied and connived, and your sons have murdered righteous men, striking them down in weakness of your own invention. You have despoiled the bodies of the dead and plundered their burying places, so their shadows will haunt you forever. You and your sons have raised up a generation of widows and orphans who will never forgive you.

"Jacob," I said, in a voice that echoed like thunder, "Jacob," I hissed, in the voice of the serpent who sheds life and still lives, "Jacob," I howled, and the moon vanished.

"Jacob shall never know peace again. He will lose what he treasures and repudiate those he should embrace. He will never again find rest, and his prayers will not find the favor of his father's god.

"Jacob knows my words are true. Look at me, for I wear the blood of the righteous men of Shechem. Their blood stains your hands and your head, and you will never be clean again.

"You are unclean and you are cursed," I said, spitting into the face of the man who had been my father. Then I turned my back upon him, and he was dead to me.

I cursed them all. With the smell of my husband's blood still in my nostrils, I named them each and called forth the power of every god and every goddess, every demon and every torment, to destroy and devour them: the sons of my mother Leah, and the son of my mother Rachel, and the sons of my mother Zilpah, and the son of my mother Bilhah. The blood of Shalem was embedded beneath my fingernails, and there was no pity in my heart for any of them.

"The sons of Jacob are vipers," I said to my cowering brothers. "They are putrid as the worms that feed on carrion. The sons of Jacob will each suffer in his turn, and turn the suffering upon their father."

The silence was absolute and solid as a wall when I turned away from them. Barefoot, wearing nothing but a shift, I walked away from my brothers and my father and everything that had been home. I walked away from love as well, never again to see my reflection in my mothers' eyes. But I could not live among them.

I walked into a moonless night, bloodying my feet and battering my knees on the path to the valley, but never stopped until I arrived at the gates of Shechem. I kept a vision before me.

I would bury my husband and be buried with him. I would find his body and wrap him in linen, take the knife that had stolen his life and open my wrists with it so we could sleep together in the dust. We would pass eternity in the quiet, sad, grey world of the dead, eating dust, looking through eyes made of dust upon the false world of men.

I had no other thought. I was alone and empty. I was a grave looking to be filled with the peace of death. I walked until I found myself before the great gate of Shechem, on my knees, unable to move.

If Reuben had found me and carried me back, my life would have ended. I might have walked and wept for many years more, half mad, finishing my days in the doorway of a lesser brother's third wife. But my life would have been finished.

If Reuben had found me, Simon and Levi would surely have killed my baby, leaving it out in the night for the jackals to tear apart. They might have sold me into slavery along with Joseph, ripping my tongue out first, to stop me from cursing their eyes, skin, bones, scrotums. I would never be appeased by their pain and suffering, no matter how ghastly.

Nor would I have been mollified when Jacob cowered and took a new name, Isra'El, so that the people would not remember him as the butcher of Shechem. He fled from the name Jacob, which became another word for "liar," so that "You serve the god of Jacob" was one of the worst insults one man could hurl at another in that land for many generations. Had I been there to see it, I might have smiled when his gift with animals deserted him and even his dogs ran from his side. He deserved no less than the agony of learning that Joseph had been torn by wild beasts.

Had Reuben found me at the gates of Shechem, I would have been there to give Rachel the burial she deserved. Rachel died on the highway, where Jacob had gone to flee the wrath of the valley, which set out to avenge the destruction of Hamor and the peace of Shechem. Rachel perished in agony, giving birth to Jacob's last son. "Son of woe," she named the little boy who cost her a river of black blood. But the name Rachel chose for her son was too much of an accusation, so Jacob defied the wish of his dying wife and pretended that Ben-Oni was Benjamin.

Jacob's fear chased him away from Rachel's poor drained body, which he buried hastily and without ceremony at the side of the road, with nothing but a few pebbles to remember the great love of his life. Perhaps I would have stayed there at Rachel's grave with Inna, who planted herself in that spot and gathered beautiful stones to make an altar to the memory of her only daughter. Inna taught the women of the valley to speak the name of Rachel and tie red cords around her pillar, promising that, in return, their wombs would bear only living fruit, and ensuring that my aunt's name would always live in the mouths of women.

If Reuben had found me, I would have watched my curse wrap itself around his neck, unleashing a lifetime of unspent passion and unspoken declarations of love for Bilhah and of hers for him. When that dam broke, they went breathlessly into each other's arms, embracing in the fields, under the stars, and even inside Bilhah's own tent. They were the truest lovers, the very image of the Queen of the Sea and her Lord-Brother, made for each other yet doomed for it.

When Jacob came upon them, he disinherited the most deserving of his sons and sent him to a distant pasture, where he could not protect Joseph. Jacob struck Bilhah across the face, breaking her teeth. After that, she began to disappear. The sweet one, the little mother, became smaller and thinner, more silent, more watchful. She did not cook anymore but only spun, and her string was finer than any woman had ever spun, as fine as a spider's web.

Then one day, she was gone. Her clothes lay upon her blanket and her few rings were found where her hands might have lain. No footprints led into the distance. She vanished, and Jacob never spoke her name again.

Zilpah died of fever the night that Jacob smashed the last of Rachel's household gods under a sacred tree. He had come across the little frog goddess—the one that had unlocked the wombs of generations of women—and he took an ax to the ancient idol. He urinated on the crushed stone, cursing it as the cause of all his misfortune. Seeing this, Zilpah ripped at her hair and screamed into the sky. She begged for death and spit upon the memory of the mother who left her. She lay on the ground and put handfuls of dirt into her mouth. Three men were needed to tie her down to keep her from doing herself harm. It was an awful death, and as they prepared her for the grave, her body broke into pieces like a brittle old clay lamp.

I am glad I did not see that. I am grateful I was not there as Leah lost the use of her hands and then her arms, nor to see her on the morning she awoke in her own filth, unable to stand. She would have begged me, as she begged her unfeeling daughters-in-law, to give her poison, and I would have done it. I would have taken pity and cooked the deadly drink and killed her and buried her. Better that than to die mortified.

Had Reuben carried me back to the tents of the men who had turned me into the instrument of Shalem's death, I would have done murder in my heart every day. I would have tasted bile and bitterness in my dreams. I would have been a blot upon the earth.

But the gods had other plans for me. Reuben came too late. The sun shone above the walls of the city when he arrived at the eastern gate, and by then other arms had carried me away.

PART THREE

Egypt

Chapter One

I LAY SENSELESS in the arms of Nehesi, Re-nefer's steward and guard. He carried me to the palace, which swarmed with flies drawn to the blood of fathers and sons. My demon brothers had lifted their knives even against Ashnan's baby, and his poor mother bled to death defending him—her arm severed trying to block the ax's blade.

Of all the men in that house, only Nehesi survived. When the screams began, he ran to the king's chambers in time to protect Re-nefer against Levi and one of his men. The queen had lifted a knife against Levi when Nehesi arrived. He wounded my brother in the thigh and killed his henchman outright. He wrested the blade from the queen to keep her from burying it in her own heart.

Nehesi brought me to Re-nefer, who sat in the dirt of the courtyard, her head against the wall, dust in her hair, fingernails caked with blood. It was years before I understood why she did not leave me to die, why the murder of her loved ones did not fill her with rage against me, who caused it all. But Re-nefer blamed only herself for the death of her husband and son, because she had wished for our marriage and made sacrifices to ensure our union. She had sent Shalem to seek me in the market and arranged for us to fall into each other's arms unhindered. She took the guilt upon herself and never put it aside.

The other reason for Re-nefer's compassion toward me was even stronger than remorse. She had hope of a grandchild—someone to build her tomb and redeem the waste of her life, someone to live for. Which is why, in the moments before she fled Canaan, Re-nefer roused herself and sent Nehesi out into the wailing town to seek me.

Her servant obeyed in silence, but with dread. He knew the queen better than anyone—better than her serving women, better than her husband surely. Nehesi had come to Shechem with Re-nefer when she first arrived, a frightened young bride. And when he found me, he wondered whether he should add to his mistress's grief by carrying still more sorrow into her presence. I lay in his arms like a corpse, and when I did stir, it was to scream and scratch at my throat until I drew blood. They had to tie my hands and bind my mouth so that we could slip out of the city undetected in the dark of that night.

Re-nefer and Nehesi unearthed jars filled with gold and silver and stole away, with me, to the port at Joppa, where they hired a Minoan boat for the journey to Egypt. During the journey, there was a terrible storm that tore the sails and nearly overturned the ship. The sailors who heard me screaming and sobbing thought I was possessed by a demon who roiled the waters against them. Only Nehesi's sword kept them from laying hands on me and tossing me into the waves.

I knew none of this as I lay in the darkness, swaddled,

sweating, trying to follow my husband. Perhaps I was too young to die of grief, or maybe I was too well cared for to perish in sorrow. Re-nefer never left me. She kept my lips moist and spoke to me in the soothing, all-forgiving tone that mothers take with fretful babies.

She found cause to hope. A new moon arrived while I lay in my own darkness and no blood stained the blankets beneath my legs. My belly was soft and my breasts burned and my breath smelled of barley. After a few days, my sleep became less fevered. I gulped at the broths that Re-nefer fed me and squeezed her fingers in mute gratitude.

On the day of our landing, my mother-in-law came to me, placed her fingers firmly on my lips, and spoke with an urgency that had nothing to do with my health. "We return to the land of my mother and father," she said. "Hear what I say and obey.

"I will call you daughter in front of my brother and his wife," she said. "I will tell them that you served in my household and that my son took you, a virgin, with my consent. I will say that you helped me to escape from the barbarians. You will become my daughter-in-law, and I will be your mistress. You will bear your son on my knees, and he will be a prince of Egypt."

Her eyes found mine and demanded understanding. She was kind and I loved her, and yet something seemed wrong. I could not name my fear as she spoke. Later I realized that my new mother had not named her son, my husband, saying nothing of his murder, nor of my brothers and their deception. We never wept or mourned over Shalem, nor did she tell me where my beloved was buried. The horror was to remain unspoken, my grief sealed behind my lips. We never again spoke of our shared history, and I was bound to the emptiness of the story she told.

When I set foot in Egypt, I was pregnant and widowed. I wore the white linen of an Egyptian, and although I was no longer a maiden, I went with uncovered head like the other women of the land. I carried a small basket for Re-nefer, but I brought nothing of my own. I had not so much as a scrap of wool woven by my own mothers, nor even the consolation of memory.

There were many wonders to see on the journey to the great city of the south which was home to Re-nefer's brother. We passed cities and pyramids, birds and hunters, palms and flowers, sandy wastes and cliffs, but I saw nothing of these. My eyes stayed mostly upon the river itself, and I stared into the water, trailing a hand into the darkness, which was, by turn, brown, green, black, gray, and once, as we passed a tannery, the color of blood.

That night, I woke clutching my neck, drowning in blood, screaming for Shalem, for help, for my mother, in a nightmare that would visit me again and again. First, I felt the weight of Shalem against my back, a wonderful heaviness that comforted me completely. But then came an unnatural heat onto my chest and hands and then I discovered my mouth was full of Shalem's blood, my nose clogged with the dusty smell of life ebbing out of him. My eyes were thick with blood and I struggled to open them. I screamed without drawing breath, though I heard no sound. Still I kept screaming, in hope that my heart and stomach would rise out of me in the scream and I could die, too.

On the fourth night of this dream, just as the blood began to swallow me and my mouth opened to seek death, I was shocked to my senses by searing pain that left me gasping. I sat up to find Nehesi above me, the flat edge of his broad sword laid against the soles of my feet, where he had struck me. "No more of this," he hissed. "Re-nefer cannot bear it."

He left me, my hair on end, struggling to catch my breath. And from that night, I woke myself as soon as I felt warmth oozing onto my breasts. Panting and sweating, I lay on my back and tried not to fall asleep again. I came to dread the sunset the way some men dread death.

By day, the sun bleached away my fears. In the morning, before the heat bore down, Re-nefer sat with me and Nehesi and recounted cheerful stories from her childhood. We saw a duck, and she recalled hunting expeditions with her father and brothers, the eldest of whom was to be our refuge. As a little girl she had been entrusted with the throwing sticks, handing them to the hunters, anticipating their needs. When we passed a great house, Re-nefer described her father's home in Memphis, and the many gardens and pools in its great courtyard. Her father had been a scribe for the priests of Re, and life had been pleasant for his family.

Re-nefer recalled every servant and slave who had waited upon her as a child. She spoke of her own mother, Nebettany, whom she remembered as lovely but distant—always at her kohl pots, happiest when the servants poured pot after pot of scented water over her back in her beautiful bath. But Nebettany died in childbirth when Re-nefer still wore the forelock of a little girl.

My mother-in-law retraced her days with charming tales and stories from her infancy until the very week that she left Egypt to be married. The preparations were elaborate, and a great dowry was assembled. Re-nefer could recall the very quantities of linen in her chests, the jewels on her fingers and neck, the bargemen who carried her up to the sea.

I leaned forward, hoping to learn some detail about life in Shechem, to hear the story of Shalem's birth or a tale from his boyhood. But she stopped just at the point she arrived in her husband's palace; a blank stare replaced her gaiety. She said nothing of Canaan, nor of her husband, nor of the babies she bore him. She did not speak the name of Hamor even once, and it was as though Shalem had never been born, nor loved me, nor bled to death in my arms.

Re-nefer's silence throbbed with pain, but when I reached out to touch her hand, she resumed a cheerful smile and turned away to chatter about the beauty of palm trees or her brother's great position as chief scribe and overseer to the priests of Re. I returned my gaze to the water and kept my eyes there until we arrived at Thebes.

The great city was dazzling in the setting sun. To the west, purple cliffs held a green valley dotted with brightly painted temples, hung with pennants of green and gold. On the east bank, there were great houses as well as temples and whitewashed warrens of smaller buildings, all glowing shades of rose and gold as the sun began its retreat behind the western bluffs. I saw white tents on the rooftops, and wondered if a separate race of people lived above the city-dwellers.

The streets that led away from the river were noisy and dusty, and we moved through them quickly, seeking our destination before nightfall. The scent of lotus grew stronger as the light faded. Nehesi asked a passerby if he knew the way to the home of the scribe Nakht-re. The man pointed toward a large building that sat beside one of the grand temples of the eastern bank.

A naked little girl opened the large, burnished door and blinked at the three strangers before her. Re-nefer demanded an audience with Nakht-re, her brother. But the child only stared. She saw an Egyptian lady who wore a dusty robe and no makeup or jewelry, a large black guard with a dagger at his waist but no shoes on his feet, and a foreigner in an ill-fitting dress who kept her head so low she might be hiding a harelip.

When the servant did not budge after Re-nefer repeated her request, Nehesi pushed the door open and walked through the vestibule into a great hall. The master of the house was concluding the business of the day, scrolls in his lap and assistants at his feet. He stared at Nehesi, startled and uncomprehending, but when he saw Re-nefer, Nakht-re leaped to his feet, scattering papers as he rushed to embrace her.

As his arms encircled her, Re-nefer began to weep—not tears of relief and happiness from a woman glad to be reunited with her family, but the raw sobs of a mother whose child had been murdered in his bed. Re-nefer howled in her bewildered brother's arms. She dropped to her knees and keened, giving voice to a broken heart.

The terrible sound brought all of Nakht-re's household into the room: cooks and gardeners, bakers and children, and the lady of the house. Nakht-re gathered his sister up and put her on his own chair, where she was fanned and given water. All eyes were fixed on Re-nefer, who took her brother's hands in hers and told him the bare details of her tale, as she had rehearsed it to me. She said that her home had been overrun by barbarians, her possessions stolen, her family butchered, her whole life pillaged. She spoke of her escape and the storm at sea. When Nakht-re asked about her husband, she replied, "Dead. And my son!" and collapsed in tears once more. At this, the women of the house commenced a high-pitched wail of mourning that crept up the flesh of my neck, like a curse.

Again Re-nefer was embraced by her brother, and again she composed herself. "Nehesi is my savior," she said, directing all eyes to where he stood beside me. "I should have died but for his strong arm and his wisdom and comfort. He brought me out of Canaan, with this girl who was my son's consort and who carries my grandson in her womb." All eyes turned to my belly now, and my hands moved, of their own accord, to the place where the baby grew.

This was a dumb show for me. I knew only a handful of words in their language, and these I had learned from my beloved in bed. I knew the words for the parts of the body, for sunset and sunrise, for bread and wine and water. For love.

But Egyptians are expressive people who speak with their hands and show their teeth when they talk, and I followed the story well enough. I watched Re-nefer's face and learned that her father had died, that her younger brother was far away, that a favorite friend—or perhaps a sister—was dead in childbirth, that Nakht-re was as successful as their father had been.

I stood by the door, safely forgotten, until I collapsed. I

awoke some time later in the dark, on a sweet-smelling pallet beside a bed where Re-nefer slept softly. The rest of the household seemed asleep as well. The silence was so deep, if I had not walked through the noisy streets of a city that very afternoon, I would have thought myself in the middle of a deserted meadow or on top of a mountain.

A bird broke the hush, and I listened, trying to find the melody in its wild song. Had I ever heard a bird sing at night? I could not remember. For a moment, I forgot everything but the sound of a bird singing to a half-moon, and I nearly smiled.

My pleasure ended the next moment, when I felt a light touch on my fingers. I jumped to my feet but, remembering Nehesi's sword on my feet, stifled my scream. A small shadow moved in a circle around me. The bird still trilled, but now it seemed to mock the joy I had felt a moment earlier.

I watched in horror as the shadow leaped onto Re-nefer's bed and then seemed to disappear. My eyes ached from searching in the dark, and I found myself weeping over the death of my good mistress, for surely the creature had killed her. I wrung my hands and pitied myself, alone and abandoned in a far land. A sob escaped me, and Re-nefer stirred.

"What is it, child?" she murmured, half asleep.

"Danger," I hiccuped.

She sat upright, and the shadow leaped down toward me. I covered my head and shrieked.

Re-nefer laughed softly. "A cat," she explained. "It is only the cat. Bastet rules the heart of the house here. Sleep now," she sighed, and turned back to her pillow.

I lay down, but my eyes did not close again that night.

Before long, light began to filter through the windows which lined the walls up near the ceiling. As sunshine filled the room, I studied the whitewashed walls, and watched a spider weave a web in the corner. I looked at unfamiliar teraphim tucked into niches around the walls, and reached out to touch the handsome leg of my mistress's bed, carved in the likeness of a giant beast's foot. I inhaled the aroma of my bed—hay sweetened with the scent of an unfamiliar flower. The room seemed crowded with elaborate baskets and plaited mats. A collection of flacons sat on an inlaid box, beside a large stack of folded cloths, which I later learned were bath towels. Every surface was dyed or painted in bright colors.

I had no place among all of these wonderful things, and yet, this was my only home.

I was barely aware of the child within me those first few weeks. My body looked no different, and I was so occupied with my new surroundings that I didn't notice the moon's progress, which Egyptian women marked with little ceremony and no separation. I stayed beside Re-nefer, who spent her first days resting in the garden, and translated when I didn't comprehend the few words addressed to me.

I was not ill-treated. Everyone in the household of Nakht-re was kind, even his wife, Herya, who suddenly had to share her home with a long-forgotten sister and her two alien servants. Nehesi knew how to make himself useful, and Nakht-re soon sent him to carry messages between the house and the temple and the tombs being built in the western valley.

I was not quite a servant and not quite a niece, a foreigner without language or obvious skills. The lady of the house patted me when she saw me, rather like a cat, but turned away before there was any need of speech. The servants did not know what to make of me either. They showed me how to spin linen so that I might help with the work of the house, but my hands were slow to learn, and since I could not gossip with them in the kitchen, I was left alone.

My main occupation was attending Re-nefer, but she preferred solitude, so I found other tasks to occupy my days. I was drawn especially to the stairways of the house and took any excuse to walk up and down, watching how the room changed with every step. I assumed the task of sweeping them in the evening and washing them in the morning, and took a mindless pride in their maintenance.

Whenever I could, I climbed all the way to the roof, where a northern breeze from the river might lift the tent hung for shade. Much of the household slept up there on hot nights, though I never joined them, fearing to bring my nightmare among others.

From the rooftop, I stared at the sun reflecting on the river and at the grace of the sailing boats below. I remembered the first great water I had seen as a girl, when my family had crossed from Haran to the south. I thought of the river where Joseph and I had been charged by an unseen power and saved by our mothers' love. When I remembered Shalem's promise to teach me how to swim, my throat closed in agony. But I fixed my eyes wide, as I had at Mamre, and stared at the horizon to keep from sobbing and to keep from walking off the roof.

The days passed in a blur of new ways and sights, but the

nights were always the same. I struggled against the dreams that left me drenched in sweat, soaking the pallet as Shalem's blood had soaked our bed, gasping for air and afraid to make a sound. In the morning, my eyes ached and my head throbbed. Re-nefer fretted over me and consulted with her sister-in-law. They ordered me to rest in the afternoon. They tied a red cord around my waist. They made me drink goat's milk mixed with a yellow potion that stained my tongue.

As my belly began to swell, the women of the house doted on me. It had been a long time since there had been a baby in Nakht-re's family, and they were hungry for a little one. I was fed amazing foods, as exotic to me as the flowers of the perpetually blooming garden behind the house. I ate melons with orange flesh and melons with pink flesh, and there were always dates in abundance. On the many feast days dedicated to gods or family holidays, there was goose made with garlic or fish in honey sauce.

But best of all were the cucumbers, the most delicious food I could imagine, green and sweet. Even in the heat of the sun, a cucumber kissed the tongue with the cool of the moon. I could eat them endlessly and never get full or sick. My mother would love this fruit, I thought the first time I bit into its watery heart. It was my first thought of Leah in more than a month. My mother did not know I was pregnant. My aunts did not even know that I was alive. I shuddered with loneliness.

Herya saw my shoulders tremble and, taking me by the hand, walked me to the vestibule at the front door. We stopped at the wall niche, and she gestured for me to remove the little goddess. It was a water horse standing on her hind legs, with an enormous belly and a huge, smiling mouth. "Taweret," she said, touching the clay figure and then moving her hand to my belly. I frowned. She squatted down, like a woman in labor, and placed the figure between her legs, and in pantomime, showed me that Taweret would ensure an easy labor.

The lady of the house thought I was afraid of giving birth. I nodded and smiled. She said, "Boy," and patted my belly again.

I nodded. I knew I was carrying a son. "Boy," I said, in the language of the house.

Herya closed my hands around the statue, indicating that I should keep it, and kissed my cheeks. For a moment the hoarse rattle of Inna's laughter sounded so loud in my ears I thought the old midwife was in the room with me chortling over her prophecy that Taweret would take me for her own.

In the next week, I felt a flutter like a bird's wing beneath my heart. I was thunderstruck at my love for the life I carried. I began to whisper to my unborn son as I lay on my pallet, and hummed the songs of my childhood to him as I swept and spun. I thought of my baby as I combed my hair and as I ate, morning and evening.

The bloody dreams about Shalem were replaced by a joyful dream of his son, whom I called Bar-Shalem. In the dream, my son was not a baby but a tiny copy of his father, nestled in my arms, telling me stories about his childhood in the palace, about the wonders of the river, about life on the other side of this life. In this dream, my beloved protected me and fought off a hungry crocodile that had come for me and the boy.

I hated to wake up and took to sleeping later and later only to remain inside this dream. Re-nefer permitted me my bed and everything else. Before we slept, she and I would watch my belly roll and shake. "He is strong," she rejoiced.

"May he be strong," I prayed.

I was not prepared when my time came. Confident of everything I had learned from Rachel and Inna, I had no concerns about giving birth. I had witnessed the arrival of many healthy babies and the courage of many capable mothers. I imagined I had nothing to fear.

When the first real pain grabbed my belly and robbed me of breath, I remembered the women who had fainted, the women who had screamed and wept and begged to die. I remembered a woman who died with her eyes wide open in terror, and a woman who died in a torrent of blood, her eyes sunken in exhaustion.

A sob broke from my mouth when my water broke and washed down my legs. "Mother," I cried, feeling the absence of four beloved faces, four pairs of tender hands. How far away they were. How alone I was. How I longed to hear their voices speaking comfort in my own tongue.

Why had no one told me that my body would become a battlefield, a sacrifice, a test? Why did I not know that birth is the pinnacle where women discover the courage to become mothers? But of course, there is no way to tell this or to hear it. Until you are the woman on the bricks, you have no idea how death stands in the corner, ready to play his part. Until you are the woman on the bricks, you do not know the power that rises from other women—even strangers speaking an unknown tongue, invoking the names of unfamiliar goddesses.

Re-nefer stood behind me, my weight on her knees, praising my courage. Herya, the lady of the house, held my right arm, muttering prayers to Taweret, Isis, and Bes, the ugly dwarf god who loved babies. The cook, on my left side, waved a bent stick carved with birth scenes over my head to ease the pain. Crouching before me to catch the baby was a midwife named Meryt. She was unknown to me, but her hands were as sure and gentle as I imagine Inna's must have been. She blew into my face so that I could not hold my breath when the pains came, and even made me laugh a little and blow back at her.

The four women chatted over my head when the pangs subsided, and cooed encouragement when the pains returned. They put fruit juice in my mouth, and wiped me down with sweetly scented towels. Meryt massaged my legs. Re-nefer's eyes shone with tears.

I wept and I yelled. I gave up all hope and I prayed. I vomited and my knees buckled. But even though their brows furrowed in response to my pains, none of them appeared worried or anxious. So I fought on, reassured.

Then I began to push because there was nothing else I could do.

I pushed and I pushed until I thought I would faint. I pushed and still the baby did not come. Time passed. More pushing. No progress.

Meryt looked up at Re-nefer, and I saw them exchange a glance that I had seen pass between Rachel and Inna at moments such as this, when the ordinary passage of life into life became a struggle between life and death, and I felt the shadow in the corner lean toward me and my son.

"No," I screamed, first in my mother tongue. "No," I said, in the language of the women around me.

"Mother," I said to Re-nefer, "bring me a mirror so that I can see for myself." I was brought a mirror and a lamp that showed me the tautness of my own skin. "Reach in," I said to Meryt, remembering Inna's practice. "I fear he is turned away. Reach in and turn his face, his shoulder."

Meryt tried to do as I asked, but her hands were too large. My skin was too tight. My son was too big. "Bring a knife," I said, almost screaming. "He needs a bigger doorway."

Re-nefer translated, and Herya answered her in a grave whisper. "There is no surgeon in the house, daughter," Re-nefer explained to me, in turn. "We will send for one now, but..."

The words came to me from far away. All I wanted to do was to empty myself of this boulder, to expel the agony, and sleep, or even die. My body cried out to push, but when the shadow in the corner nodded approval, I refused to obey.

"You do it," I said to Meryt. "Take a knife and open the way for him. Please," I begged, and she looked at me in uncomprehending pity.

"A knife! Mother!" I screamed, desperate. "Rachel, where are you? Inna, what shall I do?"

Re-nefer called out, and a knife was brought. Meryt took it fearfully. As I screamed and struggled to keep from pushing, she put the blade up to my skin and opened the door, front to back, as I had seen it done before. She reached up to move the baby's shoulder. The pain was blinding, as though I had sat upon the sun itself. In an instant, the baby was out. But instead of a joyful shout, he was greeted by silence; the cord was at his neck, his lips were blue.

Meryt hurried. She cut the cord from his throat and took up her reeds, sucking death from his mouth, blowing life into his nostrils. I was screaming, sobbing, shaking. Herya held me as we all watched the midwife work.

The shadowy dog's head of death moved forward, but then the baby coughed and with an angry cry banished all doubts. The dark corner brightened. Death does not linger where he is defeated. The voices of four women echoed around me, chattering, laughing, loud. I fell back on the pallet, and knew nothing more.

I woke in the darkness. A single lamp flickered beside me. The floor had been washed, and even my hair smelled clean. The girl set to watch me saw my eyes open and ran to fetch Meryt, who carried a linen bundle. "Your son," she said.

"My son," I answered, dumbfounded, taking him in my arms.

Just as there is no warning for childbirth, there is no preparation for the sight of a first child. I studied his face, fingers, the folds in his boneless little legs, the whorls of his ears, the tiny nipples on his chest. I held my breath as he sighed, laughed when he yawned, wondered at his grasp on my thumb. I could not get my fill of looking.

There should be a song for women to sing at this moment, or a prayer to recite. But perhaps there is none because there are no words strong enough to name that moment. Like every mother since the first mother, I was overcome and bereft, exalted and ravaged. I had crossed over from girlhood. I beheld myself as an infant in my mother's arms, and caught a glimpse of my own death. I wept without knowing whether I rejoiced or mourned. My mothers and their mothers were with me as I held my baby.

"Bar-Shalem," I whispered. He took my breast and fed in his sleep. "Lucky one," I said, overcome. "Two pleasures at once."

We both slept under the watchful eye of the Egyptian midwife, whom I knew I would love forever even if I never saw her face again. In my dream that night, Rachel handed me a pair of golden bricks and Inna presented me with a silver reed. I accepted their gifts solemnly, proudly, with Meryt by my side.

When I woke up, my son was gone. Frightened, I tried to stand, but the pain kept me pinned to my bed. I cried out, and Meryt arrived with soft packing and unguents for my wounds. "My son," I said, in her language.

She looked at me tenderly and replied, "The baby is with his mother." I thought I misunderstood her. Perhaps I had not used the right words. I asked again, speaking slowly, but she touched me with pity and shook her head, no. "The baby is with his mother, the lady."

Still confused, I cried out, "Re-nefer. Re-nefer. They have taken my baby boy. Mother, help me."

She came, carrying the baby, who was swaddled in a fine white linen blanket, bordered in gold thread. "My child," said Re-nefer, standing above me, "you did well. Indeed, you were magnificent, and all the women of Thebes will know of your courage. As for me, I will be forever grateful.

The son you bore on my knees will be a prince of Egypt. He will be raised as the nephew of the great scribe Nakht-re, and the grandson of Paser, scribe of the two kingdoms, keeper of the king's own ledger."

She looked into my confused and stricken face and tried to reassure me even as she laid me low. "I am his mother in Egypt. You will be his nurse and he will know that you gave him life. His care will be your blessing, but he will call us both Ma and stay here until he is ready for school, and for this, you can be grateful.

"For this is my son, Re-mose, child of Re, that you have borne for me and my family. He will build my tomb and write your name upon it. He will be a prince of Egypt."

She handed me the baby, who had begun to cry, and turned to leave us. "Bar-Shalem," I whispered in his ear. Re-nefer heard and stopped. Without turning to look at me she said, "If you call him by that name again, I will have you thrown out of this house and into the street. If you do not heed my instructions in this, and in all matters regarding the education of our son, you will lose him. You must understand this completely."

Then she turned, and I saw that her cheeks were wet. "My only life is here, by the river," she said, her voice heavy with tears. "The bad fortune, the evil thing that stole my *ka* and cast it down amid beasts in the western wilderness, is over at last. I am restored to my family, to humankind, to the service of Re. I have consulted with the priests my brother serves, and it seems to them that your *ka*, your spirit, must belong here as well, or else you could not have survived your illness, or the journey, or this birth."

Re-nefer looked upon the baby at my breast and with

infinite tenderness said, "He will be protected against ill winds, evildoers, and naysayers. He will be a prince of Egypt." And then, in a whisper that hid nothing of her resolve, "You will do as I say."

At first, Re-nefer's words held little meaning for me. I was careful never to call my son Bar-Shalem when anyone else was in the room, but otherwise I was his mother. Re-mose stayed with me day and night so that I could nurse him whenever he cried. He slept by my side, and I held him and played with him and memorized his every mood and feature.

For three months we lived in Re-nefer's room. My son grew from hour to hour, becoming fat, and sleek, and the finest baby ever born. Under Meryt's good care I healed completely, and in the heat of the afternoon, Re-nefer watched him so that I might bathe and sleep.

The days passed without shape or work, without memory. The baby at my breast was the center of the universe. I was the entire source of his happiness, and for a few weeks, the goddess and I were one and the same.

At the start of his fourth month, the family gathered in the great room where Nakht-re sat among his assistants. The women assembled along the walls as the men clustered around the baby and placed the tools of the scribe into his little hands. His fingers curled around new reed brushes, and he grasped a circular dish upon which his inks were mixed. He waved a scrap of papyrus in both hands like a fan, which delighted Nakht-re, who declared him born to the profession. So was my son welcomed into the world of men.

Only then did I remember the eighth day, when newborn boys of my family were circumcised and first-time mothers cowered in the red tent while the older women reassured them. My heart broke in two pieces, half mourning that the god of my father would not recognize this boy, nor would my brother Joseph or even his grandmothers. And yet I was fiercely proud that my son's sex would remain whole, for why should he bear a scar that recalled the death of his own father? Why should he sacrifice his foreskin to a god in whose name I was widowed and my son orphaned?

That night there was a feast. I sat on the floor beside Re-nefer, who held the baby on her lap and plied his lips with mashed melon and tickled him with feathers and dandled him so that he laughed and smiled into the faces of the guests who came to celebrate the arrival to Nakht-re's house of a new son.

Food and drink were brought in quantities I could not fathom: fish and game, fruit and sweets so rich they set the teeth on edge, wine and beer in abundance. Musicians played pipes and sistrums, instruments with jingling hammers that sound like nothing so much as falling water. There were silly songs, love songs, and songs to the gods. When the sistrums appeared, dancing girls ran to the floor, whirling and leaping, able to touch the tops of their heads to the ground behind them.

The headpieces given to every guest at the door were cones of perfumed wax, which melted as the evening waned in streams of lotus and lily. My baby was sticky with perfume when I lifted him, sound asleep, from Re-nefer's lap, and the aroma clung to his dark hair for days.

Among the many wonders of my first banquet was the way women ate together with men. Husbands and wives sat side by side throughout the meal, and spoke to one another. I saw one woman place a hand upon her husband's arm, and a man who kissed the fingers of his companion's bejeweled hands. It was impossible to think of my own parents eating a meal in each other's company, much less touching before others. But this was Egypt, and I was the stranger.

That night marked the end of my seclusion. My wound had healed and the child was healthy, so we were sent into the garden, where his mess did not soil the floors and where his prattle would not disturb the work of the scribes. So my days were spent outdoors. While my son napped in the flower beds, I weeded and gathered whatever the cook called for and learned the flowers and fruits of the land. When he woke, he was greeted by the songs of Egyptian birds, and his eyes widened in delight as they took flight.

The garden became my home and my son's tutor. Re-mose took his first steps by the side of a large pond stocked with fish and fowl, which he watched in open-mouthed wonder. His first words—after "Ma"—were "duck" and "lotus."

His grandmother brought him fine toys. Almost every day, she would surprise him with a ball or top or miniature hunting stick. Once, she presented him with a wooden cat whose mouth opened and closed by working a string. This marvel delighted me no less than the baby. My son loved Re-nefer, and when he saw her approach he would toddle to greet her with a hug.

I was not unhappy in the garden. Re-mose, who was healthy and sunny, gave me purpose and status, since everyone in the household adored him and credited me with his nice manner and pleasant temper.

Every day, I kissed my fingers and touched the statue of Isis, offering thanks to distribute among the multitude of Egypt's goddesses and gods whose stories I did not know, in gratitude for the gift of my son. I gave thanks every time my son hugged me, and every seventh day I broke a piece of bread and fed it to the ducks and fish, in memory of my mothers' sacrifice to the Queen of Heaven, and in prayer for the continued health of my Re-mose.

The days passed sweetly, and turned into months, consumed by the endless tasks of loving a child. I had no leisure for looking backward and no need of the future.

I would have stayed forever within the garden of Re-mose's childhood, but time is a mother's enemy. My baby was gone before I knew it, and then the hand-holding toddler was replaced by a running boy. He was weaned, and I lost the modesty of Canaan and wore a sheer linen shift like other Egyptian women. Re-mose had his hair shaved and shaped into the braided sidelock worn by all Egyptian children.

My son grew strong and sinewy, playing rough-and-tumble with Nakht-re, his uncle, whom he called Ba. They adored each other, and Re-mose accompanied him on duck-hunting parties. He could swim like a fish, according to Re-nefer. Though I never left the house and gardens, she went on the barge to watch. When he was only seven, my son could beat his uncle at senet and even twenty-squares, elaborate board games that required strategy and logic to win. From the time he could hold a stick, Nakht-re showed my son how to make images on bits of broken stone, first as a game and then as teacher to student.

As he grew, Re-mose spent more time inside the house, observing Nakht-re at work, practicing his letters, eating the evening meal with his grandmother. One morning when he took breakfast with me in the kitchen, I saw him stiffen and blush when I split a fig with my teeth and handed him half. My son said nothing to cause me pain—but Re-mose stopped eating with me after that and began to sleep on the roof of the house, leaving me alone on my pallet in the garden, wondering where eight years had gone.

At nine, Re-mose came of the age when boys tied their first girdle, putting an end to his naked days. It was time for him to go to school and become a scribe. Nakht-re decided that the local teachers were not accomplished enough for his nephew, and he would attend the great academy in Memphis, where the sons of the most powerful scribes received their training and commissions, and where Nakht-re himself had been taught. He explained all of this to me in the garden one morning. He spoke gently and with compassion, for he knew how much it would grieve me to see Re-mose go.

Re-nefer scoured the markets for the right baskets for his clothing, for sandals that would last, for a perfect box in which to put his brushes. She commissioned a sculptor to carve a slate for mixing ink. Nakht-re planned a great banquet in honor of Re-mose's departure and made him a gift of an exquisite set of brushes. Re-mose's eyes were large with excitement at the prospect of going out into the world, and he spoke about his journey whenever we were together.

I watched the preparations from the bottom of a dark

well. If I tried to speak to my son, my eyes overflowed and my throat closed. He did his best to comfort me. "I am not dying, Ma," he told me, with a serious sweetness that made me sadder still. "I will return with gifts for you, and when I am a great scribe like Ba, I will build you a house with the biggest garden in all of the Southern Lands." He hugged me and held my hand many times in the days before his departure. He kept his chin high so that I would not think him afraid or unhappy, though of course he was just a little boy, leaving his mothers and his home for the first time. I kissed him for the last time in the garden near the pond where he had marveled at the fish and laughed at the ducks, and then Nakht-re took his hand.

I watched them leave the house from the rooftop, a cloth stuffed in my mouth so that I could finally weep until I was empty. That night, the old dream returned in all its force, and I was alone in Egypt once more.

Chapter Two

FROM THE MOMENT of his birth, my life revolved around my son. My thoughts did not stray from his happiness and my heart beat with his. His delights were my delight, and because he was such a golden child, my days were filled with purpose and pleasantness.

When he left, I was even lonelier than I had been when I first found myself in Egypt. Shalem was my husband for a few short weeks and his memory had dwindled to a sad shadow who haunted my sleep, but Re-mose had been with me for the whole of my adult life. In the space of his years, my body had taken its full shape and my heart had grown in wisdom, for I understood what it was to be a mother.

When I glimpsed myself in the pond, I saw a woman with thin lips, curling hair, and small, round, foreign eyes. How little I resembled my dark, handsome son, who looked more like his uncle than anyone else and who was becoming what Re-nefer had prophesied: a prince of Egypt.

I had little time to brood about my loneliness, for I had to earn my place in the great house of Nakht-re. Although Re-nefer was never unkind, with Re-mose gone we had less to say to each other, and I felt the silence grow ominous between us. I rarely went into the house.

I made myself a place in the corner of a garden shed used to store scythes and hoes—a spot where Re-mose used to hide his treasures: smooth stones, feathers, bits of papyrus gleaned from Nakht-re's hall. He left these things behind without a backward glance, but I kept them wrapped in a scrap of fine linen, as though they were ivory teraphim and not merely a child's discarded toys.

The men who tended the garden did not object to having a woman among them. I worked hard, and they appreciated my knack with the flowers and fruit, which I supplied to the cooks. I did not want company and rebuffed the attentions of men so often that they stopped seeking me out. When I saw my son's family enjoying the shade of the garden, we nodded and exchanged nothing more than polite greetings.

When there was word of Re-mose from Memphis, Nakht-re himself brought me the news sent by Kar, the master teacher who had been his own instructor. Thus I learned that Re-mose had mastered something called *keymt* in only two years—a feat of memorization that proved my son would rise high, and perhaps even serve the king himself.

There was never any word of his coming home. Re-mose was invited to go hunting with the governor's sons, and it would not do to reject such an auspicious offer. Then my son was chosen as an apprentice and aid to Kar when the master was called to rule upon a case of law, which took up the weeks during which other boys visited their families.

Once, Nakht-re and Re-nefer visited Re-mose in Memphis, making pilgrimage to their father's tomb there. They returned with fond greetings to me and news of his growth; after four years away he was taller than Nakht-re, well spoken and self-assured. They also brought proofs of his education—shards of pottery that were covered with writing. "Look," said Nakht-re, pointing a finger at the image of a falcon. "See how strong he makes the shoulders of Horus." They made me a gift of this treasure from my son's hand. I marveled over it and showed it to Meryt, who was duly impressed at the regularity and beauty of his images. I was awed by the fact that my son could discern meaning from scratchings on broken clay bits, and took comfort in the knowledge that he would be a great man someday. He could be scribe to the priests of Amun or perhaps even vizier to a governor. Had Nakht-re himself not said that Re-mose might even aspire to the king's service? But of course, none of these dreams filled my arms or comforted my eyes. I knew my son was growing to manhood and feared that the next time I saw him, we would be strangers.

I might have vanished during those long years without anyone taking more than passing notice except for Meryt. But Meryt was always there, unfailing in kindness even when I turned away from her and gave her no reason to love me.

The midwife had come to see me every day in the weeks after Re-mose's birth. She tended my bandages and brought broth made of ox bones for strength, and sweet beer for my milk. She rubbed my shoulders where they were stiff from cradling the baby, and she helped me to my feet for my first real bath as a mother, pouring cool, scented water over my back, wrapping me in a fresh towel.

Long after my confinement was over, Meryt continued her visits. She fussed over my health and delighted in the baby; she examined him closely and gave him slow, sensuous massages that helped him sleep for hours. On the day he was weaned, Meryt even brought me a gift—a small obsidian statue of a nursing mother. I was confused by her generosity, but when I tried to refuse any of her attentions or gifts, she insisted. "The midwife's life is not easy, but that is no reason for it to be unlovely," she said.

Meryt always spoke to me as one midwife to another. No matter that I had not seen the inside of a birthing room since my own son was born; she continued to honor the skill I had shown at Re-mose's birth. When she returned to her own house after my son was born, she asked her mistress to learn what she could about me; her lady, Ruddedit, had sought out the story from Re-nefer, who provided only a few details. Meryt took these and wove them into a fabulous tale.

As Meryt told it, I was the daughter and granddaughter of midwives who knew the ways of herbs and barks even better than the necromancers of On, where the healing arts of Egypt are taught. She believed me a princess of Canaan, the descendant of a great queen who had been overthrown by an evil king.

I did not correct her, fearing that if I named my mothers or Inna the whole of my history would come pouring out of me and I would be thrown out of the house and my son cast out for bearing the blood of murderers in his veins. So Meryt embroidered my history, which she repeated to the women that she met, and they were many, as she attended most of the births of the northern precincts, noble and lowborn alike. She told the tale of how I had saved my son's life with my own hands, always leaving out her own part in it. She spoke of my skill with herbs and of the renown I had earned in the western wilderness as a healer. These things she imagined entirely on her own. And when I helped one of Nakht-re's servants deliver her first baby, Meryt spread the news of how I turned it inside the womb in the sixth month. Thanks to Meryt, I became a legend among the local women without once venturing out of Nakht-re's garden.

Meryt had her own story to tell. Though she had been born in Thebes, her mother's blood was mingled with that of the distant south and her skin showed the color of Nubia. But unlike Bilhah, whose face would appear to me while Meryt chattered on, she was tall and stately. "Had I not become a midwife," she said, "I should have liked to be a dancing girl, hired for grand parties in the great houses and even the king's own palace.

"But that life goes too fast," she said, with a mock sigh. "I am already too fat to dance for princes," slapping at the skin beneath her skinny arm, which did not budge, and breaking into a laugh I could not resist.

Meryt could make anyone laugh. Even women deep in travail forgot their agony to smile at her jokes. When he was little, Re-mose called her "Ma's friend" even before I realized that she was truly my friend, and a blessing.

I knew everything there was to know about Meryt, for she loved to talk. Her mother was a cook married to a baker, and known as a singer, too. She was often called upon to entertain at the parties of her master. Her voice

caused audiences to shudder with pleasure at its deep reso-
nance. "Had she not been bare-breasted, they would have
doubted she was a woman at all," Meryt said.

But the mother died when her daughter was still a girl
and the household had no use for her, so Meryt was sent to
the place where she lived even to the days when I knew her.
As a child, she carried water for Ruddedit, a daughter of
On, where the priests are famous as magicians and healers.
The lady looked kindly upon Meryt, and when she saw that
Meryt was clever, Ruddedit sent her to learn from the local
granny midwife, a woman with uncommonly long fingers
who brought luck to her mothers.

Meryt grew to womanhood in that house and, like her
mother, married a baker there. He was a good man who
treated her well. But Meryt was barren, and nothing could
induce her womb to bear fruit. After many years, Meryt and
her man adopted two boys whose parents had been felled
by river fever. The sons were now grown to manhood and
baked bread for the workers in the village of the tombmak-
ers, on the west bank of the river.

Her husband was long dead, and Meryt, though she saw
her sons rarely, often boasted of their skills and health. "My
boys have the most beautiful teeth you've ever seen," she
would say solemnly, for her own mouth was a pit of decay
and she chewed marjoram all day to ease the pain.

For years, Meryt spared me no detail of her life in hope
that I would share some hint of mine. Finally, she gave up
asking me about myself, but never ceased inviting me to
attend upon birthing women with her. She would stop at
Nakht-re's house and request of Herya or Re-nefer that I
be permitted to accompany her. The ladies deferred to me,

but I always declined. I had no wish to stray from Re-mose, nor had I any desire to see the world. I had not stepped outside the grounds since I arrived, and as the months became years, I came to fear the very thought. I was certain I would be lost, or worse, somehow discovered. I imagined that someone would recognize the sin of my family upon my face and I would be torn apart on the spot. My son would discover the truth about his mother and about her brothers, his uncles. He would be exiled from the good life that he seemed destined to inherit, and he would curse my memory.

I was ashamed of these secret fears, which made me turn my back on the lessons taught to me by Rachel and Inna, and thus upon their memory. My worthlessness imprisoned me; still I could not do what I knew I should.

Meryt never gave up. Sometimes, if a birth went badly, she returned afterward, even in the dead of night, waking me from my pallet in the garden shed to tell the story and ask how she might have done better. Often I could reassure her that she had done the best anyone could do, and we would sit silently together. But sometimes I would hear a story and my heart would sink. Once, when a woman had died very suddenly giving birth, Meryt did not think to take up a knife to try to free the baby in the womb, so both of them perished. I did not shield my dismay well enough, and Meryt saw my face.

"Tell me, then," she demanded, grabbing me by the shoulders. "Do not curl your lip when you might have saved the baby. Teach me at least, that I might try."

Shamed by Meryt's tears, I began to speak of Inna's

methods, her way with a knife, her tricks at manipulation. I tried to explain her use of herbs, but I lacked the Egyptian names for plants and roots. So Meryt brought her herbal kit, and we began to translate. I described my mothers' ways with nettle, fennel, and coriander, and she scoured the markets searching out leaves and seeds I had not seen since childhood.

Meryt brought me samples of every flower and stem sold at the wharf. Some of it was familiar but some of it stank, especially the local concoctions which depended upon dead things: bits of dried animals, ground rocks and shells, and excrement of every description. Egyptian healers applied the dung of water horses and alligators and the urine of horses and children to various parts of the body in different seasons. There were times that the most odious preparations appeared to help, but I was always amazed that a people so concerned with bodily cleanliness would accept such foul remedies.

Although Egyptian herbal lore was deep and old, I was pleased to find methods and plants of which they knew little. Meryt found cumin seed in the marketplace, and she was surprised to learn that it aided the healing of wounds. She bought hyssop and mint with their roots still intact, and they flourished in the pungent black soil of Egypt. No one suffered from a sour stomach in the house of Nakht-re again. Thus Meryt became famous for "her" exotic herbal cures, and I had the satisfaction of knowing that my mothers' wisdom was being put to good use.

*

My quiet life ended during the fourth year after Re-mose left the house of Nakht-re, when Ruddedit's daughter came to stand upon the bricks.

Her name was Hatnuf, and she was in a bad way. Her first baby had been born dead—full-sized and perfect in every feature, but lifeless. After years of miscarrying, another child had finally taken root, but she faced this labor in terror, and after a full day of travail, the pains had not advanced the baby's progress. Meryt was in attendance, and the lady of the house had sent for a physician-priest, who chanted prayers and hung the room with amulets and set a pile of herbs and goat dung to smoking while Hatnuf crouched over it.

But the smell had caused the mother to faint, and in falling, the girl cut her forehead and bled. After that, Ruddedit banished the doctor from the room and had him wait outside the front door, where he recited incantations in the nasal drone of a priest. Day turned to night again, and night began to brighten to another dawn, and still the pains did not abate, nor did the baby move. Hatnuf, the lady's only daughter, was nearly dead with fear and pain when Meryt suggested I be summoned.

This time, it was not a matter of being asked. Meryt appeared at the doorway of my garden hut with Ruddedit standing in the dawn's light behind her. Weariness barely dimmed the beauty in a face no longer young. "Den-ner," she said, in the accents of Egypt, "you must come and do what you can for my child. We have nothing left to try. The smell of Anubis is in the birth chamber already. Bring your kit and follow me."

Meryt quickly told me the story, and I grabbed a few

herbs I'd been drying in the rafters of my shed. The lady was nearly running. I barely had time to realize that I was out of the garden. We walked past the front of Nakht-re's house, and I remembered the day I first saw the place, a lifetime earlier. Sunlight caught the gold-tipped flagpoles in front of the great temple, where banners hung lifeless in the still of the dawn. Ruddedit's house was just on the other side of the temple, so it took no time to reach the ante-chamber where Hatnuf lay whimpering on the floor, sur-rounded by the servants of the house, who were nearly as exhausted as the laboring mother.

Death was in the room. I caught sight of him in the shadows beneath a statue of Bes, the friendly-grotesque guardian of children, who seemed to grimace at his own powerlessness here.

Ruddedit introduced me to her daughter, who looked up at me with empty eyes, but did as I asked. She moved to her side so I could reach an oiled hand up to the womb, but I felt no sign of the baby's head. The room was very still as the women waited to see what I would do or ask of them.

The dog-shaped shadow of death stirred, sensing my dismay. But his eagerness only made me angry. I cursed at his bark and his tail and his very mother. I did this in my native tongue, which sounded harsh even to me after so many years of Egyptian words in my ears. Meryt and the others thought I uttered a secret charm, and murmured approval. Even Hatnuf stirred and looked around.

I called for oil and a mortar and mixed the strongest herbs I had at hand: birthwort and an extraction of hemp, both of which sometimes cause the womb to expel its contents early in pregnancy. I did not know if they would work, and worried that the combination might cause damage, but I knew there was nothing else to be tried, for she was dying. The baby was already dead, but there was no reason to give up on the mother.

I applied the mixture, and soon strong pains seized the girl. I had the women help Hatnuf back up to the bricks, where I massaged her belly and tried to push the baby downward. Hatnuf's legs could not hold her, and soon Meryt had to take Ruddedit's place behind her, where she whispered encouragement as I reached in again to feel the baby's head, which was now near the door.

The pains became ceaseless and intolerable to the poor woman on the bricks. Her eyes turned back in her head, and she fell into Meryt's arms, senseless and unable to push.

It was full daylight now, but the shadow in the room would not let the sun's rays penetrate the gloom. My cheeks were streaked with tears. I did not know what to do next. Inna had once told a tale of freeing a baby from its dead mother's womb, but this mother was not dead. I had no other tricks to try, no other herbs.

And then I remembered the song in which Inna had taken such delight, the song which she learned in the hills above Shechem.

"Fear not," I sang, recalling the melody easily, reaching deep for the words.

> *"Fear not, the time is coming*
> *Fear not, your bones are strong*
> *Fear not, help is nearby*
> *Fear not, Gula is near*
> *Fear not, the baby is at the door*

Fear not, he will live to bring you honor
Fear not, the hands of the midwife are clever
Fear not, the earth is beneath you
Fear not, we have water and salt
Fear not, little mother
Fear not, mother of us all."

Meryt joined me in singing the words "Fear not," sensing the power of the sounds without knowing what she was saying. By the third time, all of the women were singing "Fear not," and Hatnuf was breathing deeply again.

The baby was delivered soon after, and indeed he was dead. Hatnuf turned her face to the wall and closed her eyes, wishing only to join him. But when Meryt began to pack her poor, battered womb with boiled linen, Hatnuf cried out again in the voice of a laboring mother. "There is another child," said Meryt. "Come, Den-ner," she said. "Catch the twin."

With just one more push, Hatnuf delivered a baby utterly unlike his brother. Where the first one was fat and perfect and lifeless, this one was puny and wrinkled and bellowed with the lungs of an ox.

Meryt laughed at the sound, and the room erupted in peals and gales and giggles of relief and joy. The bloody, unwashed, squalling baby was passed from hand to hand, kissed and blessed by every woman there. Ruddedit fell to her knees and laughed and wept with her grandson in her arms. But Hatnuf did not hear us. The little one arrived in a torrent of blood that would not cease. No amount of packing stanched the flow, and within moments of her son's birth, Hatnuf died, her head on her mother's lap.

The scene in the room was terrible: the mother dead, one baby dead, a scrawny newborn wailing for the breast that would never feed him. Ruddedit sat, bereaved of her only daughter, a grandmother for the first time. Meryt wept with her mistress, and I crept away, wishing I had never ventured out of my garden.

After the horror of that scene, I thought I would be forbidden to enter another birth chamber. But as Meryt told the story, I alone was responsible for saving the life of the surviving child, who had been born, she said, on a day so hated by Set that it was a miracle he drew a single breath.

Soon messengers from other important houses of Thebes came to the door of Nakht-re's garden with orders not to return home without Den-ner the midwife. These were the servants of priests and scribes and others who could not be gainsaid. I consented only if Meryt would accompany me, but since she always agreed, we became the midwives of our neighborhood, which comprised many fine houses where the ladies and their servants enjoyed fertile wombs. We were called at least once every seven days, and for every healthy baby, we were rewarded with jewelry, amulets, fine linen, or jars of oil. Meryt and I divided these goods, and though I offered my share to Re-nefer, she insisted that I keep them.

Within a year my shed was cluttered with a collection of objects I did not use or care for. Meryt looked around one day and declared that I needed a wicker box to contain my belongings. Since I owned more than enough to trade, Meryt selected an auspicious day for us to go to market.

By then I had gone out to attend at many births, still I

dreaded this venture out into the larger world. Meryt knew I was afraid and held my hand as we walked out of my garden, chattering all the way to keep me from dwelling upon my fears. I held on to her like a baby in fear of losing her mother but after a time found the courage to look upon the sights of the busy Theban quay. The harvest was still many days off and most of the farmers had little to do but wait for ripening, so the stalls were clogged with country folk who had nothing much to trade except time.

Meryt exchanged a beaded necklace from one of her mothers for some sweet cake, and we ate as we wandered, arm in arm, from one stall to the next. I marveled at the amount of jewelry for sale and wondered who could afford so many baubles. I saw sandal-makers turning out cheap shoes, made to order. A line of men waited for one particular barber, known to have the best gossip. I averted my eyes from a pile of Canaanite woolens, which might have been woven by my own aunts. Meryt and I laughed over the antics of a monkey, who held a brace of tall, hungry-looking dogs on leads and made them beg for scraps of food.

After we had taken in the sights, my friend said it was time to start our hunt, but the first basket-maker we came upon had nothing large enough to suit my needs, so we walked on, passing the wine and oil merchants, bakers, and men selling live birds. We saw many beautiful things, too: incised Kushite pottery, hammered bronze vases, household gods and goddesses, three-legged stools and chairs. My eye fell upon a handsome box with an inlaid cover that bloomed with a garden made of ivory and faience and mother-of-pearl. "Now there's a piece for the master's tomb," said Meryt, in honest admiration.

The carpenter appeared behind his work and began to tell the story of its making: where he purchased the acacia wood, and how much difficulty he had in applying the ivory. He spoke thoughtfully and slowly, as though he were telling a story rather than trying to make a sale. I kept my eyes on the box as he spoke, hearing only the warmth of his voice, and staring at his hands as they traced the design upon his handiwork.

Meryt started teasing the fellow. "What do you take us for, knave?" she asked. "Do you think we are rich ladies disguised as midwives? Who but a rich man could afford anything so fine as this? Who could lay claim to such a work of art except the king's own tomb-maker? You are pulling my leg, little man," she said.

He laughed at her words and replied, "If you think me little, you must come from a land of giants, sister. I am Benia," he introduced himself. "And you might be surprised at the bargains available at my stall. It all depends upon the buyer, my dear," he teased back. "Beautiful women always get what they want."

At this, Meryt howled with laughter and poked me in the ribs, but I said nothing, for I knew that his words had been aimed at me. In an instant Meryt, too, understood that the carpenter had been talking to me, and although I had not said a word, the sound of his voice and the gentleness of his words had moved me.

My fingers, almost of their own accord, traced the pattern of a milky-white leaf that was inlaid upon the box. "This comes from the heart of a sea creature that lives far to the north," Benia said, pointing to another part of the design.

I noticed the size of his hands. His fingers were thick as

the branches on a young fruit tree, and even longer than his massive palms, which hard work had gnarled into mountains and valleys of muscle. He caught me staring and drew his hand away, as if in shame.

"When I was born, my mother took one look at me and cried out when she saw these," Benia said. "They were far too large for my body, even then. 'A sculptor,' she said to my father, who apprenticed me to the finest stonecutter.

"But I had no talent for stone. The alabaster cracked when I so much as looked at it, and even granite would not permit me to approach. Only wood understood my hands. Supple and warm and alive, wood speaks to me and tells me where to cut, how to shape it. I love my work, lady."

He looked into my eyes, which I had raised to his face as he spoke.

Meryt saw the look pass between us and leaped into the silence like a shrewd fishwife. "This is Den-ner, tradesman, a widow and the finest midwife in Thebes. We come to the market in search of a simple basket to hold payment from her grateful mothers."

"But a basket will not do for a master," said Benia, turning to bargain with Meryt. "Let me see what you brought to trade, Mother, for I have been sitting here all day without luck."

Meryt unpacked our collection of trinkets: a carved slate for mixing malachite into green eye shadow, a large carnelian scarab too red for my stomach, and a beautiful beaded head covering, the gift of a pretty young concubine who gave birth to a fine little boy she handed directly to her mistress, without even looking at the baby. (Meryt and I saw many strange things in the birthing rooms of Thebes.)

Benia feigned interest in the scarab. "For your wife?" Meryt asked, without pretence at subtlety.

"No wife," Benia replied, simply. "I live in my sister's house and have these many years, but her husband is impatient of my place at his table. Soon I will be leaving the city to live among the workmen in the Valley of the Kings," he said slowly, speaking again to me.

At this, Meryt grew excited on her own behalf and told him all about her sons, who were bakers employed for the workmen there. "When I go, I will seek them out," Benia promised, and added, "I will be given my own house there, as befits a master craftsman. Four rooms for myself only," he said, as though he could hear his own voice echoing through the empty chambers already.

"What a waste, carpenter," Meryt replied.

As the two of them exchanged these confidences for my benefit, my fingers followed the edges of the pond that Benia had fashioned on the box cover. Before I could draw away, he covered my hand with his own.

I was afraid to look into his face. Perhaps he was leering. Perhaps he thought by making this absurd transaction— trading a pretty bauble for a masterwork—I then would owe him the use of my body. But when Meryt jabbed me in the ribs to answer, I saw only kindness on the carpenter's face.

"Bring the box to the garden door at the house of Nakht-re, scribe to the priests of Amun-Re," Meryt said. "Bring it tomorrow." She handed over the scarab.

"Tomorrow in the morning," he said. And we left.

"Now that was a good transaction, girl," said Meryt.

"And that scarab was a lucky piece to buy you a treasure box and a husband, too."

I shook my head at my friend and smiled as though she were babbling, but I did not say no. I said nothing at all. I was embarrassed and thrilled. I felt an unfamiliar tightness between my legs and my cheeks were flushed.

And yet, I did not fully understand my own heart, for this was nothing like what I felt when I first saw Shalem. No hot wind blew through Benia and into me. This feeling was much cooler and calmer. Even so, my heart beat faster and I knew my eyes were brighter than they had been earlier in the day.

Benia and I had exchanged a few words and brushed against each other's fingers. And yet, I felt connected to this stranger. I had no doubt that he felt the same.

All the way home, my step beat out the rhythm of my wonder — "How can this be? How can this be?"

As we approached Nakht-re's house, Meryt broke an unaccustomed silence and laughed, saying, "I'll deliver your babies yet. By my count, you are not yet thirty years in this world. I'll see grandbabies through you, daughter of my heart," and she kissed me goodbye.

But once I walked into the garden all thoughts of Benia were banished. The house was in an uproar. Re-mose was back!

He had arrived soon after I had left. The servants had been sent to search for me, and since I never left the grounds without informing Re-nefer first, she had grown alarmed and even sent word to her friend Ruddedit. When my mother-in-law saw me enter the yard carrying a half-eaten cake from the market, she grew angry and turned on her heel without speaking. It was the cook who told me to hurry and see my son, who had come home to recover.

"Recover?" I asked her, suddenly cold with fear. "Has he been ill?"

"Oh, no," she said with a broad grin. "He comes home to heal from the circumcision and to celebrate his manhood in high style. I'll be working from dawn till midnight all this week," she said and pinched my cheek.

I heard nothing past the word "circumcision." My head rang and my heart pounded as I rushed into the great hall where Re-mose was arrayed on a litter near Nakht-re's chair. He looked up at me and smiled easily, without a trace of pain in his face, which was now a different face altogether.

It had been nearly five years since he left me, and the little boy was now a young man. His hair, no longer shaved, had grown in thick and black. His arms showed muscle, his legs were no longer silky smooth, and his chest bespoke his father's beauty. "Ma," said the young man who was my son. "Oh Ma, you look well. Even better than I remembered."

He was merely being polite. He was a prince of Egypt addressing the serving woman who had given him birth. It was just as I feared: we were strangers, and our lives would never permit us to become more than that. He motioned for me to come and sit beside him, and Nakht-re smiled his approval.

I asked if he suffered, and he waved the question away. "I have no pain," he said. "They give you wine laced with the juice of poppies before they draw the knife, and afterward too," he said. "But that all happened a week ago, and I am quite recovered. Now it is time to celebrate, and I am home for the banquet.

"But how are you, Ma?" he said. "I am told you are a famous midwife now, that you are the only one the great ladies of Thebes will trust when called to childbed."

"I serve as I can," I said quietly and turned his question aside, for what can a woman tell a man about babies and blood? "But you, son, tell me what you learned. Tell me of your years in school and of the friendships and honors you earned, for your uncle says you were the best of your fellows."

A cloud passed over Re-mose's face, and I recognized the little boy who burst into tears when he found a dead baby duck in the garden. But my son did not speak of the taunts of his schoolmates, nor recount for me the mocking cries that followed him everywhere during the first year of his studies: "Where is your father? You have no father."

Re-mose did not speak of his loneliness, which grew as he proved himself the best of his class and the teacher took note of him and made him the favorite. He spoke only of his teacher, Kar, whom he loved and obeyed in all things, and who doted upon him.

Unlike other masters, he never beat his students or berated them for their mistakes. "He is the most noble man I ever met, apart from Uncle," said Re-mose, taking Nakht-re's hand in his. "I am home to celebrate not only my coming of age, but the great gift Kar has given me.

"My teacher asks that I accompany him south to Kush, where the trade in ebony and ivory has been revived, and where the vizier was caught embezzling from the king. The king himself has asked Kar to go and oversee the installation of a new overseer, and to take stock and report upon what he finds there.

"I will go to assist my teacher, and watch when he sits as judge and the people bring their disputes before him." Re-mose paused so I would hear the importance of his next words. "I am instructed to learn the duties of a vizier. After this journey, my training will be complete and I will receive my own commission, and begin to earn honor for my family. My uncle is pleased, Mother. Are you pleased as well?"

The question was sincere, echoing with the longing of a boy who asks his mother to pronounce upon his achievement. "I am pleased, my son. You are a fine man who will do honor to this house. I wish you happiness, a kind wife, and many children. I am proud of you, and proud to be your mother."

That was all I could say. Just as he did not tell me of the pain he suffered at school, I did not speak of how much I missed him, or how empty my heart had been, or how he had taken the light from my life when he left. I looked into his eyes, and he returned my gaze fondly. He patted my hand and lifted it to his lips. My heart beat to the twin drums of happiness and loneliness.

Two nights later, I watched Re-mose from across the room at the feast given in his honor. He sat beside Nakht-re and ate like a boy who has not been fed for a week. He drank of the wine and his eyes glittered with excitement. I drank wine, too, and stared at my son, wondering at the life he would live, amazed that he was a man already, only a few years younger than his father had been when I saw him for the first time, in his father's house.

Poised on the edge of manhood, Re-mose was half a head taller than Nakht-re, clear-eyed, and straight as a tree. Re-nefer and I sat side by side for the first time in years and admired the man-child who had given us both a reason to live. My hand brushed hers and she did not withdraw from my touch but held my fingers in hers, and for a moment at least we shared our love for our son, and through him for the unnamed son and husband of Shechem.

A pretty serving girl raised her eyes to him, and he flirted back. I laughed to think of the baby whose bottom I had washed now warming to a woman. My face ached from smiling, and yet my sighs were so loud that Re-nefer once turned to ask if I was in any pain.

It was the finest banquet I had ever seen, with much of noble Thebes in attendance. The flowers shone in the light of one hundred lamps. The air was thick with the smells of rich food, fresh lotus, incense, and perfume. Laughter, fed by six kinds of beer and three varieties of wine, pealed through the room, and the dancers leaped and twirled until they glistened with sweat and panted on the floor.

A second troupe of musicians had been hired to supplement the local performers. This company sailed the river, stopping at temples and noble houses to play, but unlike the others, they refused to play with dancers on the floor, insisting that audiences attend to their songs, said to have magical qualities. The mysterious leader was a veiled lady. Blind like many masters of the harp, she was mistress of the sistrum, the hand-held bell-drum.

According to the gossip, the singer had escaped the jaws of Anubis and won a second life, but he had bitten off her face, which is why she wore the veil. The tale was told with a wink and a nudge, for Egyptians knew how a juicy story could be used to drum up business. Still, when the veiled singer was led into the room, an expectant hush fell and the tipsy crowd sat up.

She was dressed in white, covered head to toe in a gauzy stuff that floated in layers to the floor. Re-nefer leaned toward me and whispered, "She looks like a puff of smoke."

Settled on a stool, she freed her hands from her garments to take up the instrument, and the hush released a soft gasp, for her hands were as white as her robes, unearthly pale, as though scarred by a terrible fire. She shook the sistrum four times and produced four entirely different sounds, which sobered the listeners, who quieted to attention.

First the group played a light song of flutes and drums, then a lone trumpet produced a mournful melody that caused the ladies to sigh and the men to stroke their chins. An old children's song made everyone in the room smile with the open faces they once wore as boys and girls.

There was indeed magic to this music, which could transform the blackest sorrow to the brightest joy. The guests clapped their hands high in the direction of the performers and raised their cups in gratitude at Nakht-re for the wonderful entertainment.

After the applause died down, the sistrum-player began to sing, accompanied by her own instrument and a single drum. It was a long song, with many refrains. The story it told was unremarkable: a tale of love found and lost—the oldest story in the world. The only story.

As the song began, the man returned the girl's love, and they delighted in each other. But then the tale took a sorry turn and the lover spurned his lady, leaving her alone. She wept and prayed to the Golden Lady Hathor, but to no avail. The beloved would not take her back. The girl's sorrow was endless and unbearable. The women wept openly, each remembering her youth. The men wiped their eyes, unashamed, recalling their earliest passion. Even the young ones sighed, feeling the pangs of losses yet to come.

There was a long silence after the song ended. The harpist picked out a quiet air, but the conversation ceased. No more cups were raised. Re-nefer stood and left the room without ceremony, and then, one by one, the rest of the company took their leave. The party ended quietly, and the hall emptied to the sounds of sighs and murmured thanks. The musicians packed up their instruments and led their leader away. Some of the servants slept on the floor, too exhausted to begin cleaning up until morning. The house was completely still.

Dawn was some hours distant when I found my way to where the musicians slept. The veiled one leaned against a wall motionless. I thought she was sleeping as well, but she turned, her hands out-stretched to discover who approached. I put my hands in hers, which were small and cool.

"Werenro," I said.

The sound of my accent startled her. "Canaan," she said, in a bitter whisper. "That was my name in torment."

"I was a child," I said. "You were the messenger of Rebecca, my grandmother. You told us a story I never forgot. But you were murdered, Werenro. I was there with the Grandmother when they brought you back. I saw them bury your bones. Did you truly return from the dead?"

There was a long silence and her head fell forward beneath the veils. "Yes," she said. And then, after a moment, "No. I did not escape. The truth is, I am dead.

"How strange to find a ghost of that time here in a great house by the river. Tell me," she asked, "are you dead, too?"

"Perhaps I am," I answered, shuddering.

"Perhaps you are, for the living do not ask such questions, nor could they bear the pain of truth without the consolation of music. The dead understand.

"Do you know the face of death?" she asked.

"Yes," I said, remembering the doglike shadows that attend so many births, patient and eager at the same time.

"Ah," she said, and without warning lifted the veil. Her lips were unharmed, but the rest of her face was torn and scarred. Her nose had been broken and ripped open, her cheeks were collapsed and seamed with deep scars, her eyes were milky stones. It seemed impossible that anyone could survive such destruction.

"I was leaving Tyre with a flagon of purple dye for her, for the Grandmother. It was dawn and the sky put all the tents of Mamre to shame. I was looking up when they came upon me. Three of them, Canaanite men like any others, filthy and stupid. They said nothing to me or to each other. They took my pouch and my basket and ripped them open, and then they turned on me."

Werenro began to rock, back and forth, and her voice went flat. "The first one pushed me to the ground right in the middle of the road. The second one tore off my clothes.

The third lifted his robe and fell upon me. He emptied himself into me, who had never laid with a man. And then he spit into my face.

"The second one took his turn, but he could not do the deed, and so he began to beat me, cursing me for causing his problem. He broke my nose and knocked several teeth from my mouth, and only when I was bleeding was he aroused enough to do what he wished.

"The third one turned me over and ripped me open from the backside. And laughed." She stopped rocking and sat up straight, hearing that laughter still.

"I lay, facedown on the road, as the three of them stood over me. I thought they would kill me and end my torment.

"But it was not for them. 'Why do you not cry out?' cried the one who laughed. 'Do you have no tongue? Or perhaps you are not really a woman at all, for you are not the color of woman. You are the color of a sick dog's shit. I will hear you cry out, and we will see if you are a woman or a phantom.'

"And that is when they did to me what you can see. I need not speak of that." Werenro lowered her veil and began to rock again.

"At the first sound of footsteps, they left me for dead," she said. "A shepherd's dog found me where I lay, followed by a boy, who cried out at the sight of me. I heard him retch and thought he would flee, but instead he covered me with his robe and brought his mother. She applied poultices to my face, and unguents to my body, and stroked my hands in pity, and kept me alive, and never asked me to explain.

"When it was certain that I would survive, she asked

whether she should send word to Mamre, for she had recognized the tatters of my robe. But I said no.

"I was finished being a slave, finished with Rebecca's arrogance, and finished with Canaan. My only desire was to come home and smell the river and the perfume of the lotus in the morning. I told her I wished to be dead in Mamre, and she made it so.

"She cut handfuls of my hair and wrapped it with my clothes and a few sheep's bones inside my bag. She sent her son into town, where he found a merchant headed for Mamre, who brought the Grandmother news of my death.

"The Canaanite woman gave me a veil and a walking stick and led me to Tyre. She searched out a caravan headed for the land of the great river. They took me in exchange for one of her flock, and for the promise that I would entertain them with songs and stories. The traders brought me to On, where a sistrum found its way into my hands, and now I find myself here with you, with Canaan in my mouth again." At this she turned her head away from me and spit. A snake slithered from the spot where her spittle fell, and I shivered in the cold blast of Werenro's anger.

"I would curse the whole nation but for that Canaanite woman's kindness. My eyes were put out, so I never saw her face, but I imagine it shining with light and beauty. Indeed, when I think of her, I see the face of the full moon.

"Perhaps she was atoning for some wrong she had done. Or perhaps she had once been abandoned and someone helped her escape. Or maybe no one had helped her when she was in need. She asked me nothing, not even my name. She saved me for no reason other than the goodness of her heart. Her name was goodness itself, Tamar, the sustaining fruit," said Werenro, and she began rocking again.

We sat together in the hour before dawn, silent for a long while. Finally, she spoke again, to answer a question I would never have thought to ask.

"I am not unhappy," she said. "Nor am I content. There is nothing in my heart. I care for no one, and for nothing. I dream of dogs with bared teeth. I am dead. It is not so bad to be dead."

The sighs and snores of the sleeping musicians interrupted her words. "Good souls," she said of her companions, with tenderness. "We ask nothing of one another.

"But you," said Werenro, "how did you come to speak the language of the river?"

Without hesitation, I told her everything. I leaned my head back, closed my eyes, and gave voice to my life. In all of my years, I had never before spoken so much or so long, and yet the words came effortlessly, as though this were something I had done many times before.

I surprised myself, remembering Tabea, remembering Ruti, remembering my coming of age in the red tent. I spoke of Shalem and our passionate lovemaking without blushing. I spoke of our betrayal and his murder. I told her about Renefer's bargain with me, and Meryt's care for me, and I spoke of my son with pride and love.

It was not difficult. Indeed, it was as though I had been parched and there was cool water in my mouth. I said "Shalem" and my breath was clean after years of being foul and bitter. I called my son "Bar-Shalem," and an old tightness in my chest eased.

I recited the names of my mothers, and knew with total certainty that they were dead. I leaned my face into Werenro's shoulder and soaked her robe in memory of Leah and Rachel, Zilpah and Bilhah.

Through it all, Werenro nodded and sighed and held my hand. When at last I was quiet she said, "You are not dead." Her voice betrayed a little sorrow. "You are not like me. Your grief shines from your heart. The flame of love is strong. Your story is not finished, Dinah," she said, in the accents of my mothers. Not "Den-ner" the foreign midwife, but "Dinah," a daughter beloved of four mothers.

Werenro stroked my head, which rested on her shoulder, as the room began to brighten with the first hints of dawn. I fell asleep leaning there, but when I awoke she was gone.

Re-mose left a week later, in the company of Kar, who arrived from Memphis on his way to Kush. Re-mose brought the venerable master into the garden to introduce us, but he barely acknowledged the lowborn mother of his favorite student. After they left I wondered, without pity, whether the old man would survive such a long journey.

Chapter Three

BENIA HAD DELIVERED the box as he had said he would, but I was not there to receive it. When he brought it to the garden gate, he was brusquely told that Den-ner was sitting in the great hall with her son and could not be called away by a tradesman. The box was placed in a corner of the kitchen, and I did not see it until after Re-mose had left Thebes and the house had returned to normal.

When the cook gave it to me, her curiosity overwhelmed her. How had something so elegant and rare come to be mine? And who was the man who asked after me so eagerly? I said nothing of him or the box to anyone in the house, and the gossip soon died away. I sent no word to Benia either, hoping he would take my silence as a rejection of the indirect offer he had made me in the marketplace. Although I had been moved by his words and by his touch, I could not see myself living like other women. Despite Werenro's words, I was sure that Re-mose would tell the next and final chapters of my story.

Meryt was furious at me for turning Benia down. "A man like that? So accomplished? So kind?" She threatened never to speak to me again, but we both knew that could never happen. I was her daughter, and she would never cut me off.

But Benia's box remained an embarrassment and a reproach to me. It did not belong in a garden shed. It was not made for a foreign-born midwife without status or standing. It was mine only because the carpenter had recognized my loneliness and because I had seen the need in him, too. I filled the box with gifts from my mothers, but covered its gleaming beauty with an old papyrus mat so that it would not remind me of Benia, whom I resigned to the corner of my heart, with other dreams that had died.

The weeks flowed quietly into months, the passage of time marked by the stories of births, most of them healthy. I learned that a tonic made of the red madder growing in my garden eased childbirth for many, and Meryt and I were called to ever more distant neighborhoods. Once, a barque was sent to bring us to the town of On, where a priest's favorite concubine lay dying. We found a girl far too young to be a mother, screaming in terror, alone in a room without the comfort of another woman. Shortly after we arrived, we closed her eyes and I tried to free the baby, but she, too, was dead.

Meryt went to speak to the father, who, far from bereaved, began to curse my friend and me for killing his wife and child. He rushed into the birthing chamber before I had time to cover the poor mother. "The foreigner raised a knife to her?" he shrieked. "Only a surgeon can do such a thing. This woman is a menace, a demon sent from the east to destroy the kingdom of the river." He lunged at me, but Meryt stopped him, and with strength I did not know she possessed, pinned him against a wall and tried to explain that I had cut the mother in hope of saving the child.

But I saw no reason to explain myself. I looked into his eyes and saw an odious and petty soul, and I was filled with rage and pity for the young woman who lay at my feet. "Pervert," I roared, in the language of my mothers. "Foul son of a maggot, may you and others like you wither like wheat in the desert. This was an unloved girl who lies here dead. The stench of her unhappiness clings to her. For this, you will die in agony."

Both Meryt and the priest stared at me as I spewed out my curses, and when I was finished the man began to shudder and in a terrified whisper said, "A foreign sorceress in the House of the Gods!"

The sound of our voices had drawn other priests, who did not meet my eyes and held their brother so we could leave. On the journey back, I watched the shoreline pass and remembered Inna's prophecy that I would find my heart's desire by the banks of a river. I shook my head over the irony of her vision, and returned to my garden shed unsettled and discontented.

For the first time since my childhood, I was restless. I no longer dreamed of Shalem or his death but woke up every morning haunted by visions of deserted landscapes, gaunt sheep, wailing women. I rose from my pallet vainly trying to name my disquiet. Meryt noticed grey hairs on my head and offered to make me a dye of ash and the blood of a black ox. I laughed at the idea, although I knew she used the potion and looked far younger than her years because of it. Her suggestion made me view my restlessness as nothing more than a sign of the passing years. I was nearly of the age when women stop bleeding at the new moon, and I pictured myself passing the twilight of my days in the familiar peace of Nakht-re's garden. I set a statue of Isis over my bed, and prayed for the wisdom and tranquillity of the lady goddess, healer of women and men.

But I neglected to pray for the well-being of my earthly protectors. Late one night, I was awakened by the sound of howling cats, and the next morning Nakht-re came to tell me that Re-nefer had died in her sleep. Her body was collected by priests, who would prepare her body for the next life with elaborate ritual in her father's tomb in Memphis, where a statue had been prepared in her memory. The rites would last for three days.

Nakht-re asked if I would like to attend the ritual with him. I thanked him but said no. He must have been relieved, for we both knew that there was no comfortable place for me among the celebrants.

In the days after Re-nefer's death, I cursed her as much as I wept for her. She had been my savior and my jailer. She had given me Shalem and then stolen his memory. Finally, I did not know the woman at all. I had seen little of her since Re-mose had gone to school and had no idea how she kept busy all those years; if she spun or wove, if she slept the days away, if she wept at night for her son and her husband. If she hated me or pitied me or loved me.

I dreamed in vivid detail in the nights following her death, and Re-nefer visited me in the form of a small bird flying out of the sunrise, screaming "Shechem" in a familiar voice that I could not name. The Re-nefer bird tried to lift people and objects from the ground but had no strength and beat her wings in frustration until she was exhausted and furious. Every night, she disappeared into the sun, shrieking. It seemed her troubled soul would never find peace. After seven nights of that vision, I felt nothing but pity for her.

Nakht-re died the following season, and for him I mourned without reservation. Honest, generous, good-humored, and always kind, he was the model of an Egyptian nobleman. My son was blessed to have had such a father, and I knew Re-mose would weep for the only Ba he had ever known. I assumed that Re-mose went to Memphis for the rites, though I was not told. Only Nakht-re had thought to tell me about my son's travels. With his death, I felt my connection to Re-mose weaken.

After Nakht-re was gone, his wife went to live with her brother, somewhere north in the Delta. The house would be given to a new scribe. Had Re-mose been a little older and more practiced in the politics of the temple, he might have been given the position. Instead, one of Nakht-re's rivals was chosen. Most of the staff would remain, and the cook urged me to stay on, too. But the chill in the eyes of the new mistress who came to survey what was to be her home made me want nothing less.

Meryt, too, was facing a change. Her older son, Menna, had offered her a place under his roof in the Valley of the Kings. He had been appointed chief baker and given a larger house, where his mother was welcome. Menna made the journey to see his mother and said that though many babies were born to the wives of craftsmen in the valley, there were no skilled midwives and many women had died. Meryt would be an honored citizen if she came to live among them.

My friend was tempted. Since the disastrous journey to

On, rumors had begun to circulate about the foreign-born midwife and her companion. The priest I had cursed had lost the use of his voice after I saw him, and then he went lame. There were fewer calls to attend at the births of noblewomen, though their servants and the tradesmen's wives still sought us out.

I knew that my friend relished the thought of honor and a new start, but she worried about living with a daughter-in-law and fretted about giving up the comforts of life in Thebes. She told her son that she would weigh his invitation until the following season, when the new year began. After all, she explained to me, the appearance of the dog star marked the most auspicious time for making changes.

My friend and I weighed our choices, but we often fell silent, keeping our worst fears to ourselves. In truth, I had nowhere to go. Herya had not offered me a place with her. I would simply have to stay where I was and hope for the best. If Meryt left for her son's house, loneliness would swallow me, but I kept still about that and listened as she described life in the valley.

Meryt never considered leaving without me, but she worried about asking her daughter-in-law to put up with two women in her house. My friend presented her dilemma to her good mistress, and Ruddedit begged her to stay and gave her word that I, too, would always have a place under her roof.

But the lady's husband was nothing like Nakht-re. He was a narrow-minded tyrant with a temper that sometimes broke upon the backs of his servants, and even Ruddedit kept her distance from him. My life would be pinched and furtive if I went to that house.

I might have lost heart except for the consolation I found in my dreams, where a garden of a thousand lotuses bloomed, children laughed, and strong arms held me safe. Meryt put great store in these dreams, and visited a local oracle who foresaw love and riches for me in the steaming entrails of a goat.

The new year came and Menna returned to see his mother. His wife, Shif-re, accompanied him this time and said, "Mother, come home with us. My sons work with their father in the bakery all day and I am often alone in the house. There is plenty of room for you to sit in the sun and rest. Or if you wish to continue as a midwife, I will carry your kit and become your assistant. You will be honored in my husband's house, and after your death we will honor your memory with a fine stele with your name on the west side."

Meryt was moved by her daughter-in-law's speech. Shif-re was a few years younger than I, a plain woman except for her eyes, which were large and ringed with thick black lashes, and radiated compassion. "Menna is lucky in you," said Meryt, taking the woman's hands in hers.

"But I cannot leave Den-ner here. She is my daughter now, and without me she is alone in the world. In truth, she is the master midwife, and I am her assistant. It is she the women of royal Thebes call for when their time is at hand.

"I cannot ask you to take her in. And yet, if you offer her the same hospitality, I believe you will be well rewarded in this life. She carries the mark of money and luck. She dreams with great power and sees through lies. All of this has rubbed off on me, and it will benefit you and your house, too."

Shif-re went to her husband with Meryt's words. Menna was not pleased at the prospect of yet another aging woman in his house, but the promise of luck struck a chord with him. He came with his mother and wife to my shed to make me welcome, and I accepted his offer with genuine gratitude. I took a turquoise scarab from my box and gave it to Menna. "Hospitality is the gods' own treasure," I said, placing my forehead to the ground before the baker, who was embarrassed to be shown such obeisance.

"Perhaps my brother can give you his garden for your own," he said, helping me to my feet. "His wife has no knack with growing things, and my mother tells me you have Osiris's own touch with the soil." Then it was my turn to be embarrassed at his kindness. How had I come to find so many kind people in my life? What was the purpose of such good fortune?

Menna's work called him home, so we had only a few days to prepare for our journey. First, I went to the market-place and hired a scribe who wrote on behalf of unlettered people, and through him sent word to Re-mose, assistant to Kar the scribe, residing in Kush, to inform him that his mother Den-ner had moved to the Valley of the Kings, to the house of the chief baker called Menna. I sent him blessings in the name of Isis and her son Horus. And I paid the scribe double his fee to make sure the message would find my son.

I gathered the herbs of my garden, taking cuttings of roots as well as dried plants. As I worked, I remembered how my mothers stripped their garden before leaving one life for another. I ventured into the market by myself and traded most of my trinkets for olive oil and castor oil, for juniper oil and berries, for I heard that few trees thrived in the valley. I scoured the stalls for the finest knife I could find, and the day before we left, Meryt and I went to the river and collected reeds enough to deliver a thousand babies.

I packed what I owned inside Benia's box, which had grown even more beautiful as the wood mellowed with age. Closing the lid, I tasted relief at my escape from an unhappy future.

The night before I left the house of Nakht-re I kept watch in the garden, walking around the pool, running my fingers over every bush and tree, filling my nose with the rich smells of blooming lotus and fresh clover. When the moon began to set, I crept inside the house and wandered past sleeping bodies up to the roof. The cats rubbed up against me, and I smiled, remembering my first fright at seeing the "fur snakes" of the land.

All of my days in Egypt had been spent in that house, and looking back on them in the night air, I recalled little but good: the scent of my infant son and the face of Nakht-re, cucumbers and honeyed fish, Meryt's laughter and the smiles of the new mothers to whom I delivered healthy sons and daughters. The painful things—Werenro's story, Re-nefer's choice, even my own loneliness—seemed like the knots on a beautiful necklace, necessary for keeping the beads in place. My eyes filled as I bade farewell to those days, but I felt no regret.

I was sitting outside the garden door, my box and a small bundle beside me, when the others arrived in the morning. Ruddedit walked with us as far as the ferry and embraced me before I got on the boat. She wept into Meryt's arms for a long while, but she was the only one weeping as the ferry pulled away from shore. I waved at her once, but then I set my eyes to the west.

The journey from the house of the scribe to the house of the baker took only one day, but the passage measured the difference between two worlds. The ferry was crowded with valley residents in a gala mood, on their way home from market. Many of the men had paid for the ministrations of open-air barbers, so their cheeks gleamed and their hair glistened. Mothers chatted about the children at their sides, petting them and scolding them in turn. Strangers struck up conversations with one another, comparing purchases and trying to establish a connection by comparing family names, occupations, and addresses. They seemed always to find a common friend or ancestor, and then clapped one another on the back like long-lost brothers.

They were at ease with themselves and one another like no other people I had ever seen, and I wondered what made it so. Perhaps it was because there were no lords or guards on the boat, not even a scribe. Only craftsmen and their families, heading home.

After the ferry, there was a short, steep climb to the town, which sprawled in the entrance to the valley like a giant wasp nest. My heart fell. It was as ugly a place as I'd ever seen. In the searing heat of the afternoon sun, the trees along the deserted streets looked limp and dirty. Houses crowded together, side by side, by the hundreds, each one as unremarkable and drab as the next. The doorways led down off the narrow pathways into darkness, and I wondered if I would be too tall to stand erect in the largest of them. The streets gave no hint of gardens, or colors, or any of the good things in life.

Somehow, Menna recognized one street from another and led us to the doorway of his brother's house, where a small boy stood watching. When he saw us, he shouted for his father, and Meryt's second son, Hori, rushed into the street, both hands filled with fresh bread. He ran to Meryt and lifted her up by the elbows, swinging her around and around, smiling with Meryt's own smile. His family gathered and clapped their hands as their grandmother laughed into her son's face and kissed him on the nose. Hori still had a house full of children, five in all, ranging from a marriageable daughter to the naked toddler who first spied us.

The family spilled into the street, drawing neighbors to the doorways, where they smiled at the commotion. Then Meryt was led through the antechamber of Hori's house and into his hall, a modest room where high windows let in the afternoon light on brightly colored floor mats and walls painted with a lush garden scene. My friend was seated on the best chair of the house and formally introduced, one by one, to her grandchildren.

I sat on the floor against a wall, watching Meryt bask in the glory of her children. The women brought food in from the back rooms, where I caught sight of a kitchen garden. Meryt praised the food, which was well spiced and plentiful, and declared the beer better than any she had tasted in the city of the nobles. Her daughter-in-law beamed at those words, and her son nodded with pride.

The children stared at me, having never seen a woman

quite so tall or a face so obviously foreign. They kept their distance, except for the little sentinel, who clambered up on my lap and stayed there, his thumb in his mouth. The weight of a child on my chest reminded me of the sweetness of the days I held Re-mose so. Forgetting myself, I sighed with such longing the others turned toward me.

"My friend!" cried Meryt, who rushed over to my side. "Forgive me for forgetting you." The child's mother came and took him from me, and Meryt drew me to my feet.

"This is Den-ner," she announced, and turned me around, like a child, so that everyone would see my face. "Menna will tell you that she is a friendless midwife he has taken in out of compassion. But I tell you that I am her friend and her sister, and that I am her student, for I have never seen nor heard tell of a more skilled midwife. She has Isis's hands, and with the goddess's love of children, shows the compassion of heaven for mothers and babies."

Meryt, her cheeks flushed with the attentions of her family, spoke about me like a merchant in the marketplace selling her wares. "And she is an oracle, too, my dears. Her dreams are powerful, and her anger is to be feared, for I have seen her blast an evil man out of the prime of his life for harming a young mother. She sees clearly into the hearts of men, and none fool her with fine words that conceal a lying heart.

"She comes from the east," said Meryt, now intoxicated with the sound of her own voice and her children's attention. "There, women are often as tall as the men of Egypt. And our Den-ner is as clever as she is tall, for she speaks both the language of the east and our tongue. And she gave birth to Re-mose, a scribe, the heir of Nakht-re, who will someday be a power in the land. We are lucky to have his mother among us, and the house of Menna will find itself lucky when she sleeps under his roof."

I was mortified to have so many eyes upon me. "Thanks," was all I could say. "Thank you," I said, bowing to Menna and Shif-re, and then to Hori and his wife, Takharu. "Thank you for your generosity. I am your servant, in gratitude."

I returned to my corner by the wall, content to observe the family as they ate and joked and enjoyed one another. As the light began to fade, I closed my eyes for a moment and saw Rachel holding Joseph on her lap, her cheek pressed against his.

I had not thought of my brother Joseph for years, and I could not place the memory exactly. But the scene was as vivid as my recollections of Leah's touch, as clear in my mind's eye as the tents of Mamre. Even as a child, I knew that Joseph would be the one to carry the family story into the next generation. He would be the one to change into someone more interesting and complicated than simply a beautiful man born of a beautiful mother.

Meryt's family thought I napped as I sat by the wall, but I was lost in thoughts of Joseph and Rachel, Leah and Jacob, my aunties and Inna and the days before Shechem. I sighed again, the sigh of an orphan, and my breath filled the room with a momentary melancholy that announced the end of the welcoming party.

Night was falling as Menna led Meryt and me through the moonlit streets to his house, which was nearby. Although it was larger and even better appointed than

Hori's, it was hot and airless inside, so we carried our pallets up a ladder to the roof, where the canopy of stars seemed only a handbreadth away.

I woke just before sunrise and stood up to see the entire town dreaming. They lay alone or in pairs, or in clusters with children and dogs. A cat walked down the street below, carrying something in her mouth. She placed it on the ground, and I saw it was a kitten, whom she began to lick clean. As I watched, the sun turned the cliffs pink and then gold. Women stirred and stretched, and then climbed down the ladders. Soon, the smell of food filled the air and the day began.

At first, Shif-re would not permit me or Meryt to do anything in her kitchen or garden, so the two of us sat useless, watching her work. Meryt had a horror of becoming a meddling mother-in-law, but her hands ached to be busy. "Only let me press out the beer," she asked. "I could sweep the roof," I proposed. But Shif-re seemed insulted by our offers. After a week of sitting, I could bear it no longer. Picking up a large empty jug, I announced, "I'm going to the fountain," and walked out the door before my hostess could object, surprising myself as well as Meryt. After years of fearing the street in Thebes, I rushed into this one, not entirely sure of where to go. But since there were always other women on their way to and from the fountain, I quickly discovered my route.

As I walked, I peered into doorways and smiled at naked children playing in the dust. I began to see differences between one house and the next; flowers planted here and there, lintels painted red or green, stools set up by the doorways. I felt like a girl again, my eyes open to new scenes, my day empty of work.

Near the fountain, I overtook a pregnant woman waddling in front of me. "This is not your first, is it?" I asked brightly as I reached her side. When she spun around to look at me, I saw Rachel's face as it must have appeared in the long years before Joseph was finally born to her. The woman's face twisted in anger and desperation.

"Oh, my dear," I said, ashamed. "I spoke before I understood what this means to you. Fear not, little mother. This boy will be fine."

Her eyes widened with fear and hope, and her mouth dropped wide. "How dare you speak to me so? This one will die like the others before. I am hated by the gods." Bitterness and anguish colored her words. "I am a luckless woman."

My answer came out of me with the assurance of the great mother herself, a voice that came through me but not from me. "He will be born whole, and soon. If not tonight, then tomorrow. Call me and I will help you upon the bricks and cut the cord."

Ahouri was her name, and after we filled our jars, she led me back to the baker's house. She lived only a few doorways east of Menna, and when her time came the following night, her husband came seeking the foreign-born midwife.

With Meryt, I attended as easy and straightforward a birth as any I ever saw. Ahouri sobbed with relief as she held the third child of her womb, but the only one born breathing. It was a strapping boy she called Den-ouri, the first to be named in my honor. Her husband, a potter, gave me a beautiful jar in thanks and kissed my hands and would have carried me home in his arms had I permitted it.

Meryt spread the story that I had performed some sort of wonder for Ahouri, and soon we were busier than we had been in Thebes. Most of the men who worked the valley were young, with wives of bearing age, and we attended as many as ten births in a month. Shif-re no longer had idle guests to feed, and indeed, quickly gained more dainties and extra linen than she knew what to do with. Menna was proud to have such respected women under his roof and treated me like his own aunt.

Weeks and months passed quickly, and life in the valley took on its own orderly pace. Mornings were the busiest times, before the great heat descended. The men left early and children played in the streets while the women swept out their homes, cooked the day's meals, and fetched water at the fountains, where news was exchanged and plans laid for the next festival.

While the great river was not visible from the town, it still ruled the ebb and flow of daily life in the arid valley. Its seasons were celebrated in high spirits by the craftsmen, who grew up imbibing the rhythms of farming by the Nile. After so many years in the land of the great river, I finally learned the beautiful names of its seasons. *Akhit*—the inundation; *perit*—the going-out; *shemou*—the harvest. Each had its own holiday and lunar rite, its own festive foods and songs.

Just before my first harvest moon in the valley, a scribe came to Menna's door with a letter from my son. Re-mose wrote to say that he was living in Thebes again, assigned as scribe to a new vizier called Zafenat Paneh-ah, the king's choice. He sent greetings in the names of Amun-Re and Isis, and a prayer for my good health. It was a formal note, but I was happy that he thought of me enough to send it. And that shard of limestone, written in his own hand, became my most prized possession and regardless of my protests, became proof of my status as a person of importance.

Not long after my son's letter arrived, another man appeared at the door seeking the woman named Den-ner. Shif-re asked him if it was his wife or his daughter who had need of a midwife's bricks, but he said, "Neither." Then she asked if he was a scribe with another letter from Thebes, but he said no. "I am a carpenter."

Shif-re came to the garden with curious news about a bachelor carpenter who sought a midwife. Meryt looked up from her spinning sharply and with a great show of disinterest said, "Den-ner, go and see what the stranger wants." I went without thinking.

His eyes were sadder, but in all other ways he was the same. I stood for only a moment before Benia reached out to me with his right hand. Without hesitation, I placed my left hand in it. I extended my right hand and he took it with his left. We stood like that, hand in hand and smiling like fools without speaking, until Meryt could stand the suspense no longer. "Oh, Den-ner," she called with false concern. "Are you there, or was that a pirate at the door?"

I led him back through the house to where Meryt hopped like a bird from one foot to the other, wearing the wild grin of the god Bes. Shif-re smiled too, having just learned how Meryt had spent the past months seeking out the artist who had offered me his heart along with the luxurious box that accompanied me from Thebes.

They bade him sit and offered beer and bread. But Benia looked only at me. And I returned his gaze.

"Go ahead then," Meryt said, giving me a hug and then a push. "Menna will bring your box to you in the morning and I will follow him with bread and salt. Go, in the name of the lady Isis and her consort Osiris. Go and be content."

Leaving my friend's house to follow a stranger, I was surprised by my own certainty, but I did not hesitate.

We walked through the streets, side by side, for what seemed like a very long time, saying nothing. His house was near the edge of the settlement, close to the path leading up to the tombs, many streets away from Meryt. As we walked, I recalled my mothers' stories about hennaed hands and songs for the groom and bride on their way to the bridal tent. I smiled to think of myself as being in a kind of procession at that moment, walking toward my own marriage bed. I smiled too to think of how Meryt would rush from fountain to fountain the next morning, telling everyone about the love affair between Benia the master carpenter and Den-ner the magical midwife. I nearly laughed at the thought. Benia heard the sound that escaped from my mouth as distress. He put his arm around me, placed his lips to my ear, and whispered, "Fear not."

Magic words. I laid my head on his shoulder and we walked the rest of the way holding hands, like children.

When we arrived at his house, which was nearly as large as Menna's, he took me through the rooms, and with great pride showed me the furniture he had built—two thronelike chairs, an ornately carved bed, boxes in many shapes. I laughed when I saw the easing stool, which was far too beautiful for its foul purpose. "I thought of you when I made these things," he said, shrugging in embarrassment. "I thought of you sitting here, sleeping here, putting things to right in your own way. When Meryt found me I made this for you."

He took an exquisite little box from a niche in the wall. It was unadorned but perfect, made of ebony—wood that was used almost exclusively for the tombs of kings—and it had been burnished until it shone like a black moon. "For your midwife's kit," he said, and held it out to me.

I stared at it for a moment, overwhelmed by his generosity and tenderness. "I have nothing to give you by way of a token," I said. He shrugged with one shoulder, in a gesture I soon came to know as well as I knew my own hands. "You don't have to give me anything. If you take this from my hands freely, your choice will be your token."

Thus I became a married woman in Egypt.

Benia laid out a meal of bread and onions and fruit for us, and we sat in the kitchen and ate and drank in nervous silence. I had been a girl the last time I had lain with a man. Benia had been thinking of me since that day in the market, two years earlier. We were shy as two virgins who had been matched by their parents.

After we ate, he took my hand and led me to the main hall, where the fine bed stood, piled with clean linen. It reminded me of Re-nefer's bed in Nakht-re's house. It reminded me of Shalem's bed, in his father's house. But then Benia turned me toward him and put his hands on my face and I forgot every bed I had ever seen before that moment.

Lying together was a tender surprise. From our very first night, Benia took great care of my pleasure and seemed to discover his own in mine. My shyness vanished in the course of that night, and as the weeks passed, I found wells of desire and passion that I had never suspected in myself. When Benia lay with me, the past vanished and I was a new soul, reborn in the taste of his mouth, the touch of his fingers. His huge hands cupped my body and untied secret knots created by years of loneliness and silence. The sight of his naked legs, thick and ropy with sinew, aroused me so much that Benia would tease me as he left in the morning, lifting his skirt to reveal the top of his thigh, making me blush and laugh.

My husband went to his workshop every morning, but unlike the stonecutters and painters, he did not have to work in the tombs, so he returned to me in the evening, where he and I discovered greater pleasure in each other—and the sorry fact that I did not know how to cook.

During my years in Nakht-re's house, I rarely strayed into the kitchen, much less prepared a meal. I had never learned how to make bread in an Egyptian oven or to gut fish or pluck fowl. We ate unripe fruit from Benia's neglected garden and I begged bread from Menna. Shamefaced, I asked Shif-re for a cooking lesson, which Meryt attended only to tease me.

I tried to recreate my mother's recipes, but I lacked the ingredients and I forgot the proportions. I felt sheepish and ashamed, but Benia only laughed. "We won't starve," he said. "I have kept myself alive for years on borrowed bread and fruit and the occasional feast at the house of my fellows and family. I did not marry you to be my cook."

But while I was a stranger in the kitchen, I found great joy in keeping my own house. There was such sweetness in deciding where to place a chair, and in choosing what to plant in the garden. I relished creating my own order and hummed whenever I swept the floor or folded blankets. I spent hours arranging pots in the kitchen first in order of size, then according to color.

My house was a world of my own possession, a country in which I was ruler and citizen, where I chose and where I served. One night, when I returned home very late, exhausted after attending at the birth of healthy twins, I thought I had lost my way. Standing in the middle of the street in the dead of night, I recognized my home by its smell—a mixture of coriander, clover, and Benia's cedary scent.

A few months after I moved to my own house, Menna prepared a small banquet for me and Benia. My husband's workmen sang songs of their workshop. Meryt's sons sang of bread. And then all the men, together with their wives and children, joined voices for love songs, of which there seemed to be an endless number. I was bashful at the attention showered upon us, the cups raised, the broad smiles and kisses. Even though Benia and I were really too old for such nonsense, we were giddy with delight in each other. When Meryt leaned over and told me to stop grudging people the chance to bask in the light of our shared happiness, I put aside all shyness in gratitude and smiled into the faces of my friends.

I had been right to trust Benia, who was the soul of kindness. One night we lay on our backs staring up at the heavens. There was only a sliver of moon and the stars danced above when he told me his life. His words came slowly, for many of the memories were sad ones.

"I have only one memory of my father," said Benia. "The

sight of his back, which I saw as he walked away from me in a field where I sat behind the plow breaking up clods. I was six years old when he died, leaving Ma with four children. I was the third son.

"She had no brothers, and my father's people were not generous. She had to find places for us, so my mother took me to the city and showed my hands to the stonecutters. They took me on as an apprentice, and taught me and worked me until my back was strong and my hands callused. But I became a joke in the workshops. Marble would crack if I walked into a room and granite would weep if I raised a chisel to it.

"Wandering in the market one day, I watched as a carpenter repaired an old stool for a poor woman. He saw my belt and bowed low, for even though I was only an apprentice, stonecutters who work in immortal materials are considered far greater than woodworkers, whose greatest achievements decay like a man's body.

"I told the carpenter that his respect was misplaced and that mere sandstone defeated me. I confessed that I was in danger of being turned into the street.

"The woodworker took my hand in his, turning it this way and that. He handed me a knife and a scrap of wood and asked me to carve a toy for his grandson.

"The wood seemed warm and alive, and a doll took shape in my hands without effort. The very grain of the pine seemed to smile at me.

"The carpenter nodded at the thing I made and took me to the workshop of his teacher, presenting me as a likely apprentice. And there I discovered my life's work."

Here my husband sighed. "There, too, I met my wife, who was a servant in the house of my master. We were so young," he said softly, and in the silence that followed I understood that he had loved the wife of his youth with his whole heart.

After a long pause he said, "We had two sons." Again he stopped, and in the silence I heard the voices of little boys, Benia's doting laughter, a woman singing a lullaby.

"They died of river fever," Benia said. "I had taken them from the city to see my brother, who had married into a farming family. But when we arrived at the house, we found my brother dying and the rest of his family stricken. My wife cared for them all," he whispered. "We should have left," he said, with self-reproach still raw after many years.

"After that," he said, "I lived only in my work and loved only my work. I visited the prostitutes once," he confessed sheepishly. "But they were too sad.

"Until the day I saw you in the marketplace, I did not bother to hope for anything. When I first recognized you as my beloved, my heart came to life," he said. "But when you disappeared and seemed to scorn me, I grew angry. For the first time in my life, I raged against heaven for stealing my family and then for dangling you before my eyes and snatching you away. I was furious and frightened of my own loneliness.

"So I took a wife."

I had been perfectly still until then, but that announcement made me sit up.

"Yes, yes," he said, embarrassed. "My sister found me a

marriageable girl, a servant in the house of a painter, and I brought her here with me. It was a disaster. I was too old for her; she was too silly for me.

"Oh Den-ner," he said, in a misery of apology. "We were so mismatched it could have been funny. We never spoke. We tried sharing my bed, twice, and even that was awful.

"Finally, she was braver than I, poor girl. After two weeks, she left. Walked out of the house while I was at work, down to the ferry and back to the painter's house, where she remains.

"I was resigned to making strong drink my regular companion until Meryt sought me out. She visited me three times before I would agree to see you. I am lucky that your friend does not understand the meaning of 'no.'"

I turned to my husband and said, "And my luck is measured by your kindness, which is boundless."

We made love very slowly that night, as though for the last time, weeping. One of his tears fell in my mouth, where it became a blue sapphire, source of strength and eternal hope.

Benia did not ask for my story in return. His eyes would fill with questions when I mentioned my mother's way of making beer, or my aunt's skill as a midwife, but he stepped back from his need to know. I think he feared that I might vanish if he so much as asked me the meaning of my name or the word for "water" in my native tongue.

On another moonless night, I told him as much of my truth as I could: that Re-mose's father was the son of Re-nefer, sister of Nakht-re, and that I came to Thebes after the murder of my husband, in our own bed. When he heard that, Benia shuddered, took me into his arms as though I was a child, and stroked my hair, and said nothing but "Poor thing." Which was everything I had longed to hear.

Neither of us ever gave voice to the names of our beloved dead ones, and for this act of respect, they permitted us to live in peace with our new mates and never haunted our thoughts by day or visited our dreams at night.

Life was sweet in the Valley of the Kings, on the west bank of the river. Benia and I had everything we needed in each other. Indeed, we were rich in all ways but one, for we lacked children.

I was barren, or perhaps only too old to bear. Although I had already lived a full life—close to twoscore years—my back was strong and my body still obeyed the pull of the moon. I was certain that my womb was cold, but even so I could never root out all hope from my heart, and I grieved with the flux of every new moon.

Still we were not completely childless, for Meryt often sat in our doorstep, trailing her grandchildren, who treated us as uncle and aunt—especially little Kiya, who liked to sleep in our house so much that her mother sometimes sent her to stay with us, to help me in the garden and to brighten our days.

Benia and I shared stories in the evenings. I told him of the babies that I caught and of the mothers who died, though they were blessedly few. He spoke of his commissions—each one a new challenge, based not only upon the desires of the buyer and builders, but also upon the wishes of the wood in his hand.

The days passed peacefully, and the fact that there was little to mark one from the next seemed a great gift to me. I had Benia's hands, Meryt's friendship, the feel of newborn flesh, the smiles of new mothers, a little girl who laughed in my kitchen, a house of my own.

It was more than enough.

Chapter Four

I KNEW ABOUT RE-MOSE'S message even before the messenger arrived at my house. Kiya ran to the door with the news that a scribe had come to Menna's house seeking Den-ner the midwife and was on his way to Benia's door.

I was delighted at the prospect of another letter from my son. It had been more than a year since the last one, and I imagined myself showing Benia my son's own writing on the limestone tablet when he arrived home that evening.

I stood in the doorway, anxious to discover the contents of this letter. But when the man turned the corner, surrounded by a pack of excited little children, I realized that the messenger brought his own message.

Re-mose and I stared at each other. I saw a man I did not know—the image of Nakht-re except for his eyes, which were set like his father's. I saw nothing of myself in the prince of Egypt who stood before me, dressed in fine linen, with a gold pectoral gleaming on his chest and new sandals on his manicured feet.

I did not know what he saw as he looked at me. I thought I detected disdain in his eye, but perhaps that was only my own fear. I wondered if he could see that I stood taller now that I carried less grief on my back. Whatever he saw or thought, we were strangers.

"Forgive my manners," I said finally. "Come inside the house of Benia, and let me give you some cool beer and fruit. I know the journey from Thebes is dusty."

Re-mose recovered too, and said, "Forgive me, Mother. It is so long since I saw your dear face." His words were cool and his embrace a quick, awkward hug. "I would gladly take a drink," he said, and followed me into the house.

I saw each room through his eyes, which were accustomed to the spacious beauties of palaces and temples. The front room, my room, which I treasured for the colorful wall painting, suddenly looked small and bare, and I was glad when he hurried through it. Benia's hall was larger and furnished with pieces seen only in great houses and tombs. The quality of the chairs and bed found approval in my son's eyes, and I left him there to fetch food and drink. Kiya had followed us in and stared at the beautifully dressed man in my house.

"Is this my sister?" asked Re-mose, pointing to the silent child.

"No," I said. "This is the niece of a friend, and like a niece to me." My answer seemed to relieve him. "The gods seem to have ordained that you remain my only child," I added.

"I am glad to see you healthy and successful. Tell me, are you married yet? Am I a grandmother?"

"No," said Re-mose. "My duties keep me too busy for my own family," he said, with a tight little wave of his hand.

"Perhaps someday my situation will improve and I can give you little ones to dandle on your knee."

But this was nothing more than polite conversation, which hung in the air and smelled of falsehood. The gulf between us was far too wide for any such familiarity. If and when I became a grandmother, I would know my grandchildren only through messages sent on limestone slabs meant to be discarded after they are read.

"Ma," he said, after drinking from his cup, "I am here not only for my own pleasure. My master sends me to fetch the finest midwife in Egypt to attend his wife's labor.

"No, it is true," he said, dismissing my shrug. "Say nothing to diminish your repute, for no one has taken your place in Thebes. The lady of my master has miscarried twice and nearly died from a stillbirth. The physicians and necromancers have done her no good, and now the midwives fear to attend a princess who has had so much bad luck in childbed. Her own mother is dead, and she is afraid.

"My master dotes on this wife and wishes nothing more than to have sons by her. As-naat heard of your skills from her servants and asked her husband to search out the foreign-born woman with the golden hands who once served the women of Thebes. My lord depends upon me for all things and called upon me in this matter as well," said Re-mose, his mouth growing smaller and more pursed at every mention of his master.

"Imagine my surprise when I learned that he sought none but my own mother. He was suddenly impressed by my lineage when he learned that you were a countryman of his," Re-mose added ironically. "The vizier charged me to put aside duties of state, to walk into the Valley of the Kings and accompany you to his house. He ordered me not to return without you."

"You do not like this man," I said mildly.

"Zafenat Paneh-ah is vizier in Thebes at the king's pleasure," said my son, in formal but damning tones. "He is said to be a great diviner who sees into the future and reads dreams as easily as a master scribe perusing the glyphs of a schoolboy. But he is illiterate," said Re-mose bitterly. "He cannot cipher or write or read, which is why the king assigned me, the best of Kar's students, to be his right hand. And that is where I am now, wifeless, childless, second to a barbarian."

I stiffened at the word. Re-mose noticed my reaction and colored in shame. "Oh Ma, not you," he said quickly. "You are not like the rest of them, or else my father and grand-mother would never have chosen you. You are fine," he said. "There is no mother in Egypt better than you." His flattery made me smile in spite of myself. He embraced me, and for a moment I regained the loving boy who had been my son.

We drank our beer in silence for a moment, then I said, "Of course I will follow you to Thebes. If the king's vizier commands you to bring me, I will come. But first I must speak with my friend, Meryt, who is my right hand in the birth chamber and should come with me.

"I must talk with my husband, Benia, the master carpen-ter, so that he knows where I go and when I might return."

Re-mose pursed his lips again. "There is no time for this, Ma. We must leave now, for the lady is in travail and my lord expects me every hour. Send the girl here to inform the others. I cannot tarry."

"I'm afraid you must," I said, and I left the room. Re-mose followed me to the kitchen and grabbed me by the elbow, like a master about to strike a disobedient servant.

I pulled away and looked into his face. "Nakht-re would sooner die than treat a relative—much less a mother—in this fashion. Is this how you honor the memory of the only father you ever knew? I remember him as a noble man to whom you owe everything, and whose name you dishonor."

Re-mose stopped and hung his head. His ambition and his heart were at war, and his face showed the division in his soul. He fell to the ground and bowed low, his brow at my feet.

"I forgive you," I said. "It will only take me a moment to prepare, and we will find my friend and husband on our path to Thebes."

Re-mose raised himself from the ground again and waited outside while I prepared for a journey I hated to make. As I gathered my kit and a few herbs, I smiled at my own brazenness, shaming my powerful son for his rudeness, insisting on my farewells. Where was the meek woman who lived in Nakht-re's house all those years?

Meryt waited for me at her son's door, hungry for the news. Her eyes grew large when I introduced her to Re-mose, whom she had not seen since he was a boy. She covered her mouth in awe at the invitation to wait upon the wife of the king's vizier, but Meryt could not accompany me. Three women in the town were due to give birth at any moment, and one of them was kin, the daughter of Shif-re's brother. We embraced, and she wished me the touch of Isis and the luck of Bes. She stood at her door and waved gaily. "Bring me back some good stories," she shouted, and her laughter followed me down the street.

Benia did not send me away with laughter. He and my son looked at each other coolly; Benia dipped his head in recognition of the scribe's position, and Re-mose nodded at the carpenter's authority over so important a workshop. There was no way for my husband and me to take a proper leave of each other. We exchanged our parting vows with our eyes. I would return. He would not be content until I did.

Re-mose and I walked out of the valley, saying little to each other. Before we began the descent from the valley to the riverbank, I put my hand on his arm, signaling him to stop. Turning to face home, I dropped a twist of rue from my garden and a piece of bread from my oven to ensure a speedy return.

It was dark by the time we reached the river, but we had no need to wait for the morning ferry. The king's barque, lit with a hundred lamps, waited for us. Many oars rowed us, and in no time we were hurrying through the sleeping streets of the city and into the great palace, where Re-mose left me at the door to the women's quarters. I was taken to a chamber where a pale young woman sat perched on her great bed, alone.

"You are Den-ner?" she asked.

"Yes, As-naat," I replied gently, placing my bricks on the floor. "Let me see what the gods have in store for us."

"I fear this one is dead, too," she whispered. "And if it is so, let me die with him."

I put my ear to her belly and touched the womb. "This baby is alive," I said. "Fear not. He is just resting for the journey."

At daylight, her pains began in earnest. As-naat tried to be quiet as befits a royal lady, but nature had made her a screamer, and she soon filled the air with roars at every pang.

I called for fresh water to bathe the mother's face, for fresh straw, for lotus cones to freshen the room, and for five serving women, who gathered around their mistress to offer encouragement. Sometimes it is easier for the poor, I thought. Even those without family live in such close quarters to their neighbors that the cries of a laboring mother bring out other women like geese responding to the call of a leader in flight. But the rich are surrounded by servants too fearful of their mistresses to act as sisters.

As-naat did not have an easy time, but it was nowhere near the worst labor I'd seen. She pushed for long hours, supported by women who became her sisters, at least for that day. Just after sunset, she produced a skinny but healthy son, who roared for the breast as soon as he was held upright.

As-naat kissed my hands, covering them with joyful tears, and sent one of her servants to tell Zafenat Paneh-ah that he was the father of a fine son. I was taken to a quiet room, where I fell into a dark, dreamless sleep.

I awoke the following morning drenched in sweat, my head throbbing, my throat on fire. Lying on the pallet, I squinted at the light pouring through the high windows and tried to remember the last time I had been ill. My head pounded, and I closed my eyes again. When next they opened, the light was draining from the room.

A girl sitting by the wall noticed I was awake and brought me a drink and placed a cool towel on my brow. Two days passed, or maybe it was three, in a blur of fevered sleep and compresses. When my head finally cooled and the pain subsided, I found myself too weak to stand.

By then a woman called Shery had been sent to attend me. I stared with an open mouth when she introduced herself, for her name, which means "little one," sat oddly upon the fattest woman I'd ever seen.

Shery washed the sour smell from my body and brought me broth and fruit and offered to fetch anything else I might wish. I had never been waited upon like that, and while I did not enjoy her hovering over me, I was grateful for her help.

After a few days my strength began to return, and I asked Shery to tell me the news of the baby I had delivered. She was delighted by my question and settled her weight about her on a stool, for Shery loved an audience.

The baby was well, she reported. "He is ravenous, and has nearly worn off his mother's nipples with constant feeding," said Shery with a wicked grin. She had pitied her mistress's childlessness, but found As-naat an arrogant snip of a mistress. "Motherhood will teach her everything," my new friend confided.

"The father has named the boy Menashe, an awful name that must mean something fine in his native tongue. Menashe. It sounds like chewing, does it not? But you are of Canaan as well, are you not?"

I shrugged. "It was so long ago," I said. "Please, continue with the story, Shery. It is almost magical, the way your words make me forget my aches and pains."

She gave me a sharp look to let me know that flattery did not hide my reticence. But she continued anyway.

"Zafenat Paneh-ah is truly an arrogant son of a bitch," she said, proving her trust in me by swearing about the master. "He likes to talk of his lowly beginnings as though this makes his powerful position even greater due to his rise. But this is no great thing in Egypt. Many great men — statesmen and craftsmen, warriors and artisans — are born of the lowly. Such is the case with your own husband, eh, Den-ner?" she asked, letting me know that my history was not entirely closed to her. But I only smiled.

"The Canaanite is handsome, no doubt about that. Women swoon at the sight of him — or at least they did when he was younger. Men are drawn to him as well, and not only the ones who prefer boys.

"Of course, that beauty did not serve him well when he was young. His own brothers hated him so much they sold him to a pack of slavers — can you imagine an Egyptian doing such a thing? Every day I thank the gods that I was born in the valley of the great river."

"No doubt," I said, surveying her girth, for there was no other land that could support such excess. Shery caught my meaning and grabbed at her midsection with both hands. "Ha, ha! I am a creature of amazing proportions, am I not? The king once pinched me and said that only dwarves please him more than the sight of someone as large and round as me. You would not believe how many men find this desirable," Shery said. "In my own youth," she began in a conspiratorial whisper, "I gave pleasure to the old king, until his wife grew jealous and had me packed off to Thebes.

"But that"—she winked—"is another story for another time. You want the history of this house, which is juicy enough," she confided.

"Zafenat Paneh-ah was sold into slavery, as I said, and his new masters were swine, the most Canaanite of the Canaanites. I don't doubt that he was beaten and raped and forced to do the dirtiest work. Of course, his majesty does not speak of that anymore.

"Zafenat Paneh-ah did not acquire that pompous name until recently. 'The God Speaks and He Lives,' indeed! They used to call him Stick, for when he first came to Egypt he was as skinny as his newborn son.

"When his owners came to Thebes, he was sold to Po-ti-far, a palace guard with sticky fingers who lived in a great house on the outskirts of the city. Because Stick was more clever than his master by half, he was put in charge of the garden, and then given oversight of the wine-pressing. Finally, he was set above the other servants in the house, for Po-ti-far loved the Canaanite boy and used him for his own pleasure.

"But Po-ti-far's wife, a great beauty called Nebetper, also looked upon him with longing, and the two of them became lovers right under the master's nose. There is even some gossip about who fathered her last daughter. In any case, Po-ti-far finally discovered them in bed together and he could no longer pretend not to know what was going on. So in a great show of anger and vengeance, he sent Stick to prison."

By that point I had lost interest in Shery's story, which

apparently had no end. I wanted to sleep, but there was no stopping the woman, who did not see my hint when I yawned, or even when I closed my eyes.

"The Theban jail is no laughing matter," she said darkly. "A hideous pit where men die of murder and despair as much as fever, full of madmen and cutthroats. But the warden came to pity his handsome inmate, who was neither hateful or insane. Soon he was taking his meals with the Canaanite, who spoke a good Egyptian by then.

"The warden was a bachelor and childless, and he treated Stick like a son. As the years passed he gave Stick responsibility for his fellows, until finally he was the one to determine which man slept near a window and which man was chained close to the latrine, so the inmates did what they could to bribe and please him. I tell you, Den-ner," Shery said, shaking her head in admiration, "wherever this fellow goes, power seems to move into his hands.

"Meanwhile, the old king died, and the new king had a habit of punishing minor offences against him by sending people to jail. If he was displeased by the texture of his bread at dinner, he might send the baker to jail for a week or even longer. Cupbearers, wine stewards, sandal-makers, even captains of the guard were sent to languish in that place, where they met Stick.

"Everyone was struck by his princely bearing and by his ability to interpret dreams and divine the future. He told one poor drunkard that he would not live out the week, and when he was found dead—not murdered, mind you, simply done in by years of strong drink—the prisoners proclaimed him an oracle. When a cupbearer returned from prison with a story about a jailer who saw into the future, the king sent for Stick and set him to interpret a series of dreams that had plagued him for months.

"It was not a difficult dream to divine, if you ask me," said Shery. "Fat fish being devoured by bony fish, fat cows being trampled by skinny cows, and then seven fat stalks of wheat which were beaten down, leaving seven dead stalks.

"Any half-wit magician who pulls birds from beneath baskets in the marketplace could have interpreted that one," Shery sniggered. "But the dreams haunted and frightened the idiot king, and it calmed him to hear that he had seven years in which to prepare for the coming famine. And so he elevated the jailer, an unlettered foreign-born conniver, to become his first-in-command.

"I imagine your son has already told you that this so-called Zafenat Paneh-ah is totally dependent upon Re-mose. And now that Zafenat is not only vizier but a father as well, there will be no stopping his pride," Shery fumed, bustling around the room, preparing my bed, for she had talked away the whole afternoon.

"And yesterday," she grumbled, speaking to herself by that point, "this madman demanded that his son be circumcised. Not when he is at manhood's door and able to withstand such a thing. Not like civilized people, but now. Immediately! Can you imagine wanting to do that to a tiny baby? It only goes to prove that a born barbarian does not change. As-naat screamed and carried on like a gutted cat at the order. And I can't blame her there."

"Joseph," I whispered, in horror and disbelief.

Shery peered up at me. "What?" she said. "What did you say, Den-ner?"

But I closed my eyes, suddenly unable to breathe. All at

once I understood why I had been summoned to Thebes and why Shery had told me the endless story of the vizier. But surely this could not be. It was fever that weakened my reason. Dizzy and light-headed, I lay down on the bed, panting.

Shery noticed that something was amiss with me. "Denner," she said. "Are you unwell? Can I get you something? Maybe you are ready for solid food now.

"But here is something to cheer you up," she said, looking up at the sound of footsteps. "Your son comes to pay respects. Here is Re-mose. I will bring you both some refreshment," she burbled, and left me with my son.

"Mother?" he said, formally with a stiff bow. But when he saw my face he started. "Ma? What is it? They told me you were much improved and that I might see you today," he said doubtfully. "But perhaps this is not the right time."

I turned my face toward the wall and waved him out of the room. I heard Shery go out with him and murmur an explanation. His hurried footsteps fading in the distance were the last thing I knew before I fell asleep.

Shery had told Re-mose of our conversation and repeated the word I had spoken before falling back into a fevered darkness of mind. Thus my son took "Joseph" into his mouth and, unannounced, went into the great hall, where the vizier of Egypt sat alone, whispering comfort to his firstborn son, who had been circumcised earlier that day.

"Joseph," said Re-mose, throwing the name at him like a challenge. And the one known as Zafenat Paneh-ah trembled.

"Do you know a woman called Den-ner?" he demanded.

For a moment Zafenat Paneh-ah said nothing, and then he asked, "Dinah?" The master looked into his scribe's eyes. "I had a sister named Dinah, but she died long ago. How do you come by her name? What do you know of Joseph?" he commanded.

"I will tell you what there is to tell after you describe her death," said Re-mose. "But only then."

The threat in his voice rankled Joseph. But even though he sat on a throne with a healthy son in his arms and guards ready to do his bidding, he felt bound to answer. It had been a lifetime since he had heard his own name, twenty years since he had spoken his sister's name aloud.

So he began. In a quiet voice that drew Re-mose close to the throne, he told him that Dinah had gone to the palace in Shechem with his mother, Rachel the midwife, to tend to a birth in the house. "A prince of the city claimed her for a bride," said Joseph, and Re-mose heard how Jacob turned away the handsome bride-price, and finally accepted him only on the cruelest of conditions.

Re-mose shuddered to learn his father's name from Joseph's lips, but in the next moment he learned that my brothers, his own uncles, had slaughtered Shalem in his own bed. Re-mose bit his tongue to keep from crying out.

Joseph declared his repugnance for the crime and proclaimed his own innocence. "Two of my brothers bloodied their hands," he said, but admitted that perhaps four of them had had some part in the murder. "All of us were punished.

"She cursed us all. Some of my brothers fell ill, others

saw their sons die. My father lost all hope, and I was sold into slavery."

Joseph said, "I used to blame my sister for my misfortunes, but no longer. If I knew where she was buried, I would go and pour libations and build a stele in her memory. At least I survived my brothers' villainy, and with the birth of this son, the god of my fathers shows me that I will not die forgotten. But my sister's name was blotted out, as though she had never drawn breath.

"She was my milk-sister," said Joseph, shaking his head. "It is strange to speak of her now that I am a father. Perhaps I will name the next one in her honor," and he fell silent.

"And what is Joseph?" Re-mose asked.

"Joseph is the name my mother gave me," said Zafenat Paneh-ah quietly.

Re-mose turned to leave, but the vizier called him back. "Wait! We have a bargain. Tell me how you came to know my name and the name of my sister."

Re-mose stopped and without facing him said, "She is not dead."

The words hung in the air. "She is here, in your palace. Indeed, you bade her brought here. Den-ner the midwife, the one who delivered your son, is your sister, Dinah. My mother."

Joseph's eyes grew wide in wonder, and he smiled like a happy child. But Re-mose spit at his feet.

"Would you have me call you uncle?" he hissed. "I hated you from the first. You robbed me of a position that is rightly mine, and you advance in the king's eyes because of my skill. Now I see that you blasted my life from birth!

347

You slaughtered my father in the prime of his youth. You and your barbarian brothers murdered my grandfather too, who, though a Canaanite, acted honorably.

"You ripped the heart out of my grandmother. You betrayed your sister, widowed my mother, and made me an orphan and an outcast.

"When I was a boy, my grandmother's servant told me that when I finally found my father's murderers, their names would rip my soul into pieces. His words were true.

"You are my uncle. Oh gods, what a nightmare," Remose cried. "A murderer and a liar. How dare you claim innocence in this abomination? Perhaps you raised no sword yourself, but you did nothing to stop them. You must have known something of the plot, you and your father and the rest of his seed. I see the blood of my father on your hands. Your guilt is still in your eyes."

Joseph looked away.

"There is nothing left but for me to kill you, or die a coward. If I do not avenge my father, I will be unworthy of this life, much less the next."

Re-mose's voice, raised in hatred, alerted the guards, who subdued him and led him away while Menashe wailed in his father's arms.

When I finally woke, Shery sat beside me, her face stricken.

"What is it?" I asked.

"Oh lady," she said, in a great rush to tell me what she knew, "I have bad news. Your son and the vizier have quarreled, and Re-mose is under guard in his chambers. The master is said to be furious, and they say that the young scribe is in mortal danger. I do not know the cause of their quarrel, not yet at least. But when I learn it, I will tell you immediately."

I got to my feet, wobbling but determined. "Shery," I commanded. "Listen to me now, for I will not argue or repeat myself. I must speak to the master of the house. Go and announce me."

The serving woman bowed from the waist, but in a small voice said, "You cannot go to Zafenat Paneh-ah looking as you do. Let me give you a bath and dress your hair. Put on a clean gown so you can make your case like a lady and not a beggar."

I nodded my assent, suddenly frightened by the scene ahead. What words could I use to a brother I had not seen for a lifetime? I crouched in the bath as Shery poured cool water over me and leaned back as she brushed and arranged my hair. I felt like a slave about to be paraded before a gallery of buyers.

When I was ready, Shery led me to the door of Zafenat Paneh-ah's hall, where he sat with his head in his hands.

"Den-ner, the midwife, requests an audience," she said.

The vizier stood up and waved me in.

"Leave us," he barked. Shery and all of his retainers disappeared. We were alone. Neither of us moved. We kept our places on opposite ends of the room and stared.

Though the years had cost him his smooth cheeks and a few of his teeth, Joseph was still fair of face and strong, still the son of Rachel.

"Dinah," he said. "Ahatti—little sister," he said, in the language of our youth. "The grave has set you free."

"Yes, Joseph," I said. "I am alive, and amazed to be in

your presence. But the only reason I come to you is to ask what has become of my son."

"Your son knows the story of his father's death and he threatens my life," said Joseph stiffly. "He holds me responsible for the sins of my brothers. His threat alone could cause his execution, but because he is your son, I will only send him away.

"He will not come to harm, I promise," said Joseph kindly. "I have recommended that the king give him charge of a prefecture in the north, where he will be second to none. In time, he will fall in love with the sea—they all do— and he will build a life seasoned with salt air and salt water and not wish for any other.

"You must tell him to do as I say and forget this talk of revenge," said Joseph. "You must do this now, tonight. If he raises a hand to me, if he so much as threatens me in the company of my guard, he must die."

"I doubt that my son will listen to my words," I said sadly. "He hates me, for I am the cause of his unhappiness."

"Nonsense," said Joseph, with the supreme self-confidence that made our brothers so jealous. "The men of Egypt honor their mothers like no other men in the world."

"You do not know," I said. "He called his grandmother Ma. I was no more than his wet nurse."

"No, Dinah," said Joseph. "He suffers too much for that to be true. He will listen to you, and he must go."

I looked at my brother and saw a man I did not know. "I will do as you say, master," I said, in the voice of a good servant. "But ask me for nothing else. Let me be free of this place, for it is a tomb to me. Seeing you is like stepping into the past where my sorrow lies. And now because of you, I lose all hope of my son."

Joseph nodded. "I understand, Ahatti, and it will be as you say except in one matter. When my wife comes to the bricks again—and I have already dreamed of a second son— you must come and attend her.

"You may come without seeing me if you like, and you will be well paid. Indeed, you will be paid in land if you wish, you and the carpenter."

I bridled at the suggestion that I was a pauper, and announced, "My husband, Benia, is master craftsman in the Valley of the Kings."

"Benia?" he asked, and Joseph's face crumbled into regret. "That was the baby-name for our brother Benjamin, the last-born of my mother, who died giving him life. I used to hate Benia for killing her, but now I think I would give half of what is mine only to hold his hand."

"I have no desire to see him," I said, surprising both of us with the anger in my voice. "I am no longer of that world. If my mothers are dead, then I am an orphan. My brothers are no more to me than the livestock of our youth. You and I were kin as children, when we knew each other well enough to share our hearts. But that was in another life."

The great room was silent, each of us lost in memories.

"I will go to my son," I said finally. "Then I will be gone."

"Go in peace," said Joseph.

*

Re-mose lay facedown on the bed in his handsome suite. My son did not move or speak or show me any sign of recognition. I spoke to his back.

His windows overlooked the river, which glittered in the moonlight. "Your father loved the river," I said, fighting tears. "And you will love the sea.

"I will not see you again, Re-mose, and there will be no other opportunity to speak these words again. Listen to your mother, who comes to say goodbye.

"I do not ask you to forgive my brothers. I never did. I never will. I ask only that you forgive me for the bad luck of being their sister.

"Forgive me for never speaking to you of your father. That was your grandmother's command, for she saw secrecy as the only way to keep you from the agony that cuts you low today. She knew that the past could threaten your future, and we must continue to protect you against the accidents of birth. The true story of your parentage is still known only by you, me, and Zafenat Paneh-ah. There is no need to tell anyone else.

"But now that we share this secret, I will tell you something else.

"Re-mose, your father was called Shalem, and he was as beautiful as the sunset for which he was named. We chose each other in love. The name I gave you at my breast was Bar-Shalem, son of the sunset, and your father lived in you.

"Your grandmother called you Re-mose, making you a child of Egypt and the sun god. In either language and in any country, you are blessed by the great power of the heavens. Your future is written on your face, and I pray that you will have the fullness of years denied to your father. May you find contentment.

"I will remember you in the morning and in the evening, every day until I close my eyes forever. I forgive your every harsh thought of me and the curses you may hurl at my name. And when at last you do forgive me, I forbid you to suffer a moment's guilt in my name. I ask that you remember only my blessing upon you, Bar-Shalem Re-mose."

My son did not move from his couch or say a word, and I took my leave, brokenhearted but free.

Chapter Five

RETURNING HOME WAS like being reborn. I buried my face in the bed linens and ran my hands over every piece of furniture, every garden plant, delighted to find things where I had left them. Kiya walked in to find me embracing a water jug. I sent her to tell Meryt I was home and then walked as fast as I could to Benia's workshop.

My husband saw me approach and rushed out to greet me. It seemed that we had been parted for years rather than days. "You are so thin, wife," he whispered as he held me in his arms.

"I fell ill in the city," I explained. "But I am healthy again."

We studied each other's faces. "Something else happened," Benia said, drawing his fingers across my forehead and reading something of the past days' shocks. "Are you back to stay, beloved?" he asked, and I understood the cause of the shadows beneath his eyes.

I reassured him with an embrace that earned us a loud hoot from the men in the workshop. "I will be home as soon as I can," he said, kissing my hands. I nodded, too happy to say more.

Meryt was waiting with warm bread and beer when I returned to my house. But when she saw me, she cried, "What did they do to you, sister? You are skinny as a bone, and your eyes look as though you have wept a river."

I told my friend about the fever and of Re-mose's quarrel with his master. When my friend heard that he was posted to the north, her eyes filled in sympathy.

After we ate what Meryt had brought, she ordered me to the bed and massaged my feet. All the pain of the past weeks melted as she kneaded my toes and cradled my heels. After I was at peace and still, I asked her to sit by my side and I took her hand, still warm and moist with oil, and told her the rest of what had happened to me in Thebes, including how it came to pass that Zafenat Paneh-ah, the king's right hand, was my brother Joseph.

Meryt listened in stillness, watching my face as I recounted my mothers' history, and the story of Shechem and the murder of Shalem. My friend did not move or utter a sound, but her face revealed the workings of her heart, showing me horror, rage, sympathy, compassion.

When I finished, she shook her head. "I see why you did not tell me this before," she said sadly. "I wish I had been able to help you bear this burden from the very first. But now that you entrust your past to my keeping, it is safe. I know you need no oath from me, or else you would not have told me.

"Dear one," she said, putting my hand to her cheek, "I am so honored to be the vessel into which you pour this story of pain and strength. For all these years, no daughter could have made me happier or more proud than you. Now that I know who you are and what life has cost you, I am in awe that I number you among my beloved."

After a comfortable silence, Meryt gathered her things and prepared to leave. "I will go to give you time to prepare for Benia's arrival," she said, taking my two hands in hers. "Blessings of Isis. Blessings of Hathor. Blessings of the mothers of your house."

But before she walked out the door, my friend's face regained its impish grin and with a friendly leer she said, "I will call upon you tomorrow. See if you can't get off your back long enough between now and then to make me something to eat for a change, eh?"

Benia ran in soon after, and we fell upon the unmade bed like youthful lovers, breathless and hurried. Afterward, knotted in each other's clothes, we slept the famished sleep of reunited lovers. I awoke once in the night, startled and smiling, hating to close my eyes upon the joy of being home.

After my return, I never fully lost my reverence for ordinary pleasures. I arose before Benia to study his face and breathed silent prayers of thanks. Walking to the water fountain or pulling weeds in the garden, I was overcome by the understanding that I had spent a whole day without the weight of the past crushing my heart. Birdsong brought me to tears, and every sunrise seemed a gift shaped for my eyes.

When the vizier's messenger arrived at our door, as I knew he would someday, I froze with dread at the thought of leaving for so much as a day, but to my relief, the letter did not summon me to the great house on the east bank. Joseph's dream had been fulfilled, and a second son was born to him. This one came so fast, however, that As-naat did not have time to send for me before the one called Efraem found his way into the world.

Even though I had rendered him no service, Zafenat Paneh-ah sent a gift of three lengths of snowy linen. When Benia asked me why the gift was so extravagant, I told him everything.

It was the third time I had given voice to the full story; first to Werenro, then to Meryt. But this time my heart did not pound nor my eyes fill as I told it. It was only a story from the distant past. After hearing me out, Benia took me in his arms to comfort me, and I nestled into the sheltering peace between Benia's hands and his beating heart.

Benia was the rock upon which my life stood firm, and Meryt was my wellspring. But my friend was older than I by a generation, and age was taking its toll.

The last of her teeth had fallen from her mouth, for which she claimed herself grateful. "No more pain," she chuckled. "No more meat, either," she said, with a doleful shrug. But her daughter-in-law, Shif-re, chopped and mashed every dish, and my friend remained hearty and enjoyed her beer and her jokes as much as ever. She attended many births with me, taking delight in newborn smiles, weeping over the deaths that came our way. We shared countless meals, and I always left her table chuckling. We knew her days were numbered and kissed each other goodbye at every parting. Nothing between us was left unsaid.

The morning came when Kiya appeared at the door to say that Meryt could not rise from her bed. "I am here, dear one, sister," I said when I arrived at her side, but my old friend could no longer give me greeting. She could not move at all. The right side of her face had collapsed, and her breathing was labored.

She returned the pressure of my fingers in her left hand and blinked at me. "Oh, sister," I said, trying not to weep. She stirred, and I could see that even though she was nearing death, Meryt was trying to comfort me. That would not do. I looked into her eyes and managed a midwife's smile. I knew my task.

"Fear not," I whispered, "the time is coming.

"Fear not, your bones are strong.

"Fear not, good friend, help is nearby.

"Fear not, Anubis is a gentle companion.

"Fear not, the hands of the midwife are clever.

"Fear not, the earth is beneath you.

"Fear not, little mother.

"Fear not, mother of us all."

Meryt relaxed and closed her eyes, surrounded by sons and daughters, grandsons and granddaughters. She sighed one long sigh, the wind through reeds, and left us.

I joined with the women in the high-pitched keening death song that alerted the whole neighborhood to the passing of the beloved midwife, mother, and friend. Children burst into tears at the sound, and men rubbed their eyes with damp fists. I was heartbroken but comforted by one of Meryt's last gifts to me, for at her deathbed I became one of her grieving family.

Indeed, I was treated as the oldest female relative and given the honor of washing her withered arms and legs. I swaddled her in Egypt's finest linen, which was mine to give. I arranged her limbs in the crouch of a baby about to enter the world and sat with her through the night.

At dawn we carried her to rest in a cave on a hill overlooking the tombs of kings and queens. Her sons buried her with her necklaces and rings. Her daughters buried her with her spindle, her alabaster bowl, and other things she loved. But the midwife's kit had no place in the next life, and it passed to the keeping of Shif-re, who held Meryt's tools with reverence, as though they were made of gold.

We buried Meryt with songs and tears, and on the way home laughed in her honor, recalling her delight in surprises, jokes, food, and all the pleasures of the flesh. I hoped that she would continue her enjoyment of these in the life to come, which she believed to be much like this world, only deathless and eternal.

That night, I dreamed of Meryt and woke up laughing at something she said. The following night I dreamed of Bil-hah, waking to tears on my cheeks that tasted of the spices my aunt used in her cooking. One night later, Zilpah greeted me and we flew through the night sky, a pair of she-hawks.

When the sun set again, I knew I would meet with Rachel in dreams. She was as beautiful as I remembered. We ran through a warm rain that washed me clean as a baby, and I woke up smelling as though I had bathed in well water.

Eagerly I awaited my dream of Leah, but she did not come the next night or the night after. Only at the dark of the new moon was I visited by the mother of my flesh. It was the first time my body failed to give the moon her due. I was past giving life, and my mother, who had borne so many children, came to comfort me.

"You are the old one now," she said gently. "You are the

grandmother, giving voice to wisdom. Honor to you," my mother Leah said, touching her forehead to the ground before me, asking forgiveness. I lifted her up, and she turned into a swaddling baby. Holding her in my arms, I begged her pardon for ever doubting her love, and I felt her pardon in the fullness of my heart. I went to Meryt's tomb the morning after Leah's dream and poured out wine, thanking her for sending my mothers back to me.

With Meryt gone, I was the wise woman, the mother, grandmother, and even great-grandmother of those around me. Shif-re, a new grandmother, and Kiya, about to be married, attended me wherever I went to place the bricks. They learned what I had to teach, and soon went on their own to deliver women from the fear and loneliness of birth. My apprentices became sister and daughter. In them, I found new water in the well I thought would remain forever dry after my Meryt died.

Months passed and years. My days were busy, my nights peaceful. But there is no lasting peace before the grave, and one night, after Benia and I had gone to bed, Joseph appeared inside our door.

The sight of him there, clad in a long black cloak that turned him into a shadow, was so strange that I thought him part of a dream. But the edge in my husband's voice woke me to the moment, suddenly dark and dangerous.

"Who comes into my house without knocking?" he growled, like a dog sensing danger, for this was clearly no distraught father in search of the midwife.

"It is Joseph," I whispered.

I lit lamps and Benia offered my brother the best chair. But Joseph insisted on following me back to the kitchen, where I poured him a cup of beer, which sat untouched.

The silence was thick and stiff. Benia's hands were clenched, for he was fearful that I was about to be taken from him; his jaw was locked, for he was unsure how to speak to the noble perched on a stool in his kitchen. Joseph sent me glances full of unspoken urgency, for he was unwilling to speak in front of Benia. I looked from one face to the other and realized how old we had grown.

Finally I told Joseph, "Benia is your brother now. Say what it is you came to say."

"It's Daddy," he said, using a baby word that I had not heard since Canann. "He is dying and we must go to him."

Benia snorted in disgust.

"How dare you?" Joseph said, jumping to his feet and putting his hand on the dagger at his side.

"How dare you?" Benia replied with equal passion, stepping closer. "Why should my wife weep by the bedside of a father who murdered her happiness and his own honor? A father who sent you to the long knives of men known for their ruthlessness?"

"You know the story then," said Joseph, suddenly defeated. He sat down and put his head in his hands and groaned.

"They sent me word from the north where my brothers and their sons tend the flocks of Egypt. Judah says that our father will not live out the season, and that Jacob wishes to give my sons his blessing.

"I do not wish to go," Joseph said, looking at me as though I had some answer for him. "I thought I had finished with my duty there. I thought I had even forgiven my father, though not without exacting a price.

"When they came to my house starving and seeking refuge, I twisted the knife. I accused them of theft and forced them to grovel before the mighty Zafenat Paneh-ah. I watched Levi and Simon put their foreheads to the ground at my feet and tremble. I gloated and sent them back to Jacob, demanding Benjamin be sent. I punished our father for choosing favorites. I punished my brothers, too, and kept them in fear of their lives.

"Now the old man wishes to place his hands on the heads of my boys, to choose them for his blessing. Not the sons of Reuben or Judah, who have supported him all these years and borne his moods and whims. Not even the sons of Benjamin, the last-born.

"I know Jacob's heart. He wishes to atone for the wrongs of the past by blessing my sons. But I fear for them with such a birthright. They will inherit tormenting memories and strange dreams. They will come to hate my name."

Joseph railed on as Benia and I listened. The hurts of the past clung to him, caught in the folds of his long dark cloak. He flailed around like a drowning lamb.

As he talked about fat years and lean years, about loneliness and sleepless nights, about how life had treated him so cruelly, I searched for the brother I remembered, the playfellow who listened to the words of women with respect and who once looked at me as his friend. But I saw nothing of that boy in the self-absorbed man before me, whose mood and voice seemed to change from moment to unhappy moment.

"I am a weakling," said Joseph. "My anger has not abated

and I have no pity in my heart for Jacob, who has become blind, like his father before him. And yet I cannot say no to him."

"Messages get lost," I said softly. "Messengers are sometimes waylaid."

"No," Joseph said. "That lie would finally kill me. If I do not go, he will haunt me forever. I will go and you will come with me," said Joseph, suddenly shrill, a man accustomed to power.

I did not try to hide my disgust at his tone, and when he saw my contempt he dropped his head in shame. And then my brother bowed down with his forehead on the dirt floor of a carpenter's kitchen and apologized to me, and to Benia, too.

"Forgive me, sister. Forgive me, brother. I do not wish to see my father dying. I do not wish to see him at all. And yet, I cannot disobey. It is true that I can force you to go with me, and for no other reason than to hold my hand. But you will prosper in this, too."

He stood and resumed the demeanor of Zafenat Panehah. "You will be my guests," he said smoothly. "The master carpenter will do business on behalf of the king. I go to purchase timber in the north, and I require the services of an artist who knows how to select the finest wood. You will go to the marketplace of Memphis and see olive, oak, and pine in abundance, choosing only what belongs in the king's house and tomb. You will bring honor to your profession and to your own name."

His words were seductive, but Benia looked only at me.

Then Joseph brought his face close to mine and gently said, "Ahatti, this is your last chance to see the fruits of your mothers' wombs, their grandsons and granddaughters. For those are not only the children of Jacob; they are also the children of Leah, Rachel, Zilpah, and Bilhah.

"You are the only aunt of their mothers' blood, and our mothers would wish for you to see their grandaughters. After all, you are the only daughter, the one they loved."

My brother could talk the wings off a bird, and he talked until the sun rose and Benia and I were exhausted. Although we never said yes, there was no saying no to Zafenat Paneh-ah, the king's vizier, just as there had been no saying no to Joseph, son of Rachel, grandson of Rebecca.

We left with him in the morning. At the river, we were met by a barque of surpassing luxury, filled with chairs and beds, painted plates and cups, sweet wine and fresh beer. There were flowers and fruit everywhere. Benia was stunned at the riches, and neither of us could look into the faces of the naked slaves who waited upon us with the same servility they showed Zafenat and his two sons and their noble retinue.

The lads were old enough to grow their hair, and they were good boys, curious about their father's guests but polite enough not to ask questions. Benia delighted them by carving little creatures out of wood, and naming each one. He caught me watching him, and his plaintive smile told me that he had done the same for his own sons, dead long ago.

As-naat did not come with us, and Joseph never spoke a word of his wife. My brother was attended by a youthful guard, all of them as beautiful as he had been in his youth, and I often saw him staring at his handsome companions wistfully. He and I barely spoke on the voyage north. We took our meals separately, and no one suspected that the carpenter's wife had anything to say to the powerful vizier. When we did exchange words—to say good morning or to comment about the children—we never spoke in our mother tongue. That might have drawn attention to his foreign birth, which was a sore point among many in the king's service.

Joseph kept to himself at the prow of the barque under a gleaming awning, wrapped in his dark cloak. Had I been alone, I might have sat like him, reliving the journey that had brought me to the house of Nakht-re, where I became a mother, remembering, too, the loss of my son. Had it not been for Benia, I would have thought of the impending meeting with my brothers and opened the old wounds in my heart.

But Benia was always nearby, and my husband was captivated by the sights of a journey that was, for him, like the gift of an extra life. He directed my eyes at the sails in the wind, or when the air was still, at the harmony of the rowers' oars. Nothing escaped his attention, and he pointed to horizons and trees, birds in flight, men plowing the fields, wildflowers, a stand of papyrus that looked like a field of copper in the setting sun. When we came upon a herd of water horses, his excitement was matched only by that of Joseph's boys, who crowded by his side to watch the children of Taweret splash and roar in the reeds.

On the third day of the journey, I set aside my spinning and sat quietly, watching the water lap against the shore, my mind as calm and wordless as the surface of the river. I inhaled the loamy smell of the river and listened to the sound of the water on the hull, which was like a constant breeze. I trailed my fingers through the water, watching them grow wrinkled and white.

"You are smiling!" said Benia when he came upon me.

"When I was a child, I was told that I would only find contentment beside a river," I told him. "But it was a false prophecy. The water soothes my heart and settles my thoughts, and it is true that I feel at home by the water, but I found my joy in dry hills, where the fountain is distant and the dust is thick." Benia squeezed my hand, and we watched Egypt pass, emerald green, while the sun sparked the water into countless points of light.

In the mornings and at sunset when the barque docked for the night, Menashe and Efraem would jump into the water. The servants watched for crocodiles and snakes, but my husband could not resist the boys' invitation to join them. He removed his loincloth and jumped in with a roar that was answered by childish squeals. I laughed to see my husband dive under the surface and shoot up again, like a heron, like a boy. When I told Benia of a dream in which I was a fish, he grinned and promised to make it so.

So one night, under a full moon, Benia put his finger to his lips and led me down to the water's edge. Silently, he motioned for me to lie back in his arms, where he held me effortlessly, as though I were as light as a baby and he as strong as ten men. With his hands, he coaxed and reassured me until I put my head back and unclenched my hands and lay as though on a bed. When I relaxed, my husband released me so that I felt only his fingertips on my back, while the river held me and the moonlight turned the water silver.

Every night I grew bolder. I learned to float without the support of my husband's hands, and then to move on my back, facing the waning moon. He showed me how to stay on the surface and swim like a dog, kicking and kneading the water for dear life. I laughed and swallowed water. It was the first time I had frolicked like a child since my son was a baby.

By the end of the journey north, I could duck my head underwater and even swim side by side with Benia. Whispering on our pallet afterward, I told him about the first time I ever saw anyone swimming, at the river on our way out of Haran. "They were Egyptians," I said, remembering their voices. "I wonder if they were comparing the water of that river with this just as I am tonight."

We turned to each other and made love as silently as fishes and slept like children rocking on the bosom of the great river, source and fulfillment.

At Tanis we left the river and began the journey into the hills where the sons of Jacob lived. In Egypt, farmers and even tanners were held in higher esteem than shepherds, whose work was considered the lowest and most odious of occupations. The official purpose of Zafenat Paneh-ah's journey was to conduct a census of the flocks and to select the finest animals for the king's table. In fact, this was a task beneath his station, the sort of thing usually assigned to a middle-ranked scribe. Still, it served my brother as an excuse to visit the relations he had not seen for ten years, since he granted them refuge from the famine in Canaan.

Traveling in Zafenat Paneh-ah's caravan was nothing like

the journeys of my childhood. My brother was carried on a litter by his military bearers and his sons rode donkeys behind. Benia and I, who walked, were surrounded by servants who offered cool beer or fruit if we so much as raised a hand to shade our eyes. At night, we rested on thick pallets under pure white tents.

Luxury was not the only difference. This journey was very quiet, almost hushed. Joseph sat alone, his brow knit, his knuckles white on the arms of his chair. I was uneasy too, but there was no way for me to speak to Benia without being overheard.

Only the sons of Joseph were carefree. Menashe and Efraem dubbed their donkeys Huppim and Muppim and invented stories about them. They tossed a ball back and forth between them, and laughed and complained that their backsides were black and blue from riding. Had it not been for them, I might have forgotten how to smile.

After four days, we came upon the camp where the sons of Jacob lived. I was shocked by the size of it. I had imagined a gathering like the one in Shechem, with a dozen tents and half as many cooking fires. But here was a whole village; scores of women with covered hair scurried back and forth, carrying water jugs and firewood. Babies' cries rose up from the murmur of my mother tongue being spoken, shouted, and crooned in accents both familiar and unfamiliar. But it was the smells that brought me to tears: onions frying in olive oil, the musky dust of the herds mixing with the perfume of baking bread. Only Benia's hand kept me from faltering.

A delegation of the tribe's leaders walked forward to meet the vizier, their kinsman. Joseph faced them with his sons at his sides, flanked by his handsome guards. Behind them stood servants, bearers, and slave girls, and off to one side, a carpenter and his wife. Joseph's face was nearly white with anxiety, but he showed his teeth in a large, false smile.

The sons of Jacob stood before us, but I recognized none of these old men. The eldest among them, his face deeply lined and hidden by dirty grey hair, spoke slowly, awkwardly, in the language of Egypt. He delivered formal greetings to Zafenat Paneh-ah, their protector and savior, the one who had brought them to the land in peace and fed them.

It was only when he switched to the speech of his birth that I recognized the speaker. "In the name of our father, Jacob, I welcome you, brother, to our humble tents," said Judah, who had been so beautiful in youth. "Daddy is near the end," he said. "He is not always in his own mind and thrashes on the bed, calling for Rachel and Leah. He wakes out of a dream and curses one son, but in another hour blesses the same man with lavish praise and promises.

"But he has been waiting for you, Joseph. You and your sons."

As Judah spoke, I began to recognize some of the men behind him. There was Dan, with his mother's black, moss-like hair, his skin still unlined and his eyes calm as Bilhah's. It was no longer difficult to distinguish Naphtali from Issachar, for Tali was lame and Issachar stooped. Zebulun still resembled Judah, though he looked far less worn down by life. Several of the younger men, my nephews I guessed, recalled Jacob as he had been in his youth. But I could not guess whose sons they were or which might be Benjamin.

Joseph listened to Judah without once meeting his

brother's eyes, which were fixed upon him. Even when Judah was finished speaking, Joseph did not reply or lift his head.

Finally Judah spoke again. "These must be your boys. What names did you give them?"

"Menashe is the older and this is Efraem," Joseph replied, placing his hands upon their heads in turn. Hearing their names, the boys looked up to their father, their faces shining with curiosity about what was being said in the strange-sounding tongue they had never before heard from their father's mouth.

"They barely understand why we are here," Joseph said. "I do not know myself."

Anger flashed across Judah's face, but it quickly changed to defeat. "There is no undoing the wrongs of the past," he said. "Still, it is good of you to give the old man a peaceful death. He lived in torment from the moment we called you dead, and he never recovered even after he learned you were still alive.

"Come," said Judah. "Let us go and see if our father is awake. Or will you eat and drink first?"

"No," Joseph answered. "Better to do it."

Taking his sons by the hand, Joseph followed Judah to the tent where Jacob lay dying. I stood with the rest of Zafenat Paneh-ah's servants and retainers, watching as they disappeared into the dusty village.

I was fixed to the earth, trembling, furious that not one of them knew me. But I was relieved, too. Benia led me gently to where the servants were setting up tents for the evening, and we waited there.

There was barely time to number my feelings before

Joseph reappeared, with Menashe and Efraem, their eyes fixed on the ground in fear. My brother strode past me and into his tent without a word.

Benia could not coax me to eat that night, and although I lay down beside him, I did not close my eyes. I stared into darkness and let the past wash over me as it would.

I remembered Reuben's kindness and Judah's beauty. I remembered Dan's voice in song and the way Gad and Asher mimicked our grandfather until I collapsed in laughter. I remembered how Issa and Tali wept when Levi and Simon tormented them and said they were interchangeable in their mother's eyes. I remembered how Judah once tickled me until I peed, but never told a soul. I remembered how Reuben used to carry me on his shoulders, from where I could touch the clouds.

Finally, I could lie still no longer and walked out into the night, where Joseph waited for me, pacing by the side of my tent. We walked away from the camp slowly, for there was no moon and darkness covered everything. After some distance Joseph flung himself onto the ground and told me what had happened.

"At first, he did not know me," my brother said. "Daddy whimpered like a tired child, crying, 'Joseph. Where is Joseph?'

"I said, 'Here I am.' But still he asked, 'Where is my son Joseph? Why does he not come?'

"I put my mouth to his ear and said, 'Joseph is here with his sons, just as you asked.'

"After many such exchanges he suddenly understood and grabbed at my face, my hands, my robes. Weeping, he repeated my name over and over and begged forgiveness of me and of my mother. He cursed the memory of Levi and Simon and Reuben, too. Then he wailed because he had not forgiven his firstborn.

"He named each of my brothers in turn, blessing them and cursing them, turning them into animals, sighing over their boyhood pranks, calling out to their mothers to wipe their bottoms.

"How horrid to grow old like that," said Joseph, with pity and disgust in his voice. "I pray I die before the day comes when I do not know if my sons are infants or grandfathers.

"Jacob seemed to sleep, but after a moment he called out again, 'Where is Joseph?' as though he had not already kissed me.

" 'Here am I,' I answered.

" 'Let me bless the boys,' said Jacob. 'Let me see them now.'

"My sons trembled at my side. The tent stank with his illness and his ranting had frightened them, but I told them that their grandfather wished to bless them, and I pushed them toward him, one on either side.

"He put his right hand on Efraem's head and his left hand on Menashe's. He blessed them in the name of Abram and Isaac, then sat up and roared, 'Remember me!' They shrank back and hid behind me.

"I told Jacob his grandsons' names, but he did not hear me. He stared, sightless, at the roof of the tent, and spoke to Rachel, apologizing for abandoning her bones at the side of a road. He wept for his beloved, and begged her to let him die in peace.

"He did not notice when I left with my sons."

As Joseph spoke, I felt an old heaviness return to my heart and recognized the weight I had carried during my years in Nakht-re's house. The burden was not made of sorrow as I had thought. It was anger that rose out of me and found its lost voice. "What of me?" I said. "Did he mention me? Did he repent of what he did to me?

"Did he speak of the murder of Shechem? Did he weep for the innocent blood of Shalem and Hamor? Did he repent for the slaughter of his own honor?"

There was silence from the ground where Joseph lay. "He said nothing of you. Dinah is forgotten in the house of Jacob."

His words should have laid me low, but they did not. I left Joseph on the ground and stumbled back to the camp by myself. I was suddenly exhausted and every step was an effort, but my eyes were dry.

After Joseph arrived, Jacob stopped eating and drinking. His death would come within hours, days at the most. So we waited.

I passed the time sitting at the door of my tent, spinning linen, studying the children of Leah, Rachel, Zilpah, and Bilhah. I saw my mothers' smiles and gestures, and heard their laugher. Some of the connections were as clear as daylight. I recognized an exact copy of Bilhah in what had to be Dan's daughter; another little girl wore my aunt Rachel's hair. Leah's sharp nose was evident everywhere.

On the second day of Jacob's deathwatch, a girl approached, a basket of fresh bread in her hands. She introduced herself in the language of Egypt as Gera, the daughter of Benjamin and his Egyptian wife, Neset. Gera was curious to discover how a woman of my status sat and spun while the others who attended Zafenat Paneh-ah cooked and fetched and cleaned all day.

"I told my sisters that you must be nurse to the sons of the vizier, my uncle," she said. "Is it so? Did I guess well?"

I smiled and said, "You made a good guess," and asked her to sit down and tell me of her sisters and brothers. Gera accepted my invitation with a satisfied grin and began to lay out the warp and weft of her family.

"My sisters are still children," said the girl, herself still a few years away from womanhood. "We have twins, Meuza and Naamah, who are too young even to spin. My father, Benjamin, had sons in Canaan as well by another wife who died. My brothers are called Bela, Becher, Ehi, and Ard, and they are good enough fellows, though I do not know them any better than the sons of my uncles, who are as numerous as our flocks and just as noisy," she said, and winked at me as though we were old friends.

"You have many uncles?" I said.

"Eleven," Gera said. "But the three oldest are dead."

"Ah," I nodded, bidding farewell to Reuben in my heart.

My niece settled in beside me, drawing a spindle from her apron and setting to work as she unraveled the skein of our family's history. "The eldest was Reuben, son of Leah, my grandfather's first wife. The scandal there is that Reuben was found lying with Bilhah, the youngest of Jacob's wives. Jacob never forgave his firstborn, even after Bilhah died, even though Reuben gave him grandsons and more wealth than the rest of the brothers combined. They say my uncle wept for Jacob's forgiveness when he died, but his father would not come to him.

"Simon and Levi, also born of Leah, were murdered in Tanis when I was a baby. No one knows the whole tale there, but among the women there is talk that the two of them tried to get the better of a trader in some small matter. For their victim they chose the most ruthless cutthroat in Egypt, who killed them for their greed."

Gera looked up and saw Judah walking into Jacob's tent. "Uncle Judah, son of Leah, has been clan leader for many years. He is a fair man and bears the burdens of the family well, though some of my cousins think he's grown too cautious in his old age."

Gera went on, teaching me the story of my brothers and their wives, pointing out their children, reciting the names of nieces and nephews, flesh of my flesh, with whom I would never exchange a word.

Reuben had three sons with a wife named Zillah. His second wife, Attar, bore him two girls, Bina and Efrat.

Simon had five sons by the odious Ialutu, whom Gera remembered as an awful scold with bad breath. He had another son by a Shechemite woman, but that one walked into a flooded wadi and drowned. "My mother says he killed himself," said Gera in a whisper.

"That man over there is called Merari," she said. "The miracle in him is that he is a good fellow despite the fact that he was born to Levi and Inbu. His brothers are as bad as their father was."

A slack-jawed man shuffled up to Gera, who handed him a bit of bread and sent him away. "That was Shela," she explained, "Judah's son by Shua. He is feeble-minded, but sweet. My uncle had a second wife named Tamar, who gave him Peretz and Zerach, and my best friend, Dafna. She is the beauty of my family in this generation.

"Over there is Hesia," she said, nodding to a woman nearly my own age. "Wife to Issachar, son of Leah. Hesia is the mother of three sons and Tola, who has taken up the midwife's life. If Danfa is heir to Rachel's beauty, Tola has her golden hands."

"Who is Rachel?" I asked, hoping to hear more of my aunt.

"That is your master's mother," she said, surprised at my ignorance. "Though I suppose there is no reason for you to know her name. Rachel was the second wife, Jacob's beloved, the beauty. She died giving birth to Benjamin, my father."

I nodded, and patted her hand, seeing the shape of Rachel's fingers there. "Go on, dear," I said. "Tell me more. I like the sound of your family's names."

"Dan was the only son of Bilhah," Gera said. "She was Jacob's third wife, Rachel's handmaid and the one who lay with Reuben. Dan has three daughters by Timna, named Edna, Tirza, and Berit. All of them are kindhearted women; they are the ones who tend to Jacob.

"Zilpah was the fourth wife, handmaiden to Leah, and she bore twins. The first was Gad, who loved his wife, Serah Imnah, with a great love. But she died giving birth to her fourth child, her first daughter, Serah, who is gifted with song," said Gera.

"Asher, Gad's twin brother, married Oreet," she continued. "Their eldest was a daughter, Areli, who gave birth to a daughter last week, the newest soul in the family, whose name is Nina.

"Leah's Naphtali fathered six children upon Yedida, whose daughters are Elisheva and Vaniah. And of course, you know the sons of Joseph better than anyone," Gera said. "He has no daughters?" she asked.

"Not yet," I replied.

Gera caught sight of two young women and, pointing at me, nodded her head emphatically. "Those are two of the daughters of Zebulun, son of Leah. Their mother, Ahavah, produced six girls who are their own little tribe. I like it when they include me in their circle. It's a merry group.

"Liora, Mahalat, Giah, Yara, Noadya, and Yael," she said, counting out their names on her fingers. "They have the best gossip. It was they who told me the story of the Shechemite woman's son who killed himself. He went mad," she said, lowering her voice, "when he learned the terrible circumstances of his birth."

"What could have caused him such despair?" I asked.

"It's an ugly tale," she replied coyly, leaning in to whet my interest.

"Those often make for the best stories," I answered.

"Very well," Gera said, setting down her spinning and looking me straight in the eye. "According to Auntie Ahavah's story, Leah had one daughter who lived. She must have been a great beauty, for she was taken in marriage by a Shechemite nobleman, a prince, in fact. The son of King Hamor!

"The king brought Jacob a handsome bride-price with his own hands, but it wasn't enough for Simon and Levi. They claimed that their sister had been kidnapped and raped, and that the family honor was demeaned. They put up such a noise that the king, bowing to his son's great passion for Leah's daughter, doubled the bride-price.

"Still my uncles were not satisfied. They claimed it was a plot of the Canaanites to take what was Jacob's and make it Hamor's. So Levi and Simon tried to undo the marriage by demanding that the Shechemites give up their foreskins and become Jacobites.

"Now comes the part of this story that makes me think it is nothing more than a tale that girls tell each other. The prince submitted to the knife! He and his father and all the men in the city! My cousins say this is impossible, because men are not capable of such love.

"In the story, though, the prince agreed. He and the men of the city were circumcised." Gera lowered her voice, setting a dark tone for the sorrowful ending.

"Two nights after the cutting, while the men of the city groaned in pain, Levi and Simon stole into the city and slaughtered the prince, the king, and all the men they found within its gates.

"They took the livestock and the women of the city too, which is how Simon came to have a Shechemite wife. When their son learned about his father's villainy, he drowned himself."

My eyes had been fixed upon my spindle as she recounted the tale. "And what of the sister?" I asked. "The one who was loved by the prince?"

"That is a mystery," said Gera. "I think she died of grief. Serah made up a song about her being gathered by the Queen of Heaven and turned into a falling star."

"Is her name remembered?" I asked softly.

"Dinah," she said. "I like the sound of it, don't you? Someday, if I am delivered of a daughter, I will call her Dinah."

Gera said nothing more about Leah's daughter, and prattled on about feuds and love affairs among her cousins. She chatted until late in the afternoon before thinking to ask about me, and by then I could excuse myself, for it was time for the evening meal.

Jacob died that night. I heard one woman sobbing and wondered who among his daughters-in-law wept for the old man. Benia folded me in his arms, but I felt neither grief nor anger.

Gera had given me peace. The story of Dinah was too terrible to be forgotten. As long as the memory of Jacob lived, my name would be remembered. The past had done its worst to me, and I had nothing to fear of the future. I left the house of Jacob better comforted than Joseph.

In the morning, Judah prepared to take Jacob's body to lie with his fathers in Canaan. Joseph watched as they lifted his bones onto his gold-covered litter, which he gave for the funeral voyage.

Before Judah left to put his father into the ground, he and Joseph embraced for the last time. I turned away from the sight, but before I reached my tent I felt a hand on my shoulder and turned to face Judah, whose expression was a map of uncertainty and shame.

He held out a fist to me. "It was our mother's," he said, struggling to speak. "When she died, she called me to her and said to give this to her daughter. I thought she was out of her mind," said Judah. "But she foresaw our meeting. Our mother never forgot you, and although Jacob forbade it, she spoke of you every day until she died.

"Take this from our mother, Leah. And may you know peace," he said, pressing something in my hand before walking away, his head hung low.

I looked down to see Rachel's lapis ring, Jacob's first gift to her. At first I thought to call Judah back and ask him why my mother had sent me the token of Jacob's love for her sister. But of course, he would have no way of knowing.

It was good to see the river again. After the heat of the hills, the embrace of the Nile was sweet and cool. And at night in Benia's arms, I told him all that I had heard from Gera and showed him the ring.

I puzzled over its meaning and prayed for a dream to explain the mystery, but it was Benia who gave me the answer. Holding my hand to the light and peering at it with eyes practiced at seeing beauty, he said, "Perhaps your mother meant it as a token that she had forgiven her sister. Maybe it was a sign that she died with an undivided heart, and wished the same for you."

My husband's words found their mark, and I recalled something that Zilpah had told me when I was a child in the red tent, and far too young to understand her meaning. "We are all born of the same mother," she said. After a lifetime, I knew that to be true.

Although the journey was uneventful and my hands were idle, I was exhausted by the trip home. I longed to return to my own house, to see Shif-re and Kiya's baby, who had been born during my absence.

I was terribly restless during the three days' stop in Memphis, but kept my impatience to myself because of Benia. He returned from the marketplace every evening, overflowing with the beauty he had seen. He exclaimed at the silkiness of the olive wood, the pure black of the ebony, the aromatic cedars. He brought back scraps of pine and taught Joseph's sons to carve. He bought me a gift too, a pitcher in the shape of a grinning Taweret that made me smile every time I looked at her.

The vizier's barque trailed a barge laden with fine timbers when we sailed out of Memphis for the last part of the journey to Thebes. Joseph and I said goodbye in the darkness of the last night. There was no need for sorrow at our parting, he said lightly. "This is only a farewell. If As-naat bears again, we will call for you."

But I knew we would not meet again. "Joseph," I said, "it is out of our hands.

"Be well," I whispered, touching his cheek with a hand that bore his mother's ring. "I will think of you."

"I will think of you, too," he replied softly.

In the morning Benia and I eagerly turned to the west. Once home, we resumed the order of our days. Kiya's new son was goodnatured, and he learned to crow happily when his mother handed him to me on nights she went to attend at a birth. I rarely accompanied her past sunset, though, for I was growing old.

My feet ached in the morning and my hands were stiff, but still I counted myself lucky that I was neither feeble nor

dull. I had strength enough for my house and to care for
Benia. He remained strong and sure, his eye ever clear, his
love for his work and his love for me as constant as the sun.

My last years were good ones. Kiya had two more babies,
another boy and a girl, who took over my house and my
husband's heart. We received countless sweet-breathed
kisses every day. "You are the elixir of youth," I said, as I
tickled them and laughed with them. "You sustain these old
bones. You keep me alive."

But not even the devotion of lithe children can stave off
death forever, and my time arrived. I did not suffer long. I
woke in the night to feel a crushing weight on my chest, but
after the first shock there was no pain.

Benia held my face between his great, warm hands. Kiya
arrived and cradled my feet between her long fingers. They
wept, and I could not form the words to comfort them.
Then they changed before my eyes, and I had no words to
describe what I saw.

My beloved turned into a beacon as bright as the sun,
and his light warmed me through and through. Kiya glowed
like the moon and sang with the green and solemn voice of
the Queen of the Night.

In the darkness surrounding the shining lights of my life,
I began to discern the faces of my mothers, each one burning
with her own fire. Leah, Rachel, Zilpah, and Bilhah. Inna,
Re-nefer, and Meryt. Even poor Ruti and arrogant Rebecca
were arrayed to meet me. Although I had never seen them,
I recognized Adah and Sarai as well. Strong, brave, wonder-
struck, kind, gifted, broken, loyal, foolish, talented, weak:
each one welcoming me in her way.

"Oh," I cried, in wonder. Benia held me even tighter and

sobbed. He thought that I suffered, but I felt nothing but excitement at the lessons that death held out to me. In the moment before I crossed over, I knew that the priests and magicians of Egypt were fools and charlatans for promising to prolong the beauties of life beyond the world we are given. Death is no enemy, but the foundation of gratitude, sympathy, and art. Of all life's pleasures, only love owes no debt to death.

"Thank you, beloved," I said to Benia, but he did not hear me.

"Thank you, daughter," I said to Kiya, who had put her ear to my chest, and hearing nothing, started to keen.

I died but I did not leave them. Benia sat beside me, and I stayed in his eye and in his heart. For weeks and months and years, my face lived in the garden, my scent clung to the sheets. For as long as he lived, I walked with him by day and lay down with him at night.

When his eyes closed for the last time, I thought perhaps I would finally leave the world. But even then, I lingered. Shif-re sang the song I taught her and Kiya moved with my motions. Joseph thought of me when his daughter was born. Gera named her baby Dinah. Re-mose married and told his wife about the mother who had sent him away so that he would not die but live. Re-mose's children bore children unto the hundredth generation. Some of them live in the land of my birth and some in the cold and windy places that Werenro described by the light of my mothers' fire.

There is no magic to immortality.

In Egypt, I loved the perfume of the lotus. A flower would bloom in the pool at dawn, filling the entire garden with a blue musk so powerful it seemed that even the fish and ducks would swoon. By night, the flower might wither but the perfume lasted. Fainter and fainter, but never quite gone. Even many days later, the lotus remained in the garden. Months would pass and a bee would alight near the spot where the lotus had blossomed, and its essence was released again, momentary but undeniable.

Egypt loved the lotus because it never dies. It is the same for people who are loved. Thus can something as insignificant as a name—two syllables, one high, one sweet—summon up the innumerable smiles and tears, sighs and dreams of a human life.

If you sit on the bank of a river, you see only a small part of its surface. And yet, the water before your eyes is proof of unknowable depths. My heart brims with thanks for the kindness you have shown me by sitting on the bank of this river, by visiting the echoes of my name.

Blessings on your eyes and on your children. Blessings on the ground beneath you. Wherever you walk, I go with you.

Selah.

Acknowledgments

I WOULD LIKE to thank Barbara Haber, curator of books at the Arthur and Elizabeth Schlesinger Library on the History of Women in America at Radcliffe College. At her suggestion I applied for a library fellowship at the Schlesinger, which was kind enough to support a project far afield from its stated mission. Radcliffe College also provided me with help from a wonderful undergraduate research partner, Rebecca Wand.

Thanks to the Women's Studies Department at Brandeis University for my appointment as visiting scholar, and to the Museum of Fine Arts, Boston, for permission to photograph the Statue of the Lady Sennuwy. Ellen Grabiner, Amy Hoffman, Renée Loth, and Marla Zarrow—the members of my writing group—provided three years of encouragement, careful reading, good advice, and friendship that sustained me. Long-distance colleagues Eddy Myers and Valerie Monroe held my hand (mostly via e-mail) before, during, and after.

Thanks to Larry Kushner, who introduced me to Midrash.

For their various contributions, thank you to Iris Bass, Professor Mark Brettler, Jane Devitt Gnojek, Judith Himber, Karen Kushner, Gila Langner at *Kerem* magazine, Barbara Penzner, David Rosenbaum, Janice Sorkow at the Museum of Fine Arts, Boston, and to Diane Weinstein.

My brother, Harry Diamant, introduced me to my agent, Carolyn Jenks, who in turn introduced me to Bob Wyatt, a thoughtful editor and a full-fledged mensch.

My husband, Jim Ball, has been infinitely patient. My mother, Hélène Diamant, and my daughter, Emilia Diamant, cheered me on. My father (whose memory is a blessing) always thought I would write a novel someday.

Visit **www.panmacmillan.com** to read more about all our books and to buy them. You will also find features, author interviews and news of any author events, and you can sign up for e-newsletters so that you're always first to hear about our new releases.